The Bedroom Games Series

Alisha Rai

The Bedroom Games Series

Edited by Sasha Knight
Cover by Bree Bridges

The Bedroom Games Series

Play With Me

Chapter One

I WANT TO KEEP you bound to my bed forever. Black leather ties encircling those dainty wrists, those slender ankles. Stretched wide for me. You'd never be able to escape.

Inhale.

Even if I make a fortune some day, it won't compare to how rich I feel every time you open your thighs for me.

Exhale.

I love you. Always.

"Ma'am?"

Tatiana Belikov snapped the manila folder in her hands shut, hiding the pile of old and tattered letters she'd made the mistake of skimming—though the words weren't new to her—while waiting for the receptionist to finish her phone call. She was all too aware of the slight sheen of sweat on her upper lip. She stuffed the folder in her oversized bag as she rose to her feet, her trembling hands making the job more awkward. "Yes. Hi."

The woman gave her a warm smile. Tatiana didn't have a vast working knowledge of the hiring practices of rich and powerful men, but television had taught her the waiting area would be guarded by a sexy, slinky shark of a woman.

Wyatt's assistant looked like she should be playing bridge somewhere. "I'm so sorry about that. Now, what can I help you with?"

Your boss and I popped each other's cherries years ago. Can you please tell him I'm here? She cleared her throat. "I was hoping I could see Mr. Caine."

"Do you have an appointment?"

"No, I don't."

The other woman—Esme Schmidt, her desk tag read—turned away from her computer, her frown genuinely regretful. "I apologize, dear. But Mr. Caine doesn't see anyone without an appointment. If you'd like to leave a message, I can see that he receives it."

The waiting room wasn't packed—only one other person was present, a frowning, shifty-eyed baby boomer clutching two briefcases bulging with documents. Still, Tatiana couldn't imagine how much work went into running an operation of this size. Showing up with no notice wasn't the best tactic, but alas, she hadn't really thought about it until it was too late to call off this crazy venture.

"Can you please give him my name? I know he'll see me." She didn't know that he would listen to her, or even speak with her for very long. But curiosity alone should get her a couple of minutes. A couple of minutes was all she needed.

Maybe not all she *wanted*. But all she needed.

When the older woman hesitated, Tatiana pushed, injecting equal amounts of charm and confidence into her plea. "We're friends. He'll be so disappointed if he knows I left without seeing him. Please." She clutched the strap of her bag, the letters weighing it down. “Tatiana Belikov.”

The older woman pursed her lips. As she reached for the phone, Tatiana heard her mutter something that sounded like, “It’s your funeral.”

“What now, Esme?”

The low, annoyed voice came through the receiver, too deep and booming to be contained by a small piece of plastic. A small chill ran down her spine. It had been roughly a decade since she’d heard that voice, and it still managed to make her sit up and take notice.

He sounded harder. Tougher. And not happy.

He was about to get even more unhappy.

“There’s a young lady here to see you.”

“Is she on my schedule?”

“No, sir.”

“Then she doesn’t exist.”

Esme cast her a reproachful glance, and Tatiana winced, mouthing, *Sorry*. She was sorry. She also wasn’t budging.

Esme continued. “She says to tell you her name is Tatiana Belikov.”

Tatiana didn’t know what she expected. A laugh. A guffaw. Or worst of all, a “Who?”

Instead, resounding silence greeted the announcement. Tatiana’s breath caught as she waited for…something. Anything.

A creak brought her gaze from the phone to the mahogany double doors leading to what was assuredly the lion’s den.

Back straight, head up. Oh, but her hands. What to do with her stupid, restless hands? Worry urged her to link them together. The stirring of her girlish heart had her longing to twirl her hair.

Her pride took over. She clenched those hands into militant fists.

The door opened wider, revealing a man she barely knew, yet at the same time, knew all too well. He was larger now, a full-grown male instead of the gangly youth she'd known. He wore a solid black suit, harsh against his very white shirt. His tie was bright red, a splash of color that should have been garish but instead added a dash of charm and whimsy to his otherwise stark appearance. He wore the suit well—but then, was there anything he wouldn't wear well? He still had the physique of the common laborer he'd been, not the executive he was.

Had he been any other man, she would have accused him of posing for her. But he'd never had much vanity about his body, using it as other people did a tool. He moved, placing his large hands on his hips and pushing back his suit jacket, as if to display the trimness of his waist and stomach.

Dear eyeballs, anytime you want to stop eating this guy up with a spoon, that would be good. But it was so damn hard. The man had aged well, and she had never been immune to his appearance. As a bumbling, awkward freshman in high school, she'd drooled every time she'd looked at the hottest senior. Even when they'd broken up, she'd had to battle that tug of attraction.

He could have at least gotten a bald spot. But, no, he had a full head of hair. He'd worn it long when they'd been lovers, as suited a young rebel. Now, the coal-dark strands were cut short. She tightened her fists until her nails cut into the skin of her palms, the better to resist the temptation to see if he still liked a woman running her fingers through that cool silk.

His eyes were as dark as his hair, framed by a fringe of lashes so thick he'd been teased into more than one fistfight over whether he wore eyeliner. Those eyes were trained on her, piercing through her thin armor, right into her soul.

"Tatiana Belikov." His voice was emotionless, as if they were acquaintances meeting at a dinner party, not standing face-to-face for the first time since the finale of their tumultuous relationship.

She raised her chin. She might look delicate, but she was no pansy. "Wyatt."

He cocked his head. "What a…surprise."

"Mr. Caine? The young lady said you were friends. Do I need to call someone?"

Her boss's reaction was disturbing Esme. Tatiana wondered if women frequently had to be bodily removed from Wyatt's office.

"That won't be necessary, Esme. I do know her." His smile was a flash of white in his swarthy skin. "And yes. We're old friends."

She shivered, though she wasn't sure why. The lush, climate-controlled office wasn't cold. "I apologize for barging in like this so unexpectedly." He didn't speak, didn't rush to reassure her that she wasn't barging in. She wasn't sure she expected him to. "I need to speak with you about an important matter."

Wyatt's only reaction was a raised black eyebrow. His expression was closed, remote, sardonic. Déjà vu. He'd worn this same face countless times as a teenager. Wyatt had perfected the careless-rebel role back then, which she had sworn, in her dreamy, girlish way, she could see beneath to his squishy, warm heart.

Not that she was fooling herself into thinking she could see anything now. A lot of time had passed, and they were both different people.

"How curious. Of course. Far be it from me to deny a lady."

Was she the only one who noticed the emphasis on that last word? Wyatt glanced idly around the waiting area, and she followed his gaze to the other occupant in the room. The man sitting on the sofa made no secret of his avid interest in their exchange. "Esme, reschedule this gentleman's appointment to tomorrow."

The man scowled, transferring his gaze to Wyatt. "What? No. I need to see you today!"

Wyatt gave him a cold look. "You'll reschedule to tomorrow."

A pang of guilt made Tatiana turn around and peer at the man. "I really am sorry—"

"Well I don't care if you're sorry—"

"I think you're forgetting," Wyatt cut him off cleanly, with the precision of a surgeon wielding a blade, "who's here begging a favor from whom, hmm? You want to help dull the memory of how you screwed me over last time we did business? You'll reschedule. To tomorrow."

The man opened his mouth, but something he saw in Wyatt's face made him shut up. Paling, he shook his head, muttering as he fished out a handkerchief and mopped his forehead.

"Come into my office," Wyatt said to her, his voice smoother, lower.

Will you walk into my parlour? said the Spider to the Fly. She bit her lip. Nerves were making her belly jump.

At least, she hoped it was just nerves. A low-level buzz of caution around this particular shark was a good thing. It would keep her on her toes. Lust would be far more troublesome.

Damn it, Wyatt. If not a bald spot, maybe some chub. Really, is a paunch too much to ask for?

"Tatiana."

Uttering her name should not make the fine hairs on her arm stand up and salute. It was the way he said it that was magic, all cool command and expectant.

Goddamn it. It wasn't just nerves.

She resisted the urge to fan herself and took a step toward Wyatt. He shifted and held the door open, waiting for her to precede him.

She walked inside the office, unable to stop herself from adding a twitch of attitude to her ass. A glance over her shoulder proved it was wasted—he was closing the door, his back to her. Her lips compressed. Fine. She would give him some other opportunity to slaver over her still-pert body.

He wasn't the only one who had aged well. And any minute now, she would stop sounding so freakin' defensive.

To occupy herself, she glanced around the luxurious office. The cherry desk was huge and uncluttered, save for a sheaf of papers piled on the surface. The chair was plush black leather, and its price tag alone could pay her bills for a month. A wet bar graced one corner of the room; probably de rigueur for a man who owned a casino. The floor-to-ceiling windows that made up the fourth wall showcased a glorious view of Las Vegas.

The walls were a creamy off-white, and while a few tasteful paintings decorated them, there wasn't a single picture of family or friends. Which made sense, since she knew his mother was dead, his father had barely been more than a sperm donor, and he'd had no other real family growing up. Her quick research of the low-key CEO of Quest Casino had turned up the news he had never married nor had children. According to Wikipedia, at least. A private detective she wasn't.

"You have a nice office," she said, in order to break the heavy silence. She turned to find him standing at the door, one hand on the wood as if he were barring others who might try to enter.

Or to keep her from leaving.

He dropped his hand. "Thank you." Still expressionless.

"The whole place is nice." Tatiana waved, to encompass the large building she stood in. She supposed, compared to the Mirage or Caesars, Quest was a small entity. However, what the hotel and casino lacked in size, it made up for in exclusivity and class. In the five years since it had been established, it had hosted politicians, heads of state, and millionaires—all of whom were guaranteed discretion and the opportunity to indulge their vices with no commoners about to carry tales. One article she'd read had written, *What happens in Vegas stays in Vegas, but what happens at Quest...no, nothing ever happens at Quest.*

Wikipedia was a freaking *fountain* of information.

"You've played here?"

The question was posed innocently enough, but she thought there was a bite of mockery in it. *You have the means to play in my sandbox?*

Her spine stiffened. "No. I've never been here before today. I meant it seems nice."

"Thank you. You don't live here, I take it."

"I live in San Francisco now."

"San Francisco? That's far from New England."

"So's Las Vegas."

His lip curled. "Touché. But I had no real ties to the East Coast. I'm surprised you were able to leave your beloved family behind."

The knot between her shoulders seized up. "I see them on the holidays."

"That's enough for them? Hmm."

The rush of defensive words beat in her head, dying to pour out of her mouth. The girl she'd been would have let them spew. The woman she was now had learned some semblance of self-control. "Yes. We miss each other, but I like living out here." Plus, she had some newly discovered family within a day's drive, or a short plane ride. Right here in Vegas, even. *Coincidence, you're a cruel bitch.*

He stared at her, those black eyes unsettling. "You're looking well." His glance was a quick one, up and down her body. Her skin still felt seared.

"Thank you." She fought the urge to fidget with her clothes. The simple grey sheath dress paired with a dark blazer was her go-to classy outfit for when she needed to disguise her normally artsy style and meet with a client or a gallery owner. She'd needed confidence, though, so she'd added one of her favorite necklaces, multiple strands of coiled, interconnected hammered gold that hung between her breasts. "You are as well. Have to say, I never saw you as a businessman. And running a casino, of all things."

When they'd broken up, he'd been taking college classes part-time, so though he was three years older, academically he'd still been around her level. Every other spare minute he'd had had been spent working: a bookstore, so he could learn during his breaks; construction, so he could fall back on a trade; a waiter, for the free meals. Not to mention anything else he could get his hands on.

Her physicist parents hadn't been able to stand that. *Tatiana, you need a boy who will put his education first.*

"You know how much I like to be unpredictable."

"How did you get into it?"

He just looked at her.

She tucked her hair behind her ear. "If you don't mind my asking." She should probably get down to the purpose of her visit, but small talk wasn't a bad thing. Plus…she was curious. Wildly curious.

Wyatt shrugged. "I came to Vegas with some guys and won a shitload of cash in a poker game."

She raised her eyebrows, not expecting that.

He tapped the side of his head. "Turns out I have a knack for cards. Used the money to buy into bigger and bigger games. Ended up meeting some people who had more money than me and an interest in investing in a place here in town. It worked out."

"Yeah, it did. What luck." And what a deliberate downplay, she was certain, of the amount of work and energy Wyatt had poured into this venture.

"You make your own luck. This city is good for that sort of thing."

She sure hoped so.

"And what is it you do?"

The question was no doubt a polite response to her own inquiry. Still, she perked up at his interest. "An artist. I design jewelry."

He cocked his head. "Really? Last I heard you were a bio major. Big change."

It had been a big change—and Wyatt knew very well she had only been a bio major to please her adoptive parents. "I dropped out of college during the last semester of my senior year," she said, keeping her voice even. She refused to fall back into that need to prove him wrong about her so-called slavish devotion to her family.

Even if he had been right all those years ago. No nineteen- or twenty-year-old wanted to be told their parents controlled them.

He turned away from her and walked to the wet bar. He poured a glass of amber liquid and swallowed it back in a single gulp. He immediately helped himself to another serving. Well. Maybe he wasn't quite as cool as he looked.

He faced her and raised the glass. "Sorry. Drink?"

"No. Thank you."

Wyatt took another sip, slower this time. "My surprise over what you do for a living is surpassed by the fact that you're here at all."

"I know." She hesitated before launching into the speech she'd carefully prepared on the plane ride over. "Thank you for seeing me. I know we didn't part on the best of terms, but I want—"

"Sit."

"Um."

He gestured to the brown leather sofas arranged on the far side of the room. "If you like. You can sit."

"Yes. Okay." So civilized. They were so very civilized. She crossed to the little seating arrangement and perched on the edge of the loveseat. He strode over, and she tried to not notice how the fabric of his pants clung to his thighs. Tried. And failed.

Hold steady, girl.

She breathed in and then out. The material of the couch was warm against the backs of her thighs. Her skirt had ridden up when she sat down. She shifted, wishing she could stand and adjust the fabric but not wanting to call attention to the length of bare leg that was exposed.

Too late. The attention had been garnered. His gaze dipped over her legs before gliding up over her chest.

She could easily clear her throat and put him in his place.

You wanted him to see you still had it…

So she didn't.

He glanced up from his leisurely perusal. Not a trace of shame crossed his face when he realized he'd been caught ogling her. He sat back in his seat. "You were saying?"

What had she been saying?

"You want…" he prompted, his voice caressing the two words.

Yes. She wanted. A hazard of her fair complexion: blushes were too obvious. "I wanted to speak with you. I have a proposition for you."

"Is that right?" A slow smile crossed his thin, slightly cruel lips. "That sounds…interesting."

"Not that kind of proposition."

The smirk spread. "I don't know what you're talking about."

Her, on her knees. Hands bound. Him, holding her head steady.

That kind of proposition.

She tried to banish the images—the memories—from her mind by focusing on something else. But all she could see was *him*. His wide shoulders, his powerful legs, the masculine beauty of his face.

"I found my birth family," she blurted out in an effort to say something, anything that wasn't *Can I feel your biceps?*

If the abrupt words startled him, he didn't show it. His gaze turned to his glass. The ice in the drink clinked together.

"Did you now? Congratulations."

"Thank you."

"That must have been a big deal for you." He rolled his glass between his hands. "You spoke of it a lot as a teenager."

A lot was an understatement. Her parents, who had adopted her when she'd been a few days old, were as kind and loving as they were infuriating and meddling, but she'd always felt vaguely out of place with them. She was petite; they were sturdy and tall. She was a dreamy, impulsive artist; they were practical scientists. Discovering her roots had been a frequent fantasy.

"It happened recently. About a year ago. My brother—my biological half-brother—he was the one who found me."

"What's it like to be a sister?"

The easy conversation, too, was familiar. Tatiana's stiff posture relaxed as she settled into the luscious couch. "Weird. Normal."

"That makes sense."

She gave a half laugh and struggled to clarify her answer. "I've always been an only child. And then there's someone in your life who looks like you and automatically cares about you on that basis alone, before they even know you." Still bemused by it all, she shrugged. "He's just…family. It was right. New, but right. Know what I mean?"

"Maybe. I've felt that way a time or two." He studiously avoided looking at her. "Never about blood relatives."

Tatiana sobered. The place they'd grown up in was small enough to have a designated town drunk, and Wyatt's father had been it. After his wife had died, he'd abused his son emotionally until the day Wyatt turned eighteen and moved into his own apartment.

Talk about his home life had been high on the list of taboo topics. Their fights over him not allowing her to meet or even talk about his dad? Epic.

All you could freak out about was your hurt over him not sharing. You barely gave a thought to why he would keep something like the pain he'd endured private. Ugh. Relationship hindsight was brutal. Sympathy and regret made her voice scratchy. "Yeah."

"So. No other new relatives?"

Her lips twisted. "None that matter. My brother was raised mostly by his father, which from what I understand was a good thing. His—our—mother lives in L.A. She…she wasn't interested in meeting with me." Or, really, even speaking to her. Her childish dreams of becoming biffles with her birth mom had died a swift and nasty death. She'd shaken it off, helped by her brother's delight in getting to know her.

"I'm sorry." Wyatt took a sip of his drink. The slight

jiggle of his knee caught her attention, unusual for such a controlled guy.

Now that she thought about it, his shoulders did look tense. That was strange. She was the one who should be anxious.

She spoke a little faster, some of her ease vanishing. "It's her loss. But my brother. He's a sweet boy. He's got a really big heart and a loving personality. He has a wife and a small baby, and they've invited me for Thanksgiving and driven to San Francisco to see me—" She shook her head, unable to express the wonder of this blessing that had unexpectedly come into her life. "They've been—are—wonderful."

"That's good. I'm happy for you." He glanced at his watch. The move was discreet, but Tatiana caught it.

She needed to get to the point. The poor guy was probably wondering what, if anything, all her bleating had to do with him, and rightly so. Tatiana bit her lip. "Well, you see. It turns out that my little brother—and you're going to laugh about what a small world this is—his name is Ronald West. I understand he used to work for you."

Oh. His fingers tightening around the glass until the knuckles turned white was not a good sign. "Indeed." His voice was soft. "He not only worked for me. He stole from me."

"I know." She licked her lips. "But if you only knew…his wife's mother was sick, and they went into debt. He was desperate." She didn't understand the level of desperation it would require to commit embezzlement, but despair had been obvious in Caitlin's voice when the younger woman had called her yesterday, hysterical. *It's all my fault, Tatiana. He did it for me. I don't know what I'll do if he goes to jail.*

"I don't know if you remember this, Tatiana, but I had a few desperate times in my past. Yet I never stole."

Tatiana flinched. "I remember. I know. But you have to understand, Ronald's not like you." Ronald was actually frighteningly similar to her, with her tendency toward dreaminess and impulsiveness, but magnified about tenfold. Not for the first time, Tatiana was grateful she'd had her strong, pragmatic parents as role models. "He's not a criminal, not at heart. He knows he made a mistake." Or at least Tatiana assumed he knew that. It had been hard to understand what he was saying on the phone. His tears kept getting in the way.

Except his boss's name. That had come through loud and clear. She'd been disbelieving at first, but a Google search had turned up the fact that yes, her Wyatt Caine was indeed *the* Wyatt Caine.

After her third glass of wine, she'd booked her flight to Vegas. Had it been two in the morning? Three? It was a little blurry.

"He sent you to plead his case." Wyatt shook his head. "Hiding behind a woman's skirts? That doesn't convince me he's a paragon."

"He doesn't know I'm here. Or that we knew each other." She'd come straight from the airport to see the man Ron had stolen from. The man she oh so coincidentally had slept with once upon a time.

"So, what? He told you he was in trouble, so you decided you should use the fact that we've fucked before to your advantage—"

Sorry, had he said something past the word *fucked*?

'Cause if he had, she hadn't processed it. The word sounded harsh and vulgar on his lips, the way it should be. The way she liked it.

Her hands fluttered, and she grasped them together, stilling their motion. "I was surprised to discover who you were. I didn't know until yesterday."

"I wasn't hiding."

"Neither was I," Tatiana snapped, suddenly annoyed. "Yes, I may have come here instead of going through a lawyer because of our past relationship, but it's not so crazy that this is the first time we've spoken after all these years. It's not like you ever came looking for me after we broke up either."

They froze, and Tatiana wished she could recall the words. Needy, grasping words, just lying between them. Wyatt captured her gaze, his black eyes boring into her soul. "I didn't realize you wanted me to contact you."

Her face felt stiff and frozen. "I didn't. That is. I never thought about it." She lifted her chin, determined to get through this. "And I know you never thought about me after we broke up. I moved on. You moved on."

"Until now."

"Yes. Until now."

"So tell me. How exactly were you going to use my nostalgic memories of you to get me to drop the charges against your brother? Was I supposed to be overcome with lust at the sight of your body? Remember the way it felt to sink my cock inside your virgin cunt?"

She trembled. With outrage. It was totally outrage.

He leaned closer, placing his glass on the table between them. The clink was too loud, making her flinch. "I do remember that, sweetheart. You were so tight. Your eighteenth birthday, right? I don't know how I waited that long."

No. She wasn't going to stand here mute while he ripped into her. "You waited that long because my father would have killed you for touching me before that."

"It might have been worth it." He inched forward, farther into her space. "So what's in the script, Tatiana? Aren't you supposed to be begging prettily for your brother's life?"

She eyed him, trying to draw the tattered remnants of her cool around her. "I came here because I thought you might be reasonable. All I want to do is work out some sort of payment plan. I have savings. I can loan that to Ron, and he can repay his debt. If, in return, you agree to not press criminal charges."

"He *stole* from me. I can't abide thieves. And fifty thousand dollars is hardly chump change."

Oh. My. God. Neither Caitlin nor Ron had gone into the details, beyond saying thousands. Perhaps naively, Tatiana had assumed they had meant, at the most, ten thousand. Ron was a blackjack dealer who would be hard-pressed to find any kind of job if word of this got out. Caitlin stayed at home with the baby. How could he have ever thought he could replace this kind of money? Did he honestly think no one would notice it?

Anger at her brother overwhelmed her, but she tried to focus. She'd rip the kid a new one later.

She looked Wyatt in the eye and reached into her bag. Her fingers brushed against those damn letters, but she dug past them to her checkbook. "Fine." She pulled it out, slid her pen free, and looked up at him. "Give me the exact amount, and we'll make this right."

Oh, she loved the way he eyed her in that superior way. He named a figure, obviously expecting to call her bluff.

She briskly filled in the blanks, trying not to think of the fact that she'd never put so many zeros on a check. Years of living the life of a starving artist, unwilling to take a dime from her parents after she'd bucked them and left college, had made her appreciate her success when she had achieved it. She'd saved like a squirrel hiding nuts for a cold, hard winter.

Wintertime was here, she supposed. Family above all. Plus she would get it back, if slowly, from Ron. It was worth it to save her stupid, loveable brother from prison. She made a mental note to transfer the necessary funds from her savings account that evening.

Wyatt watched her tear the check off and lay it on the coffee table. "You don't have that kind of money."

She capped the pen, tucking it back into her checkbook. "What makes you say that?"

"Your dress and shoes. If they even came from a department store instead of a supercenter, I'd be surprised." His gaze dipped to her neck. "The gold in your necklace is real, I'll grant you, but it's hardly a liquid asset you can tap into."

"Since when did you get so good at women's fashion?" He *was* good, too. She'd bought her dress and shoes at Target. On clearance.

Oh she loved shopping. But not for boring, conservative clothes like these. Floaty fabrics, slinky dresses, impractical shoes, unnecessary accessories. If she splurged, those were her weaknesses.

"Since my job consists of assessing the depth of my opponent's pockets."

"Is that how you see everyone playing downstairs? Your opponents?"

"They're betting against the house, aren't they? I *am* the house. And I always win."

"Well, you're wrong this time. The fact that I'm not wearing expensive clothes right now doesn't mean I don't have money." She hooked the necklace in her finger and lifted it. "This *is* real. Wearable, precious art. And people pay dearly for my creations, Caine."

His black eyes glinted with an avaricious gleam as he studied the necklace, as if he was cataloging its weight and price tag. "You're talented."

The small compliment smoothed some of her ruffled feathers. "I know." She allowed the necklace to drop, to lay against her breasts. "I may not be as wealthy as you, but I've been as successful in my field as you've been in yours."

His lashes dipped. "Apparently."

She placed her fingers on the check and slid it across the table. "So I can afford to pay back my brother's debt. I'll speak with Ron. There's no need to bring legal pressure against him."

"This feels like hush money."

"It's not. It's restitution."

"And if I don't take it? What then?"

She met his gaze evenly. "Then maybe I do beg prettily a little."

He stilled. She didn't know how long they were locked in a staring contest. Frankly, she didn't care. Part of her, a frighteningly large part of her, was enjoying it too much.

She'd handed him everything, all the power, and he

knew it. She could pull out those letters she had as well. Remind him of the things he'd said to her, in his own words. Really strip them both bare.

Wyatt leaned back on the sofa. "What if I said I would promise not to press charges against your brother…" he spread his legs slightly, putting his palms on his powerful thighs, "…if you spent a night in my bed?"

Chapter Two

HER HEART STOPPED. She had to struggle to find words. The right words, the socially appropriate ones. Ones that didn't betray her illicit spurt of lust. "I would slap your face and tell you I'm not a whore."

He cocked his head. "You played one for me occasionally."

Ah, yes. She remembered that memorable night. Remembered showing up at his crappy apartment in the fishnets and old trench coat she'd procured at Goodwill. Remembered how she'd begged him to pretend that he'd purchased her for the night, his to use at his will.

He had used her that night. As much as she'd used him.

They'd explored each other's likes and dislikes from their third date onward. No one had told her a teenager wasn't allowed to fantasize. She'd read dirty books voraciously when her mother wasn't looking, downloaded smut from the low-tech version of the internet that had existed then, and imagined doing every single dirty, wrong thing with her sexy rebel boyfriend. He had happily complied, both of them learning kink and games turned their cranks hard. They might have been virgins when they met, but there had been nothing innocent about their relationship.

"I'm not a real whore," she said, aware of how ridiculous that sounded. "And I'm certain you don't want or need a martyr in your bed."

"I don't know. A martyr could be hot. It reminds me of all those coercion scenarios we used to act out."

Don't ask me if I remember those. Don't.

"Remember?"

Christ.

His voice roughened, deepened. "You dirty little whore. You'll take my cock and you'll like it."

She knew he was only mocking her by repeating words from their past, words that were probably echoed in those letters of his. She knew she should walk right out of here.

But she stayed and watched him, her nipples painfully hard.

"Take those goddamn clothes off," he taunted. "Before I rip them off you." His gaze lingered on her throat, aware, she was certain, of every beat of her heart. "You like the way my cock feels, don't you? I felt you come, you little slut."

He wasn't any more immune to his words than she was. A quick glance down showed her the hard bulge beneath the fine twill of his trousers.

"Remember?" he asked softly.

Who was he kidding? She'd always remember Wyatt. That was the problem with having your first lover be spectacular in the sack and so attuned to all your dirty needs. Other men might be equally proficient, but he was the only one with whom she'd felt that particular *click.*

Still. She wasn't *really* a whore. She only played one in

bed sometimes.

She raised her chin. "The difference is I don't barter in sex. Um, for real, I mean."

He studied her for a beat of time before giving a shrug that was a little too casual for her to believe. "Fair enough. Would it make a difference if I told you I've already dropped the charges against your brother?"

Her mouth fell open, and she straightened. "What. Did. You. Say?"

"I dropped the charges against your brother earlier today. The publicity would have been an annoyance I can deal without. We agreed to a payment plan, so I won't need your money." With that, Wyatt picked up her precious check and ripped it cleanly in half, letting the paper flutter to the table.

"I'm supposed to believe you? Boom, like that?"

He rose from his seat, towering over her. With a few long strides he was at his desk. He picked up the sheaf of papers there and brought them back to her. "I got these from my attorney not long ago."

Regarding him warily, she accepted the crisp papers. It took her barely a few sentences to see past the legalese and realize it was, indeed, an agreement between Wyatt and one Ronald West, to accept responsibility for the stolen money and set up a payment plan.

"I'm surprised your brother didn't call you."

Mentally, Tatiana groaned and placed the agreement on the table. "I never took my phone off flight mode." She reached inside her deep bag and pulled her phone from its cluttered depths. She switched it on and waited a few seconds. Sure enough, she had four missed calls and a text from her brother. *Boss agreed to drop charges!!!!!! AMAZEBALLSSSSS.*

Tatiana hit reply, lest her brother be worried over her lack of response. *Yeah. Amazeballs. TTYL.* She slipped the phone back into her purse. "Well. It wouldn't have hurt you to tell me about this when it became clear I had no idea you'd already dropped the charges."

"You caught me off guard. And you may not remember, but I really hate someone sticking their nose in my business. Even if it is a pretty little nose."

Ugh. She did remember that, and if she had been using her brain, she might have realized that a different, more subtle approach was called for in dealing with this man.

Still, that didn't make her any less annoyed. "What the hell was up with that proposal? What do you think this is, some cheesy movie? *I'll drop the charges if you sleep with me.*" She mimicked his deep, cool voice.

Was that…? Yes. That mischievous glint in his eyes might have been swiftly disguised, but she'd seen it before. Back when teasing her had been his favorite pastime. He shrugged. "I wanted to see your response."

She rose to her feet, unable to stand him looming over her any longer. Sadly, he was much, much taller than her, so this only decreased the extent of his looming instead of banishing it altogether. She stalked forward until they were toe to toe and poked him in his chest. His firm, muscular…

No!

"I'm not a bug under some microscope. When I was a teenager, all of this emotionally unavailable brooding crap was sexy, but I'm an adult now. Do you think women enjoying feeling cheap like that?"

He grabbed her wrist before she could poke him again and drew her in until she was so close his hot breath fanned her cheek. His hand surrounded her wrist completely, his fingers overlapping.

She loved feeling delicate and small. It fed her fantasy of being taken. No! No, she wasn't being taken. Not right now.

"It wasn't meant to make you feel cheap." His lips touched her ear. "It was meant to make you hot."

A tremor ran through her.

"Because the girl I remember would have found that kind of proposition very, very hot. Are you still that girl, Tatiana?"

"I'm not a whore."

"There was nothing to barter over. It was a fantasy."

"Only you knew that."

"Yeah. And it still got you hot, didn't it?"

"You're a freak," she whispered.

"The best kind. Why did you come here?" Very delicately, he licked the outer curve of her ear, as if he couldn't stop himself from tasting her.

"I told you."

"You didn't have to come see me. You could have called or sent me an email. If you're as wealthy as you say, you could have hired a lawyer to rival my team."

"So why did I come here?" *Tell me. Because I don't know if I can even figure it out.*

The pause before he spoke told her he was giving the question serious consideration. "Because you were curious. Curious to see if I was still the man you remembered. If you still found me appealing, or if I'd turned into a disgusting toad. If you still responded to me the way you used to. If the sex was as good as you recall. Basically everything you wonder when you meet a former lover again. A former lover as memorable as me, at least."

"You're pretty arrogant."

"I'm smart, not arrogant."

He was. He was very smart. From the second she'd learned who Ron's boss was, she'd been bombarded with fantasies. They had grown with every glass of wine, and had become overwhelming when she'd dug through her memory chest for his letters, letters she hadn't glanced at in years and years.

She could have gotten back in touch with him, as he'd listed, in a number of less personal ways. She could have done nothing, let Ron handle it all, and given her brother financial and legal support quietly in the background.

But she'd been curious. Her curiosity would be the death of her.

Like now, with her fertile imagination wondering if he could still keep up with the horribly dirty scenarios her brain kept spinning about him. And her. And the things they could get up to as adults, things they'd barely scratched the surface of as kids.

Him, wrapping her hair around his fist.

Her, on her knees.

Him, binding her hands.

Her, surrendering.

The low hum of attraction she'd felt since the moment she'd heard Wyatt's voice flared into full-blown arousal. Her nipples tightened beneath her practical dress, her thighs trembling.

No. This was a monumentally stupid idea. Not only did they have this new *thing* with her brother lying between them, it was never a good idea to have a one-night stand with an old flame. She didn't know who he was anymore. He could have grown up into a sadistic monster. The games she played required a certain amount of trust. Could a person change from a sensitive, attentive lover to a monster in a decade? Possibly. Was it likely? Probably not.

Still. Stupid idea.

It was like he could sense her hesitation, knew that she needed just a little push. "I wouldn't fuck you in exchange for your brother's freedom. But I'd fuck you in exchange for a night of really hot sex."

The words lay between them. She should pull away. She should leave.

"Am I your memorable former lover, Wyatt?" Her voice was tremulous, but it was an act, the uncertain tone belying the coy demand hidden in the words. It had always been an act with Wyatt, but one that was conversely more honest than anything she'd ever had with anyone else.

They were still so close, their lips inches away. His gaze dipped to her mouth. "You know very well what you are."

"You must have gorgeous women throwing themselves at you all the time."

"I do."

She couldn't even take offense with his cavalier acknowledgment of his own charms. "I'm probably nothing compared to them."

"You don't need me to tell you how stunning you still are. And I know exactly what you can do with that body." The flick of his gaze felt like the touch of fire. "To answer the question you've been wondering since you decided to come here: Yes. I've gotten even better at sex, Tatiana. Have you?"

She totally had. But she didn't want to boast. Eh. Fuck it. "I'm sure your conquests outnumber mine, but I've had my fair share since you."

"Were they as good as me, though?"

What a male thing to ask. "Some were."

"Did they play well with your fantasies, Tatiana? The way I did?"

"Some did."

His eyes darkened further, and she was experienced enough to label the emotion gripping him now as lust with a heavy dose of jealousy. It was silly to be thrilled over that jealousy. He had no rights over her. Hadn't had any rights in a long time. "Did kissing them feel like you were getting burned alive?"

This was stupid. But… "It's been so long. I barely remember what kissing you felt like," she bluffed.

His lips were easing over hers almost before she finished speaking, brushing lightly, sending small tingles through her nerve endings. There was a spark.

And, then, without warning, he fanned that spark into a fire.

One arm went around her waist and he yanked her close, kissing her so brutally she swore her panties spontaneously combusted.

It was the kiss of a marauder and a pirate, taking everything she had to give and more. His tongue swept into her mouth, stroking, thrusting, mimicking sex. He allowed her a brief second of air before he kissed her again, this time growling over her easy surrender.

He slid one hand in her hair, holding her still for the violent kiss, while his other hand swept down her back to her bottom. His fingers clenched on her flesh, and she cried out in his mouth. Christ, but he tasted good. When he picked her up so her mound cradled his hard erection, she did whimper. He lifted his head. His cheeks were flushed, his eyes unfocused. "Well. Do you remember now?"

She tried to hide her smirk and licked her swollen lips. "Kind of."

He lowered his head for another kiss. A spurt of sanity had her turning her head. "Wyatt."

As if a weak evasive maneuver like that could stop Wyatt. He pressed a hot kiss against her neck. "Yeah?"

"We shouldn't." It would help her case if her voice wasn't so damn tremulous.

It was all his fault. Clearly Wyatt could still make her drop her social façade and tap into the wild creature inside of her. Maybe because he had helped develop it all those years ago.

He licked up to her ear and caught the lobe between his teeth, biting down gently. "You smell so good. You taste even better."

"Wyatt, wait. We need to talk."

He scraped his teeth along her earlobe. "Talk."

"This situation with my brother's between us. It complicates things."

"I told you. I don't want to talk about your idiot brother anymore."

"He's not an id—Oh fine. He did something pretty idiotic." She cast about for another excuse, but it was hard when he was… Dear God, his mouth. "We have a history. This would be stupid."

"This?"

"You know where this is leading."

He pulled away. His eyes were glazed with lust, underscored by something that looked an awful lot like…resignation? "Of course. I knew from the moment I heard your name."

Skeptical, she cocked her head. "Before you even saw me? How'd you know I didn't gain three hundred pounds and a hunchback over the last decade?"

His lips twisted. "I met you when you were chubby and had frizzy hair and acne."

A gasp escaped her lips. So she'd had a bit of an awkward phase. Bringing it up now was hardly gentlemanly. "Shut up, Caine."

"My point is, I wanted you then. I still want you now. When I walked away from you all those years ago, I knew that wanting would never stop." He tucked a strand of hair—sleek, not-frizzy hair, thank you very much—behind her ear. "Prettiness helps, Tatiana, but you and me? It's always been *more.* We're like a moth and a flame."

"Who's the moth?"

"Who cares?"

Really, when it felt so good to be on fire, who did care?

He leaned forward and delicately licked her neck, little flicks, as if he were sampling her. "It's pointless to resist this. Give in. I did."

"We're adults. Not impulsive kids ruled by our hormones."

"Then let's do some adult things."

"I could have a husband. Or a boyfriend."

"No. Or you wouldn't be here."

"No." Despite herself, she tilted her head back to give him access to the hollow of her throat. "You?"

"Not a single boyfriend," he said, dry as ever. "And no female either."

She was a little too relieved over that. "Just because we're both single—"

"Tatiana." He grasped her shoulders and held her back from him. "Tell me. Tell me you don't want me. I'll let you go. Stop kissing you. Stop licking you. Stop thinking of sucking your nipples or sinking my tongue in your pussy. Stop wondering if you still like having your hair jerked hard when you're sucking cock. Stop imagining how you'll look when you're getting pounded by my dick. All you have to do is tell me."

Her chest rose and fell, pragmatic thought blown out of her mind. Yes, please. All those things sounded perfect. A smorgasbord of lust and pleasure.

He kissed her, a quick, hard claiming. "Or, tell me you want this. And I'll make it the best night of your life."

Hmph, male ego. Natural competitiveness rose, and she found her voice. Her hoarse, excited voice. "You don't think it would be the best of *your* life?"

"We could find out." His lips captured hers again, kissing her until her lips felt bruised and sensitive. He drew away to whisper, "One night. No brother. No past. No coercion, unless you want to play at it."

There was no way this would end well. "And we'll be no different from old flames who hook up at their high school reunions? In the morning, we'd go back to our own lives?"

Dear Tatiana, when your brain says something is a stupid idea, maybe, I don't know, listen *to it.*

There was a pause. "Certainly."

Her body trembled as her good common sense did battle with her bad erogenous zones. What he was proposing was mad.

And she liked it.

Oh, for crying out loud. Her impulsive nature revved the engine. *Wheeeee.* What was life, anyway, without a few mistakes?

She licked her lips, loving the way his eyes immediately jumped there and darkened. "I wouldn't be averse to us pretending that you're coercing me. A little."

If he hadn't been holding her, she wouldn't have felt the shudder roll through him. That familiar sexual power rose inside her.

He smiled. It was the first real smile he'd given her, fond and amused. "You did have a thing about being handled rough."

She lifted her shoulder in a delicate shrug. "My liking for it has grown over the years." Some boyfriends had found it exciting, others abhorrent. She'd learned to judge who would respond to her tastes.

"What a coincidence. So has mine. Yes, then?"

"Yes."

He tightened his grip on her. "Safe word."

She responded to the urgency in his touch and voice. "Peanut."

"Too close to penis. I might think you're begging for more."

She bit the inside of her cheek, though safe words were

no laughing matter. "Candle."

He nodded. A shutter descended over his face, and when he next spoke, his voice was cold.

The curtain had lifted. The act had started, in earnest.

Chapter Three

"MAYBE YOU'RE RIGHT, Tatiana. Maybe we shouldn't do this. After all, that kiss was nice, but I can't imagine we'll be kissing all night, will we?"

She shook her head mutely, stopping when his large hand sank into her hair. She was never so grateful that she'd left it loose and unbound. The tug on her scalp made her eyes want to cross in pleasure.

"I think you need to give me a sample of what you're offering, honey." The slight pressure on her head made his desire clear. Her mouth watered, her attention darting down to where his cock was hard and prominent beneath his expensive clothes.

Still, she resisted. That was her favorite game, after all. "I don't know if we should. In the office. In the middle of the day."

"For the rest of the day and night I own you, Tatiana. If I want you to suck me off in front of an audience of twenty, you'll do it. Otherwise, you can leave right now."

She bit her lip and lowered her gaze, hoping to hide the hot lust detonating inside of her. "I don't want to leave."

"Then show me. On your knees."

She sank to her knees, loving the feel of the Berber carpeting beneath them. Loving the way his eyes followed her. Loving how his pants tented even more. Loving the supplication. She reached for the buckle of his belt, fumbling more than she needed to if only to raise the anticipation and excitement between them. Playing into the fantasy of the young ingénue and the ruthless pirate. She unzipped and unbuttoned his pants, and his cock leapt out to greet her.

Nothing had changed here. His cock was still as long and hard as she remembered, her hands too small to grasp as much as she'd like. She stroked down to the base, loving the decadence of soft skin stretched taut over tensile strength. His hand tightened on her hair when she slid her palm over the head of his cock, moistening her hand.

She resisted the steady pressure on the back of her head. Not because she didn't want her mouth on him, but because her character shouldn't.

"Stop playing," he growled.

"Am I playing?" She cast a glance upwards from beneath her lashes, her hand smoothing below his shaft to cradle his balls in her palm. She rolled them slightly, and he jumped, the muscles in his thighs tensing.

"Enough. Suck me."

Her pussy clenched so hard, she almost came right then and there. "But…I've never done that before," she said, in as breathless a tone as she could muster.

Lies. And he knew it, since he had been her tutor in oral sex. They'd spent many a heated afternoon in her bedroom, in his car, with his hand on her head and his body captive to her mouth.

His lips quirked upward. "Then you'll learn." The pressure on her head became a notch more insistent.

She gave in to the silent command, leaning forward to swirl her tongue around the head of his cock. Oh. Oh my. He didn't taste as good as she remembered. He tasted better, all manly and hot.

"Swallow me."

Poor man. If only she could. But where would be the fun in giving it all up right away? Deliberately awkward, she gave a few shallow bobs, letting her tongue glance over the sensitive underside of his shaft.

He growled in warning. "Tatiana."

She gave him a delicate lick, rubbing her tongue along the slit of his penis. He jumped and swore.

Tatiana drew away and nuzzled her cheek along the wet tip. "Yes?"

Wyatt's hand clenched on her head. "More. I want my entire dick wet with your saliva."

"Is that what you want?"

He wrapped one hand around the base of his shaft, stroked all the way up to that luscious fat tip and slicked it back down. "It's what you want, too."

Truth.

His hand pumped that thick shaft twice more, long, slow pulls, teasing her as much as she'd teased him. "Or I could come like this," he said, taunting her. "You can sit there. Watch me. Take it on your pretty face. I don't need you to suck me."

Oh, didn't he? She moved forward, pulling up short when his fingers tangled in her hair.

"Change your mind?" Wyatt dragged his cock across her

cheek, leaving a trail of his precome.

"Wyatt." The twinge of irritation she was feeling must have made itself apparent, because he chuckled and pressed his erection to her lips.

He wasn't laughing when she inhaled his cock until it just breached her throat. Since she knew he loved feeling like he was more than she could handle, she allowed herself to gag. She retreated, only to have him sink both hands in her hair. He held her head steady, his thumbs resting in the hollows of her cheeks. "Look at you. I never could forget how much you love this," he murmured, breaking out of his ruthless character. "Your eyes get so big when I thrust deep."

He put the words to action and groaned. She tried to swallow, breathe around the obstruction blocking her throat, though it was difficult. He withdrew and thrust again, shallower this time. She attempted to bring some suction into play in an effort to gain power, force him to lose control, but he figured out her game. A low growl sounded in his chest.

"Uh-uh, honey. This is my show. My body to use how I want. Isn't it?"

She nodded around the cock in her mouth, the body he'd spoken of firing up and heating.

"I'm going to fuck this pretty little face. And you're going to kneel there and take it. And if you do a very good job, maybe I'll let you come."

God, she needed that, wanted it. She nodded more furiously.

He set an unpredictable pace, never allowing her a chance to get comfortable in the depth and speed. His taste, his moves, they were both different and curiously nostalgic. He'd been forceful back then, but it had been fueled partially by the eagerness of a boy desperate to get off. Now, the force was tempered by a man who knew exactly how much pressure to exert. A man who had an intimate knowledge of female bodies and what they could take. What they needed. What she needed.

Her hands teased the parts of his shaft she couldn't swallow, spreading her saliva all over him until the wet rhythm accompanied his increasingly heavy breathing. She marked the instant his need became too urgent to control. His hips became more frantic, his balls tapping against her chin with each drive. She was nothing more than a receptacle for his lust, an object for him to play with.

It should have angered her.

It should have disgusted her.

Instead it freed her.

Freed her to admit she loved this, more than anything.

Wyatt had unlocked her brand of kink when she'd barely been old enough to know what it meant. It was only right he see how proficient she was in this role now.

He grunted above her and thrust deep, coming in thick pulses on her tongue. He withdrew while still coming, letting the semen mark her chin. He grabbed his cock and milked it, aiming the final spurts at her neck and chest, the neckline of her practical dress wetting under the evidence of his lust.

Her chest rose and fell as he stumbled back a step. He recovered his cool faster than she would have hoped, tucking his cock inside and buttoning and zipping his trousers up. "Not bad. Your technique has improved over the years."

Bitch, please. It had been better than not bad. She had his release staining her clothes to prove that. He was staying in character, however, and she would appreciate that the second she got hers. She fisted her hands on her thighs, ready to rip her own clothes off if he wasn't quick enough about it. "What about me?"

That black eyebrow rose. "What about you?"

The pout forming on her face wasn't faked. "You said you would let me come."

"I said maybe I would let you come."

Yes, yes, yes. Her toes curled. Having an orgasm was fun. But the anticipation of waiting for it, teased with it? That was bliss.

"Then, again," he was saying. "I suppose it would be cruel to make you—"

"You bastard," she interrupted smoothly and slipped her hand up his thigh. "I need it so bad."

He barely missed a beat. "I know exactly what you need. You need to wait, until this evening. It'll make things even more explosive, don't you think? After all, now that you've taken the edge off for me, I won't be in any hurry."

A slow Wyatt was dangerous. Her pussy clenched.

He gave her his hand, and she rose to her feet, conscious of his sticky release on her chin and neck. "Tell me you have a shower hidden away in a secret panel somewhere?"

He studied her, satisfaction in his gaze. "No. Though that sounds like something I should have." One large finger swiped at the mess on her chin, bringing it to her lips. Hungry for the taste of him, ready to take any chance she could to tease him, she greedily licked him clean. He pressed his finger deeper, until he was inside her to the knuckle. The digit felt too small after the huge thickness of his cock, her mouth swollen and sensitive.

Wyatt withdrew his touch all too soon. "My suite isn't far. You can shower there."

A jolt of surprise ran through her. She hadn't quite expected that he'd be raring to head to a hotel room right away. A civilized assignation would allow her time to go to the lodgings she'd booked elsewhere, get dressed properly for the night, pamper herself. "Are you done working for the day?"

"No. But if you think I'll let you step foot off these premises and give you a chance to change your mind, you're mad. You'll wait for me in my home. It's right upstairs."

The logistics of his directive were troubling. "You expect me to walk out there…"

"And into the hallway and into the elevator, where you will obviously be going to my bed."

She rolled her eyes. Men. "I need a Kleenex. A towel. Something."

His gaze dropped to her chest. "Ah. Yes." He leaned away and pulled a handful of tissues from the box on his desk. Batting away her hands, he cleaned her off, buttoned up her blazer, and dropped a kiss on her nose. "There. No one will even know you took a bath in my come." He dropped his voice. "Though that might be fun, too. For people to see what a dirty little slut you are?"

That *would* be fun. She imagined what his employees, his guests, might think if they saw her all messed up, clearly heading up to his bed.

"You like that." It was a statement, not a question.

"Maybe."

He smirked. "Duly noted." He pulled a key card from his pocket. "Take this. You'll need to swipe it in the elevator, and again at the door for penthouse access. Feel free to make yourself at home."

"I need clothes, since you destroyed mine. My suitcase is in my car."

"Forget your suitcase. I'll send up someone from the spa and a selection from the clothing shop downstairs."

A lifetime of paying her own way prompted her to frown. "I don't want you buying things for me."

He surveyed her lazily. "But that's part of the fantasy. I want to pamper you. I want you to prepare yourself for me from the skin out. I want to know I put every piece of clothing on you, so I won't feel bad when I tear it off."

Tatiana wouldn't be a female if those words didn't give her a thrill of guilty pleasure. "Maybe just this once..."

Done with conversation, Wyatt checked his watch. "You have two hours, approximately, before I'll expect your time to be my own."

A shiver of delight ran down her spine. She couldn't resist a final teasing parry as he guided her to the door. "You're so presumptuous. I could have had things to do before our night."

He smiled and leaned down to whisper in her ear as she exited. "Ah, but, pet, the only thing you'll be doing for the indefinite future is...me."

Chapter Four

TWO HOURS.

Somehow, he had to wait two hours to see Tatiana again.

That was going to be hard, no pun intended.

Wyatt rubbed his forehead and stared at the computer screen. He had no idea what document he had open, or what it was about. No, there were numbers on it. So it was related to numbers. Probably had something to do with the business he'd spent years slaving over. His baby. Until not too long ago, the sole focus of his existence. No big.

"Jesus Christ." He buried his face in his hands. *It's always been more.* Yes, some indefinable *more* that he'd never captured with any other woman, no matter how much he liked or cared for them.

When he was young, he could remember playing at his mother's feet with a mechanical toy she'd treasured from her own childhood. After it was wound up, a pair of skaters would dance around the perimeter of the circular surface, come together for a brief moment for the crescendo of the song, and then skate off again for the chorus.

When he and Tatiana had called it quits, part of him had hoped they'd never meet again. The pain of the breakup was that excruciating. Another part of him—a secret, hidden part—had wondered if they were like that mechanical couple. Crashing together, twirling around, maybe drifting off. But always returning.

Even though he'd been half-waiting for her to come back into his life for what seemed like forever, seeing her again had been a punch to the gut. The gray and boring real world had disappeared, leaving only the two of them and all the things they knew they could do to each other. A buffet of Technicolor fantasy.

Their crashing together was inevitable. She'd twitched her tail at him, and he'd started counting down the minutes to locking his lips with hers. Lips and…other things.

Forget work. Forget his schedule. Forget everything else in the world. All that mattered was her.

Wyatt pinched the bridge of his nose. There were no words to explain how hard he'd had to restrain himself from escorting her to his rooms. If he had, he would have stayed. For that matter, he was vibrating with the urge to head upstairs this very minute, to make sure she had actually gone to his home instead of taking the elevator in the opposite direction. No. He pushed that possibility out of his mind. Of course she had stayed. He couldn't possibly be the only one who was this worked up.

Maybe she was showering, or better yet, ensconced in the bathtub he'd chosen for its luxurious decadence and never used, because really, who had time for baths when they worked nineteen-hour days?

He'd like to see Tatiana soaping up. Washing his come

off so he could make her dirty again.

But no. He inhaled. Tatiana would be combustible later if he made them both wait. The woman had a perverse love of testing his limits. The more he controlled himself, and by extension her, the hotter she got. Or at least that's the way he remembered things from their seven-year relationship. He'd almost forgotten, until she'd cued him. Clever girl.

His eyes strayed to the clock on the bottom of the screen. One hour and thirty-eight minutes to go.

He wrapped his fingers around the Montblanc pen on his desk and squeezed hard. Only the ridiculous cost of the thing and his fear of cracking it made him ease up. Paying more than a dollar for a pen. Fucking ridiculous.

His door opened, and he tensed. He didn't have to look up to identify the steady, heavy footsteps of his assistant. Damn it. He had been hoping the woman would sit quietly at her desk for the rest of the day.

He hired his people partially for their ability to keep their mouths shut. But behind closed doors, Esme didn't bother pulling her punches or remaining silent around him. He didn't remember much about his mother, since she had died when he was barely eight, but he liked to think if she had lived, she would treat him the way Esme did. With a sort of calm and rock-steady concern.

It wasn't manly to crave mothering, so he told himself Esme was also his friend and right hand, and she was. He would be crippled without her. Really, though…he liked the idea of someone giving a damn about him. So she stayed. And he allowed her some liberties when it came to meddling in return for cookies at Christmastime and invitations to her family's events.

That didn't mean he wanted maternal interference right now. Not when his brain was filled with images of a slick Tatiana. Was she washing her hair right now? When they'd been younger, she'd had a straight, honey-colored waterfall to her waist. Her cut was shorter now, more mature, but the strands were still long enough for him to wrap around his fist.

"Yes?" he asked, in as curt a manner as possible. An hour and thirty-six minutes now.

"I need these signed, sir," she said in her deceptively soft, grandmotherly manner.

Soft, hah. The woman was a piranha. Disguised as a flounder.

Brusquely, he used his ridiculously expensive pen to sign at the indicated tabs and handed the sheaf of documents back to her.

"You didn't even read them," she remarked.

Curses. It had been a test. "Did I need to?"

"No. They're all standard. It's just not like you."

He avoided looking at her and clicked the mouse. She couldn't see his screen, or she'd know he was merely switching back and forth between browser tabs. "I'm busy, Esme. Can I help you with anything else?"

"Are you okay?"

Click. Click. "Sure."

"You don't seem okay."

"I'm fine."

"That girl…she's beautiful."

"She is."

"She rattled you."

Esme saw way too much sometimes. "No."

"I'm not saying it's a bad thing. I haven't seen you acknowledge a woman at all in a while, let alone like that."

What? Why, he'd had a date just last…

His mind blanked. Hell. It was a bad sign when you couldn't remember the last time you'd wanted to ask a woman out.

He was careful with his image. He and Tatiana had discovered their predilections early enough that they'd understood it was something they shouldn't share with everyone, and it was important for him to keep a moderately low profile anyway. In a town full of larger-than-life pleasure palaces, his was carefully designed to appeal to those who wanted to partake of Sin City without their faces showing up online the next day.

That didn't mean he was a monk. His staff had seen women on his arm and even in his penthouse, women he liked and respected and were as discreet as him. Maybe not lately, though.

"Plus," Esme continued, "there's the fact that she went up to your place right away. That's fairly unusual too."

He huffed out a breath. "Is there anything that happens around here that you don't know, Esme?"

The woman patted a gray hair back into place. "Not really."

"We dated when we were younger." Years of love and fights and passion boiled down to a few words. "High school, college." She'd been in college. He'd been taking classes whenever he could fit them in around basic survival.

"Ah." A wrinkled hand dropped onto his shoulder, the weight comforting. "An old flame, then."

"Yes."

She squeezed. "A bad breakup?"

"Yes." At the time, they'd told themselves it was amicable, but his pain after hadn't felt friendly at all. A decade later, he no longer had any idea what had led to their separation, except for a series of stumbling blocks, one after another. Her parents' constant disapproval of him. Him accusing her mom and dad of controlling her. Her jealousy of any woman he so much as spoke to. His feeling that he had nothing to offer her. They had been young and tempestuous and unable to cope.

Sometimes he wondered what would have happened if they'd been a little older. A little wiser.

A little more like who they were now.

He shut the door on that dangerous train of thought. He might know who he was now, but he didn't kid himself that he knew Tatiana at all anymore. Except that she still had some sort of crazy *it* factor that made him want to drool at first glimpse.

He glanced at the torn check lying in pieces on his coffee table. Her success pleased him nearly as much as her continued smoking-hot appearance. Sure, maybe she'd had parents to fall back on while he had none, but it sounded like she'd bucked them and carved out a niche of her own in a competitive industry. Just like him.

There was no joy in dominating a weak female. But a strong, successful woman, an equal, who *allowed* him to push her to her knees?

Yes. Hot.

He took a deep breath, trying to diffuse some of his anticipation. This sexual encounter still didn't mean anything. This…whatever they were embarking on, didn't mean anything.

Other than she was as hungry now for the same brand of kinky sex she'd been eager for years ago. Luckily, he hadn't lied—his skills in that area had only grown.

"Well. Since you're obviously seeing her again, I hope things work out better this time around."

He glanced at Esme. "We're having dinner, maybe some conversation. Catching up. That's all." Sometimes he felt like an alien, searching to hide his nature under words that were socially acceptable to the masses. *We're having a date* was far more palatable than *we're fucking each other silly within hours of meeting each other again.* "This isn't a relationship or anything."

Her blue eyes were soft, concerned. "Would it be so terrible if it was?"

His mouth twisted. "I'm quite content with my life as it is, Esme." No more living hand-to-mouth, wondering whether his next paycheck would cover the rent and the groceries. All he'd had to do was work like a dog and give up having a social life and a family. Who needed any of that when you had things? Things like a huge hot tub.

That you never use.

"Of course, sir."

A thought occurred to him. "If you hear any gossip about Ms. Belikov, please let me know the source. And squash it." He'd never sent up staff from the salon and the boutique to tend a woman in his penthouse, though they offered such personal services to their guests. The employees wouldn't breathe a word about their clients' identities, but he understood a deviation in their boss's routine might titillate them.

No one would dare speak about Tatiana. Not if they valued their job. And yes, he would be this protective of any woman's identity and reputation.

Liar.

A militant look entered his assistant's eyes. "Don't you worry, Wyatt. I'll handle it."

"Thank you."

"I'm going to take off a little early if that's okay. Celia's bringing the baby around."

Esme doted on her granddaughter. The kid was cute, he supposed. He didn't know much about children, except they were loud and looked vaguely smooshed for the first few months of their life. "Sure. Have a good night."

"You too." The older woman gave him another assessing look, a final pat, and left. Wyatt almost called her back. Her concern might be unwarranted, but at least it kept his brain from dwelling on what Tatiana might be doing right this minute.

Was she hot? Was it painful to keep her fingers away from her swollen sex? He regretted he hadn't seen it yet, but he could hardly torture her without denying himself.

Besides, he knew what was waiting for him. A decade couldn't dull the memory of the hot little pussy he'd explored for years with his cock, mouth, and hands. He could still visualize every puffy pink fold shining with her juices. It had been a privilege to be the first man inside that territory. Such a privilege, he'd waited to lose his own virginity far longer than most guys did. He hadn't wanted to fuck just any girl. He'd wanted to fuck Tatiana.

It also hadn't been such a hardship, since an adolescent's idea of what constituted sex was far more fluid than an adult's. The things they'd done…

He shifted, annoyed when he realized he still had a solid hour and twenty minutes left. Wyatt shoved back from his desk and raked his hands through his hair. His skin felt too sensitive, as if every inch of him was screaming for her touch. He needed her *now.*

He paced to the window and stood, clenching his hands behind his back. When he got her under him, he didn't know if he'd be able to let her up to breathe for a while.

You only get a few hours.

That was good. It was better to have an expiration date on their time together. For this kind of sex, he'd be willing to toss everything else out the window, starting with his precious business.

And wasn't that a scary thought.

Chapter Five

TATIANA LINGERED IN the foyer for a while after she gained access to Wyatt's penthouse, clutching her blazer tight to her throat like a nervous virgin.

Or like a harlot concealing sin.

Yes. Yes. She was a harlot, a daring and brave woman. And she would not be intimidated by the absurd display of wealth in front of her.

Tatiana tightened her lips and walked into the living room. Even after she had started earning regular commissions and paychecks, she had never seen the need to flaunt her money. She lived in the same small apartment with the same comfortable furniture and drove the same reliable car. Wyatt, however…oh, he flaunted it.

The suite matched the rest of the casino: large, luxurious, and expensive. She ran her hand over the cool black leather of the large couch, fingering the thick red blanket draped over its back. It was the sole homey touch to the otherwise sterile black-and-white décor. Did he live here primarily? Did he have some other place where he kept all his knickknacks and clutter?

Curious, she walked into the open kitchen. It looked like a chef's wet dream, filled with granite and stainless steel. Unable to shake the feeling that she was snooping, she pulled open the fridge door. It wasn't packed, but it was stocked with enough perishables to last a single person for the week. So odds were, yes, he did live here regularly.

She walked back out into the living room. Like Wyatt's office, no personal effects decorated the walls or tables or bookshelves. There were some paintings, abstract paint splatters Tatiana hated on sight. The Wyatt she remembered would never have picked those out.

But then, you don't know this Wyatt. Maybe he loved abstract art. And other things she hated with a passion. Like Brussels sprouts. Had there been Brussels sprouts in his fridge? What kind of monster liked Brussels sprouts? Tiny alien brains.

Don't you dare talk yourself out of the fun now. She was having trouble reconciling this elegant place with the dingy apartments Wyatt had lived in when they were lovers, that was all. Hell, she couldn't really reconcile this with anything in her reality. Her parents and most of her friends were still firmly middle-class.

But rich wouldn't cow her. Money was paper, a way to buy things. She squared her shoulders and kicked off her boring, sensible heels. A hum of delight left her when her bare feet met the plush white carpet. She bent to scoop up her shoes.

First things first. She needed to clean up. The door to a half bath stood open in the foyer, but Tatiana assumed there was a full one somewhere.

The first door she wandered through was a bedroom.

She knew even without prying through the closets or the drawers of the mahogany dresser that this was Wyatt's room. It smelled like him, all warm and spicy.

The massive four-poster bed with rich black bedding dominated the room. A renewed pang of arousal went through Tatiana at the thought of Wyatt dominating *her* on it. Soon. Soon.

Her, on her hands and knees, his hands clenching her hips, serving her pussy up for his possession…

She clenched her hand on the doorframe and breathed deep. Maybe she should opt for a cold shower.

The bathroom was as decadent as the rest of the place, with gold-veined-shot chocolate marble decorating the floor, tub, and shower enclosure. She eyed the tub wistfully but feared if she sank into it, she'd never leave, not even when Wyatt came to the door.

He could join you.

Oh, that was a nice possibility. She'd table that, for later in the evening. If she waited for him in the tub, she'd likely be a prune by the time he got home.

The shower was the best type of consolation prize. Enclosed on three sides by glass, there were four waterfall showerheads and controls that looked like they had been designed by NASA scientists.

She made quick work of her clothes and stepped inside. After a couple of minutes, and a face blast of water, she figured out how to operate the damn thing and stood under perfectly angled sprays of water.

She tipped her head back, enjoying the experience. This. She could get behind this kind of indulgence. Pleasure-wise, this ranked up there with splurging on strappy gold sandals.

Slicking her hair back from her face, she glanced at the ledge that held soap and bottles of shampoo. Two of the bottles sported labels from high-end salons. She opened one of those pink bottles and sniffed, choking on the strong floral notes. No wonder it was full. No way would Wyatt choose to smell like this.

She put it back and picked up a vaguely familiar blue bottle. It was a two-in-one shampoo and conditioner. Almost exclusively a man's shampoo, designed for no-fuss shoppers.

Her lips curved, remembering a long-ago evening and Wyatt's annoyance when she bought him a separate shampoo and conditioner. *Tatiana, who the hell cares if this will condition my hair better than my usual stuff?*

He still used that three-dollar shampoo from a drugstore. Even when he could buy and sell a whole salon full of expensive men's hair products.

She liked that. She liked it so much she used the two-in-one though the more girly products were probably meant for females like her who weaved in and out of his life.

She would rather smell like him than them.

Leaving the water was tough, but she needed time to ready herself and see about the clothes Wyatt had said he would send up. She dried off in the steam-filled room, the rough terry of the towel turning her skin pinker.

When she was bundled in a robe, she stepped outside the bathroom, only to pull up short at the clear, brisk sound of feminine voices outside the bedroom door.

Hoping it wasn't a trio of serial killers, Tatiana steadied the towel wrapped around her head, cinched her belt, and opened the door. The polished young women standing just outside turned as if they were one creature and smiled with professional distance.

"Ms. Belikov," one of them said. "My name is Cher. We apologize for disturbing you, but Mr. Caine sent us up to take care of your needs."

I'd like Wyatt to take care of my needs.

But for that, she would have to wait. She glanced at the rack of colorful clothes they'd brought with them, as well as the wheeled salon chair. "Ah, I see. I'm not certain what needs I have."

The same girl spoke, studying her intently. "Waxing."

Tatiana wanted to cover her eyebrows in shame. Yes, fine, they had been a little neglected lately.

"And we can do your hair and nails and makeup, of course. While we're doing that, Jean here…" she gestured to the blank-faced blonde standing next to her, "…can model the outfits for you until you find one that meets with your approval."

Jean was the same size as her, roughly. Wow. There were people in the world too wealthy to even try their own clothes on?

In for a penny.

"That's fine," she responded.

Cher nodded once, and that was apparently a signal to the other women to briskly go about their duties. "Come." Cher gestured to the salon chair. "Katya here will be doing your nails. I will handle the waxing."

Tatiana bravely blinked back tears when the torture on her eyebrows was completed. Cher moved around to face her. "Would you like anything else waxed? Legs, arms, bikini, Brazilian?"

Tatiana glanced up. “I, uh, just shaved my legs this morning.” Briefly, she entertained the possibility of a more intimate wax. Wyatt had never stated an opinion when they’d been dating, but then they’d both been young enough to care more about getting naked than grooming preferences. A shot of uncertainty ran through her. As he’d matured and refined his tastes, had he grown to dislike the natural look? Maybe he was one of those guys who wanted no obstacles in their way.

These ladies may know what Wyatt’s other lovers prefer.

As soon as the thought emerged, she shoved it aside. No. Thank you. She didn’t want to think of those women at all, let alone their vaginas.

“I’m not sure,” she admitted.

Cher was expressionless. “It’s a matter of taste.”

“Do you think…do you think a waxed look is better?”

Katya, silent until now, paused in filing Tatiana’s nails and cleared her throat. For a second, Cher’s professional mien slipped and amusement shone through, but she sobered in a blink. “I don’t think it matters. It should be what you prefer. I will tell you, if it’s your first time, the area might be sore for a couple of days afterward.”

Bless her, she was telling Tatiana in as subtle a way as possible that sex may not be the best activity to engage in after a waxing treatment. Besides, she thought, mildly annoyed with her brief moment of insecurity, it *should* totally be what she preferred. “I think I’ll skip that then.”

“No problem.” Brisk, Cher unwound the towel around Tatiana’s hair. “Your hair’s beautiful. We’ll just give it some volume, hmm?”

“Sounds good.” Back on more familiar footing, she let

them fuss and flutter around her. If such a thing were possible, they spoke even less. Tatiana preferred the lack of chatter. This way, her thoughts could linger on what Wyatt might be doing downstairs. Was he thinking of her? Was he counting the minutes, the way she was? Was he remembering what her body looked like, wondering how she'd changed?

Sex was so much more fun when anticipation was added to the mix.

Jean modeled one outfit after another. At first, Tatiana tried to be tactful, but after her second glass of champagne, she felt no compunction about sending the model off with a wrinkled nose. *This is kinda fun.*

While Jean was donning the final dress, Cher spoke to Katya, who was putting the finishing touches on Tatiana's toenails. "Call down to the shop and tell them to send up another rack of dresses. These are no good."

Tatiana grimaced. "Oh, no. No. I'll pick one of them."

"Don't feel obligated. I agree, none of these would look right on you."

Jean opened the bedroom door and came out to the living room, a small grin on her face. "I think you'll like this one. I should have put it on first."

Tatiana inhaled. *Oh my, yes.*

The dress was her favorite color, green. It was made of some floaty kind of chiffon, and was short, just covering the model's ass and hitting the tops of her thighs. The skirt consisted of layers of vertical strips that flirted with her skin. The bodice was a halter, and it cupped the model's small breasts, pushing them high. She turned around, and Tatiana had to restrain herself from drooling over the bare expanse of back that was revealed.

"This one," she said definitively.

"Absolutely," Cher agreed. She checked her watch. "We'll help you dress and then bid you good night. Mr. Caine wanted you ready by six for dinner."

Dinner, huh?

Tatiana glanced at the model, imagining the dress on her own body.

Well. He was certainly going to eat her up. And she would absolutely let him.

Chapter Six

WYATT PAUSED OUTSIDE the door of his suite, hesitation and a foreign emotion making him pause. She was inside. *She* was inside his home.

Déjà vu swamped him. They'd done this before. Back then, he'd come home to his apartment, his muscles and arms aching, and she'd be waiting for him. Oftentimes studying. Occasionally, she'd brought him some dinner, but really, all he'd ever wanted to nibble on was her.

He shook his head hard, trying to dislodge those memories. *Do not mix up tonight with the past.* This was different. Like an anonymous one-night stand. Just because he'd never had one of those before didn't mean he didn't know their rules.

He'd been so good lately, hadn't he? Guarding his image as an upscale businessman, someone who could run a discreet den of sin. People handed him their money and their secrets, trusted him. He had wealth, power, prestige. Respect tinged with a small amount of fear. What more could a man want?

Nothing. Except maybe a night between the thighs of

the woman waiting inside his home.

He pressed his hand against the pad next to the door. The door beeped and admitted him.

He stepped inside, opening his mouth to call out something dry and witty. But then he saw her.

Fuck it all.

He was lightheaded. That's what happened when every single drop of blood in your brain raced to your cock.

It was dim inside the suite—she hadn't turned the lights on, and the sun was setting. She stood with her back to him across the expanse of plush white carpet, staring out the floor-to-ceiling windows.

She wore a dress, a scrap of green gauze the same color as her eyes. It skimmed over her round ass and brushed the tops of her thighs. Her back was bare, exposing the long, elegant line of her spine. Her skin was white there, a contrast to her sun-kissed face and arms.

He knew she was aware he was there. She was posing for him, no fool as to her effect on a man. Her eyes met his in the reflection of the glass.

Ever so slowly she turned, allowing him to process the rest of her. The skirt was a game of peek-a-boo, a bunch of strips held together by some miracle of modern dress design. The top he could easily rip away and bare the round, succulent breasts that were swelling up from the neckline.

She licked her lips. Her slick, glossy lips, painted a whore's red. She'd done something to her eyes to make them darker and more mysterious. Her cheeks were flushed, and he wasn't sure if that was makeup or arousal.

He should compliment her. Tell her she looked stunning, as stunning now as she had a decade ago—no, even more stunning. Ask her if she wanted to order dinner here, or go out somewhere to eat. Feed her body, and then let her feed his hungers.

Instead, he heard himself speaking, sounding rough and foreign. "Have you changed your mind?"

She swallowed. Like a helpless puppet, he watched her throat bobbing.

He wanted to be in that throat when she swallowed. He could live in her mouth. He entertained a stray vision of chaining her to his desk and forcing her to give him blow-jobs when he required. It would be a continuous, endless round of fellatio. A barbaric fantasy. But she liked him barbaric.

"No." Her voice sounded no better than his, scratchy and thin.

It was difficult to follow her response, though he had been the one to ask the question. No, she hadn't changed her mind. Excellent. Thank God.

Oh yeah. He didn't care anymore if this was a bad idea.

Time to take control. While he would be happy fucking her any which way he could get her, he wanted them both to get their rocks off.

He cleared his throat and deliberately made his tone hard, commanding. "Is this the way you learned to greet a man?"

Slowly. Oh so slowly, so he would be left in no doubt that she was obliging him because of her own needs and not his, she sank to her knees. The skirt of her dress billowed out around her creamy thighs. She glanced up at him from beneath her long eyelashes. "Good evening."

"Good evening…?"

A corner of her mouth kicked up. "Do you like to be called Master now?"

He prowled closer, until he stood directly in front of her. His crotch was at her eye level, leaving her in no doubt of how aroused he was. She may as well have not sucked him off in his office a couple hours ago.

He felt like he was sixteen again. At least as far as his stamina went. He grabbed hold of her hair, which had been done in a fetching topknot, a look that made him want nothing more than to shove his hands in it and mess it up. Women and their sneaky tricks.

He pulled hard enough that she winced, and a glint of wariness entered her eyes.

"You will address me with respect," he said quietly. "You will do everything I say. Or you will be punished. Do you understand me?"

"Yes," she breathed.

He used his grip on her head to give her a small shake. "Yes, what?"

"Yes…sir."

"Good." He released her hair and walked over to the minibar. He didn't precisely need a drink, but he had to occupy his hands before he tore the dress off her and plunged his cock into her tight pussy. He pulled out a bottle of scotch, casually checking the label. "Did you masturbate when you came up here?"

"No, sir."

"Why?"

"Because you told me not to."

"Will you always do what I tell you?"

She paused. "In the bedroom, you know that I will."

He had to bite back a smile at the caveat, and poured the scotch. "Undo that halter. I want to see your tits."

She didn't hesitate, which told him that she needed to come almost as badly as he did. He watched in the mirror behind the bar as she lowered the top, baring her small breasts. They were round and firm, with hard apricot-colored nipples topping them. That gold necklace was still around her throat, the twisted strips of gold falling between her curves. A pagan sacrifice, all for him. Wyatt pressed his cock into the wood of the bar in the hopes of some relief. "Play with them."

She cradled them from below, as if offering the flesh to him. Slowly, she circled the nipples, letting them grow harder and longer.

The mirror wasn't enough for him. He turned to watch her, captivated by the way the sun bathed her from behind. It lit her hair so it glinted like a honey-colored nimbus around her face, burnishing her skin to a golden tone.

Her head was tilted back, a small frown wrinkling her forehead as she concentrated on the sensations in her body. He liked her focus, but at the same time, wanted to ruffle her up some more.

"Are you wet?"

"Yes…sir."

He made a mental note of the hesitation, probably purposeful on her part. If ever he'd seen a woman who craved a good spanking, it was her. "Lift your skirt. Let me see."

She kept one hand on her nipple, pressing it hard between her finger and thumb, and dropped the other to her thigh. Kneeling as she was, the fabric of her skirt had separated, the strips between her legs falling down to cover her. He would swear she was in even better shape now than she had been at eighteen.

Yeah. He was a jerk enough to be a little put out over that. He had spotted some grays in his hair the other day. Was it so much to ask for an ex to not look better than him?

Actually, he decided when she brushed the material of her skirt away so it bared her panties, scratch that. He was very, very happy with her appearance. Very happy indeed.

"I hope you don't mind, sir," she whispered. "I know you sent up some lingerie, but I felt more comfortable in my own underwear."

She also knew him too well, knew that the plain white cotton bikinis would tantalize him far more than the raciest of crotchless lace panties. He took a sip of his drink to give himself something to do, barely tasting the fiery alcohol.

There was a wet spot on her panties that had probably been there since he'd kissed her in his office. "Push them aside."

Her French-manicure-tipped finger hooked the crotch of her panties and pulled them to the side, revealing a mound with trimmed blonde ringlets and her puffy pink pussy lips.

"Put your finger inside."

She obeyed, sinking her finger deep and closing her eyes. A gasp left her lips, and she threw her head back, that topknot trembling. She used her other hand to grab her breast and squeeze, hard.

But, he noted with approval, she didn't do anything with that finger but insert it. He shifted, betraying his excitement. "How does that feel?"

"Good."

"Stir it around. Get it really wet."

She pulsed her finger in and out of her pussy a few times and made a small mewling sound.

"Do you want to fuck it?" he asked, as calmly as he could.

"Yes."

"Fuck it then. Only five strokes."

She pushed her finger in and out exactly five times and then stopped, waiting. Her breathing was so fast her pretty little tits were trembling. "Please. I need more."

"More strokes?"

She licked her lips, eyeing his crotch. "More…everything."

"Aren't your fingers thick enough for you?"

"No, sir."

"Aren't they long enough for you?"

"No, sir."

Every tremulous *sir* out of those lips raked across his balls. Jesus Christ. He drained his glass and placed it on the counter of the bar. He paced back over to where she knelt and stood over her. He tucked a tendril of hair behind her ear, and she shook.

Good. One day he would teach her to come when he touched her cheek. When he looked at her across the room.

You won't have her one day.

Wyatt paused. Right. Whatever. He'd just have to debauch her thoroughly now.

He ran his finger down her cheek. "You look like such a good girl, Tatiana. But you're so hungry for cock, aren't you?"

"Your cock. Sir."

The flattery was part of the game, but it still pleased him. He grasped her nape. "Take your fingers off your body and unbutton me."

She obeyed, eager, and he could smell the scent of her body on her finger where she fumbled with his fly. Once she had his trousers open, she reached inside and pulled out his cock.

He didn't know if he'd ever been so engorged. "Get it wet. No." He stopped her when she moved her head forward, mouth open. "I want to feel your pussy on me."

She nodded, her hand sinking between her legs and under her panties before he even finished speaking. The sight of her fingers rubbing her muff would be one of those images he'd replay when he was aching and alone, fucking his own fist.

He hissed when she wrapped her wet hand around him, the heat from her body scalding him. Christ. He had hoped to drag this out a little longer, but they were both too excited, too turned on. Her hand stole away for more lubrication—and maybe just to tease herself with her touch, though she didn't linger. If he was capable at all of pretty speech, he'd heap praise on her for the way she was polishing his dick.

"Get up," he said instead, guttural.

Sinuous as a cat, she released him and got to her feet. Her skirt dropped, hiding her pussy from his view. No. No. Nothing should conceal that pussy. She should walk around always bare and ready for him. Or in nothing but those tight, white, oh-so-easy-to-rip bikinis.

"Go stand in front of the window."

She glanced behind her at the huge glass wall. The sun

had sunk, dusk settling over the valley beneath them. "But…"

"But what?" He didn't have to force the sharpness of his tone. His cock wanted in this woman, damn it. The poor bastard didn't understand the delay.

"Couldn't someone see us?"

"Maybe." He walked over to the wall and hit the light switch, sliding it down so they were bathed in dim light. "Now they can, if anyone's looking."

Her eyes narrowed, and for a second he found himself praying she would argue, if only so he could punish her insolence.

But instead, she turned and walked to the window, her breasts proudly bared and her shoulders straight. He reached into his pocket and pulled out a condom. His pants were bunched beneath his balls, but he liked being fully clothed while she was in disarray. It appealed to him. "Press your breasts against the window, Tatiana. Give everyone a good show now."

"I don't want to." But she didn't utter their safe word.

"Do you want this cock?" He passed his hand over it, fighting not to grimace. His own fist felt distasteful after the softness of her fingers, the wetness of her mouth. After he fucked her, he'd really be ruined.

Her glance over her shoulder was full of yearning. "Yes, sir."

"Then you'll obey."

Hesitant, she pressed her breasts against the window. A gasp left her.

"Is it cold?"

"A little. Now that the sun is gone."

The desert nights could get wickedly cold. "Is it cooling down that fire in your pussy?" He ripped open the foil package, grateful she had her back to him. She wouldn't be able to see the way he had to fumble the latex on.

"No, sir."

He came to stand beside her, only then realizing she could see his face and his shaking hands in the reflection of the glass. He grasped her hips a little harder than he needed to. Both to show her he was still in control, and also because he knew it would ramp up her excitement. "What will?"

"You."

Before she could finish breathing the word, he pulled her feet and hips backward until her back arched. She made a startled noise and braced her hands on the window.

He shoved her wispy skirt up and made a low growl at the sight of her round ass, still encased in the white panties. So many options. He could have that ass naked, but he knew he'd treasure the sight of his dick shoving the fragile cotton out of its way. Ruined innocence. Though innocence wasn't something either of them had ever cared much for. Not even when they'd had virginities to speak of.

He pulled the panties to the side and grasped his cock, arrowing it into the hot wet slit he knew was waiting for him.

He had to thrust hard to get past the initial tightness of her body. He wanted to remain silent and in control, but how could he be silent when he was sinking into heaven? If there was a way to bottle this feeling, getting sucked into her hot flesh, he would make a fortune. A small growl left his lips. "Has it been a while?"

"Yes," she gasped.

How long? Is this better? Am I *better?* He bit back the words, and pressed her up against the window, until she was sandwiched between him and the glass. She pulsed her hips back at him in a subtle motion to get him to move, but he clamped her hips hard, holding her in place to be skewered by his cock. She whimpered.

"You're so tight, Tatiana. Like you're a fucking virgin again. Do you remember that? Remember that first night? I took you missionary, fucked you gentle." He layered his body over hers until he could whisper in her ear. "We didn't stick to missionary for long, did we?"

"No. We didn't."

"Or gentle." Their debauchery had started when she came to him one night with a shy request to tie her down—something she had read in a dirty book that had turned her on. He'd made it clear she didn't need to be timid about asking for whatever she wanted. Particularly since the idea of domination had always turned his crank too. Hell, anything involving the two of them naked turned his crank. But especially the naughty stuff.

Neither of them had been made for vanilla.

She turned her head, resting her cheek against the cold glass, and cast him a glance. "We did gentle. In our own way. Did you forget?"

He froze. No. No, he hadn't forgotten, but it was easier to pretend he had. The sex had always been explosive and raw and dark. But then they'd cuddled. Or she'd rubbed his back after a hard day of work. He'd made her sandwiches when she was studying late at night.

They'd been gentle with each other. In their own way, as she said.

Thought this was supposed to just be a hot fuck?

It was. Is.

"Eyes forward," he said, voice hoarser than he would have liked.

Maybe she was awash in memories too, but she clearly saw the wisdom of his directive because she turned her head until her forehead rested against the glass. He tightened his hold on her hips and rammed inside, the blood rushing in his ears making her cry of pleasure sound distant.

Yes. This. This was all he wanted. All he needed.

Chapter Seven

WYATT'S FIRST THRUST made her toes curl. His second made her head want to explode.

She cried out, thankful he'd been smart enough to ignore her bleating about gentleness and kindness. This was all she craved, all she had signed up for. This hard, driving rhythm, a fucking to clear her head and tide her over for the blander partners she may have to settle for in her life.

Her musings over whether the man could still fuck? Fruitless. Holy crap could he fuck.

The glass was smooth and possibly the most diabolical thing for him to fuck her against, since there wasn't a single damn thing she could grab and brace herself with. His hands captured her wrists, pinning them to the window. Her entire body followed suit when he used his thrusting hips to press her tight against it, her breasts flattening, her clit loving the hard pressure. She was caught, helpless as his cock moved inside of her in tight, rapid jabs.

"Is it still cold?"

Smug bastard. She shook her head and squeezed her eyes shut. Cold was the least applicable adjective. The glass was slick and hot. Her necklace ground into her skin, the bite of metal delicious. He chuckled and released her to insert his hand between the window and her clit. His thick cock continued to rock inside of her, his thrusts becoming more fierce. Two fingers found her clit and pinched it. Even if she wanted to get away, she couldn't. He was in front of her, behind her, inside of her, and she'd never be able to escape him.

His breath came hot and fast on her neck, the panting telling her he was as overwhelmed with sensation as she was. "Come on my cock. Let everyone see who owns this little pussy. Who's always owned it."

Always? Yellow cautionary lights flashed in her brain at his too-intimate words, but they were eclipsed by her body's *hell yes*. Her body was ruled by a ho.

She strained, her hips trying in vain to work his pistoning hard-on, but he easily held her still, forcing her to accept only what he gave her. She loved that he could overpower her.

She stopped struggling and let her orgasm build, her fingers curling. It coursed up from the balls of her feet, sensation exploding, her pussy clenching around him in tight contractions. He dropped his head to her shoulder and gave a short groan, his hips jerking against her. The condom muted the heat of his release, and she briefly fantasized that he was bare, filling her with his come. Since he was the only man she'd allowed that particular liberty, she knew exactly how she would feel, all luxuriously creamy and overfilled, the thick semen dripping out of her when he pulled away.

He grunted when another small orgasm rocked her, and nipped her shoulder like a stallion correcting his mare. She dropped her hand to his thigh, the muscle hard and tense beneath his trousers.

"I'm going to fall down," Tatiana whispered. Weakness—real weakness, not the play weakness she reveled in in bed—was one of those things she'd rather die than admit, but she was pretty certain all that was keeping her boneless body up was him and the glass.

He muttered something that sounded like, "Me too," but she wasn't sure. He pulled away from her, his still-large cock slipping out. Its absence left her empty and aching.

She made a subtle movement backwards, as if she could recapture him inside of her. He cupped her hip, his touch oddly protective. "I'll fill you up again soon, Tatiana. Don't worry. The night's just starting."

She wasn't sure if that was a threat or a promise. Frankly, she really didn't care.

TATIANA WAS LOOKING shakier than he'd like. Only his own wobbly knees kept him from sweeping her up and carrying her to the couch. He led her there instead, and after she had collapsed on to the leather, he fled. No. Walked. He walked calmly, at a rather brisk pace, to the bathroom.

His motions were mechanical as he tossed the condom and rebuttoned his pants. He turned the faucet on and after washing his hands, splashed the cold water on his face. It didn't clear the fog in his brain one little bit. Wyatt braced his hands on the counter and hung his head, watching the running water swirl down the drain.

Holy shit. What had happened?

An orgasm, yes, but possibly one of the best orgasms of his life. Her body wasn't just more amazing now. She was more amazing now. *They* were more amazing now.

No. No, no, no. It was the novelty. The excitement of being with an old flame. Nothing more than that. It had been a while for him. They had been together for a long time. She knew how to push his sexual buttons. All she wanted was for him to play the stud and service her, not think or feel. *So be a man, stop trying to Dr. Phil this to death, and get out there and fuck her some more.*

He took a deep breath, ran a hand through his hair and went back out into the living room.

Tatiana remained where he'd left her on the couch, still bare-chested, and of course his cock gave a leap at that pretty sight. He couldn't read the expression on her face, but then, reading women outside of sex wasn't his strong suit.

Her attention was fixed on the window. He followed her gaze and smiled at the smears they'd left on the previously spotless glass. "Housekeeping is going to be confused."

She jumped, her breasts giving a slight jiggle, and turned to look at him. "What?"

He gestured to the window. "The maid. When she cleans tomorrow. Then again, I may try to preserve the image of your breasts there."

Ah, he loved that she could still flush. Pink stained her cheeks. "I didn't think of that."

Neither had he when he'd ordered her to press herself against the window. Nor would he tell her that he fully intended to clean up any signs of their rendezvous before any maids stumbled across them. Spraying a bit of Windex wasn't so far beneath him.

"Are you hungry?" he asked, changing the subject.

She paused. "Yes. I guess I am."

"Pasta, beef, or chicken?" *Pasta.* She'd never been a big meat eater.

"Pasta. Thank you."

He went to the phone and lifted it, dialing down to the kitchen. "Send up a full spread for two, please. One beef, one pasta. Chocolate for dessert." He hung up. "It should be here in about fifteen minutes."

"That's fast."

"It's a fast kitchen. And I write their paychecks."

She smiled faintly, but there was a hesitancy about her that hadn't been there earlier. Was she also blown away by their coupling? He didn't know. Couldn't ask.

He did know that her continued toplessness was both sexy and strange, seeing as how they weren't smack in the middle of one of their games. He cleared his throat. "Do you want to do up your…?" He gestured to her chest.

Tatiana blinked and glanced down. "Oh."

"Did you forget you were half naked?"

"Maybe." She peeked up at him. Her hesitancy had diminished, coy teasing directed his way. "Plus, you didn't tell me to cover myself. Sir."

His cock stirred. "Good girl. You can fix your dress."

Her lashes dipped down, and she retied her halter, removing those pretty tits from his sight. Belatedly, he kicked himself. He should be maximizing naked breast time, yeah? Moron.

But with both of them clothed, he was moderately more comfortable sitting next to her on the couch, arm extended to drape over the back. He shifted. Shifted again. The sofa felt uncomfortable and alien. Strange. This was his favorite piece of furniture in the entire place, one he'd personally chosen for its butter-soft leather and cushioning embrace.

It's her. She was the reason behind his discomfort. There wasn't much distance between them. The fact that there was any bothered him.

Not questioning the urge, he reached across the small gap and pulled her on to his lap. She was so petite, her weight barely registered. Wyatt adjusted her until she was arranged to his satisfaction, her round ass caressing his cock.

She was pliant, but he still felt as if he needed to explain himself to her. "I want you here," he growled.

"Then I'm here." She kissed him, her warm lips moving over his, her tongue flitting out to flirt. There were no hidden meanings in her words. And even if there were, he wasn't going to dwell on them. He was too busy enjoying these sweet, unhurried kisses, reminiscent of the beginning of their relationship. Other kids at school had thought he was a big stud, but he'd barely kissed girls before Tatiana came into his life. For the first couple of dates, they'd sat in his car, giving each other these slow, drugging kisses, until he'd had to break away, play the good guy, and drive her home. The great thing about being a grownup was the ability to indulge desires. The passion boiled over fast, the kiss turning hard and deep. Pulling her panties to the side, he loosened his pants to release his cock and sank home.

Mentally, he grimaced over the fact that he was essentially repeating the same moves a second time tonight. Next time, he consoled himself, next time he'd manage something more creative than simply shoving clothes away and himself inside of her.

Or maybe this time. When she tried to turn, to straddle

him, he kept her sitting sideways, which he knew would add to her feeling of helplessness. She couldn't move, couldn't even try to get away.

He kissed his way down her throat, adding small love bites to her flesh. Her skin was delicate, and he bet she still bruised easily. He wanted to mark her so she would see his possession for days afterward. He *needed* to mark her.

She shifted in his lap, her tight pussy nearly tempting him to change her position and ram himself until he came inside her.

"You're not wearing a condom," she gasped.

Goddamn. No wonder she felt so scalding hot.

He hadn't been with a woman bare since…her. She'd been the only one. Back when they'd both been too young and stupid. He was older now, but still stupid enough to mutter, "Give me a second," and steal another kiss while he reveled in the feeling of her pussy rubbing against his naked cock. Christ, talk about nostalgia.

"Now, Wyatt."

He groaned, but he wasn't a complete moron. They no longer had the luxury of having been each other's only lovers. Or being in a long-term relationship with other precautions in place. The rules were different now. He pulled out, cursing when his cock met air, too cold after being inside her heat.

The condom was, blessedly, in his pants pocket. She lifted herself off him slightly while he donned it, and then he yanked her back down on his lap. They both groaned when his cock sank inside of her again. She whimpered and squirmed on him, trying to gain some purchase and ride him.

The knock startled them both. She turned and looked at the door, the small glittery earrings in her earlobes swinging at the movement. "Who…?"

"Room service. Shit, the staff is too fast."

She gave a breathy laugh and braced her hand on his shoulder. "We can finish this once they're gone."

He stayed her, a glimmer of an idea taking place in his brain. A naughty, bad idea. "Or we can finish it while they're here."

"Wha—?"

He pulled the blanket off the back of the couch. Esme had bought the thing for him last Christmas, a huge bulky monstrosity he couldn't figure out where to put. She had appeared so proud, he hadn't the heart to tell her that he wasn't much the type for cozy afghans sprinkled around his home.

Besides, it had kept his feet warm a time or two. Now it could keep Tatiana's pussy warm for him.

He draped the blanket around them so they were covered from the waist down, and shifted to reach for the remote on the coffee table, a movement that ground him deeper into her wetness. She gasped. He swore. He clicked the TV on, tugged her closer as a movie began playing at low volume, and cleared his throat. "Come in."

Chapter Eight

WAS THE MAN mad?

Mute with aroused alarm, Tatiana had her answer a second later when he bid room service to enter. "What are you doing?" she gritted out.

His arm was braced around her back. He tightened it, pulling her closer. "Don't make a scene, love. They won't know where my dick is unless you tell them."

She tried to control her erratic breathing as the door swung open and two young men wheeled in two carts. Objectively, she supposed Wyatt was right. To the entire world, they looked like a couple cuddled on the couch, watching a movie and waiting for dinner.

Only she and Wyatt knew that his cock was so deep inside of her she could practically feel it in her throat.

The men nodded to Wyatt. "Sir."

"Thank you for being so quick," Wyatt said warmly. But what did he care, she thought. He would get a high-five if they knew what he was doing right now. Men.

His hand brushed her thigh, and she inhaled. He'd worked it beneath the blanket, while the other casually held the remote in plain view. Thankfully, the afghan was thick enough and large enough that the men wouldn't notice what was going on beneath it. She hoped.

"Where would you like us to set the food up, sir?"

Just leave, so I can fuck this man.

Wyatt paused for an agonizingly long beat of time, while his hand drew circles on her inner thigh. "Tell me," he asked her, all solicitous concern, "did you want to eat here, or on the dining table? There are candles there. Might be more romantic."

She didn't miss his emphasis on the word candles. Or the dancing mischief in his eyes. One utterance of the safe word, and the men, the risk, the threat of being caught by his employees would vanish.

Like she would miss this?

"Here," she finally cooed, calling his implicit dare, raising the stakes. "Why don't you set it up on the coffee table in front of us? It's so cozy here, we don't want to leave."

His hand tightened on her thigh, and he jerked the leg toward him, opening her up to where she was impaled. "It is cozy."

Both men wheeled the carts over and started to set out the plates on the oversized table. She was conscious of every inch of Wyatt pressed up inside of her, of the scent of their bodies and sex in the air. Wyatt's fingers pinched her clit at the exact second they opened the first silver dome. She gasped. One of the waiters glanced at her, and she gave him a weak smile. "It…looks so good."

Wyatt's chest vibrated against her back. "Why don't you try a taste? Here, John, hand her that plate of calamari, why don't you?"

The other man beamed and hastened to do as he was told, handing her the small appetizer, as well as a hand towel. She accepted them with a murmur. Her finger brushed against the waiter's just as Wyatt's thumb rubbed her clit in a slow circle. His cock flexed, stimulating the tissues.

She bit her cheek to keep from whimpering and quickly popped a calamari into her mouth.

"Is it good?" Wyatt asked her, bumping his hips up as much as he could before it became obvious he was inside her.

She could barely taste the food. "It's hot," she said, hoping that would explain the flush in her cheeks.

"Hot's not a bad thing." He didn't cease his circling exploration of her clit, continuing the subtle pulsing of his hips. How he had the self-control not to toss her over and fuck her hard and deep, she didn't know. Craving was making her burn, and she couldn't believe he was unaffected.

"It has its place."

He smiled at her almost sweetly, the innocence a far cry from the lewd things he was doing to her hidden from view. He flicked her clit rapidly, his cock flexed again, and she manfully struggled to keep from climaxing.

The waiters finally—*finally*—finished arranging the dishes and stood expectantly. Wyatt chuckled, the sound vibrating inside of her. "I don't have any cash, guys. Do you have the bill?"

"Sure thing, sir." One of them held out a small leather folio.

Wyatt withdrew his hand from beneath the blankets.

She could smell herself on him. Tatiana waited in an agony of worry for the waiters to become scandalized upon realizing where it had been.

Instead of taking their pen, he reached into his shirt pocket and pulled out his own shiny black pen. He added a more-than-generous tip and handed the check back.

With wide smiles, the waiters nodded and left. The instant the door clicked behind them, Wyatt shoved the blanket off her, and she gasped in relief from the lack of the stifling material.

"Do you think they knew?"

"Doubtful. You were quite a good little actress. As always." The smile he gave her was respectful, one player to another.

"I told you I'd gotten better."

"My apologies for doubting you." He rolled the pen between his fingers. "But then, there were only two men. No telling how you'd do in front of a larger audience."

She bit her lip as his cock flexed inside of her. Was he imagining her sitting on his cock in the five-star restaurant downstairs? Maybe trying to remain motionless and quiet at a show on the strip? Silently sweating as he ground up inside of her in an exclusive boutique? "That sounds like a dare. But I need you to fuck me too much to take it right now."

He chuckled and placed the pen under his nose, sniffing it appreciatively like a cigar. "It seemed cruel to taunt those boys by spreading your juices all over their pen. I'd rather they be on mine."

"I'm sorry I ruined your pen."

"Please. It's finally worth the price I paid for it."

He used the tip of the pen to trace the bodice of her

dress, pushing it down to trace her tight nipple with the hard plastic. She arched her back, hoping he would take the hint to replace the damn pen with his mouth or hands. Instead, he slid it down her body, using it to brush aside the fabric of her skirt until they could see where she was impaled on his cock. Her panties were scrunched tight against the crease of her leg.

"You were a very good girl, Tatiana. I think you deserve a reward."

Back when they'd been dating, she'd learned to get wet at the sound of the word *reward.* Also, *punishment.* Also, most everything else he'd uttered.

He smirked, not missing her response. He lowered the pen until the hard tip was directly touching her exposed clitoris. "I don't think this smells enough like you, though. We should fix that." The pen circled. She whimpered and squirmed. He didn't move his cock at all, except for that flexing, a subtle pulsing.

He adjusted the pen until it was lengthwise against her open pussy, the metal clip brushing her clit, and rubbed it up and down, forceful and deliberate. Responding to her sighs and jerks and cries, he sped up his motions. His arm flexed with the force of his movements, the veins standing out as he worked her exposed sex and let her clench on his cock. His face was focused, grim, his entire attention on making her come. The instrument became wet and slick. *You creative bastard.*

"Now," he rasped.

The one word was all she needed to give free rein to the hunger inside of her. She keened and came on him, her pussy milking his unmoving cock, way better than any dildo she'd ever played with. With an acute knowledge of her body, he slowed down the pen, gentling his stimulation until finally he simply held it in place against her.

She slumped on him, breathless, spent, yet all too aware of his still-hard cock lodged within her.

He licked her throat. "You're a *very* good girl."

Chapter Nine

WYATT HADN'T COME. After she had lain against him for a few precious minutes to regain her breath, he surprised her by slapping her hip and picking her up off his lap. He shook his head, giving her a tight smile when she made a murmur of protest. "Let's eat first. Then we can play some more."

So after hastily repairing their clothes, they ended up on the floor between the couch and the coffee table, side by side. They dug in, and Tatiana smiled at the picture they must have made. They were both still garbed in their expensive designer clothes, but that was all she could really say about the outfits. Both were wrinkled beyond belief and showed evidence of their grasping hands and mouths. Well, she thought with a dose of humor, the dress had looked nice before he'd gotten his mitts on her.

"Here. Try this. It's a tender bite." Wyatt held a piece of steak to her mouth. It was the fourth piece of meat he'd fed her. They were both ravenous, but while she flitted from appetizer to appetizer, he had dug straight into his main course with gusto. Healthy boys needed their iron.

She chewed, in agreement even though she wasn't a big fan of beef. "It's good steak."

"It's the best."

She twirled pasta around her fork and took a bite, closing her eyes over the savory and spicy sauce. "Whatever you're paying your chef, double it."

"Don't worry. He already holds this corporation hostage, and he knows it."

They ate in silence for a while, broken by the sound of their silverware on the fine china plates. It was a companionable silence, not awkward at all.

Tatiana glanced at him sideways, catching him dipping his steak in sauce. "Remember prom?"

A smile curled his lips, and his hands paused. His face was unguarded, and he suddenly looked younger. "I remember I couldn't afford a tux, a hotel room, and dinner. So I had to axe the dinner, because there was no way we weren't going to have that hotel room. Not after you told your parents you were staying over at a friend's."

"We had dinner."

He cut into his steak with obvious relish. "It was hardly a dinner."

"We ate. In the hotel room. Just like this, on the floor. Burger King."

"No. It was McDonald's. You hated Burger King because their fries were too soggy."

She grinned. "You're right. I had forgotten that. I like their fries now."

"I can have someone run and get you some, if you like."

She snorted, because he sounded like he was about two seconds away from snapping his fingers and summoning his minions. "Nah. Thanks, though." She picked up a piece of calamari and took a bite, able to actually appreciate the taste of the appetizer now that he wasn't driving her mad with his cock and fingers. "This is a long way from a Days Inn and McDonald's, Wyatt."

He picked up his wine. "I won't apologize for the money. I worked hard for it."

"I'm sure you did."

His lips twisted. "Is that sarcasm?"

"What? No. I meant it. You always were the hardest-working person I knew. Sometimes I felt like I floated through life, but you…you powered through and got things done."

He was silent so long she glanced at him, only to find him watching her with a small furrow between his brows. "Thank…you."

She shrugged. "It's the truth. When I found out what you'd accomplished, I was only surprised you managed it as quickly as you did. But I knew you'd eventually do something big."

"Wow."

"Why are you so skeptical?"

He shrugged his broad shoulders, his gaze on his fork pushing around his pile of potatoes. "When we broke up, I was pretty certain you thought I was worthless."

"What?" She was genuinely shocked. "I never said that."

"Please. College girl and the construction worker? 'Uptown Girl' was written for us."

That was an uncomfortable truth. Wyatt had taken college classes, but he'd been all about survival back then. Her parents had been delighted when she and Wyatt had parted ways her junior year. "I always thought you were smarter than me."

His jaw looked tense. "I graduated, finally, you know."

She hated the defensiveness in his voice. "Like I said, I didn't." She paused, thinking over their fights during the decline of their relationship. "If I ever gave you the impression that I thought I was superior to you just because you were going to school part-time instead of full-time, I'm sorry. I never meant to. And I never believed that. My parents placed a lot of emphasis on school and academic success." Her lips twisted wryly. "I may have subconsciously adopted that attitude. Even if I didn't believe it."

He studied her, and then gave her a small nod, his attention returning to his steak. "What made you leave school?"

"I finally realized it wasn't making me happy. The only thing that did was art and jewelry design. Not the art history courses I was taking, but actual design. So I told my parents, packed everything up, and headed for the West Coast." It was a simplified version of events, but she didn't want to get into the years of lean living and the dues she'd paid before an exclusive store owner had taken a shine to her work.

"I'm sure your parents freaked out."

"They did, but they came around. They really are good people, and they love me. Everything they did, they did because they love me."

He nodded slowly. "Yeah. My feelings toward them were probably a little excessively angry back then."

"I was so grateful for that love, maybe you're right, I was more deferential to them than I should have been…" She struggled for words. "They never kept my adoption a secret from me, and I suppose in the back of my head I just wanted to make sure they never gave me up either."

"Like your birth mom did."

"Yeah."

"Sorry she wasn't all you dreamed of."

"It's okay. I got Ron out of it."

He lifted his head, and she held up her hand. "Do *not* ruin this civil conversation by calling him names. He stays out of this, remember?"

Wyatt subsided, looking disgruntled. "Fine."

"Is your dad…still around?"

"Last I heard." It was no surprise when he changed the subject, gesturing to her food. "Eat. Stop pecking. No wonder you're still so small."

She arched an eyebrow at him and nibbled on a bite of pasta. "Are you complaining?"

"Hardly. But you need to keep your energy up." A wicked look. The vibe in the room abruptly altered from civil conversation to looming sexy times. "Frail women worry me. They break, you know."

"Oh, darling, if there's one thing you should know about me, it's that I don't break."

He cocked his head. "That sounds like a challenge."

"To break me?"

"Breaking sounds cruel. Maybe to see how far you can…bend."

She placed her fork carefully on the plate. "I'm pretty flexible."

He mirrored her movements, pushing his plate away. They had better things to do with their hands and mouths than eat. "I haven't even seen you naked yet."

"You're missing out," she purred.

"Take off your clothes then. Let me see how much you can take."

She didn't protest, curious to see where he would take this. She stood and untied the halter at her neck, letting the dress drop off her hips to pool around her feet. She stepped through it and her panties, kicking them aside.

She'd never been that self-conscious about her body. She worked hard to take care of herself, running daily even when she was in the grip of a feverish new design or project.

But since Wyatt's head was right at the level of her pussy, she couldn't help but be a little self-conscious. Should she have waxed? Shaved? Added sparkly jewels? Maybe installed a music box?

Stop.

Whatever doubts she had were banished when he gazed up at her like a supplicant at her feet. He brushed his hand over her hip. "I was missing out."

She tried to swallow past the scratchiness in her throat. "I told you."

He stretched up far enough to take her necklace between his teeth, tugging on it before releasing. "Take this off. I don't want to make it dirty."

The snap of tone from praise to orders was sudden but not unexpected. Yet…*Dirty?* Intrigued, Tatiana reached behind her neck and released the catch, dropping the expensive trinket into his palm without the care she usually showed her pieces.

Without breaking her gaze, he placed the jewelry on the coffee table. "Hands behind your back. Spread your legs. I'm still hungry."

Shivering, she obeyed. "Am I your dessert, Wyatt?"

"No." He picked up the plate of chocolate cheesecake from the table. "This is my dessert. You can be my dish." Crooking his fingers, he dipped them into the cake. "I like cheesecake," he said conversationally. "It's so easy to spread."

The first touch was on her belly, and her stomach muscles contracted at the coldness of the dessert. "Jesus."

"Too chilly for you?"

The last two words took the question from a solicitous inquiry to a rough taunt. "Not at all."

He swirled the chocolate around her belly button in a design only he knew. "Do you ever work on canvas?"

"No..." She bit the inside of her cheek as his fingers crept downward, teasingly close to her mons. He looked like he was totally absorbed in his creation, painting long curlicues over her hipbones and down her thighs.

"I think I'd be good at this whole art thing."

Her thighs tightened when he added more "paint" to his fingers and dabbed it into the curls at her vagina. Wyatt frowned. Leaned back a little and studied her, as if he really was using her as his canvas. Cupped her whole sex in his hand and ground upward. Quick, fast, not there long enough for her to rub against and find release.

Her breathing picked up, her breasts trembling. The crude smearing of creaminess over her vagina highlighted the seductive designs he'd painted on her thighs and stomach. The man was displaying a fairly good understanding of contrasts.

Most men would probably have started licking her off by now, but Wyatt apparently didn't consider her pussy the finish line. He gathered more cake in his fingers and smoothed it over the curve of her breast. She thrust forward, trying to get his attention on her nipples.

She got it. Fire raced through her and her toes curled when he raised his hand and slapped at her nipple. Not hard enough to hurt, but definitely hard enough to sting. The remnants of cake on his fingers stained her flesh, chocolate mixing with flushed pink. "Don't move."

Before she could respond, he delivered a tap to her other breast.

"I didn't move!"

He glanced up at her, wickedness making his eyes glint. "I know. I wanted your nipples nice and hard." He compressed the tip between two fingers. A sizzle of delicious pain ran through her. "I wish I had something to decorate these. Remember those green jeweled clamps we had?"

Wyatt's naughty smile. "I got green to match your eyes."

Speech was becoming a challenge. "You don't keep an arsenal of sex toys?"

"If only. I would love to see you with a butt plug up your tight little ass. Or whip marks on your back. What do you like?"

Any of those things. All of them.

"Yes. Too bad I'm not more prepared. We'll have to save those things for another time," he murmured.

Another time? There wouldn't be another time. Before she could marshal her thoughts to answer, he slapped her nipple again.

She cried out, and he paused. "Hurt?"

"Yes."

Wyatt returned to working the nipples with his fingers, both soothing and inflaming the sting. "Too much?"

She narrowed her eyes at him. "Shut up and spank my tits, Caine."

His mouth curved down, and she knew he was trying not to laugh. He delivered a few spanks to each side. By the time he stopped, her head was tossed back, her pussy clenching with every beat of her heart. Pain and pleasure sizzled through her nerve endings, heightening every sensation. Her hands were fisted behind her back, the nails making imprints into her skin.

Cold enveloped her hot breasts, and she gasped, her eyes shooting open. "Wyatt!"

He finished piling the dollops of cheesecake on top of her nipples and sat back. The plate landed on the table, the large slice of cheesecake reduced to a denuded graham cracker crust.

He didn't break their gaze as he wiped his fingers off on a towel. Ever so slowly, he undid his already askew tie and slid it free. "Turn around."

"You don't need to tie me. I haven't moved my hands." *Yes. Yes, tie me.*

"Turn around."

Her thighs were wet with her arousal, she was so turned on. She obeyed. The fabric, still warm from his body, whispered over her skin, a gentle kiss. The ends brushed over her ass as he knotted it securely. Silk and strength. She was his.

He smacked her ass. "I wish I hadn't used the whole cake on your front." He clasped the cheek he had slapped and squeezed, opening her up. "God, this ass. I just want to…"

His teeth closed on her, and she yelped.

Another bite, and he gave a low laugh. "Swivel. I bet you taste even sweeter with chocolate."

Finally. Tatiana turned, fully expecting him to fall on her, ravenous. But he was busy unbuttoning his shirt, turning a simple masculine chore into a striptease. He drew the shirt off and tossed it aside, his bare torso gleaming in the dim light.

How had his body gotten so much better with age? Ropy muscles lined his arms. His chest was wide and hard, his stomach still nice and flat. And his chest hair. *Unf.* He still had the perfect amount, neither too much nor too little. The dark hair arrowed in a line down below his navel, disappearing into his pants. Many hours had been spent with her tracing that happy trail with her tongue. She moistened her dry lips. "You know, artists should clean up after themselves."

Wickedness glinted in his eyes. "You're so right." He rose to his knees, one arm going around her waist while he served her breast to his mouth. He enveloped her nipple, eating her as if she were a creamy dessert. Switching, he made sure her other breast received the same treatment, pulling hard enough at her nipple that his cheeks hollowed and she cried out.

He sucked and licked and bit his way down her body, missing some spots, spending far too much time at others. He avoided her desperate pussy and thoroughly cleaned off her thighs and hips. Her hands were curling into claws. "For fuck's sake, Wyatt."

There were no delicate getting-to-know-you-again forays into her pussy. He was nuzzling her thigh one second, and the next he had his face buried in her. He wasn't as interested in the chocolate covering her sex as he was in the juices inside, his tongue uncurling to press deep. One thumb settled on her clit and the other hand clenched her hip so hard she knew she'd have bruises tomorrow. Taking his cues from her writhing body, he took control, moving her so she was fucking his tongue. Her hands struggled against her bonds, desperate to grab his head, his hair. Not because he was doing anything wrong, but because he was doing everything right. What if he stopped?

Her legs trembled. Standing would become impossible soon. "Let me lie down."

He sucked her clit, letting it pop free of his mouth to come up for air. "You taste so good," he muttered. "Ready to come, Tatiana?"

"Yes." She arched her hips, an infinitesimal movement that his observant eyes couldn't miss.

He lapped at her belly. "Ask me nicely."

Ah. She stilled, trying to get her breathing under control. So this was the game. She could succumb, since she was in such dire straits. Or. She could see what kind of pleasure she would receive in return for refusing.

No-brainer. She made her voice rough and uncaring. "Fuck you."

The heat that flared in his eyes told her she'd made the right decision. He withdrew and came to his feet, a study in contrasts himself with his bare gleaming chest and tented dress pants.

"Not nice enough." He grabbed her by the neck, his hand feeling large and heavy. "Get in the bathroom."

"The…what?" Not the bedroom? Had she heard him wrong?

"You said artists clean up their messes." Those hooded eyes surveyed her. "I've made you awfully dirty."

Some of the imminent fire in her pussy cooled. Was this a break in their play? A pragmatic interlude in their otherwise fantastical night?

Yeah, it was really responsible of him to want to make sure his sheets didn't get chocolate on him. He couldn't help the fact that she needed a good hard fucking right now.

His thumb swept over the hollow of her throat. "Come on." He released her and placed a hand at the small of her back.

"Aren't you going to untie me?"

"No."

Oh. Huh. Maybe this wasn't a scene break.

Okay.

She walked a couple of steps ahead of him, certain to add a little twitch to her hips, letting the ends of the tie flirt with her ass. They made it through the darkened bedroom, directly into his master bath. The towel she'd used earlier was still askew where she'd tucked it to hang dry.

Wyatt turned on the shower and gestured, expressionless. "Get inside and rinse off."

"Um. You aren't going to help me?" She rolled her shoulders, as if to remind him of her tied-up state.

"Do the best you can."

What the fuck? He was missing prime, wet, sexual-antics time here. Eyeing him askance, she got inside and let the hot water course over her body.

Out of the corner of her eye, she caught movement through the glass enclosure. Turning around, she watched Wyatt adjusting the taps on that decadent bathtub, pouring something inside. *Oooh.*

The man was full of great ideas. Had he figured out how much she coveted that tub? He came back to her, reaching inside and shutting the water off. The combination of hot anticipation and steam in the bathroom kept her from shivering from cold. "That would have been more efficient if I had hands to help me," she couldn't resist grumbling.

He held her arm as she got out. "Don't worry. I'm going to go over every inch of you and make sure you didn't miss a spot."

She gave him a flirtatious glance from beneath her eyelashes. "And if I did?"

"Then I'll punish you for being such a dirty girl."

"Fair enough."

He urged her into the tub, helping her maintain her balance when she might have toppled, tied as she was.

She sank into the warmth of the water, sitting in the center of the tub. The sound of a zipper prompted her to glance up in time to see Wyatt's pants and underwear hit the ground. His cock looked huge and swollen, its mushroom-shaped tip round and voluptuous. Semen glistened on the tip. Enraptured, she leaned forward slightly as he stepped inside the tub, his strong legs spread on either side of her, his cock right at the perfect level for her to…

A wordless noise escaped her when he grabbed her head, stilling her. His chest rose and fell with his heavy breaths. He didn't correct her, but he did slowly bring her head forward until the velvet skin of his cock brushed against her lower lip. She kissed him, a chaste peck. His fingers rubbed her scalp in a tender manner. "You want it, don't you? Tell me where. I'll stuff you full, anywhere you want."

She almost told him before she remembered. The game. She cast him a militant look and pushed back against his hands. "Thought you were cleaning me up."

He gave a chuckle and released her, before kneeling in the tub. His knees brushed against hers, the hair on his thighs scraping her legs. "I couldn't resist. You looked so hungry."

"We both know you need me more than I need you."

As soon as she said the words, uttered out of rashness and possibly jest, Tatiana wished she could recall them. They meant something. She wasn't entirely sure what, but they meant something. He froze, his face wiped clean of humor. Her muscles locked as well. Tension vibrated between them, becoming as thick as the steam in the bathroom.

"I…I didn't mean…"

"Shh." He placed his fingers over her lips. His face was set, hard.

She spoke around his hand. "I was just playing, you know. Trash-talking."

"Yeah. Me too." He moved his hand down over her throat to her breasts. He massaged them roughly. "You're still so dirty, Tatiana."

"My hands are tied," she pointed out, breathless. She felt like a ping-pong ball, the way she kept bouncing up to the height of desire. Her unnecessarily intimate faux pas took a seat on the back burner.

He lifted one breast up, leaned down, and bit at it. She squealed.

"Beg me."

Do it. Finish this. "No," she heard herself say.

A growl sounded in his chest. He pushed her back until she was sprawled in the tub and he was straddling her. He shut off the water, the cessation of sound leaving only their panting breaths in the room.

He swept over her belly and down her legs, paying lip service to cleaning her off, his real intent to arouse her nerve endings with his calloused touch. He stroked back up to her pussy, using the heel of his hand to grind down on her clitoris. With his other hand, he shoved two fingers deep inside her.

She cried out, her head tipping back against the dark marble.

He leaned in close, his hot breath fanning her ear. "My fingers are bigger than yours. But they still aren't thick enough, are they?"

They weren't. She needed…

"They aren't long enough." He thrust lazily a few times. "They can't reach deep enough. They can't hit that spot that makes you squeal when I'm fucking you."

No, they weren't nearly long enough.

"You need my cock. Say it."

Tatiana wasn't sure how she managed it, but she kept stubbornly silent.

He gave a humorless laugh and reached over her head. With a whir of noise, the jets in the tub started. She expected the ones placed around the side of the tub. It was the rush of water below her that really startled her, streams blasting against her legs, another right below her ass, the water hitting her sensitive skin.

Wyatt arranged her like a doll, forcing her to sit right on top of one of the forceful jets, so it tunneled between her legs. "Jesus Christ, Wyatt!"

"I've never used these before. Tell me if I'm doing it wrong."

Bastard. They both knew he was doing everything exactly right. His gaze was locked on her face, two fingers moving by touch alone as they opened up her pussy lips, giving her no place to run from the directed water. She squirmed against the bonds he'd tied, trying to free herself so she could…she didn't know what. Grab him and force him to fuck her?

He thrust three fingers inside of her this time and combined with the jet, she nearly climaxed. Ten years ago, it had taken the two of them three books and a weekend of fingering before Wyatt had figured out how to stimulate her G-spot. Now, he hooked those fingers inside of her and rubbed, finding her G-spot as easily as if he had never forgotten it. "Well, hello, old friend," he murmured as she writhed.

"Wyatt," she sobbed, straining to get away, or get closer, she wasn't sure which.

"Just say it." He stroked harder.

"Please," she bit out.

He kissed her hard, sucking on her tongue as if he would consume her. His fingers never relented their torture below. "Say it. Say you want my cock."

"I want your cock. Please." She gasped when he twisted his hand on the downward thrust and adjusted her so the water hit her clit directly.

"Say you need my cock."

"I need it. I need your cock so bad."

His teeth closed on her earlobe and he whispered, "Say

you need *me*."

Her breath caught. "I need you. I need you."

"Why? Why do you need me?"

The words slipped past her lips, unable to be contained. "Because I've never had anyone as good as you."

There. She couldn't regret the words. The fact that she'd said them in the throes of sexual bliss didn't make them any less true.

As if he'd been spurred, Wyatt removed his fingers and surged up, the displaced water splashing both of them. He slammed the jets off and hoisted her to her feet.

"Please," she said, unable to stop begging now. "Please fuck me, Wyatt."

"I want you in my bed." He helped her out of the tub and spun her around, cursing as his fingers slipped over the wet knot tied at her wrists. There was barely a second for her to shake out her arms before he picked her up off her feet, carrying her out of the bathroom and into the bedroom.

She didn't even notice the cold air on her wet body—the fire in her pussy warmed her all over. She wrapped her arms around his neck and pressed frantic kisses on his neck and chest. "Please. Please, sir. Please fuck me."

"Shh."

Contrary as always, she couldn't shut up now that he allowed her to. "I want your big, thick cock so badly. You can tie me to your bed and stay inside of me. All day and all night, just fucking me, coming in me." She bit his neck, tonguing the area to soothe it.

"I don't think I've ever heard such a tempting idea." He forced her to stand on her wobbly legs, facing the huge king-sized bed. His palm slid up her spine until he grasped the back of her neck.

He exerted pressure, forcing her down until her cheek pressed against the mattress. She was arched over the side of the bed, her ass high in the air. She flattened her hands on either side of her body. A wet chunk of hair slid over her face, tickling her nose.

"Stay," he said, his voice cold and a little mean.

He left her like that, and she heard the rustle of foil that told her he was donning a condom. She jumped when his hands coasted over her ass cheeks, petting, shaping her flesh. "I love your ass. Your skin is so white." One hand drew away, and then it was back in a stinging slap. He gave a dark laugh when she cried out. "I think I'd like it even more all pink and hot." He gave another spank. "Too bad I can't wait."

With a grunt, he spun her around. His body came over hers. In the dark, he looked demonic, almost possessed, a marauder, his face a mask of selfishness. He pushed her thighs wide and sank inside her. "Make yourself come if you like," he said, almost coldly. "This fuck is for me. That's your punishment for being so difficult."

And it was for him, she realized, as he began a driving rhythm, his face frozen in a determined expression. But the deep thrusts were perfect for her, detonating a chain reaction in her body. She opened her legs wider, giving him more room. He made a savage sound, grasping her legs beneath her knees and using the grip to open her completely, until her ankles were in the vicinity of her ears. Each stroke rubbed the base of his cock against her clitoris. She whimpered and pinched her nipples. Cursing, he leaned down and bit at the hard buds. The rough nip was just what she needed. She arched her back and came, keening.

"Fuck, yeah. I love the way you milk me," he growled, his teeth clenched. His words triggered another small climax. The heavy bed moved as he thrust harder, shoving himself in so deep, she wondered how she'd ever dislodge him. He panted into her ear and ground against her, holding her tight as he came. "No one but you, Tatiana. No one."

No one.

For long minutes there was only silence and the sound of their breathing, exhaustion hanging heavy between them. Finally, he hefted himself up and cursed softly, lowering her legs so they weren't pressed up in a gymnast's pose. He rubbed feeling back into her limbs, looking everywhere but her eyes.

She opened her mouth, her natural sassiness struggling to assert itself in the face of the serious mood. "Told you…" Her voice broke. She cleared her throat. "Told you I was flexible."

His lips quirked, a mockery of his usual smile. "Yeah. You weren't lying."

"Yoga," she rasped.

"Hm. God bless yoga."

Her grin was shaky. It faded as they stared at each other.

No one.

He pushed himself off the bed. "I'm going to… I'll be right back." He staggered to the bathroom, his legs looking about as steady as hers felt.

She lay there, still breathing hard, their combined sweat all over her body. The room wasn't that warm, the desert night naturally cooling the apartment. She shivered and realized her limbs were splayed wide.

She flushed and sat up, closing her legs and curling them underneath her. The sink ran in the bathroom for a long time, and the door opened, silhouetting Wyatt. He switched off the light, and his large shadow came toward the bed. He sat next to her. A towel dropped over her head, and he patted briskly, drying her still-wet hair.

"Thanks," she murmured when he pulled the towel away and stroked it over her body, drying off the remnants of water and perspiration.

"No problem."

So polite. The formal note in his voice was sharply at odds with their nudity. Worry wiggled through her. She didn't know what the protocol was. It was late. Was she supposed to leave? Were they done with each other? Was sleeping together part of their deal?

He dropped the towel carelessly on the ground and gave a sigh that came from the bottom of his soul. Wyatt reached past her to lift the comforter. "Get in."

Okay. "So I should stay?"

He looked at her. In the darkness of the room, his eyes were unreadable. "Yeah. You should stay."

Tatiana swallowed and scrambled over the bed to crawl under the blanket. He slid in next to her. Immediately, his body heat warmed her, and she sought it out, curling into his side. Chilliness plagued her. What she wouldn't give to have a heater like Wyatt in her bed every night. "The comforter on that side is wet," she whispered. The mattress too, possibly.

"It's fine."

Unable to resist, she rubbed her nose against his pec. He grunted and moved so her legs and arms were tangled up with his, her cold feet and hands finding a natural resting place against his limbs. She breathed in his scent. Drugstore shampoo mixed with boutique bubble bath. So familiar and foreign. Exhaustion tugged at her. "Wyatt?"

"Hmm?"

"I'm…" Happy? Content? Glad?

His large hand passed over her head, pressing her closer to his chest. "Hush."

Yes. There was no point in talking, not when she wasn't sure what words she'd say. What words needed to be said.

She fell asleep with the touch of his lips on her forehead.

WYATT KNEW SHE was gone within minutes of waking.

God damn it. She'd worn him out so much he hadn't even stirred when she slipped away. He hadn't felt so rested in years, but that was cold comfort. He stared up at the ceiling and listened carefully, straining to hear noises in the kitchen or bathroom that proved him wrong. Nothing.

You set the parameters. You can't complain now.

Back when they'd broken up as kids, he'd gone on a two-week-long bender. But he was older and wiser, and this wasn't a seven-year-long relationship that was ending, just a one-night stand that had run its course.

Calling himself a sentimental fool, he swept a hand over the empty space in his bed where she had snuggled next to him, frowning and sitting up when his hands met paper.

An unassuming file folder rested next to him. He picked it up and read the scrawled writing on the front.

There's no one like you, either. I'm amazed at who you

grew up to be. Thank you.

Thank you? Thank you for what? He cleared his throat, trying to dislodge the sudden lump there and opened the folder. At first he didn't understand what he was looking at, until he spotted his own signature at the bottom of the worn paper.

Letters. Letters he'd written Tatiana a decade ago. Though she'd been the academic, she preferred the phone. He'd always been the one to write her when or if they had to be apart, something about the method of communication appealing to him. Tatiana had called him a closet romantic, and he'd scoffed.

She had kept these? All these years? Why? What did that mean?

No one like you.

He *wasn't* a romantic. Pragmatism was his middle name.

But…maybe there was a tiny kernel of hope blooming in his chest. Bemused, he leaned back against his pillows and began to read the words he'd written long ago.

Chapter Ten

EVERY MINUTE DRAGGED by as if it had been dipped in molasses. It had only been three hours since Tatiana had left Wyatt sleeping in his bed, and not a second had passed without her trying to come up with a reason to go see him again, and just as many reasons why that was a horrible idea.

He's not looking for a relationship.

They were so good in bed together.

You came here to help your brother. Even if that's resolved, that little issue of theft might make family get-togethers weird.

It wasn't only the sex. There was still something emotional between them. Something that should be teased out.

One night doesn't mean you know him at all. Not who he is now.

Damn it, she wasn't a moron.

Even if she did feel like one. Groaning, Tatiana laid her head on the steering wheel. That note. Why had she left that note? And his letters? What had she been hoping to accomplish there, some sort of closure?

A soft curse left her lips. They might have sat abandoned in her closet for years, with only an occasional glance, but she fiercely regretted losing those letters. She blamed their loss on the ooey-gooey sentimentality running through her system this morning. Which, indirectly, could be blamed on Wyatt and the orgasms he had given her. They had addled her mind. That bastard.

She'd been sitting in Ron and his wife's driveway for a couple of hours. It had been too early when she arrived to knock on the door, but she'd had no place to go.

Last night was a fantasy, a dream best forgotten. Today is reality.

Reality was doing a predawn walk of shame from Wyatt's bed to the hotel she usually stayed at in Vegas, flushing as the expressionless clerk checked her bedraggled self in.

Reality was showering and leaving said hotel room to come sit in a driveway, because even the modest suite reminded her of Wyatt's more lavish rooms.

Reality was facing her brother shortly, and lecturing him on the stupidity of embezzling funds.

Reality was not seeing Wyatt anytime in the near future.

Maybe we can have another one-night stand in a decade.

Oh God. So depressing.

Her bag was vibrating. Listlessly, she reached for it, but a tap on the glass made her abandon the quest for her phone. Startled, she sat straight up, glancing out the window to find her brother's surprised, cherubic face.

When he gestured and gallantly stepped back, she forced a smile and opened the driver's side door.

"Tatiana?" he said, pleased amazement written all over him. "What on earth are you doing here?"

"Hey, Ron." She stepped out and let her long-lost sibling draw her into a bear hug. Ron was of average size, which meant he was still much larger than her. Though he was in his late twenties and a husband and father, he had a bit of baby fat around his face that brought out all of her protective feelings. She pulled back to smile up into his concerned green eyes. Her eyes.

Ron studied her. “Why did you come out here? You should have called me. Didn’t you understand my text? I worked things out with my boss.”

“Ron… Oh! Tatiana.” Caitlin appeared in the doorway, baby Pete on her hip. Like her husband, the pretty redhead was dressed in pajamas and a faded robe. The strain of the past couple of days had left their mark on the woman’s face and in her bloodshot eyes. “I wondered what was taking Ron so long to get the paper.”

Tatiana smiled at her sister-in-law, but before she could speak, Ron grabbed her arm, all easy affability. “Come in, sis, come in. It’s always good to see you.”

Caitlin stepped back as they entered. “Tatiana, did you drive out here?”

“I flew in yester—I flew in.” No need to explain where she’d been last night.

Ron frowned. “You didn’t have to do that. Everything’s going fine.”

“Yes. Fine.” Caitlin’s tone wasn’t as certain as her husband’s, and she pulled Pete closer to her chest. The four-month-old blew spit bubbles at Tatiana and waved his fist. Tatiana made a face at him, smiling when he did the same. She wasn’t an expert with babies or kids, but she was a fan of this one.

“Come into the kitchen. We were just about to have breakfast.”

It was a short walk to the kitchen. The home was modest, yet pleasant, open and airy. Caitlin arranged Pete in his highchair and gave him a spoon to play with.

"Pete's still not sleeping in his so-called nursery, so you can have that room, Tatiana."

"I got a hotel room."

Ron made a shushing noise. "My sister isn't staying in a hotel room."

She gave a faint smile, used to his unthinking generosity.

"Not that we don't love to see you, Tatiana, but you really didn't need to fly out," Caitlin said, her voice soft.

She shrugged and leaned against the counter. "Yes. But I wanted to." Wanted to help her brother. Wanted to see Wyatt again. So many wants.

"I think Caine's going to send over the agreement today for me to sign." Ron cheerfully cracked eggs into a bowl. "The man's a god. I don't know what I would have done if he'd pressed charges."

"You did a really stupid thing, Ron."

"I know." He frowned for a moment, his calm mask slipping. "It was wrong of me. Trust me, I don't ever want to be in this position again."

"We're not home free yet. We still have to pay the man back." Caitlin dragged a hand through her hair.

Her husband shot her a warning look. "I'm going to get two jobs. Don't you worry. We'll make it work."

Tatiana thought of the useless, torn-up check she'd left sitting on Wyatt's table. "I'll give you the money."

Ron scowled. "No."

Caitlin didn't protest. But then, Tatiana'd already figured the other woman was the more sensible half of the couple.

"I have the money, Ron. Let me do this for you."

"I'm not taking a dime from you. That's not what this relationship is about."

"This relationship is about family. Family helps each other out."

"Not a chance."

"Ron—" Caitlin started.

"No."

"We can do it as a loan if you like," Tatiana offered. "You can pay me back."

"I'd rather be in debt to your sister than some man we don't know," Caitlin interjected.

Her brother's jaw was set. "I did something bad and wrong. I have to pay for it, one way or another."

"You did it for me. For my family. How do you think that makes me feel?" Caitlin whispered.

Instantly, Ron abandoned the eggs and walked around the counter to pull his wife into a hug. "Stop that. Right now. You and your mom *are* my family."

"I won't stop feeling awful until we've paid that man back. You don't know how filled with guilt I am. Please, Ron. We don't have room for pride right now."

Ron's jaw worked, and he looked at Tatiana. "I'll demand the same plan I worked out with Caine. Interest and everything."

She nodded, relieved that a lecture wouldn't be necessary. Her brother might have done something stupid, but at least he was trying to man up and be an adult. "Sure. Whatever you want. Pay him back in the installments you agreed upon, though, so he doesn't think you stole the money from someplace else." Or more accurately, so Wyatt didn't realize she'd fronted her brother the money he'd refused to take directly from her.

"That's smart." He looked down at his wife and smiled tenderly. "See? No need to worry anymore."

The woman sniffled. "Thank you so much, Tatiana. And I swear, I'll get a job too, and we will pay you back as quickly as we possibly can. As long as I don't have to keep worrying about us defaulting and Ron being sent to jail, I can actually get some sleep at night."

"Wyatt wouldn't send Ron to jail." Not now that Wyatt knew they were related. Maybe. Probably.

Caitlin wiped at her eyes. "You can't know that. You don't know him."

Oops. "Um. Yeah."

Ron didn't appear to have heard her slip. "He's been surprisingly decent. Furious at first, of course, and he let me sweat things out for a while, but that offer from him was more than I deserved."

"He seemed like such a tough boss," Caitlin mused. "We were both so stunned when he called yesterday."

"He was a tough boss," Ron answered. "I'm guessing the deal is partly to keep a lid on publicity. Though he said he was only making an exception for me because we had a mutual friend."

Tatiana froze. She straightened. "What was that he said?"

Ron glanced at her. "He said that he thought I had learned my lesson. And he was cutting me some slack because we have a mutual friend he thought very highly of."

No. It couldn't be. "Do you know who the friend is?"

"No idea. It's not like we move in the same circles. I suppose it could be someone else who works at the casino, but he doesn't exactly socialize with the people on the floor."

"When did he say this?" Tatiana knew her tone was sharp, but she couldn't help it.

"Yesterday. Yesterday morning, when we spoke."

Yesterday morning. Before she had marched into Wyatt's office and revealed her connection to Ron.

Suspicion pulsed through her veins, followed by anger. Anger…and a tiny, tiny speck of anticipation? No. "Oh. *Really.*"

"Yeah. Hey—where are you going?"

Tatiana stomped toward the door. "I'll come back later. I have to see someone."

"Do you want to eat breakfast first?"

"After, maybe." She might work up an appetite…kicking Wyatt's ass.

Chapter Eleven

YOU RAN OUT on me. We're not done. Call me back.

Tatiana tightened her grip on her phone.

I was going to wake you up with my face between your thighs, sucking your clit. Tie you down first so you'd have no choice, eat you all day long. Call me back.

The elevator opened. She pressed the button to end her voicemail and shoved the phone into her jeans pocket, holding on to her mad in the face of temptation. They *weren't* done. But probably not in the way Wyatt meant.

Esme was the only occupant of the waiting room today. Busy at her desk, she glanced up when Tatiana thundered into the waiting room. The older woman's look of polite inquiry relaxed into welcome. "Ms. Belikov. How nice to see you again."

Wyatt's assistant had been kind to her. That was the only reason she managed to swallow her temper enough to speak civilly. "Nice to see you, too. Is Wyatt in?"

"Yes—ah. Ms....?"

Tatiana waved one hand and strode to the door of his inner sanctum. "No need to announce me. Cancel his appointments."

"But Ms. Belikov, Mr. Caine said—"

Ignoring Esme, she opened the door, wishing it wasn't so heavy. She'd give anything to really fling it wide. Maybe with smoke and crashing music announcing her appearance.

Even without dramatics, her entrance caught Wyatt's attention. The man looked up from his desk and froze at the sight of her. For a second, she caught a flash of something—happiness? Excitement?—on his face before his cool, controlled mask descended. "Well. Hello."

"Surprise." She kicked the door closed behind her, keeping her gaze locked on his, though she was tempted to check out the way his broad shoulders filled out his blinding white dress shirt. It was important to never take your eyes off a predator. Especially a sneaky one.

"You got my messages, I'm guessing."

"I got both of them."

"Both?" His brow furrowed.

"Yeah. Nice imagery on the second one there." Nice imagery, but no sign that he was yearning for anything more than chastising her for running away.

"Are you…okay?" He gave her a quick onceover. Like an automatic response, her body heated and warmed for him, just as it had the last time she'd walked into his office.

Yesterday, however, she hadn't known how good of a lover Wyatt had become. Now, her skin was itching to feel his hands on her one more time. *Focus.* "Swell."

"I'm glad to hear it." He leaned forward and placed his arms on the desk. His strong forearms were revealed by the rolled-up sleeves of his shirt. He fiddled with a pen between his long fingers. Was it the same pen that had fiddled with her? "Tatiana—"

"How could you not contact me before this?" The words flew out of her mouth, filled with all the anger and annoying lust boiling inside of her.

He blinked, and the confusion on his face only made her madder. "Before this? I called you when I woke up…"

"I'm not talking about today. Before before!"

He opened his mouth. Closed it again. "I don't think I get what you're saying."

Fists. Her hands were fists. "I want to *throw* something at you. But I'm scared I'll miss and hit your window. Can you go stand in front of the wall please?"

"No. Tatiana. Calm down, and let's talk."

Oh, that tone. She *hated* his let's-be-reasonable tone. How had she forgotten that tone?

Yet she still wanted to bone him. Argh. "You knew."

"I knew what?"

"You knew Ron was my brother. Before I told you yesterday."

He winced, his body deflating in his chair. "Figured that out, did you?"

That he didn't even bother to deny it made her anger flare brighter. "Why else would I be here?"

A heavy silence descended before he cleared his throat. "Why, indeed." His hand fidgeted on his desk. The flash of gold caught her eye. Her necklace was instantly recognizable, as was the familiar stack of papers next to it.

He followed her gaze. "You forgot something."

Funny. She hadn't realized she'd left the expensive trinket behind. Nor did she particularly care. Tatiana walked to the desk. Instead of reclaiming her jewelry, she went for the letters.

Wyatt got there before her, his big palm slapping down and sliding the pile toward him. "No."

"They're mine."

"You gave them to me."

"You gave them to me first." Tatiana barely resisted the urge to stick her tongue out at him. He'd probably take it as an invitation. "Besides, I changed my mind, you lying—"

Wyatt made an exasperated sound. "You have the same eyes."

"What?"

His lips tightened. "I was down on the floor one day and see this baby-faced boy dealing cards. This boy with your eyes."

"Lots of people have green eyes."

He glanced down and shifted a paper. "'I love your eyes. I could spend hours drowning in them, an emerald sea at dusk.'" His smile was wry. "Cheesy, but a twenty-year-old kid can't be anything but, can he?"

Her heart leapt at the sound of the words he'd written so long ago coming from his very adult mouth. There was naughty stuff in those letters, yes. But pure sweetness was interspersed between the racy promises of sex and kink.

He'd deny it to his dying day, but her tough rebel had been a hopeless romantic.

Wyatt shook his head at her, as if he was disappointed. "Do you really think I would confuse your eyes with any other human being on the planet? No. He had *your* green eyes. Your coloring. Your nose, the line of your jaw. The similarities were striking enough to investigate."

"When was this?"

No longer the image of a powerful and controlled businessman, he squirmed. Like a small boy called on the carpet by his principal. "Two years ago."

Her legs felt watery. She braced herself on the desk. "That was before he found me."

"Yes."

"Wyatt. Did you…did you have anything to do with Ron tracking me down?"

"Maybe."

"Maybe?"

He sighed. "Fine. I had a private investigator dig around a little, found out his mother had given a baby with your birth date up for adoption. I made sure that information was made available to him, anonymously. He was the one who pursued it."

Did he think she was stupid? Finding one's birth family wasn't an easy lark, or she would have attempted it eons ago. The enormity of his actions staggered her.

She'd figured that he'd simply known about hers and Ron's relationship. Not that he'd *engineered* it. He was the reason she had her brother and sister-in-law and nephew, hell, even her bitter old mother, in her life. "That's unbelievable."

"It's a small world."

"Why would you do something like that?"

He shuffled the papers again and quoted softly, "'I can't imagine a world without you in it. Sometimes I think I'll die if I lose you.'"

She didn't want to hear what he'd said at twenty. She wanted to hear what he was saying now.

He continued. "You weren't just an old flame, Tatiana. You were my first. First best friend, first love. When we ended it, things were going badly, but…" He shook his head. "You can't just wipe away your first."

"Why…why didn't you find me then? Why didn't you pick up the phone and call me and tell me about Ron yourself?" That was what really galled her. The second he'd come back on her radar she'd booked a flight to see him on a pretense. Okay, fine. She got tipsy and nostalgic, and then booked a flight to see him on a pretense. Same thing.

His smile was sad and a little wistful. "I told the PI to only tell me if you were alive and well, and if you could have a connection with this kid. I didn't want your phone number or your address or even your email."

Her pride smarted, and she raised her chin, ready to blister his ears, but he spoke before she could. "But then I changed my mind." He reached inside his shirt pocket and withdrew a tattered scrap of paper. "Didn't you wonder how I got your cell phone number? I've had it for years. Just this, nothing more. It was safer than having your address, because I knew I would write you some blubbering letter when I got lonely or when I thought of you. This…this, I could just keep." His long fingers caressed the paper. "You don't know how many times I've almost picked up the phone. When you stormed in? I was sitting right here, psyching myself up to call you."

"Why didn't you? Why was it so hard?"

"Because I was too much of a coward to take a chance on falling for you all over again. Hell, I lasted, what, half an hour yesterday? Before I was seducing you into my bed? Lying to myself, telling myself it would only be sex, when I knew…"

"Knew what?"

"Knew that you and I…we're so much more, Tatiana. I fought it because I barely survived losing you once, and our parting was mutual then. I have people who depend on me now, who rely on me. You're a distraction I can't afford."

Stung, she reared back. "I'm no femme fatale."

"No. But what you said last night, that wasn't a joke. I always needed you more than you needed me."

"That's not true," she rasped. Didn't he get it? He was hurting her, clawing away at her.

"How could it not be? You were this beautiful, golden angel. And I was…me. You could have done better. Everyone knew that." He lifted his chin, proud even in his vulnerability.

She pressed her fingers to her temple, trying to parse through the glut of information he was shooting her way.

First things first. "I'm no more an angel than I am a whore, Caine," she growled. "Then, or now. But, I'll grant you, I do demand full attention. I don't think that's a bad thing."

A muscle in his jaw clenched. "No. I realized when I woke up this morning, that maybe it's not. I'd somehow forgotten."

"Forgot what?"

"How happy it always made me to be distracted by you."

Unable to stand another second of this without doing something with her restless hands, she grabbed hold of his tie and pulled his delicious, surprised face across the desk. He half rose, making a startled noise as she devoured his lips, giving him a kiss filled with every emotion warring within her: gratitude, annoyance, irritation, and yes, hope.

He'd given her a brother. Even though her family had always been a point of contention between them, he'd made an effort to investigate a man who happened to look similar to her and make sure they were reunited. Because he'd remembered, a decade later, how much she'd wished to meet her birth family.

Their kiss was long and lingering. He braced his hands on his desk and leaned farther over the wide expanse to get closer to her. She finally drew away. "Apologize," she whispered.

He scowled, his lips wet from hers. "For what?"

"For not telling me about my brother earlier. For quietly pulling strings behind the scenes like a control-freak wizard."

"I was trying to—"

"Apologize."

He glared at her. "You never let me get away with anything."

"Nope."

"Fine. I'm sorry—umph."

He'd barely finished speaking when she took his mouth again. This time the kiss was hot, wild, and out of control.

She separated from him, giving him a parting lick across his lips, and released his tie. He didn't straighten right away and his eyes were dazed enough to stroke her ego. "Thank you," she murmured. "For giving me more family."

He shook his head as if to rid the cobwebs from his brain. "I don't want your thanks. If anything, I should be thanking you."

"For what?"

"For following your impulse to come here. I used to

criticize you for playing it safe, for playing by your parents' rules, but you were always ready to risk more than I was. Otherwise you never would have taken a chance on me all those years ago."

She gave a small sniff. "Oh, Wyatt."

He rifled through the letters. "Why did you keep these? For all these years?"

"Because you never forget your first." He'd always hold a piece of her heart, just as, it appeared, she held a piece of his. Because he was a good man, a kind man, and there was a reason she had loved him so much when they were young. "You really are wrong. You needed me enough to write those. I needed you enough to keep them. It was a two-way street with us. Always. Even if we pretended otherwise sometimes." Blast it, those were not tears making her vision foggy.

He swallowed, his mask slipping, as it tended to around her. "Why did you give them back to me, then?"

Tatiana gave a half laugh and dashed an arm over her eyes. "At the time, I might have been thinking in terms of closure. But I think really, deep down…I simply wanted you to know I kept them. That they—you—meant a lot to me. Then. And always."

His broad thumb rubbed the wetness on her cheek. "Tatiana Belikov, confess. That's not the only reason you left these."

"Oh?"

"No. You knew I'd start wondering *why* you kept them. Wondering whether you ever really got over me. Realize I never quite got over you." He cocked his head, his natural arrogance returning. A smirk played on his firm lips. "Track you down. Demand we see each other again, because whatever we have between us is too explosive not to explore."

Had a tiny part of her entertained exactly the scenario he painted? Well. Possibly. "Wow. I must be pretty manipulative." She bit his thumb when it strayed too close to her mouth, not bothering to be gentle.

A slow smile crossed his face. "You're as manipulative as I am, woman." The underlying admiration took the sting from his words.

"I admit nothing. Except…our break up wasn't painless for me either. It's easier to strip yourself physically than it is emotionally." She gathered up the letters and closed the file, resting her hand on top. "These are mine."

"I wrote them."

"Yeah. To me. They're mine. I may not read them on a regular basis, but I like to know I have them. That I was loved like this."

Wyatt placed his hand over hers. "They're yours." He raised an eyebrow. "So. I left you three messages. Not two."

Three messages. "Did you? What did you say?"

"You should listen to it."

Intrigued, she pulled the phone out of her pocket and redialed her voicemail, passing over his previous saved messages to get to the final one.

You and me, Tatiana, we're always going to crash into each others lives. I figured that out a couple years ago, and I've been fighting it all this time.

A pause. *I think we need to talk about some stuff. We also need to give the universe a break. I don't want to wait another ten years.*

There went another tear, leaking out of the corner of her eye.

Let's see each other again. Call me. Please.

She hung up when it became clear the message was over. Trying to think past her excitement was tough. "Oh."

"Let's get to know each other now that we're all grown up. Distract me, Tatiana. Please. I need it."

"Oh."

"Why don't you come over here…" a tug on her hand, a glance from beneath those ridiculously long lashes, "…and we can discuss a more in-depth answer."

Calm yourself. Don't be impulsive. Impulsiveness will only… Oh, fuck it. Sometimes the only way to get ahead was to take a leap. "I don't need to discuss it. I already know my answer."

His grin was blinding. "Yeah? Come give it to me, then."

Her eyes narrowed at his cockiness. "You think you're winning."

"I told you." He lifted her hand to his lips. "I'm the house. I always win. But I'll make sure you share in the prize."

"Hmm. In that case, my answer is…" She disengaged from him and linked her hands primly in front of her. "I would like to go on a date."

Left holding air, Wyatt blinked. "A…a date?"

"Not right now. Right now, I think I'll go check out of my hotel. Ron invited me for breakfast, and I'll probably end up staying with them for a couple of days. See the sights. Spoil my nephew. But tonight. I'd like to go out on a date tonight."

"Is this...?" He squinted at her. "Is this part of a game?"

Tatiana laughed. "No. No game. I want a nice, respectable date. In public, where we have to show off our social skills and behave like normal, boring people. Dinner. A show, perhaps. Is that so crazy?"

A slow smile curled his firm lips. "No. Not crazy at all. I like the idea of a date. I can pick you up at six? Text me the address."

She released a breath she hadn't realized she was holding. "Good. That sounds good. Get ready, because you're going to have to be civil to my brother."

He frowned and opened his mouth, but she beat him to it. "If you want to see me, you'll definitely have to learn to be nice."

Looking annoyed, he subsided. "Fine."

"Oh, and I almost forgot," she exclaimed, totally making things up as she went along, "we won't be having sex with each other. Not until the fourth date, at least."

"What?" He reared back. "You can't be serious."

"Do I look like I'm joking?"

"What, you're such a good girl now?"

She dropped her voice. "I've always been a very good girl, Wyatt."

The flare of lust in his gaze warmed her. "I know. That's why I think you should reconsider..."

"No." This was fun. A new act was starting, and it was going to be so much fun.

He gnashed his teeth, ready to negotiate terms 'til the bitter end. "Just so I'm clear, when you say no sex, are we going by our adolescent definition of sex?"

Only a fool would turn away all the pleasurable alternatives he was alluding to. She pretended to think about it. "Yes."

A lascivious look crossed his face. "Does last night count as one of the four dates?"

"I'll see you tonight, Wyatt."

"Until tonight. I can't wait."

"Even though you won't be getting lucky?"

He tipped his head, eyes bright. "I won a second chance at getting to know you. How much more luck could I ask for?"

Bonus Short Story

This bonus short story takes place shortly after the events in Play With Me.

"IS THAT A vagina?"

Tatiana Belikov sipped her wine and cocked her head, studying the painting of the bright red poppy that graced her living room wall. "Where do you see a vagina? It's a flower."

Wyatt Caine placed his half-finished wineglass on her coffee table, an old steamer trunk she'd found at a garage sale. "Aren't all flowers secretly vaginas?"

"Only if you're a perv."

Wyatt nodded. "That explains it. I *am* a perv."

"Or your vision has been impaired by the hideous abstract crap you have at your place."

He raised an eyebrow. "You have no idea how much that crap cost."

"Oh, I know." Tatiana shook her head. "Sadly, you can't buy taste."

"Those paintings are an investment."

"An investment doesn't have to be painful." She nodded

at the art. "That's going to appreciate, and I love looking at it."

"Who's the artist?"

"A friend. I traded with her for a bracelet. Isn't she phenomenal? Undiscovered yet, but look at these brushstrokes."

"Yeah. The strokes on that vagina are inspired."

Rolling her eyes but secretly amused, Tatiana curled her legs up underneath her. "My, you have vaginas on the brain."

He shot her a pointed look. "Gee. I wonder why."

She fluttered her eyelashes at him, as innocent as can be. "Me too."

They subsided into a comfortable silence, lulled by the radio she'd turned on. She snuck a glance at Wyatt, marveling that he was sitting right there. She felt like she'd barely scratched the surface of the man he was now, though they had spent one lovely night fucking each other's brains out last week when they'd reunited in Vegas.

As exciting as it was to tentatively embark on the relationship they'd decided to rekindle, Tatiana hadn't been able to quell her nerves when he'd kissed her soundly at the Vegas airport and announced that he'd be coming to San Francisco this weekend. This was her territory, after all.

And his large frame took up most of that territory. His navy suit was still crisp and pressed, the sophistication a contrast to her cluttered space. Tatiana didn't understand how people could travel in suits. It was probably one of those things businesspeople were simply adept at doing. Like not napping after downing martinis at lunchtime.

He ought to have looked out of place in her world, this new, wealthy Wyatt. But he fit in perfectly, another mismatched piece in her mismatched life.

Mentally, Tatiana exhaled, a long sigh of relief. No need to fret, not right now. This felt....right.

He shifted, reached behind him and pulled out one of her throw pillows, this one shaped like a mushroom. After pondering it for a moment, he placed it aside. "You have an interesting place."

She followed his gaze around her small, beloved apartment, wondering what he saw. Color, for sure. From her crimson couch to her purple armchair to her bright green bookcase and her red walls, she embraced color.

She liked what she liked, and oftentimes, none of what she liked complemented anything else. Some of her accents were whimsical and cheap, things that caught her eye at the flea market. Sprinkled amongst them was priceless art she purchased from galleries or, preferably, bartered from local artists she knew.

Some people would find her taste gaudy, or even nauseating. Curious, Wyatt took it all in. His sharp black eyes missed nothing as he catalogued every detail of the room before glancing back at her. "This suits you."

She straightened and smiled. "Does it?"

"It does." He scooted closer, tossing the mushroom pillow to the floor.

She made a mental note to tell him the cushion's market value later. It might flabbergast him.

"I remember how annoyed you would get that your parents wouldn't let you decorate your room as you wished. So the minute you got to college, you painted the walls of your dorm room yellow."

The recollection of her hall director's irritation made her

nose wrinkle. "Ugh. They made me paint it back right away. Totally unfair, since I was the one who had to live with that ugly off-white for eight months."

His mouth kicked up at the corner. "I'm sorry. Who had to slap on four coats of white to cover up that yellow?"

A rush of affection ran through her at the memory of young Wyatt. *Jesus, Tatiana. Couldn't you express yourself with posters?* His frustration with her hadn't stopped him from grabbing a paint roller. "You helped."

"Helped?"

"Helped a lot," she modified. She'd done some of the work. Or tried to. Painting a wall a boring color was, well…boring.

He pulled her wineglass from her fingers and placed it next to his on the table. Coming closer, he curled his hand around her neck. "I like your style."

She was an experienced woman, hardly a shy virgin. Yet her stomach fluttered when he looked at her that way. "Thanks."

"Mmm." He leaned in closer until his breath fanned her lips. "Are you going to take me on a tour?"

"This isn't your hotel, Wyatt. You don't need a tour to navigate a space that's eight hundred square feet."

"I haven't seen your bedroom."

No, that was not a blush creeping up her cheeks! She was not a blusher. But she couldn't help it. The way he said that word, *bedroom*, was criminal. "Maybe we can do the tour after dinner."

His finger swept over the pulse beating in her neck. "Did you make plans for us tonight?"

A shiver ran down her spine at the intent in his gaze.

The man had some plans in mind. Naked plans, probably. "There's a great Thai place down the street. It doesn't look like much, but they make an awesome panang curry."

"Hmm." He dropped his hand from her neck. She mourned its loss. His fingers worked his tie, until it hung in two strips. "I can get Thai in Vegas."

"Jamaican?" Her breath caught when he loosened the top three buttons of his shirt, those long, elegant fingers nimble, revealing the tanned column of his throat.

"Same."

"What can't you get in Vegas?"

A slow smile crossed his lips, filled with enough wickedness that her tummy flip-flopped. "I know for a fact that you can get that all over Vegas. On every street corner, in fact," she said archly.

He pulled the tie off and placed it between them. She stole a glance at it, imagining it wrapped around her wrists or her ankles. Totally an oversight, not dating more businessmen. They had kinky bindings with them at all times.

"Not with you."

She swallowed, her throat dry. "I'll give you that."

Another button. "Will you give me *you*?"

Ah, fuck. There came that blush again. It was the novelty and excitement of the situation that was making her revert to a giddy schoolgirl. A new, tentative relationship with the guy she had loved long ago? Things were all shiny and sexy and fun. So the blush was justifiable, damn it.

As was her yearning. Oh, yeah, she'd love to lie down, spread her legs, and let Wyatt have his way. She knew it would be time well spent. The man had been good at fucking ten years ago. He was *great* at fucking now.

So. Much. Temptation. But she'd made a decision, and she'd stick with it. "I told you. Four dates. Four dates before we jump back in bed with each other."

His lips twisted. "But this is date number *five*."

"It's two."

Scowling now, he counted off on his fingers. "One, our first night together. Two, our date the next night. Three, I took you to that godforsaken magic show you mentioned you wanted to see. Four, I drove you to the airport. Five, tonight."

Tatiana rolled her eyes. "First of all, you can't ever count going to the airport as a date."

"We grabbed coffee on the way."

She ignored that. "In any case, I'm counting that whole trip to Vegas as one date. This is our second."

His mouth dropped open. "Are you—? You have got to be kidding me. What, is this weekend going to be counted as one date?"

She pretended to think about it. Rules were highly entertaining when you made them up along the way. "Yes."

"Tatiana."

"Wyatt."

"I'm a man of my word. I'd be happy to give you time. But what is the purpose of this arbitrary period of enforced celibacy again?" He spoke through gritted teeth.

"I don't want lust to blind us." My, that sounded appropriately dramatic and noble.

"Not fucking each other isn't going to make us any less lustful. In fact, my lust is pretty much through the roof right now."

She batted her eyes at him. "Is it?" Of course it was. After their first night together, the most they had engaged in was a few minutes of heated necking. Sexual tension was a living, breathing thing between them, always present.

He stopped and considered her. "You know, I'm not a sex machine. I'd have no problem with this absurd rule, if I didn't know you're only fucking around with me to see how much you can get away with."

She placed her hand on her chest, gratified when his hot eyes darted right there. Her blue top was cut low to make the best of her cleavage. "I don't know what you're talking about."

"Right. Don't think I can't tell a power play when I see it."

It wasn't a power play, per se. Part of her, the mischievous, impulsive side, just wanted to see how much she could tease them both before they exploded.

Wyatt may not be a sex machine, but she kind of was.

And because of her aforementioned love of sex, she'd ensured there was a safety valve built into this nonsense. Go four dates without jumping the man's bones? Impossible. She lifted the tie and ran it through her fingers, testing its strength. "I think you're forgetting something about my absurd rule."

Instantly alert, he leaned forward. This was her comfy suede couch, her life, and still he managed to dominate it. "What's that?"

"Our definition of sex." She peered up at him from beneath her lashes. "Our adolescent definition."

He paused for a moment, and then gave her a wry grin. "Of course. That leaves a lot on the table, doesn't it?"

Their teen definition of sex had been about as loosey-goosey as some politicians. Vaginal penetration? Sex.

Everything else? Um. Not sex. Especially if they could do it in the backseat of his car.

"You tell me." She let the tie slip out of her fingers.

His gaze was hot enough to singe. "You hungry?"

Only for you. "No." She sidled closer, dropped her hand on his chest. Like a heat-seeking missile, her fingers flew to his buttons, toying with them.

"You have no idea how much I've been tormenting myself with thoughts of your hands on me for the past week."

No. She had an idea. At odd moments of the day, she'd stare off into space, unable to think of anything but his hands, mouth, and cock on her and in her. The daydreaming would have been annoying if it wasn't so arousing. She hummed. "Poor baby. Were you getting pumped up? Thinking this was the fifth date?"

"Knowing it was the fifth date."

She hid her smile and unbuttoned the crisp white shirt, excited to have him stretched out for her exploration. "Well. I'm happy for both of our sakes that I can still put my hands on you."

When she was finished unbuttoning his shirt, she spread the halves wide, her toes curling at the sight of his strong, tanned chest. She scraped her fingers over his hard belly, loving the way the muscles contracted and tightened at her touch.

Broad shoulders, narrow hips, defined abs. A delicious body. A body that could be justified by the hour he spent in his home gym every morning when he woke up at dawn.

Eager to eat him up with her eyes, her hand dropped to his belt. After unbuckling it, she attacked the fastening on his pants.

His hand covered hers, stopping her. "You're overdressed."

She knocked his hand away. "I want to suck you."

The words might have been initially intended to shock and arouse him, but as she said them, Tatiana knew they were for her benefit, too. She squirmed at the mere thought of having this man captive to her mouth. His eyes darkened to pure black, a curse hissing between his lips.

She unzipped his pants, carefully maneuvering over the impressive bulge between his legs. His black boxer briefs did nothing to hide his cock.

She licked her lips, and his cock jerked. "Hello there. Aren't you tempting?"

His hand covered his cock, and he squeezed. "Does this tempt you?"

"You know it does."

"It's too bad you don't want it inside of you." He rubbed his dick through the cotton. "What a shame that you're determined to deny both of us pleasure."

She cast him a flirtatious look. "I'm not denying either of us anything." She lowered his boxers and pulled out his hard cock. It was thick and long, precome wetting the tip. She bent over and lapped her tongue over the head, tasting him.

Breathing harsh, he fisted the root of his cock with one hand and sank the other into her hair. "Yes."

He didn't use his grip to make her deep throat him, which she appreciated. Oh, there were times when she was more than happy to get face-fucked, but she wanted to tease right now, this first time since they'd slept together, and he knew that. She licked him all over as if he were a melting ice cream cone, enjoying his increasingly desperate groans above her.

Finally, finally, she wrapped her lips around him and sucked. His fingers clenched in her hair hard enough to make her scalp sting, and he pulled her away. He dispatched her top in seconds, humming with pleasure when he caught sight of her breasts cupped in virginal white lace, a bra she knew he'd love.

So maybe she'd entertained the possibility that they would engage in some naked shenanigans.

He stood, his cock wet and curving out of his underwear. "Take your clothes off," he ordered, and did the same, tearing off his garments in the amount of time it took her to wrestle her jeans and panties down.

He rested one naked knee on the couch next to her hip. He reached behind her. With a flick of his wrist, he had her bra undone.

"You're still pretty good at that." Tatiana shrugged her bra straps down her arms.

"It's one skill a man doesn't forget. Especially if a man has you for a teacher."

An odd pride ran through her. Yes, she had taught him that. She'd been his first after all, and had stamped herself on his life the same way he had on hers.

Unable to resist, she stroked the cock staring her in her face and leaned in to flick it with her tongue. He grasped her head and gave her a small shake. "No."

"You don't want a blowjob?"

His slow smile made her heart pound. "Not exactly." Dropping to his knees on the carpet between her spread legs, he wrapped one arm around her and brought her close, kissing her deep, his tongue flicking against her lips. Because she knew it would drive him crazy, she remained prim, keeping her mouth closed.

Sure enough, he growled, one hand cradling her head, his thumb pressing down on her chin. "Let me in," he muttered against her lips.

She allowed him to pressure her lips into opening. He stroked inside, exploring her, his tongue dominant and strong. He bit her lip when they separated, dragging on the sensitive flesh. "Do you know what I haven't had in a long time?" he murmured.

"What?"

His smile was curiously tender. He brushed aside a lock of her hair. His hand drifted down over her throat, to her breasts. He shaped the flesh and cradled it. "Do you remember what I used to love to do to you? In the backseat of that old Civic I had?"

"Um, everything."

His thumb rubbed over her nipple. "Yes. But since I saw you today in that cock-teasing shirt, all I've been able to think about is fucking these tits."

If it were possible to spontaneously combust of arousal, Tatiana would be there right now. Her thighs clenched, her pussy dampening. Especially when he came closer and drew her nipple into his mouth, each tug a direct line to the place between her legs. She looked down when he switched breasts. His long lashes fanned over his cheeks, his expression concentrated. With a final suck, he pulled away. A cry escaped when he deliberately rasped his ever-present stubble over one wet, sensitive tip.

His fingers toying with the nipples he'd left, he ran his tongue over the valley between her breasts and the inner slopes, rough swipes of possession.

His chest was rising and falling almost as quickly as hers when he released her. He nodded to the couch and stood. "On your back."

She shifted to lie on her back, the soft couch making her nerve endings tingle. He stared down at her for a long minute. Vaguely self-conscious, she covered her belly with her arm. "What is it?"

"Nothing. You're so fucking beautiful."

Tatiana had a fairly good opinion of her looks, but that kind of heartfelt compliment was always appreciated. Relaxing, she ran her fingers over her stomach, a subtle taunt. "Thank you."

"I thought about buying you some jewelry, you know. But that seemed silly, when you can make anything you like." He stroked her collarbone. "But I can give you a pearl necklace."

Cheesy as his words were, she smiled. "I do love pearls."

"Me too. Especially these." He straddled her, his cock dragging over her stomach. Reaching above her, he grabbed the arm of the couch, inching up until the tip of his cock nestled between her breasts.

His cock was still damp from her mouth and his pre-come, and her breasts were wet with his tongue, but she knew that wouldn't be enough. "We need lube."

He rubbed his cock over her nipples. They both gasped. "Where? Bathroom? Bedroom?" The tightness in his voice reflected what he thought about that. Small though her apartment might be, that was too damn far.

"Drawer on the side table."

He got up and headed for the table she gestured to, back in a flash with a still-sealed bottle in his hand.

"You keep edible lube in your living room?"

She shook her head, expecting the question, though maybe not the moody possessiveness underlying it. "I'm acquainted with both of our libidos. Figured we wouldn't make it more than an hour before we were ripping clothes."

He gave a harsh bark of laughter, straddled her again, and opened the bottle. He squirted a generous amount on her breasts and his cock. Unable to resist that shiny, taut flesh, she grasped his penis in both hands and spread the lube up and down while he did the same to her breasts, making the simple act into a sexy massage. When they were both gleaming, he adjusted his position. "Push those pretty tits together and let me fuck them."

She obeyed, breathless, creating a warm, wet valley for him to fuck.

His face looked pained, and he closed his eyes and breathed hard as his cock slid between her breasts. He let go of the armrest to tweak her nipples, and she cried out, the sharp pleasure making the wetness between her legs unbearable.

"This feels so good." He compressed her nipple harder. "You don't even know."

She knew. She knew exactly what it felt like, to have your brain short-circuiting, your body primed for release. One touch against her clit and she'd be done. She raised her head to look down her body. His penis popped her breasts up with every thrust, her nipples bright red and aching for his touch.

"Jesus. Yes. Tighter. I'm going to come."

Unable to string words together in any intelligible fashion, she let her actions speak for her. She craned up further, opening her mouth to lick and suck the head of his cock as it emerged from between her breasts. He froze for a second and thrust again, hard enough to shove her up the couch. Her neck bent against the armrest at an awkward angle, but she didn't care. Her entire focus was on his cock and the pleasure on his face, pleasure that looped around to tie into hers.

He groaned, thrust into her mouth a final time, and came. He pulled out, leaving a trail of semen on her tongue and chest and neck.

Wyatt dragged his hands through his hair. "God. I needed that." He took a few deep breaths, his face carved in lines of strain, before he straightened and surveyed her, satisfaction obvious. "Perfect."

She clenched her thighs, both amused and annoyed. He'd gotten his, after all, while she most assuredly had not. It would be so easy, too; she was that turned on. "What about me?"

"Poor thing," he crooned. He moved back to sit between her legs, his slick cock still semierect. "Let me take care of you."

"Or I could take care of myself."

His teeth flashed white. "When I'm near you, I take care of your orgasms. Not you." He flattened his palms against her thighs and spread her legs wider until one foot was touching the floor, the other pressed tight against the back of the sofa. He dipped his head down to her pussy and inhaled. "God you smell good."

At the first touch of his tongue, she shouted, her body arching up to welcome him. He licked all around her pussy lips and then finally flattened his tongue, sliding in and stroking out. Again and again and again, holding her open with his fingers.

"My clit," she gasped.

He used his nose to nudge the hard bud while he ate her out. When she clenched on his tongue and grabbed handfuls of his hair, he drew her clit into his mouth while shoving two fingers into her pussy. It wasn't his cock, but it filled her up enough to trigger her orgasm.

He pulled away, his face shiny with her juices. Appropriate, since his semen marked her neck and chest. They were all over each other, which was how it should be.

She stretched languidly. "That was pleasant."

"I could make it more pleasant." He sat back on his heels and fisted his cock.

"I bet you could." She smirked. "In two more dates."

"You know what's strange, in light of this rule of yours? That unopened box of condoms I spied in that side table. Don't trust yourself?" He made the pulls on his cock more explicit.

Oh, she trusted herself. No one had ever called her a pushover. Even if he did have the most beautiful penis she'd ever seen. "I was trying to be forward-thinking. Figured we'd use them in a few weeks." She said the words carelessly, but those excited nerves did a little tap-dance in her stomach.

They were too combustible to call it quits any time soon, even if they did live in different cities, right? After all, fate had thrown them together again. It seemed a shame to let a short plane ride stand in their way. By default, things might proceed slowly, but that was probably good. Cautious didn't normally describe Tatiana, but the pain of their last failed attempt at a relationship had made an impression on her.

A smile lit his face, calming her. "Damn right we'll use them." He got up off the couch and bent down, picking her up easily. "If you don't mind, I'd like to see what you've painted the bathroom. Fuchsia? Teal?"

"Yellow." She kissed his cheek.

He grinned. "Of course. Why don't we go have some not-sex in the shower? Clean ourselves off before we grab some food."

She linked her arms around his neck. His skin was hot, his muscles hard and strong. Would it be possible to spend the whole weekend rubbing herself all over him? Something told her he wouldn't object. "Sounds perfect."

Risk & Reward

Chapter One

"GET IN MY car. And take off your clothes."

Tatiana Belikov gave a jerk of surprise at the low rumble in her ear, fumbling her large handbag. Delight replaced her shock in the next heartbeat. Oh, that voice. That low, gravelly voice alone made her want to strip and wriggle in happiness.

"They told me Vegas was dangerous, but I didn't realize I'd get accosted the minute I stepped foot off the plane," she purred.

A large, possessive hand settled on her waist. "You should have. You came here to see me. Accosting beautiful women is my specialty."

She turned and attempted a frown, though she was too excited to pull it off successfully. "Women, plural?"

The tall, lean man slipped his arm around her. "I misspoke. Woman. Singular. A very singular woman."

"That's better." Unable to keep her cool, her grin broke free, and she stretched up to bring her lips to his answering smile. The kiss was more eager than sexy or seductive, her lips and tongue excited to taste him.

Tatiana hadn't known it was possible to crave someone as much as she craved Wyatt Caine. Chocolate, yes. A person, no.

Wyatt bent over her, cradling her head and angling her so his tongue could make a deeper foray into her mouth. He hauled her closer to him, until his muscular thigh insinuated itself between her legs. His teeth caught her lower lip, scraping the flesh, sending a shiver down her spine.

She slid her hands down his chest, tugging on his tie. It was dark plum, and one she fondly recalled draped over her bedpost not long ago. Had it also been used to bind her limbs at some point? Maybe blindfold her as he licked his way down her body? Probably. She had a fairly intimate knowledge of his neckwear collection by now. "What are you doing here? You said you had meetings all day."

"I cancelled one." He licked her where he'd nipped her, soothing the sting. "I didn't want to wait until tonight to see you."

Tonight. The same pang of guilt that had been dogging her for the better part of a day popped up again. *In a second. We can talk about it in a second.* She mock pouted and leaned back. "And you didn't come meet me inside?"

"Sorry, I ran late, or I would have met you at baggage claim."

"I had no bags to check." In the past seven months that they'd been dating, Tatiana had learned there was no point in packing heavy for her visits. Wyatt insisted on keeping her naked for almost the entire trip. Not that she was complaining.

"Good. Saves us time." He took hold of her carry-on and loosely linked his fingers with hers. "This way."

Tatiana stole a glance at him as they walked down the long line of limousines and luxury sedans, a small thrill going through her. He was...beautiful. There was no other word to describe him, though as a self-respecting manly man he might balk. He had the face of a fallen angel, all dark and perfectly chiseled. No matter how often he shaved, a faint five o'clock shadow lingered. His lashes were so long, she was surprised they didn't tangle when he blinked.

His hair shone blue black, the strands cut close to his head. The suit he wore fit him impeccably, outlining his lean and muscular physique. She might get annoyed sometimes that he was so effortlessly attractive when she had to put work and effort into looking good, but then that annoyance was drowned out by the knowledge that he was hers. All hers.

Tatiana smiled at the familiar, fit young man who stood rigidly at attention next to a black limousine. "Sal. Good to see you again."

The driver's face was expressionless. As usual. If she ever saw him emote, Tatiana might drop dead of shock.

"Ma'am." He opened the back door.

Tatiana slid in first, arranging her handbag next to her. Wyatt followed, taking the seat opposite hers. The car was large enough that his long, stretched-out legs didn't touch her feet, which were primly crossed at the ankles. Still, his presence was so big, the luxurious cabin felt smaller than it should.

She recrossed her legs. "Why'd you bring the limo?" Normally, he sent his town car. The first couple of times she'd visited, she'd booked her own rental car, wanting to have freedom to move around if she wished to.

Having a car was like having lots of clothes—completely wasted when you spent your entire trip naked in a bedroom with a hot guy.

So she'd attempted a taxi from the airport…once. Wyatt, who had barely tolerated the rental car, had found her taking public transportation to be some sort of personal affront, though she still wasn't sure why. Hence, the chauffeur pickup.

"I like the divider in this car." Wyatt loosened his tie.

"The divider?" She instinctively glanced over his head. The solid black glass was already in place, separating them from Sal.

"I knew I'd take one look at you and want to fuck you. Even if Sal could see us. Figured the divider might come in handy."

She shifted, the subtle movement of the powerful car vibrating under her legs. "So when you told me to get in your car and take off my clothes…"

"You're in my car. Now take off your clothes."

She ran her finger along the hem of her skirt. "But we're going to the hotel."

"You are." He glanced at the gold watch on his thick wrist. "I have exactly enough time to take the edge off. Sal will drop me off at my next meeting. Now take off your clothes."

"You sure know how to sweet-talk a girl."

"I don't need to sweet-talk my girlfriend. Do I?"

Oh, she loved that. She especially loved that he couldn't quite suppress the tiny jump of delight in his voice every time he said girlfriend. She wasn't the only uncool one in this relationship. "You always have to sweet-talk me."

"Fine." He leaned back, his smile lascivious. "Baby, it's a felony for a woman to look as good as you. But if you want to suck my dick, I'll get you off with a warning."

"You are possibly the worst sweet-talker I've ever heard."

Lazily, he rubbed his thumb over his bottom lip. "My mouth is better suited to other activities. I've demonstrated that."

Those lips capturing her nipples, her clit. Cheeks hollowing with every suck. Her stomach clenched. "You have."

"Take off your clothes. Before I rip them off. It's been too long."

"It's been three weeks."

"Three weeks is too long."

This had been one of their longer separations. They'd been doing pretty well, all things considered. Since Tatiana's profession as a jewelry designer was far more portable than Wyatt's as a casino mogul, she had been able to arrange longer visits to see him. The times when she either needed or wanted to be in San Francisco, Wyatt had flown to visit her on the weekends.

"We video chatted," she offered weakly.

His dark eyes were locked on hers. "Beating off to you touching yourself is hot, but it's a poor substitute to what I really want."

"Are my live sex shows getting poor reviews? I should have known I couldn't compete with the ones here in town."

"Oh, I give you two thumbs and a cock up." He smiled at her giggle. "But I want to touch that pussy. It's mine, isn't it?"

The softly spoken demand made her humor vanish. The

vibe shifted from playful reunion to darker need. "You know it is…sir."

His shoulders tensed, the one word ripping into whatever façade of calm he'd managed to don. Just as she'd intended it to.

Wyatt leaned back into the plush seat and gazed at her from beneath heavy lids. His muscular thighs spread open wider, as if to give the thick bulge between them more room.

He knew exactly how to tempt her. She was as desperate for his penis as he was for her pussy.

She slid from the seat to kneel on the floor, the carpet softer than in most other cars. Good. She was vain enough to not want visible rug burn. "Is the divider soundproof?"

"No. You'll have to be quiet."

Another woman might roll her eyes, get up, and tell her man to wait, in that case. She wasn't other women. An illicit thrill shot through her. Oh, the joy of almost discovery.

Undressing for Wyatt hadn't gotten old, because no matter what order she went in, what article of clothing she removed first, she was confident of his full and lustful attention. Still, she gave the task all due consideration. Should she begin with her skirt this time? No. She'd rather work her way up to the main event. Crossing her arms, she pulled the tank top over her head, revealing the purposefully virginal white lace bra she wore. Since starting to date Wyatt, her investment in white underwear had shot up. Only the fact that he ripped so many of them to pieces kept her lingerie drawers from overflowing.

"The bra, too."

She obeyed, dragging the straps down her arms with the

kind of hesitancy she figured a more innocent woman might display, pushing the cups below her breasts before unhooking the garment. The car went over a pothole, giving her flesh a bit of added jiggle.

Wyatt licked his lips, his hand going to his cock, squeezing it hard through his slacks. "The skirt."

She had to tear her attention away from the rude rubbing he was giving his dick. Curling her fingers under the hem of her skirt, she pulled it up. Slow. Slow enough that it would torture him, but quick enough that he wouldn't attack and shove it aside.

Part of the fun was the reveal.

He didn't disappoint, freezing when her trimmed bush came into view. A low growl sounded in his chest. "Were you bare-ass naked under this skirt for that whole flight?"

"Would that bother you?"

"That anyone could catch a glimpse of your snatch? Hell, yeah."

"But wearing no panties makes things so much easier." They were whispering now, quieter than they probably needed to be, lest the driver overhear.

"Things?"

"Like when I start thinking about you. I can reach under that thin little airline blanket and..." She trailed off, opening the lips of her pussy to bare herself to him.

"And what?" His words were still hoarse, but there was cold steel there. Annoyance and lust. The poor guy didn't know whether to scold or fuck.

The best combination, because then he'd give her both.

She glanced up at him from under her lashes, full of faux coyness, a marked contrast to the way she held her pussy open for his hungry gaze. "You know."

"I think I do know." He gave a jerky nod to the seat that ran the length of the car. "Lie down."

She got up and stretched out, raising her arms above her head. One foot she propped on the seat, the other flat on the floor. With her back arched and her legs open, the position was lewd and inviting. Like her. "Is this good?"

He removed his suit jacket and left it folded neatly on the seat next to him. Crawling over, he came to kneel between her legs. "Perfect." With no warning, his thick finger speared into her. She bit her lip to keep her whimper contained. Yes, three weeks had been too long. Her fingers and toys could never compete with him.

"Tell me. So I'm clear. Is this what you would do on the plane?"

"Yes."

He thrust hard enough to make her breasts jiggle. "And this?"

"Yes."

"But anybody could have seen you." His thumb dipped inside her, gathering moisture. "The man sitting next to you. The flight attendant. They would have known how hungry this pussy is."

"I was… Oh God."

He pinched her clit hard. "You were what?"

"Careful."

"And did you come on that plane, you dirty little slut?"

The words were a barely audible growl, but she heard every drop of appreciation in them. "Yes, sir."

"Hmm." In the next instant, his hand was gone from between her legs. She opened her eyes to find him carelessly using her discarded shirt to wipe his fingers clean before he sat back against the seat. "Then I suppose you don't need to be fucked right now."

He was kidding. He had to be kidding. "What?"

"You've already taken care of yourself. On the plane."

She licked her lips, desperate to have his hand back on her, in her. "I was kidding." Yeah, she'd gone panty-less, but it had been an impulsive whim, in the restroom after she'd landed, and mainly to get in the sexy mood for Wyatt.

"I, however," he said, as if he hadn't heard her, "do need to be fucked right now. As I've made very clear." He unbuckled his belt, unbuttoning and unzipping his finely made slacks. She shivered and rose on her elbows as his cock came into view. His penis was a work of art, perfectly shaped—no funny kinks or bends, large enough so he could be arrogant about it, but not so huge as to scare her.

He pulled a condom from his pocket and ripped the foil, rolling the latex down his ruddy cock. *Something else we need to discuss.*

Later. This. You waited so long for this.

He leaned over her, his broad shoulders blocking whatever light managed to stream in through the tinted windows. His face was set and intense, his jaw clenched. "This won't last long."

She didn't mind. Their separation and the anticipation of reuniting ensured that her pump was primed. There was no need for anything right now but a fast, hard fuck.

The tremble in his hands as he pushed her thighs wider thrilled her, a sign of his rapidly failing composure. He made room, fitted himself to her pussy, and pressed his thick cock deep inside.

They both groaned as he thrust, retreated, and pushed in again, going deeper with every rock. "You feel so good," he murmured.

"Right back at you." She twined one leg around his narrow hips, loving the contrast of his still-clothed body on her naked skin. He ground his hips hard enough to shove her up the slick leather seat.

Wyatt hissed a warning and pulled her back by the waist, demanding she remain still for his penetration. He moved faster and faster, her breasts bouncing with the force of his thrusts, drawing his attention.

Using one hand to support himself, he fondled her tits, cupping and squeezing forcefully, the way she liked it. He leaned down and bit her nipples, the sharp sting of pain traveling right to her pussy, making her clench around the erection penetrating her. Reaching between them, he used his fingers to open her up.

She gasped when he twisted his hips, angling his cock to reach that perfect place inside her while abrading her clit with the wiry hairs of his groin. "Yes. Yes. Just like that. Yes, that's what I nee—"

His lips covered hers, swallowing the words that might have given away their backseat shenanigans, the kiss sloppy and desperate. "Shh," he drew back to whisper. "Be quiet. You don't want Sal to hear, do you? Hear that you're getting fucked? He'll know how hot you are for me. How you couldn't wait to get to a bed."

Every word scraped over her, driving her arousal higher. She shook her head, frantic. "Wyatt, I'm going to..."

His body moved faster inside of her, and he shoved his palm over her parted lips. His skin tasted salty with sweat.

"Bite me."

She bit down, hard, her shriek muffled by his flesh. The tension curled into a tight ball in her stomach and exploded, her body arching to milk as much of him with her pussy as she could. He gave an approving growl, the pounding picking up speed until he froze, buried deep. His cock jerked inside of her as he came. He gave a ragged sigh and rested his forehead on hers.

She stroked his shoulders, hoping for his sake he hadn't sweat through his shirt. "Christ, I needed that."

"Me too."

"I'm glad you came to the airport. Beat my plan."

"What was your plan?"

"To barge into your office and blow you under your desk during whatever meeting you were in."

He lifted his head, eyebrows raised in interest. "Well, now. That sounds intriguing. Don't toss that plan completely."

"Mmm."

He sat up and pulled out of her slowly, both of them appreciating the way her body tried to keep his softening cock inside. "Is that why you were panty-less?"

"Yes. I took them off after I landed, by the way. I wouldn't fly commando. Kinda unsanitary."

"If you had taken my plane, you could have gone naked." He grabbed tissues from the box of Kleenex on the console, taking care of the condom.

"The whole private-jet thing is a little out of my comfort zone." After her initial shock over the decadence of his luxurious lifestyle, Tatiana had made a conscious effort to not dwell on Wyatt's wealth, a far cry from the blue-collar kid she'd dated in high school and college. It helped that for the most part he treated his hard-earned wealth as a tool. The fine clothes were an image enhancement, acquired with the same level of careless attention he'd once applied to purchasing jeans and T-shirts. *Nothing attracts a high roller like the challenge to be the richest dick in the place,* he'd cynically told her when she questioned his ordering a slew of suits, the season's latest, after barely glancing at the catalog his assistant had provided. *I have to make them want to beat me. That's what lures these people in.*

Not that he didn't actively seek out and enjoy some of his luxuries, particularly the toys. When they were younger, she'd often found dog-eared car magazines lying around his apartment. Sometimes he'd stopped and drooled over this or that gadget. It delighted her that he could now indulge his champagne tastes.

Even if it did occasionally discombobulate her. The limo and the fancy penthouse, okay. Though she was conservative with her money, she could fathom someone she knew, who was roughly her age, owning those things. A private airplane? That was ludicrous.

"One day, I'm going to drag you onboard. Fuck you ten thousand feet in the sky."

They'd gotten comfortable saying things like that. One day. Someday. Next time. Eventually. Nothing definite, of course, but vague indications of them being together at some point in the distant future.

Because they were good together. The sex was awesome, no complaints there. They made each other laugh. Conversation rarely faltered, and if it did, their silences were comfortable. They'd both grown up to be fairly independent, so crowding wasn't much of an issue.

Yes. It was perfect. She was so happy when she was with

him.

Too happy.

She shook her head, trying to clear it of the insidious thought. There was no such thing as too happy. "We'll see."

"Fine, fine." He casually did up his pants.

She took a deep breath. "Listen. Is it okay if we go to dinner tonight?"

"Dinner? Out, you mean?"

She didn't fault him for his surprise. When they spent a week apart, let alone three, they were desperate to spend the first night in bed.

"I guess so. Is there someplace in particular you want to go?" Wyatt straightened his tie.

"I thought Eduardo's. If that's okay."

He bent to gather her clothes and handed them to her. "Yes, that's fine."

It didn't matter where they went, but Eduardo's had a great vegan selection. Tatiana sat up. "The thing is…"

His phone beeped, and he pulled it out, frowning at the screen. "Esme. She's stalling the people I'm supposed to be meeting."

"Oh."

"I'll let you get out here and I'll run. I'll be home by six."

That was when she realized the car had stopped. "Are we at the hotel? When did we get here? Oh my God." She shoved her skirt down and hurriedly put her bra on. "Sal could have opened the door."

"Relax. It's barely been a minute." Wyatt flicked a piece of lint off his shoulder. "Besides, he knows not to just fling open the door. Guy drives around some of my guests. Do you have any idea what sort of depraved things they get up to? Yeah, no one does."

She tried to put herself to rights. Wyatt handed over her bag, and then wrapped his hand around her neck, bringing her in for a deep kiss. "Mmm," he murmured against her lips. "Pamper yourself for the rest of the day. But don't touch yourself. I want you crazy for cock by the time we're done with dinner."

She didn't know if he'd be talking to her after dinner, but she gave him a weak smile. No time now to explain tonight's surprise to him. When he came home. She'd tell him then. Completely blindsiding him wasn't an option.

Even if she feared losing *this.*

"I may go shopping."

"Good." He pulled out his wallet and casually extracted a credit card.

She stared at the platinum piece of plastic, annoyance replacing some of her anxiety. "If you don't want me to shove that card up your ass, you'll put it away."

He made an irritated sound. "You think too much when it comes to spending your money."

"And you think I'll think less if I'm spending someone else's money?"

"Not someone else's, my—Damn it." His phone beeped again, and he scowled. "I have to go."

"I'm going to buy something ridiculously expensive. With my money." She settled her bag on her shoulder and reached for the door.

"That'll show me."

Tatiana threw him a scowl. "Quit being cute."

"Impossible, sweetheart."

Chapter Two

IN THE SHORT drive to his lawyer's office, Wyatt struggled to wipe the grin off his face. The goofiness of it might alarm anyone who spied him.

Smiling when Tatiana was around was nothing new. The past half a dozen months or so had been amazing. When they were together, he felt like...more. A better person, a better human. The sex was phenomenal. They fucked like rabbits on Viagra. She was his absolute equal in bed and out, able to handle anything he threw at her.

There was a level of comfort that existed simply because they had known each other before they'd achieved professional success. With other women, he felt pressured to maintain a particular image. Tatiana didn't expect him to be suave and cultured all the time. In fact, he thought she liked him more when he was crass.

It was a certainty that he liked that part of her. Her sweet, golden appearance had always disguised a dirty, sassy soul that delighted him.

She had changed over the past decade, of course, as had he. It intrigued him, made him feel like he was putting together a fractured puzzle, reconciling the old Tatiana with the current one. He'd always loved puzzles, and each minute he spent with her gave him something new to chew on and study.

It had gotten to the point that when they weren't together…

Wyatt's smile faded. It wasn't just the sex he missed when they were apart. It was her. He resented the phone or computer between them. He wanted to see her when they texted or spoke. When they video chatted, he went crazy with the need to touch her.

Wyatt didn't want a repeat of their seven-year-long adolescent relationship. Back then, they'd started talking marriage when Tatiana was a senior in high school. Soul mates, Tatiana had called them, and he'd secretly agreed.

That kind of thinking had made their eventual breakup that much harder. Because if you couldn't make it work with a woman you considered the love of your life, who could you make it work with? They'd been young, he'd told himself over the intervening years, when he reflected. They hadn't even known what love was.

But he'd never had a relationship half as good as the one he'd had with Tatiana. Granted, that last year had been tense, filled with constant yelling and escalating stress. When Tatiana had finally, bitterly suggested they call it quits, it had been almost a relief to agree.

Almost. He grimaced, hating that he could still remember the aching throb of losing her.

When it had been good, though…it had been great.

Perhaps that was why, when she'd walked into his office that fateful day a little over six months ago, he'd gone a little mad, proposing a one-night stand, a brief respite from both of their lives.

He hadn't expected that it would be an explosive night that would lead to an attempt at actually reconciling. Nor had he realized that he would want such a thing. But right now? He was about as happy—no, happier—than he'd been even in the early years of their young romance.

Though his rash impulsivity had been rewarded, he was trying to keep a tight lid on himself as they came to know each other all over again. Neither of them had used the L word yet, and that was good. He was older, she was wiser, and he figured they had a tacit agreement in place to let this unfold however it did, no expectations.

The long-distance thing wasn't ideal, but he'd started delegating some of his day-to-day responsibilities so he could free up time for visits. They spent most of those visits naked, so he had an immense amount of fun. Aware that sometimes Tatiana might wish to try a non-fucking activity, he occasionally attempted to normalize their time together. Like tonight, she'd wanted to go out to dinner, so he'd mentally said sayonara to the plans he'd had to keep her tied to his bed. Thank God he'd rearranged his schedule to come fuck her on her ride home from the airport, or he'd be suffering by night time.

Tatiana was happy, too. Each of her smiles beamed their way into his heart. She couldn't fake that sort of pleasure.

So, why, he wondered as he slipped his credit card back into his wallet, did he feel as though something was vaguely…off.

Wyatt trusted his instincts. He was a poker player, after all, adept at reading his opponents and the situation. And right now, they were screaming that he and Tatiana were on the verge of some sort of impasse. Like those old Choose Your Own Adventure books, where the protagonists either lived happily ever after or died tragically.

His resolve hardened, strengthened by fear. He would choose right, this time. Another decade with a barren personal life while he scraped and slaved to build a second or third fortune? No thanks.

His lips quirked as the car slowed, and he tucked his wallet back into his pocket. God knew she wouldn't take his money. She didn't need his connections. The nostalgia factor could only go so far. All that was left was him. Adult Wyatt needed to be enough for Adult Tatiana.

He hoped he was.

Chapter Three

RED WAS FOR courage.

Tatiana leaned in close to the mirror and slicked the lipstick on over her lower lip, her mouth forming an O. When she was finished, she pressed her lips together and examined her appearance critically.

The bright red of her lips was reflected on her nails and dress. It was too much, perhaps, especially in contrast to her fair skin and honey-colored hair, but she liked the shock and awe of it all.

It helped overcome the nervousness that had grown with every minute of the day.

She smoothed her hand over her stomach. Grasshoppers were ricocheting around in her belly.

Wyatt was going to kill her. She should have told him last night, the second she'd gotten off the phone with her parents, even if it had been late. Hell, she should have told him when he'd grasped her arm at the airport today.

What was wrong with her? He was going to be so freaking angry. And she couldn't blame him.

As if she'd conjured him, the front door opened and

closed. Those grasshoppers did another tap dance. "Tatiana," came Wyatt's faint voice.

"In here."

The bedroom door opened, and Wyatt stepped in. "Sorry I'm late. I won't change, we can—" His gaze met hers in the mirror, and his words dried up. She was gratified by the insta-lust that filled his gaze as his eyes dipped down over the front of her body. "Well," he murmured. "Don't you look nice?"

She smoothed a hand over the dress she'd spent a solid five hours shopping for on the strip earlier today. A futile effort at distraction from her mounting anxiety. "I spent a fortune on it. So shut up about me being cheap."

His eyes tracked her hand and where it settled on her hip. "Worth every penny. You know red's my favorite color."

"Yeah, yeah, you shark you," she joked, trying to stay normal. "All that blood in the water turns you on."

"Nah." He walked closer until he was nestled in behind her, his hands replacing hers on her hips. His cock was semierect beneath his trousers, and he ground it against her ass. "It reminds me of you."

"How's that?"

"The color your nipples get when they're all hard and aching. The color of your clit when you're almost ready to come. The color of your ass when I spank it."

The tension in her body transferred from nervousness to a sexual need. "No wonder you like it so much," she managed.

"Mmm." He slid his hands inside her bodice and massaged her breasts, watching in the mirror as he pushed them up to plump over the neckline. "God, I almost forgot what these look like."

"You saw them a few hours ago." She gasped when he pinched her nipples rougher than usual.

"I barely got to touch them." He shoved the neckline down, and she thanked God she had splurged for an expensive label. Cheaper fabric may not have held up to his rough treatment. He pulled her breasts out and let them rest on the shelf of her bodice. "Look at how much these babies missed me."

She shook her head even as she tried to keep from gasping when he tweaked each nipple. "Wyatt."

"You know…" he licked her ear, "…if you lived closer, I could do…this…whenever I needed it. Whenever you needed it."

She froze. He wasn't suggesting they move in together, was he?

They hadn't talked about a more permanent arrangement, not really. In her deepest heart, she couldn't imagine anything better than waking up with Wyatt every morning and going to bed with him at night. She'd done it before. When she'd gone to college in a neighboring city, he had an apartment near her. Though they hadn't lived together in truth—Tatiana hadn't wanted to break her parents' hearts—they'd spent enough time sleeping over with each other that she had a fairly good idea of what the experience would be like.

And, she feared, she knew how it would end. With *their* end.

The arguments. She couldn't remember what each fight had been about. They all blended together in her mind, an amalgam of jealousy, anger and bitterness, the causes probably not even that important.

They were careful this time around. They didn't fight, not at all. What was there to fight about? Everything was smooth and hunky-dory.

Or it had been, until tonight.

He bit her ear and laved the spot. "What are you thinking?"

She opened her mouth, her fears and distrust and worries dying to come spewing out. But then she glanced at her watch. Yikes. One battle at a time. "We'll be late for dinner."

"So hungry? The food's not going anywhere." He cupped the back of her neck in a warm hand. "You know, when I had them move this table in here, all I could think about was you bent over it. All your bottles and things knocking together as I fucked you." He exerted a familiar pressure.

She gripped the edge of the vanity. Small and delicately carved, it was a marked contrast to the dark and heavy furniture in the rest of the room. "Is there anything you don't imagine fucking me over?"

He gave that consideration. "No."

Her smile was real. "Wyatt."

He paused at the finality in her voice, attuned as ever to her cues. "What? You're serious? You'd rather go eat?"

She turned to face him, and his hand dropped away. After adjusting her dress so her breasts were covered again, she linked her fingers together in front of her in an effort to stop them from nervously fidgeting. "We need to talk."

"You're worrying me." The words were light, but she

knew the sentiment was real. "Hey. What's up?"

She couldn't bear his concern. Not when she was about to royally piss him off. "My parents are in town."

She might as well have told him her father was in the bedroom with them. Wyatt backpedaled, creating a giant space between them. Not just physical space, but emotional too. A cold, remote filter descended over his face.

She hadn't seen that mask in a while. A part of her heart mourned its return.

"What?" he asked, low and harsh.

"My mom. And my dad."

"I understand the definition of *parents.* What do you mean they're in town?"

The cold snap in his voice was also expected. Still, it made her heart seize in dread. "They're staying at the Wynn for a couple of days."

His sneer for his rival was automatic, though he remained on topic. "Oh really? How funny that they showed up today and surprised you. What a coincidence."

The cutting sarcasm in his tone made it very clear he didn't believe in coincidences.

"How long have you known they would be in town, Tatiana?"

Her tongue snuck out to lick her lips. "My mom called me yesterday. Late. It was unplanned. My dad was invited to speak at this conference when the scheduled guy canceled, so they decided to make a trip out of it. They were going to come see me in San Fran after, but since I'm here…"

"And you couldn't tell me this yesterday? Or this morning…" He straightened, and Tatiana could see the gears in his brain working. "When you asked if we could go out tonight."

Too smart, this guy. "Wyatt…"

"Tatiana. Are you serious right now?" His voice was deadly quiet. "Are you fucking serious? You didn't tell me they would be here, and now you're blindsiding me with them at dinner?"

Be calm. He has a right to be mad. "They know we're seeing each other again. When they found out I would be here too, visiting you, of course they invited us both."

Wyatt pointed his finger at her. "This is fucking manipulative, even for you."

Her mouth dropped open. "I wasn't trying to be manipulative."

"Then what do you call it?"

"I was scared!"

The words lay between them. He shook his head in disbelief. "Scared of what?"

She faltered. "I don't know. Scared you wouldn't come." *Scared you'll never want to come.*

"Well, I don't have that choice now, do I? You took that away from me." He jerked at his tie and spun away.

"Wyatt, wait, let's talk…"

"We don't have time to talk." The *thanks to you* was left unsaid, but message received.

"You don't have to come," she said quietly. "I'll tell them you had to work. Or an emergency cropped up. They'll understand, since it was short notice. They're in town for a couple of days. You can see them some other night." *Or not at all.*

He paused, as if he was thinking that over, contemplating the out she was offering. Her heart pounded, ticking away the seconds of the clock.

Finally, Wyatt gave a shake of his head. "No. That would be rude."

The rebel she'd known in high school wouldn't have given two fucks about being rude, but the gloss Wyatt had acquired over the years had made him sensitive to proper social etiquette. When he was out with her, Tatiana noticed that he even spoke with more proper diction. Hell, he usually knew better than her what fork to use. Another illusion for the world.

Wyatt threw his jacket and tie on the bed and started unbuttoning his shirt. There was nothing she liked more than watching him undress. But the rough, furious motions he was displaying right now had everything to do with barely suppressed anger and nothing to do with passion. He tossed his shirt, followed quickly by his pants and boxer briefs. His round, tight buttocks flexed as he stalked away.

She locked her fingers together. "Are you changing?"

"Showering. If we were just going to eat, I wouldn't bother, but since I fucked you in these clothes earlier, I'm a little wary of meeting your father like this."

She took a tentative step forward. "Wyatt. I don't want you to go if you're this mad."

The glance he gave her was filled with annoyed comprehension. "I'm not about to tell them that their daughter tricked me into coming. They already hate me, so that would hardly endear me to them, yeah?"

"Hate you? My mother is eager to see you again." Maybe eager was reading too much into her mother's emotions, but the other woman was the one who had suggested the chance to get reacquainted with Wyatt.

He slashed his hand through the air. "Leave me alone, Tatiana."

She bit her lip. Not cowed, not exactly. But…cautious. She'd seen Wyatt angry, furious even, filled with this controlled and cold-burning temper. But not since they'd reunited. Not at her.

She swallowed down the nauseous dread rising up inside her throat. Her makeup was already on, her hair done, tasks that rarely took her long anyway. She should have waited. It would have given her something to do, instead of gingerly sitting on the edge of Wyatt's bed, feeling like an interloper as he showered in record speed. He barely glanced at her when he came out, a large white towel wrapped around his lean hips. His hair was dripping water onto his shoulders, the rivulets streaming down his chest.

Any other time, she would have slinked her way over, traced that water with her tongue. Any other time, she would have been certain he wouldn't shove her away.

Instead, she fiddled with the silver chain of her necklace. After ten minutes passed without a peep from the closet, Tatiana nervously glanced at her watch. If they didn't leave soon, they would run the risk of being late.

Since her parents were her parents, they were used to her getting caught up in one of her projects or getting lost in traffic and losing track of time. But Wyatt liked punctuality. The fact that they were running behind would only key him up more. As evidenced by the loud curse that erupted from the closet.

Despite his order to leave him alone, Tatiana couldn't take it anymore. She walked to the large closet and stood inside the doorway. It was rather ridiculous to call this a closet, since it was more like a small room. Had she lived here, it would have been bulging with all her clothes and possessions. Wyatt, though he probably had more suits than most men, barely took up a third of it. The clothes she'd brought with her, along with the handful she'd left behind on past visits, were neatly arranged on the empty half.

Standing only in boxer briefs, Wyatt dumped a pair of trousers on the floor. They lay crumpled along with a handful of once-pristine clothes. "Wyatt?"

The look he gave her was a little wild. "Esme ordered my latest suits. All the pants are cut too slim. If I look like a fucking hipster, your father will never let me hear the end of it."

He was…worried about his outfit?

Guilt wracked her. And why not? If she wanted to make a good impression on someone, she agonized over her clothing choices. Why should he be any different because he was a man?

She cast an eye over the rack and pulled down a gray suit she'd seen him wear multiple times, as well as a nice white shirt. "What about this one?"

"It's older."

"It still looks fine," she said brightly, and thrust it at him.

He set his teeth and snatched the suit. "Great. Not like I have time."

She winced, not missing the emphasis on time. He dressed quickly, grabbed a tie at random and draped it around his neck, knotting it with rough jerks. It sat a hair crooked, and her fingers itched to correct it.

"Wyatt, I am so, so sorry."

He ran his hands through his drying hair and sighed. "Whatever. Let's get this nightmare over with."

Nightmare. The word pounded into her brain as they descended to the ground floor. The limo was waiting for them, an expressionless Sal holding the door open.

She climbed in, and he entered after, sitting next to her, both of them staring ahead at the divider that had allowed them to explore each other's bodies not more than a few hours ago. Had he chosen the limo so they could engage in a little backseat shenanigans on the way to what he thought was their date?

"Your tie's crooked," she tried again, and reached out to tidy it.

He allowed her to fix it, but didn't so much as turn his face to look at her. She placed her hands back into her lap.

Nightmare.

A dangerous emotion rose inside of her, almost as fierce as her guilt, and she throttled it back. *He's entitled,* her conscience murmured. *You have to take it.*

She wasn't good at taking it. Silence had its moments, but at times like this, it made her want to climb the walls and scream like a banshee.

Fuck it. This was going to be a really long night if she had to play at this timid shit. "I said I was sorry."

Brooding silence.

Her belly tightened, and she breathed in deeply. Calm. She turned to face his stony profile, not caring that the move creased her pressed dress. "Can we put this in perspective? It's not like I asked you to have dinner with your mortal enemy. Or worse, one of those magicians that are crawling all over this city."

Her joke fell flat. "No. Just your parents."

"Right. Just my parents. If this is about whatever antagonism you guys had in the past, remember that we're adults now. I'm not some sixteen-year-old bringing a boy home for Mommy and Daddy's approval." She dared to put her hand on his flexed arm. "I know you don't want to hear this, but they've met other guys I've dated, and they've learned to be at peace with whoever I choose. And I choose you."

Was that a subtle softening in his jawline? "It was a shitty thing you did, not telling me."

True. It had been a shitty thing to do, to not give him advance warning, but things had been going so well.

Because you haven't had to deal with any problems yet. And though she might have hoped otherwise, between her father's sneers and her brother's embezzling, her family had always been a problem for them.

It was a problem that wasn't going anywhere. And she couldn't stand the thought of delaying the confrontation anymore. "Would it have changed anything? Beyond giving you time to put product in your hair?"

His nostrils flared. "I do not put product in my hair."

"Figuratively speaking, that is." She rubbed his arm. "You wouldn't have come, Wyatt. And I…I wanted you to."

"You said you would make excuses for me, that I didn't have to come."

Logic. Wyatt had it in spades. "I would have been pissed if you'd taken me up on that offer."

His chest moved in an involuntary silent laugh, and she smiled in return. His hand came to rest over hers. Tentatively, not with his usual confidence, but it was a voluntary move, a crack in his otherwise icy composure. "Women. Say one thing, mean another."

"Nah. I'm special. Woman. Singular." She turned her hand so she was palm to palm with him. "They're my parents. I love them very much. And you're…also important to me."

His gaze seemed to search hers. "Am I?"

"You know you are."

His shoulders relaxed, the tension easing out of him. He squeezed her hand. "Yes. You're right. I suppose I'd have to see them again eventually. Better to rip this Band-Aid off now."

Her heart seized. There it was again. *A nightmare. A Band-Aid.*

You've won. Let it go.

But this was her *family*. A family she didn't see eye to eye on in every subject, but who the hell did? She loved them, and they loved her, and she knew they hadn't made it easy for the guy when they were young, but she was sick unto death of the way Wyatt utterly…dreaded them.

Once upon a time, she would have snapped back at him for his poor choice of words. But the car was slowing, and that meant they were probably close to Eduardo's. "I'm sorry," she repeated.

He nodded once, and she knew he had accepted her apology. The lines of strain were still around his mouth, but his fingers brushed against hers, and the chill in his eyes had receded.

He had calmed down. She'd been forgiven for her admittedly shitty avoidance technique, which was pretty awesome seeing as how she could barely verbalize why it was so important for him to come tonight.

So she would keep her cool. Even though a fresh wave of annoyance ripped through her when he cupped her elbow after they disembarked and said, "Let's get this over with."

They walked into the restaurant, and Tatiana stood on her tiptoes. Wyatt, so much taller than her, had no such problems. "I see your mother." He nodded in the direction of the bar.

She glanced that way. The crowd parted enough for her to spy the tall, lean black woman standing at the bar, dressed in a blue linen cocktail dress that managed to be both elegant and practical, a sharp contrast to Tatiana's own frothy crimson silk dress.

Something within Tatiana eased at the sight of her mother, though she was well past the age where she expected the other woman to be able to fix everything with a wave of her hands. She started her way, startled when Wyatt's hand slipped from her arm. She glanced at him.

"Go on. I'll make sure our table is ready."

Tatiana forced a smile and continued on to her mother, feeling the lack of his presence at her side sharply. Her mom spotted her as she approached, a bright smile spreading across her still-unlined face. Within a second, she was enfolded in her strong arms and inhaling a familiar baby-powder scent.

"Hey, Mom," she said, her voice muffled from where her face was smooshed against her mother's boobs. When she was young, before she'd fully understood what adoption entailed, she'd hoped she'd grow up to look like her mother. Being a small blonde moppet had its perks, but her mother had been and remained all strength and power.

"My baby."

She gave her mom a final hug and disengaged herself. "It's good to see you."

"It's been too long since Christmas. Could Wyatt not make it tonight?"

"No, he's here, checking on our table."

"It's a lovely restaurant. I'm glad you picked it." Her mom looked over Tatiana's shoulder, her warm smile dimming, her face rearranging itself into the polite mask she wore when greeting acquaintances. "Wyatt Caine. My goodness. You haven't aged a bit."

Wyatt accepted the hand she held out and shook it formally. "Neither have you, Dr. Belikov."

"Please. I thought it was silly for you to persist in calling me that once you were done with high school. We're definitely all adults now. Call me Janet."

"Janet."

"I feel like I've gone back in time, seeing you two together again."

Tatiana looked up at Wyatt. "Sometimes it feels like that to us, too."

Wyatt's hand brushed the small of her back. "Though we are, as you said, adults now. Some things are different."

Tatiana clung to that, the words that never failed to make her feel better when she secretly wondered if they could resurrect a relationship that had failed once already. Maybe she wasn't the only one who consoled herself with them.

"We missed you at the holidays, Wyatt. We were quite

looking forward to seeing you, but of course we understood about your work."

Wyatt didn't respond to her mother for a second. Had he forgotten? She'd told him that her parents had invited him for Christmas. He had declined. *After he finished laughing.*

She bit the inside of her cheek. She'd let that slight go by then, and she would now, too. *Not important. Not worth fighting over.*

"Yes." Wyatt finally said. "The holidays are a busy time for us."

"I'm sure they are."

"Where's Daddy?" Tatiana asked.

"Right here, my pumpkin," came a voice from behind her. Despite decades in the States and a fully American wife and daughter, her father clung to his thick Russian accent.

With a smile, she turned and embraced her father. "Daddy. I thought maybe the speaking engagement tired you out and you were resting."

Large in height, width and spirit, her father puffed out his chest. "I am not so old a little talking exhausts me." He kept one arm around her and brought her to rest at his side. Shrewd blue eyes, cold as ice chips, surveyed the man she'd brought with her. "Wyatt Caine." Tatiana half-expected him to add something like *so we meet again*, but her dad stopped there.

Wyatt nodded, as watchful as a gunslinger sizing up his enemy. "Sir."

"So you and my daughter, you are together again."

"That's right, Dr. Beli—Nikolai."

Her father cocked his head. The overhead light made his bald scalp gleam. "You may call me Dr. Belikov."

"Nikolai!" her mom snapped.

"Daddy."

A thin smile crossed his lips. "Kidding."

Chapter Four

WYATT ASSUMED THERE were more awkward things than a dinner with two people who had once heartily disapproved of you dating their only daughter. He just didn't know what they were.

They had foregone appetizers, for which he was grateful. Maybe that would cut down on the amount of time they needed to be here.

"Wyatt." Janet smiled at him after they placed their orders. She was a beautiful woman, as tall and statuesque as her husband. Tatiana looked like a fairy dining amongst a table of giants. "We were so pleased to hear you and Tatiana were seeing each other again, weren't we, Nikolai?"

Nikolai made a noise that could have signaled anything from happiness to disgust.

Wyatt gave a tight smile and took a sip of his wine. Wished it was hard liquor. *Make an effort.* "I'm sure it came as a surprise. It did to both of us."

"Not really. The only surprise was that you managed to run into one another after so many years. What a small world it is."

Tatiana leaned toward him. "It was fate."

Her father's snort was loud enough to be audible.

Wyatt set his teeth. Despite Tatiana's words in the car, he couldn't help but feel like he was eighteen again, being judged and found wanting. In an effort to dispel the emotion, and out of politeness, he spoke. "I didn't realize you were going to be in town this week, or I would have told you sooner, but you're both welcome to come stay at Quest. I'll arrange a suite for you, with a great view."

"How kind of you. Nikolai, wouldn't that be—"

"The Wynn is nice."

Wyatt's arrogance wouldn't let that lie. "I assure you. My place is nicer."

"Nikolai's conference is at the Wynn. It would probably be more trouble than it's worth to travel back and forth for it."

The two hotels were within walking distance, and if it really was necessary, Wyatt could arrange for a car and driver, but he didn't feel obliged to insist. "Of course." He didn't look at Tatiana, but he hoped she was sticking this under his "he tried" column.

Janet bit her lip. "But thank you so much, Wyatt. We've heard amazing things about your place and would still love to see it. I was so excited when Tatiana told us you'd become a casino owner, of all things."

Because you always thought I'd amount to nothing.

No, that wasn't entirely fair. Of the pair, Nikolai had been the overtly hostile parent. Still, Wyatt had never missed the worried glances Janet had tossed his way when she thought he wasn't looking. *What will you do to my baby?* they'd seemed to say. *How will you drag her down?*

Well, he hadn't dragged her down. He'd left before he could. "Yes. It's different."

Nikolai grunted. "Didn't know you were taking business classes in college."

"I was. My degree is in business. I have an MBA as well." Not from any well-known school, and he frankly hadn't cared enough to put his diplomas on his wall, but he had them.

The older man sipped his wine. "Gambling seems an odd choice. Janet, was it Howard who became addicted? Told his family he was having an affair to hide his trips to a casino. They lost everything. He ran off, left his wife alone with two young children and a giant mountain of debt."

Wyatt opened his mouth. Shut it again. Was he supposed to say something in response to that?

Janet set her glass down precisely on the table. "Howard was a miserable toad of a man, and he wasn't lying about the affair. The gambling was possibly the least of his flaws."

"Gambling." Morose, Nikolai shook his head. "No one can ever win. Terrible pastime."

"I'm sure Wyatt hardly sits around playing slots all day."

His past was no secret. "No. But I played poker on the professional circuit."

Nikolai squinted. "Professional."

"Yes." He'd lived and breathed the cards for a few years, eager to make a name for himself. He hadn't wanted to stay in that world long-term. Poker had better odds than some games, but at the end of the day, the player was basically working on generating income for the house.

That was why he'd always intended to be the house. Playing had given him the capital and connections he'd needed to move up in the world.

Nikolai drummed his fingers on the table. "I see."

"To go from playing poker to owning your own place is quite amazing. It must have been a great deal of hard work," Janet interjected.

"The casino was already here, yes?" Tatiana's father eyed him as if he'd snuck in and stolen the keys from the previous owners.

"The structure was there," Tatiana jumped in, and he wasn't sure if he was annoyed or pleased that she recognized her precious daddy's third degree for what it was. "Wyatt and his investors took the Quest and turned it into something magnificent."

"Hurrumph." The older man scowled at him. "I Googled you. You are not as well known as the other places."

"I attract a certain clientele." Curious tourists didn't have the kind of dough necessary to play at his tables or purchase his staff's discretion over other sinful vices.

"The deviant sort."

Goddamn it. He was too old to be made to feel like a pervert by a woman's father. "Sometimes."

The awkward silence lasted a solid minute before Tatiana cleared her throat. "Daddy, what are you speaking about at the conference?"

For the first time that evening, the older man perked up. "It is on a new flywheel capable of kinetic energy storage…"

Wyatt was grateful for the distraction, since it took the man's attention off him. Janet looked on fondly, occasionally interrupting her husband to correct or argue with his speech. But then, she was a physicist as well, as renowned as her husband. Though Tatiana hadn't gone to school for this stuff, she'd grown up with two brilliant minds, and she knew the language. She listened intently, frowning, asking an intelligent question here and there.

He had no idea what a spinning mass was, or a wobble, or resonance. So he sat there, drinking his wine and praying dinner would come soon.

When it did, there was a brief period of silence while they attacked their food. "So, Wyatt," Janet started. He mentally groaned and cast his mind around for some question that would set them off on one of their scientific monologues. "We understand you and Tatiana met when you fired her birth half-brother for embezzling money from your company. Has that caused any tension?"

"Mother."

Janet cast her daughter a quizzical glance. "It's a reasonable question, darling. I was curious."

Wyatt coughed. He'd forgotten that Tatiana's parents were as unconventional in their own way as she was. Her artsy dreaminess sometimes put her out of step with normal society; their scientific absorption with curiosities resulted in the same.

"No," he admitted. "Ronald has been good about repaying his debt, and we barely see each other." He hadn't told Tatiana, but he was keeping an eye on the kid, who had taken a job as a dealer with one of his competitors. Another corporation wouldn't be as generous as he was. Tatiana wouldn't handle her brother being in prison very well.

"Hmm." Janet frowned. "But Tatiana said that since she's been with you, she's seen Ron more than ever, since she comes here so often."

"I see him when Wyatt's working," Tatiana said quietly.

Nikolai paused, and then continued eating.

A warning signal pinged in Wyatt's brain. *Something is off.*

"Ah." Janet smiled, and Wyatt was distracted by the worry tingeing it. Yes. Yes, that was the look he remembered all too well. *You're going to hurt my baby,* it said. "Well, I certainly know how busy work can get. Hopefully you'll get a chance to get to know him better. Nikolai and I have only met him a couple of times, but he seems like a sweet boy. He and his family came out for the holidays, and it was lovely."

"Flighty and overly cheerful," Nikolai grunted. "But good-hearted."

"Sounds like you're one big happy family." Wyatt cut into his steak. That's right, Tatiana had mentioned that her brother had gone East with her, that her parents had happily pseudo-adopted the half-brother she'd been reunited with.

He'd wanted to enjoy the holidays with her. It had been lonely to spend Christmas Eve in the suite Esme had professionally decorated for him, eating the cookies she'd baked, watching DVRed TV in an effort to find something that wasn't holiday themed. It had been a momentary pang, gone when Tatiana had returned and celebrated New Year's in his bed.

Yes, he'd wanted to spend the holidays with her. But not enough to spend it with her family.

He glanced at Tatiana, not surprised to find her pushing her pasta around her plate. She always played with her meals, but tonight she hadn't taken more than a couple bites while her parents had both made dents in their tofu burgers, and his steak was half gone. Worry made him frown.

Janet noticed his regard. "The food here is delicious. I swear, since Nik and I became vegans, we don't even miss meat."

"The way meat is processed in this country would make you ill if I told you," Nikolai said with a certain amount of relish.

Wyatt paused while cutting into his steak. Cooked rare, like he liked it. Vegans. Of course they'd become vegans. He turned to his potatoes.

Nikolai cleared his throat. "Tatiana, Alfie Jamison became engaged."

Tatiana stilled. Wyatt didn't miss the warning glower she directed at her father. "That's nice."

"Tatiana dated Alfie. After you. A nice boy. Doctor."

Wyatt's fingers curled tighter around his knife. "Is that right?" He shot her a look filled with what he hoped was cool amusement and not creepy jealousy. "Alfie, huh? That sounds like a can of dog food."

Janet chuckled. "He did look like a puppy."

"Looks are immaterial. A woman needs a good provider with a stable job—oomph."

This time Janet was the one giving Nikolai a warning glance. "Darling. Let's not get started on how women need a man to provide for them."

Wyatt allowed the reluctant smile tugging at his lips. No, Tatiana hadn't come by her feminist core by accident.

"Alfie's bride does not seem to mind his earning capacity," Nikolai muttered.

"I'm sure she doesn't," Tatiana responded. "But it'll be a cold comfort when he cheats on her with whatever hot young thing is working in his office next month."

Wyatt stilled. "He cheated on *you*?" Cheating on anyone was a shitty thing to do, but a man would have to be stone-cold stupid to risk losing Tatiana in such a manner.

"What?" Nikolai glowered. "You did not tell us this."

Tatiana wrinkled her nose. "It wasn't a big deal. I was going to break up with him anyway. Caught him with a nurse."

"What was his full name again?" Wyatt asked.

Tatiana eyed him warily. "Not telling you."

"Alford Jamison," her mother supplied helpfully. She had abandoned her burger and was watching the exchange with much interest.

Wyatt made a mental note. "Excellent."

"You are not doing anything, Wyatt."

"I know where he lives," Nikolai said grimly. "I can handle him."

"I've got this." Wyatt stabbed his potato.

"What can you do from across the country?"

Wyatt smirked and snared the older man's gaze. "You'd be surprised."

"I have connections."

"As do I."

Nikolai's eye twitched, but neither man broke their staring contest.

"Nobody is handling him," Tatiana cut in.

Janet leaned back in her chair. "Well, this will be awkward, seeing as how one of your men might kill or ruin Alfie, but his mother asked if you could design a bridal set for his fiancée."

Tatiana flicked a glance at her mother. "I would love to.

Tell her to stop by my website first, though. My style may not be what they're looking for."

Janet shrugged. "It would simply need to match her dress. All gold. I don't think they care about style or design."

"You'd be surprised at how much that matters," Tatiana said diplomatically.

"Our little artist." Nikolai's smile was not unkind. "I suppose each piece of metal speaks to you, eh?"

Unable to resist, Wyatt butted in. "Tatiana does create art." He took a sip of his wine, figuring that the alcohol was more necessary than the food. "Her work has been in galleries as well as boutiques."

Nikolai raised a bushy brow. "I am aware of what my daughter does, Caine."

Tatiana often called him that, Caine. But when she did it, it didn't ring of derision.

You're imagining it.

Was he, though?

"I'm just clarifying. She's not some vendor in a mall, churning out baubles for bridezillas."

If possible, Nikolai became grimmer, his face flushing redder than the inside of Wyatt's steak. "As I said. I am aware of my daughter's skill."

"Calm down," Tatiana whispered. "Wyatt didn't mean to imply anything."

"Oh, but he did. Tell me, Caine, why you think my grown daughter needs defending from her own parents?"

Whoa. "She doesn't. I was only speaking for Tatiana's work."

"She does not need speaking for."

"Let's all take a deep breath, Nikolai," Janet interjected.

The older man lifted his napkin and placed it over his half-eaten tofu burger. "You may have changed your clothes and your hair, boy, but you have not changed at all."

Each word scraped across his heart, but beyond the tightening of his fingers around the stem of his wineglass, he didn't let it show. He had already donned the cold layer of ice that protected him. "You are entitled to think that."

"Daddy." Tatiana's words were a sharp rebuke. "You are out of line. Wyatt was a good man when we were young, and he's a good man now. He didn't need to change."

"He did, if he wanted a chance at a lasting relationship with you. I told Janet, when Tatiana told us about this..." he waved his hand between the two of them, "...I told her this was a bad idea, that it would never last."

Tatiana's lips firmed. "You can't know that. What a terrible thing to say."

"Compatibility is a simple equation, my darling. You adore your family. He never has, and he will go out of his way to avoid us. How long do you think you will be happy choosing between him and us, this time?"

Nikolai wasn't a surgeon, but each word cut into Wyatt's soul with the precision of a scalpel, slicing him open.

"Wyatt doesn't control me." Tatiana's voice was like a whiplash. "He never forced me to make that sort of choice. Not then, and not now."

"So you say." The older man stood. His wife rose, reluctance and displeasure in every tight line of her face. "We will go. I have seen all I need to see. Tatiana, I hope we will meet with you again during our trip. While he is at work perhaps."

Wyatt spoke up when Nikolai reached for his wallet. "I will pay."

Nikolai's face grew mottled. He pulled out a wad of cash and threw it on the table. "They are my wife and daughter."

"And she's my girlfriend." He couldn't savor the word this time, as he normally did.

"For now."

Janet lingered for a moment after her husband stomped off. "Wyatt…" She shook her head. "Excuse my husband, please. He spoke hastily."

Maybe he shrugged or made some noncommittal noise. He didn't know.

"Tatiana, call me tomorrow, please. We can make plans." She came around the table and gave her daughter a kiss on the cheek and him a tight, anxiety-ridden smile.

Not good enough. Not nearly good enough.

Yeah. There were a lot better ways they could have spent this night.

Chapter Five

TATIANA DIDN'T REMEMBER much of what happened after her parents departed so dramatically, except that Wyatt hustled them to the limo. She stared out the window, numb. Too numb to decipher all of the feelings thrumming right below the surface of her faux-calm demeanor. Wyatt didn't try to make conversation in the car, for which she was grateful.

When they entered Wyatt's suite, she let him take her coat and came to stand in front of the floor-to-ceiling windows. They afforded a glorious view of the Vegas skyline. She pressed her fingers against the glass. This was the first place Wyatt and she had had sex.

This time, during this relationship. The first place they had ever had sex had been in a saggy bed in his apartment, on the stroke of midnight of her eighteenth birthday. Unrealistic, some might say, that they had dated for three years without consummating their relationship, but Wyatt had said he wanted to do things right.

Not to mention, Tatiana wasn't an idiot. Her academic dad could be a real hard-ass where his baby girl was concerned, particularly when said baby girl had been dating a guy a few years older than her. Once, she'd heard her father casually ask Wyatt if he had researched the state law on statutory rape.

For a month, the poor kid hadn't even wanted to risk sticking his hand under her shirt.

Tatiana's lips curled up. She traced a finger over the glass. There had been a few inklings of Wyatt's expensive tastes back then, though he hadn't had two pennies to rub together. That night, he'd purchased silk sheets and surrounded the bed with candles. Afterward, they'd eaten pizza and blown the flames out. Except for one. With that candle, he'd shown her how good hot wax could feel.

Wyatt came to stand behind her. They hadn't turned the lights on, but the bright glow from the skyline was sufficient. She could see his reflection in the glass.

"Do you want a drink?" Wyatt asked.

She focused on the circle she was drawing, making it perfectly round. "No. Thanks."

"Coffee?"

"No."

A sigh. "What do you want?"

She could hear it in his voice, a shutdown and rejection of what was coming. Her belligerence and snark, her goddamn emotions, which she had learned to manage but could never truly extinguish. She was angry, and sad, and maybe it was dramatic of her, but she felt despair.

You knew this would happen. This yawning distance between them would always be the result of any problem. Of course she'd been doing her best to keep everything smooth and easy. "It wasn't necessary." The words blurted out of her, despite her best efforts to restrain them.

"What wasn't?"

In for a penny. "What you said to my parents. Defending my work."

He paused. When he spoke, his tone was ice cold. "You don't want me to defend you?"

"There was nothing to defend. They're my parents. I don't need defending from them." *Not fair. Daddy deserves your anger, too.* But her father wasn't here, and she could successfully deal with him later. Wyatt was, and it was important he know what he'd done wrong.

"You're okay with them treating your work with that kind of disrespect?" He snorted. "Tatiana, once, just once, I heard your neighbor ask if you were still making 'little necklaces', and I thought you were going to rip that old lady a new one."

The batty old neighbor wasn't the first one who had felt the sharp edge of her tongue when they made the mistake of diminishing her work to nothing. But her parents were different. They weren't just people, and she'd figured out a long time ago that she'd rather have them in her life, vaguely disapproving, then cut them off or constantly be at odds with them. "A part of them is always going to think I've wasted my life by doing this as my profession, no matter how much money I earn or how much people love my work. There's nothing I can do about it." She gave a helpless shrug. "It is what it is."

A small snort came from behind her. She twisted around. "What?"

"Listen to yourself. 'There's nothing I can do about it'? That doesn't sound like you."

Tatiana's temper ratcheted up a notch. *They're brainwashing you. Do you really want to study biology? You dread each class.* Back then, maybe it had been true—she'd been eager to please, and trying to live up to the high academic standards of her parents had been her way of showing them her love. She'd found her spine, though, and kept it. "I'm not a pushover."

"Then stop sounding like one."

She whirled around. "You don't get it."

"Whoa." He lifted his hand in warning. "Let's not shout."

Her back teeth ground together. "Let's not talk about me in the third person, then."

He dipped his head in acknowledgment of the point. "What don't I get?"

"Family stuff."

"Oh, right." Ice could crystallize on his words, they were so frigid. "Because I only had a dysfunctional family. How would I know how to have any kind of emotional attachment with someone?"

"Don't put words in my mouth. I didn't say that."

"But you agree with it." Wyatt slashed his hand in the air. "You know what, forget it. We both need to cool off."

"We need to talk."

"No." He drew his rigid control around himself like a finely crafted suit. "This is not how I pictured the night going."

No, this wasn't how she'd pictured the night ending either, especially since the visit had started out so well, with him relaxed and warm. She'd ruined it.

Ruined it how, exactly? By asking him to do something as

simple as meet your parents?

He turned and started to walk away.

Panic mixed with anger spurted through her. "Where are you going?"

"To bed. I can take the guestroom tonight."

She supposed that was the equivalent of sleeping on the couch. Hell, this was a hotel. The man could have an entirely different suite, if he wanted. There were so many places for him to run to.

"Don't walk out on me."

He paused in the middle of yanking off his tie. His back was stick straight. "Don't use that tone with me, Tatiana. I told you not to shout."

The warning in his otherwise emotionless voice made her reckless. God, she hated when he did that, when he made her feel like she was being hysterical and loud. "Then don't you dare leave this room."

He pivoted slowly and stalked over to her, every step making her back up until the hard glass pressed against her spine. Wyatt loomed over her, the tension in his shoulders and face making him look larger than he usually did. He leaned down until his hot breath fanned over her lips. "I think I do a good job putting up with you, Tatiana. You don't get to give me orders, too."

Her eyes narrowed. "Put up?"

"Yes."

"Men would beg to get a chance to 'put up' with me, Caine."

"I'm not men. I'm me. Don't think you can push me around the way you do every other poor sap."

Her spine went rigid. "I don't think I like the way you

consider me some sort of bitch."

He leaned in closer. "Then stop acting like one."

Their breaths had gotten heavier and deeper with every word, until they were both panting. The aggression and emotion arching between them twisted into something darker. "Wyatt." The one word was weak.

His nostrils flared. "Yes."

"I'm not done discussing this."

His blunt finger traced the scoop of her neckline. "I told you. We need to cool off. I don't want to talk."

That's the problem.

Her eyes flew open. Yes. That was exactly the—

His finger dipped below the neckline and brushed her nipple, and every logical thought shot out of her brain. Damn it. Foiled by her tits. Story of her life.

"So," Wyatt continued. "We can either go to bed and sleep. Or we can do something else that doesn't require words." His fingernail scratched against her nipple, and her body heated up.

There wasn't even a choice. She wouldn't get a lick of sleep if she kept these emotions bottled inside of her. There had to be an outlet, or she would literally go insane. Sex shouldn't be the only release valve open to them. But she'd take it for now, take the pleasure, and deal with it after. She wrapped her hand around his wrist, and he stilled. One word, the first syllable of their safe word, and she knew he would back off. The bridge of trust they had between them had been started years ago. In the past seven months, it had been remodeled, renovated, but it was still there. In the bedroom, at least, their bodies listened to one another.

She swallowed. "Standard rules."

"Candle" as their safe word, or she'd hit the ground three times. His reply was instant. "Yes."

"Wyatt."

"Yes?"

"Force me."

"What?"

The heat between them shot up, the two illicit words making them both breathe faster. She bridged the gap between their mouths and bit his lower lip, tugging at it. "You heard me. I want it rough."

His hands slid down her sides to span her waist. "I'm not sure that's wise, after the night we've had."

"If you're not feeling it, tell me."

"I didn't—"

She cut him off, grabbing his face between her hands. Surprise was on her side, or she'd never have been able to turn them until it was his back shoved against the glass. "Or, if you like…I can force you."

She kissed him again, her lips aggressive. It took him a second to catch up, but the instant he did, he slid his hands into her hair, twisting the strands between his fingers and arching her head back in an angle that was one tick away from uncomfortable. His tongue thrust into her mouth, mimicking what he would be doing soon, all too well, with his cock.

He pulled her head away, his natural bossiness asserting itself. "I like the first plan better."

Aw, shucks. She wouldn't have minded getting a little handsy with him, maybe tie him up and have him at her mercy. Though she did love it when he put her on her knees and growled out orders. "You always do."

"Are we…okay? With everything else?"

He was talking about the debacle with her parents, with her clumsy feelings. Hoping, probably, that they'd never have to examine or think about it. "Later." Or, more likely, never. But the sex would provide a distraction for now.

Old habits.

Shut up, brain.

The relief on his face swiftly evaporated when she tugged at his shirt. He pushed her back a step and yanked at his tie. She loved watching him loosen that tie. The quick yet deliberate movements of his fingers as he undid the knot, the swish of silk on silk as it slid free. Like a Pavlovian response, she could see neckwear and get wet now, thanks to him.

The two ends hung loose. He undid the first couple of buttons of his shirt with practiced flicks of his fingers. His thin, borderline-cruel lips moved, framing a single word: "Run."

Yes. Yes, this was what she needed.

Lifting her skirt high, she spun around and darted through the darkened living room. The suite was large but hardly huge. The kitchen was partially enclosed, but the living room, dining room, and foyer were all part of one sprawling room. Three bedrooms extended off the main room—one office, one a guest bedroom, and one Wyatt's bedroom.

They were all his, really. This whole damn place, the whole building was his.

Was she his? She didn't know.

With no real plan in place except that she wanted to get caught more than she wanted to run away, she darted to the front door. Wyatt had only thrown the deadbolt when they entered, so she flipped it with unsteady hands and started to open the heavy wood.

A heavy palm slammed against the door and shoved it closed. "Where the fuck do you think you're going?"

The tremble in her voice couldn't be faked. "Away from you."

"You can't get away from me. You're stuck."

"Please. Please let me go." Every plea that fell from her lips made her wetter.

"If I let you out this door, do you know what will happen?"

"What?"

"I'll have to fuck you in the hallway. Is that what you want?"

Up against a wall. Her legs spread open, her back supported by the plaster and drywall, Wyatt's narrow hips pistoning his cock into her.

There was one suite on this top floor, with an elevator that could only be accessed by certain staff. But still, the elevator could open, admitting someone. "I don't want you to fuck me," she breathed. Lies. All lies.

"If you're a very good girl and suck my cock for me, maybe I won't."

Her thighs tightened at the taunting words, and she nodded. "Yes. I-I can do that."

He spun her around and looked down at her, his eyes cold. "On your knees."

She slid down the door until she was on her knees, the cold marble of the entryway a delicious counterpoint to her otherwise heated body. She stroked his hard cock through the gray suit pants.

His hand brushed over her head, an implicit promise and a threat. "Take me out."

TATIANA MADE THE unbuckling of his belt and loosening of his zipper into a dance of seduction. He knew she could probably undo his clothing blindfolded, with one hand behind her back, but she infused hesitance and fumbling into the act.

It was always an act, but one in which they could connect at a level that otherwise wasn't possible.

He pushed the troubling thought away. No, they connected outside the bedroom. Tonight was a small bump in the road. They had been great until this evening, right? There was history between her parents and him, long-standing tension, and it had come to a head.

When she'd calmed down, she'd see that there was nothing for her to be angry over. He'd done the best he could with the hand she'd dealt him. Hell, if he had to see her parents again, he would be more prepared, and they could behave like civilized adults. It wasn't like they had to run into each other all that much.

He and Tatiana would go back to the easy relationship they'd been in until tonight. In the meantime—he hissed when she wrapped her hand around his bare cock—he'd enjoy this mutual blowing off of steam. His hand tightened in her hair. "Suck me."

She obeyed, glancing up at him with a mixture of manufactured fear and true desire. Oh, he loved this game of theirs. Each order he gave made his cock swell, and every time she acquiesced made his heart do the same.

She was on her knees in front of him, wanting him enough to obey his every command because it made her burn. He couldn't find a more perfect mate.

So you can't lose her again.

Anxiety made his voice rougher. "If you don't make this good, I'll have to fuck you."

Her lashes fluttered down to make dark crescents on her cheek as she leaned forward and drew the tip of his dick into her mouth. Her eye makeup had smudged, and her lipstick had stained her lips red. With her breasts plumped up over the neckline of her dress and her cheeks hollowing with every tentative suck of her lips on the head of his cock, she looked like a debauched socialite, a ruined woman.

Ruined by his hands, his fantasy whispered. Even if reality told him her depravity was firmly in her own control.

His breath came faster, and his thumbs caressed her cheekbones. "You can do better than this." Gripping her head tight, he gave her a few inches more, keeping his motions controlled and shallow.

Tatiana pulled away. "Too rough," she gasped, an almost whine in her words.

He twined his hands in her hair and tilted her face up. "You haven't seen it rough yet, love."

Her little pink tongue flicked out nervously. "Haven't I?"

A dare as much as it was a question. He held her steady and breached her mouth again, allowing her to suck at him. He thrust into her mouth until he could feel her throat close around the tip of his cock. She could deep throat him—he knew she could—but that would kill the fantasy. So instead of stopping her gag reflex, she let it come, let the smooth muscle convulse around him.

Fucking her face sent him to some perfect nirvana where he lost track of time and space. All that mattered was the hot, tight wetness surrounding his dick, the silken strands of her hair tangled around his fingers, the smooth skin of her cheeks beneath her thumbs. He glanced down and studied the perfect crescents of her lashes, made darker and longer by some feminine trick.

"Use your hands. Jack me off."

Her lashes fluttered, and she obeyed, wrapping one hand around him to work the part of the shaft she couldn't swallow, the other reaching under to cradle his balls. His spine tingled as she fondled the sensitive flesh. "Good girl. Play with my balls."

She squeezed a little harder, and he grunted, a tingling in the base of his spine telling him he was close. Her mouth retreated, and though he knew she was merely following the rhythm he had set, he held her tight.

"Don't move." One thrust, two, and he was undone, giving a low moan as the pulses of his release shuddered through him.

His cock was still hard when it slipped from her lips, the sight of his semen spilling out of her mouth keeping his arousal at a slow simmer. He staggered back a step, his hanging belt buckle hitting his thigh.

Tatiana delicately wiped away the come from the corner of her lips and gave him a powerful, smug smile. Right before she came to her feet and darted out the front door.

Chapter Six

TATIANA'S HEART BEAT accelerated when the front door closed behind her. No point in running…she wanted him to catch her.

Still, her steps toward the elevator quickened when she heard the door open and his heavy tread. It took him a few long strides to catch up with her, and then he had her wrist clenched tightly in his hand. He drew them forward a couple more steps before pushing her up against the wall.

"What," he asked, his voice low and dangerous, "do you think you're doing?"

"Why? Are you angry?"

"Yes."

"Good," she muttered, breaking the game enough to let her true emotions shine through.

An incredulous silence. "Did you say good?"

"Yes. Good." She couldn't verbalize why it was good. But she wanted him mad. Furious even. She took a deep breath and slipped back into character. "You said you would let me go if I sucked you off."

"I never said that."

"I want to go home," she lied.

"That's not an option." He licked her ear, not tender or seductive, but a rough swipe of ownership. "I'm going to fuck you. Your choice if you want to enjoy it. And where. I'm fine in the hallway too."

She started to struggle, and he leaned in close, trapping her. "You're forgetting. There are people watching the entire building. Including this floor."

She stilled, her eyes flicking up at him.

"Funny enough, there's a blind spot right here." He nodded at either end of the hallway. "About a five-foot gap none of the cameras cover. A silly oversight I've been meaning to fix since I found out about it, but it hasn't been a priority." His voice dropped, became menacing. "You move three feet to the left or two feet to the right and anything we do will have some interested viewers. You know how vigilant my security is." He slid his hand down her side, over the curve of her ass. "They'd see me tear this pretty, expensive dress off. Rip your panties. Get inside you and drill you into the wall."

The oxygen had left her brain, leaving her lightheaded and dizzy. "They would come and help me."

His laugh was mean and sadistic. "No. They wouldn't dare. They know I own you. No one would save you." He gripped her ass. "This is mine. Your tits, your pussy, your ass, you're all mine."

His hand slid to the small of her back, and he pressed until she was flush against the wall. "What do you want? Want to try to run? Maybe, after we're done, I can invite them up. Have a little party. They can watch me fuck you live."

She imagined multiple men's eyes on her, watching as Wyatt used her, despoiled her in a hallway. His woman, in the building he essentially owned.

She shuddered. Yes, she wanted that. But the fact that Wyatt paid their salaries made it both hotter and impossible. Their fantasies occupied a very definite niche in their lives, a quiet, secretive one.

Now, if they were in some different place? And the ones who were watching were strangers? Well. That was a fantasy that could be explored another time.

"Make your choice. It's the last one you'll have all night."

"I don't want this."

His expression didn't alter. In the bright hallway lighting, he looked foreign, some stranger inhabiting Wyatt's large, strong body. "Too late. This is what you get. Sex show or not?"

"Not. I-I don't want anyone to see." So many lies.

"Good choice." His hands went to the bodice of her dress. As he had earlier in the evening, he grabbed the material and yanked it lower so her breasts spilled out. Her nipples were already tight, ready for his hands and mouth.

His gaze was cold as he looked down and surveyed her, a master checking his goods. "You say you don't want me to fuck you. Why are your nipples so hard?"

"It's chilly."

His fingers pinched her chin, and he forced her to meet his gaze. "You liar. You want this."

"No."

His thumb pressed enough to open her mouth. Two of his fingers shoved inside, thrusting shallow. Unable to resist, she brought her teeth down on his flesh, not breaking the skin, but reminding him that she could.

He cursed and removed his hand, lips firming. "Oh, Tatiana. You are so fucked."

Yes, yes, yes.

Fisting large handfuls of her skirt, he hauled the silky material up. "Hold it."

Her fingers complied, bunching the material up farther so her white thong was revealed. She didn't know what she expected—for him to open his own hurriedly zipped trousers and fuck her, or maybe spin her around and do the same. Instead, he sank to his knees and yanked her panties down until they pooled around her ankles.

His palms slapped against her thighs and widened her stance as much as her stretched thong would allow, and then his tongue and lips and mouth were on her naked pussy. She groaned and leaned her head back against the wall, her fingers biting into the skirt of the dress.

Wyatt was a master at giving head. There was no tentativeness, no asking permission, he just fucking went for it, seeming to delight in the taste and feel of her sex. His nose rubbed against her clit as his jaw worked, thrusting his firm tongue into her channel. She glanced down and could see his biceps flexing as he worked his cock. She wished they were on a bed so they could properly 69.

He drew away and tugged at the hair on her mound, pulling at her sensitive, wet flesh. "I love this," he murmured, his voice dreamy, breaking character for a brief second.

She did the same. "I thought guys liked it bare."

"Normally I don't care how the fuck a woman decorates

her pussy as long as I can get inside it. But this." He tugged again, harder this time, and leaned in to scrape the stubble on his jaw over her clit. She yelped, her legs turning wobbly as pleasure shot through her. "I like that you didn't change it. It makes me feel like I'm nineteen again."

The wistfulness in his voice made her heart pulse. She scratched her hand through his hair, and a deep rumble came from his chest.

They had tender sex, but at the moment that didn't jive with the emotions roiling inside her. She used her grip on his head to bring him forward to her pussy. In a show of rare subservience, he let her, sliding his slippery tongue back inside, fucking his face against her, his nose bumping against her clit. She returned to clutching her skirt, out of his way while he ate her out in the hallway of his hotel. Her head lolled to the side, and she eyed the elevator not far from them. A ding—that's all the notice they would have if someone were to come up and catch them in the act.

It would be hotter if they didn't even have that much notice.

Her climax came fast, rushing over her like a freight train, leaving her weak and slumping against the wall.

He rose to his feet, his cock curving out of the fly of his unbuttoned and unzipped pants. He pulled a condom out of his pocket and donned it, his hand giving his cock long pulls. His face was shiny with her juices. He licked his lips smugly, back in his role of coercer. "I thought you didn't want it."

Ever scrappy, she stiffened her spine. "I figured I might as well have some fun if I'm going to get fucked anyway."

His big hands wrapped around her hips. Easily, he lifted

her up until she was free of her panties, and held her against the wall. His cock dragged over her thigh. "Nothing you can do could stop me."

Recognizing the dare, she let loose with her hands, slapping at his chest and face with all her force, letting him feel her anger.

She stopped, panting. Unmoving, he waited until she paused. "You done?"

"No." She slapped him across the face, so hard his eyes gleamed.

She expected him to bind her wrists, maybe with the tie still draped around his neck. He didn't bother.

He crowded closer, until she was pinned to the wall with his body weight. His cock burrowed tight against her pussy, a thick, long threat. A broad palm settled on her throat. Not squeezing. Just there, a heavy, weighty reminder of how big he was. How much larger than her. How helpless she was. She stilled.

"Nice," he murmured. His thumb stroked her skin. "You're going to be good now, aren't you?"

"Is that what you want? A good girl?"

"I want you."

Did he? Did he really? Or did he only want the ease of a relationship with an idealized memory?

She bit her lip, losing the thought when he pressed his cock inside of her, pushing slowly past the initial resistance of her body. She was slick and wet from her arousal and his tongue, but she still made him work for it, tightening the muscles of her pussy until sweat beaded on his brow.

And that hand, still on her throat. A threat and a promise. She bucked, and he tightened his fingers. There. The tiniest amount, enough to make it very clear that he could do so much more.

She wanted more. When he loosened his grip, she pressed her hand over his and increased the pressure. His eyes flashed. "Yeah?"

Her lips were beyond dry. "Yeah."

His motions were controlled as he fucked her, each steady thrust rocketing her arousal higher. He varied the tempo of his hips, sometimes hammering her, other times shafting her slowly, until the need coiled inside her.

"Don't come," he ordered.

Was he crazy? Of course she would come.

His fingers twitched on her throat, enough pressure that he cut off her air. He released almost immediately, but that small restriction, that second of illicit danger was enough for her to clench down on his hard cock and shatter.

He grunted. "You dirty little whore."

The words were distant but appreciated. She gasped as he surged above her, thrusting deep before collapsing against her with a muffled shout. His body tensed as he came, his hands holding her tight. Between them, sweat made for a peculiar sort of glue.

She had a fleeting thought for her dress, so expensive and brand new. Ah well. Dry cleaning could possibly take care of it.

He let her down slowly, holding her steady when her legs would have collapsed. It took him a few seconds to repair his clothes, and he scooped down to pick up her panties and shove them into his suit coat pocket. He readjusted her bodice, but not before bending and pressing a reverent kiss on each nipple.

She glanced at the cameras on either end of the hall. "This *is* a blind spot, right?"

"Of course." He arched a brow. "I wouldn't lie about that."

"Don't you think they'll wonder why we ran out but never made it to the elevator?"

"They're focused on watching the casino floor and the guest areas, or they should be. There are other safeguards in place to make sure no one unauthorized comes up to this floor."

She shook out her skirt. Wyatt might be a sex machine, but he knew exactly how far to take things without making a mockery out of their games.

He was…perfect. Fear made her tighten her fingers on her skirt.

Attuned to her body language, he paused. "We are okay, right?"

"Of course." The tension that the sex had given her a temporary reprieve from found its way to the base of her spine, lingering but numbed by their fast and furious coupling and a solid postcoital glow.

She could read the exhaustion in his face, in the tired ghost of a smile he gave her. He offered her his arm, and she took it. They strolled back to the apartment door, looking for all the world like a rumpled version of the civilized couple who had returned from their earlier night out.

She rested her head on his shoulder as they walked back in, breathing in the scent of his cologne and the sex they'd had. *Dear Lord. Please don't let me screw this up.*

Chapter Seven

SHE WOKE UP to her hair being stroked back from her face. Wyatt was already showered and dressed and sitting on the side of the bed, staring down at her with an intent expression. "Hey."

She stretched and regarded him somberly. "Hey."

With those two words, she knew things were still strained. They were being cautious with each other, or he would have tickled or kissed her awake.

"I have to get to work. I tried to clear my day out to spend it with you, but there's some things..."

"No, it's okay," she responded quickly. "Go do what you normally do." When they visited each other, neither of them worked as much as they normally did, conscious of their finite duration of time together. The perils of a long-distance relationship.

"Did you bring work?"

"I have a commission I can work on. But I think I may go visit my parents first." She threw it out there casually, like it was no big deal. Like the subject of her parents wasn't some great gaping injury.

Was there something twisted in her that liked to stick her fingers in these wounds and dig them around when there would be no payoff or resolution? She knew what his reaction would be, and he didn't disappoint. Wyatt's face became emotionless, and he dropped his hand away from her, making a show of checking his watch. "Yeah. I have to run. Why don't you call me when you're done, and I'll come meet you somewhere."

Done? How would she ever be done with her family? Her father's insidious words from the night before whispered in her mind. Heart heavy, she nodded. "Sure thing."

He hesitated. "Tell your mom…tell her I regret that last night was uncomfortable."

She nodded, her sarcastic side certain that the words were simply another manifestation of his relatively newfound social skills training. *Emily Post says when your girlfriend's parents storm out of dinner, be sure to convey your deepest regrets.* "Yup."

He leaned down and pressed a kiss against her forehead. "I ordered breakfast for you. It should be up when you're done with your shower."

She closed her eyes, drinking in the consideration as well as his affection. "See you later."

With a last half smile, he left her. Lingering in bed would have been nice, but all she would accomplish was moping. Instead, she hopped up to go take her shower.

She made plans with her mother via text while she ate, and then left the suite. The hotel was large enough that she didn't know all of the staff, but they knew her. She received nods and smiles from bellhops and the front desk as she departed.

She raised a brow when she came outside and found Sal waiting for her outside a sleek town car, his face expressionless and his uniform crisp despite the already mounting heat. "I don't need a car today, Sal."

Though she knew Wyatt had ordered him to take her wherever she needed, Sal nodded. That's what she liked about him. He didn't put his boss's orders above her own.

She set out down the street, appreciating the low-key morning energy of the Strip. Las Vegas was different from her normal digs, and not just because the heat was a sharp contrast to the foggy bay chill that marked San Francisco. Part of her liked going back and forth. Exploring two cool cities meant she was rarely bored.

This area was walkable, helped by the elevated crosswalks taking her across traffic. In no time at all, she was at the Wynn. She'd been here once or twice before, so she was aware of the location of the adults-only pool her mother had suggested for a meeting spot. Her large tote slapping against her thigh, she made her way through the bar and entered, spotting her mother's head over the rows of chaises.

She walked toward her, gasping when she came closer and saw the smooth line of her mother's back, a skort-style bottom her only nod to modesty.

"Mom," she said quietly, in an effort to hide her complete mortification. This was like the time her mother had chaperoned her junior prom and started dancing to Madonna. Only worse. Much worse. "Why are you topless?"

Her mother turned her head, keeping her arms stacked under her cheek. "Hello to you, too, darling."

"Hi." She sat in the lounger next to her. "Mom, seriously."

"It's an adults-only pool, Tatiana. European style. Sunbathing is expected."

She was well aware of the adults-only/European-style concept of the pool. Wyatt even had something similar at Quest, though his was more exclusive, geared toward smaller, private parties instead of hordes of sunbathing guests. They hadn't personally tried it out—

Note to self: Make sure you drag Wyatt to the pool. For al-fresco fucking possibilities.

—but she knew of its existence.

She glanced around. Only a few women had foregone their tops, and she had to admit, the level of male gawking was at a minimum, if nonexistent.

Still, that didn't explain why her mother was topless. Not that she was an ugly woman, but she was her mom, and she was naked in public, and that was wrong in and of itself. "What would Daddy say if he knew you were out here naked?"

Her mother's shoulders shook, and she gave a little snort. "Oh, honey. He'd be out here as soon as humanly possible, and it wouldn't be to tell me to put my top back on."

Ewwwwwwwwwwwwwwwwwww.

Her mom rose on her elbows to turn around, and Tatiana slapped her hand over her eyes. "Mom! Please."

She heard a gusty sigh and the rustle of clothes. She peeked to find her mother readjusting the straps of her bathing-suit top. "Honestly, Tatiana, you're an adult now. No need to be so prudish."

She imagined Wyatt—hell, any of her past lovers—chortling over that statement. But her mom didn't know about her sex life, which meant Tatiana was doing things perfectly right, as far as she was concerned. She'd figured out how to be discreet when she was fifteen and Wyatt Caine had snuck his hand under her bra for the first time. "You raised me, so I suppose it's your fault." Satisfied her mother was appropriately covered, she slipped out of her sundress to reveal the relatively modest bikini beneath.

Her mom reached into her beach bag and pulled out a bottle of sunscreen. "You always forget."

Touched when she realized it was the same SPF she usually used—much higher than any her mother, with her skin's natural tolerance to the sun, would ever buy for herself—she slathered it on. "Remember the first time I got badly burned?"

Janet rolled her eyes and readjusted her sunglasses. "How could I forget?"

Tatiana had been four or five, but she could still recall her mother's frantic tears and calls to the pediatrician after her father had taken her to the beach, become absorbed in explaining the physical properties of marine vertebrates, and forgot to put sunscreen on her.

They sat in silence for a few minutes, soaking in the hot rays of the sun. "Have you spoken to Clarissa?" Janet asked softly.

Tatiana's birth mother. Not her real mother. "Not since the last time." They'd only communicated twice. Once to make initial contact, and a second time because Tatiana hadn't received the hint that the woman wasn't interested in pursuing a relationship.

"I'm sorry."

"It's okay." And it really was. Tatiana held nothing

against the woman who had given her up for adoption. Maybe it was a sign of her maturity, or maybe it was because her half-brother had given her that sense of genetic connection she'd wanted. Either way, she was fine. She stirred. "You didn't want to attend the conference?"

"Other than your father, the speakers are morons. It wasn't worth arguing with them the whole day when it's so nice out."

"Good thing you came here instead of San Fran then. It's been super chilly there."

"I like San Francisco though. Maybe next time." She hesitated. "If you're still living there, of course. I don't know what yours and Wyatt's plans are."

"Oh." She paused, thought about it. "Neither do I, really."

"Hmm."

Her mom didn't push, for which Tatiana was grateful. She wasn't a pusher, not since Tatiana had dropped out of college and left the coast to pursue her dreams. She figured her parents had decided the same thing she had—that they'd rather be in each other's lives, even if they didn't agree on every point, than cut each other off completely.

This time, however, Tatiana was itching to talk to someone. The words bubbled out before she could halt them. "Last night was kind of a disaster, huh?"

Her mother tightened her lips and then released a small sigh. "I agree. I'm sorry, love. I had told your father to be on his best behavior, but you know the man. He has always been very protective of you. Something about Wyatt rubbed him the wrong way when you were young, and I suppose that hasn't changed. I told him that he needed to stay open-minded, but, well…"

"It wasn't all Daddy. Wyatt shouldn't have been so defensive. And it's my fault too." She winced. "I kind of sprung dinner on him. About a half an hour before."

"Oh, Tatiana."

"I know. He wasn't pleased."

"Why did you do that?"

Tatiana squirmed, fidgeting until her legs were curled up under her. "I was scared he wouldn't want to come."

Janet frowned. "Does he dislike us so much? We haven't even seen him in a decade."

Tatiana relaxed at the note of genuine curiosity in her mother's voice. She had hoped the other woman wouldn't take a sign of Wyatt's aversion personally. "No. I don't know. I don't think he dislikes you as much as he dislikes what you stand for." Tatiana glanced down at her hands. "I mean, Daddy was always riding Wyatt pretty hard when we were kids—"

"Honey. If your daddy wasn't morally opposed to firearms, he would have been cleaning guns any time a boy came to the door."

She smiled at her mother's dry words. "Yeah, so I think he has pretty not-fond memories of that. Plus, we fought about you guys a lot back then." Wyatt would make cutting, sarcastic remarks and she would explode. All the damn time.

"Us? Why did you fight about us?"

"Because…" She rolled her neck, trying to relieve the tension. She'd never formally confronted either of her parents, and she wasn't particularly keen on doing so now. "He said you were controlling me. Pushing me into a major I hated, a life I didn't want. No girl wants to hear that. I would get mad, he'd get more annoyed, and then we'd storm off."

Her mother signaled a passing waiter. "Can you get us a pitcher of sangria, please?" She turned to Tatiana. "He was right."

"What?"

"He was right, back then. We were absolutely forcing you into a life you didn't want. Not maliciously, of course, and we didn't realize you didn't want it, but we were still doing it."

Tatiana stared at her mother, unprepared for the casual admission of guilt.

Her mother smiled at the waiter's return and poured them both a glass of the fruit-filled alcohol. "You were such a sweet child, Tatiana. So eager to please. We had no idea you didn't want to follow us into the scientific world, not until you up and quit school."

"I know. I should have said something."

"We may have had difficulty listening. This world, this is my life, your father's too. We don't fully understand anything else. If you'd told us you wanted to be an artist, we might not have taken you seriously, probably would have bought you some canvas and told you to make it a hobby. And you, sweet child, would have agreed. So even though I don't understand what you do or why you feel the need to do it, I'm grateful you took such a stand and ran away to live your life, because I can see that it makes you happy. And it's made you a strong woman, one who can stand on her own two feet." Her mother sipped the sangria. "If Wyatt was one of the motivating reasons behind you striking out on your own, I'll kiss him the next time I see him."

"Well." Tatiana took a big gulp of her drink. "This is interesting."

"I only ever wanted your happiness, Tatiana." Her mom clasped her hand.

Tatiana returned the squeeze. "I know. I'm so glad I was the lucky kid who ended up with you and Daddy."

Her mother's long lashes hid the sheen of moisture in her eyes. "Yes."

Tatiana studied her mother's hand in her own, naked except for her plain platinum wedding band. The woman worked with her hands too much to fuss with bracelets or rings. A necklace, Tatiana thought. Gold, twisted like a Mobius Coil, with chips of red rubies peeking out. Her fingers itched to draw it, to get started on it right away, but she filed the image of it away in her mind. Later. It would make a lovely birthday present.

Her mother sniffed. "Well, in any case, that extends to Wyatt. He made you happy back then, and I can see and hear it in your voice that he makes you happy now."

"He does." So happy it was making her crazy.

"It's unfortunate that we all fell back into old patterns last night."

A chill that had nothing to do with the icy drink in her hands ran down her spine. "Don't say that. The last thing I want is to fall back into old patterns. I want to make this work this time, which means we have to do things differently."

Her mom stopped mid-drink. "Wait a minute. Were we the reason you broke up when you were in college?" Distress crossed her otherwise-smooth brow. "Oh, honey, that would—"

"No. I mean, yes, we argued about you, but we argued about a ton of things." She gave the response she'd said to herself so many times. "I don't know exactly why we broke up, not anymore, but it wasn't exclusively because of you."

"Hmm."

"What?"

"Nothing. Just that it's strange, because he did make you so happy. Neither of you cheated on each other—"

"Of course not." Betrayal wasn't something she'd ever be comfortable with.

"Or lied to each other, or somehow transgressed hugely, so it's strange that something you can't remember would destroy your relationship."

Tatiana shifted, struck. "Yeah. I suppose it is kind of weird."

They drank in silence for a minute. "With the exception of last night, how are you trying to keep yourself from old patterns?"

Tatiana considered that question. "Well, I think we're naturally more considerate of each other's time. When we were younger, we didn't really respect what the other person did. Wyatt assumed his work was more important than my schoolwork, and vice versa."

"It's clear that Wyatt is proud of your business."

A small, pleased smile crossed Tatiana's lips. Yes, she wasn't happy Wyatt had jumped to her defense with her parents, but she generally liked his fascination and pride in her skill.

It wasn't a business, not to her. Wyatt understood that. Even though her mother, with her unconditional love, didn't. "He is."

"Good. It's hard to find a man who appreciates a woman for her brain and talent."

Since her mother was something of a genius, Tatiana knew she was aware of what she spoke about. "Yes. We're also not fighting. I mean, we're super careful to make each visit with each other peaceful and happy, not chaotic."

Janet released a crack of laughter. "If you figure out how to sustain that whole no-fighting thing, let me know. Your father and I have been quarrelling for almost forty years."

Tatiana laughed along, but unease slithered through her.

Her mom sobered. "In seriousness, Tatiana, be careful, please. Long-distance romances are tough because it's hard to address all of the important issues when you're trying to pack a lot into short visits with one another."

"I know."

The other woman gave a sigh. "Good. And please, tell Wyatt I'm sorry. And that we'd really like to start fresh with him. I swear, I will make your father be civil. We don't want to be the cause of any tension between you and the man you're with."

Tatiana nodded. The concession was kind, but she wouldn't be able to relax unless she knew Wyatt was on board with making nice in the future. "He asked me to convey his regrets as well."

"Did Ronald call you? He wants to have a barbecue tomorrow, while we're here. Maybe Wyatt can come to that. It'll give him and your father a chance to be around each other in a more relaxed atmosphere."

The bitter laugh spilled from her lips, shocking her. Yeah, sure. During the past seven months, Wyatt had gone out of his way to avoid her brother, like he had gone out of his way to avoid the rest of her family.

Her mother was staring at her, concerned, so she tried to force a grim smile. No need to paint Wyatt any blacker in her parents' eyes.

He's making you choose. Making you separate your worlds so they won't ever have to touch.

Tired of the effort it took to conceal her worries, Tatiana leaned back in the chair. "Yeah, sure. We'll see." No doubt tomorrow she'd have to sneak off and see her family like they were some terrible secret. Hard to do when it was Saturday, but Wyatt would probably find some excuse to bury himself in work if he had the slightest notion he would otherwise have to interact with her kin.

"Good. They will come around."

Her skepticism must have been obvious, because her mom laughed. "Trust me, I know how to handle a proud, arrogant man. Arrange them around a grill, and they'll all start to bond. Now…" Her mom wiggled her eyebrows. "Let's see how many pitchers we can finish before your father gets his lunch break."

"Do I get to drunk yell at him for being mean last night?"

"Certainly, darling. I'll help."

Chapter Eight

TATIANA LET HERSELF back into the penthouse and dropped her tote to the ground. Exhaustion rode her, the kind of satisfying tiredness that comes from a whole lot of lying around in the sun. Her limbs were loose from the cocktails she'd downed and the catharsis of chastising her unhappy father.

"He is not good enough for you," he'd muttered.

She'd poked at his chest, careful not to spill her fruity drink. "You remember how you used to sneer at poor Alfie whenever he came around? You never think anyone is good for me!"

He'd given her a flabbergasted look. "Because they cannot be. You are perfect."

Lord save her from men who thought she was perfect. At least he hadn't completely refused to entertain the possibility of accepting Wyatt's presence in her life. She viewed his grumbling and stomping away with a lot of hope. Sangria-fueled optimism.

She exhaled and pulled her dress up over her head as she strolled into Wyatt's bedroom, dropping it to lie in a heap on the carpet, making a mental note to pick it up later. Wyatt was military neat, and he gave her The Look of Displeasure when he found her clothes strewn around. Which was unfair, since he didn't have a problem doing the actual strewing.

A smile crossed her lips. Despite her annoyance with him, she wished he were here now. Especially since she was in a swimsuit, oiled up, and moderately tipsy. He'd attack her at first glance.

She pulled off the bikini top as she padded into the bathroom, her nipples beading at the chill in the air-conditioned room. Her breasts were lighter than the rest of her skin, thanks to the sun she'd received today. Had it not been her mother accompanying her, she might have been tempted to go sans top.

She'd definitely go without if Wyatt dragged her out to one of the grottos on his property, small pools shaded by foliage planted for privacy as much as for beauty.

Strip. Or I'll rip those bottoms off of you.

That's what he would say, all growly and intense. She shivered and hooked her thumbs in the bikini bottoms, shoving them down her legs, concentrating to retain her balance as she squirmed her way out of the still-damp spandex.

Balance. So. Hard.

Tatiana toppled to land on her butt on the cold marble tile, blinking at the tangled scrap of hot pink wrapped around one ankle. Scissoring her legs, she managed to yank it off.

Phew. Mission accomplished.

Getting up was so much work, but she managed to

make it back on her feet. Maybe she would buy a more revealing bikini before she and Wyatt embarked on exploring the private pools. Or no, even better, a modest white one piece, cut low on the legs and high on the chest. They could play the reluctant tourist and the coercive, blackmailing casino owner.

What would he be blackmailing her over? Why, her plot to steal…something. Something cool and shiny. Eh, they could work all of that out.

She didn't realize she was stroking her own body until her hand grazed her nipple. She instantly paused, unused to touching herself when Wyatt was within a ten-mile radius.

Don't touch yourself.

Keep those pretty hands out of your panties.

This body is mine.

Her eyes narrowed. But he hadn't given her any of those orders today. They'd been too busy tiptoeing around each other, the explosive sex during the night not enough to wipe out the lingering awkwardness of their aborted fight.

So she could play with herself. Take her pleasure into her own hands. Watch herself in the huge mirror that spanned the length of one wall. She turned slightly, displaying her good side, liking the way the recessed lighting flattered her skin. Tatiana coasted her hand over the slope of her breast.

There were some problem areas, spots she could never quite tone, an odd scar and blemish here and there. But hot damn. Wyatt was a lucky guy.

He should be here. Her gaze went to the lip of the giant Jacuzzi tub. He would watch her, lounging there.

Bound.

The shiver that trickled through her told her that her body liked that idea, though having a helpless man had never been one of her favorite fantasies. He wouldn't be helpless, though—Wyatt could be hogtied and his eyes would still blaze with dominance, the mantle of control resting easily on his shoulders.

Naked, tied-up, watching her. Unf. She tweaked her nipple, her breath accelerating as she slid her hand down her belly to the tuft of hair that Wyatt had professed to like. Her pussy was wet, ready for a cock. On legs made more unsteady by arousal, she made her way to the vanity and fumbled a drawer open. In his nightstand, Wyatt kept the essentials: lube, condoms, a couple of vibrators. Annoyed once when he had to interrupt their play in the Jacuzzi...and the kitchen...and the living room...to go fetch necessities, he had started keeping the same things in a drawer or cupboard in every room in his home.

Withdrawing a large, wickedly curved dildo about the size of Wyatt's cock, she ran her fingers along the tip of it and glanced in the mirror behind her at where she imagined Wyatt would be sitting.

Use it. Fuck that cock.

She dragged the nubby silicone over the tips of her breasts. Her nipples were tight and aching, ready for his mouth and his big, calloused hands.

Stop teasing me. You're hungry for it.

But she could tease him, because in her fantasy he was helpless. He had to watch her and be grateful for every scrap of mercy she showed him.

Your pussy's hot for me.

It was. She dragged the dildo down her belly, loving the

way it slicked over the sunscreen moisturizing her skin.

Only for me.

Yes, only for him. The bright pink plastic skated over her mons.

You've never been so hot for anyone. You never will be so hot for anyone.

She whimpered. Bracing her hand on the vanity, she inserted the cock inside of her and pushed.

Yes. Fuck it. Good girl.

Greedy and well aware of what she needed to get off, her hand sped up, fueled by the visual in the mirror, the flush building on her chest and neck, the sway of her breasts, the hardness of her nipples, the flex of the small muscles in her arm as she fucked herself. This was what Wyatt would see. This was what he did see.

Um. *Fucking* lucky, that guy.

You don't even need me around. You could just make love to yourself.

She gasped out a small laugh at what she expected Wyatt's dry reaction would be to her vanity. After sucking her fingers into her mouth, she brought them to her nipples, making them glisten, the way they would if Wyatt had sucked them.

So close. She used the dildo exactly as Wyatt might, with short, sharp thrusts. He'd wrap his other hand around her waist, draw her back against him, give her something to claw and strain against. Grab her breast tight and squeeze. *That's right, baby. Give it to me.*

Everything would be better if he were here. But she needed to get off, and this tool was literally at hand. A series of gasps left her lips as she withdrew the dildo and ground it against her clit.

Panting, she straightened and cleaned the sex toy off. She supposed she should feel mildly embarrassed at the way she had shamelessly come on a fake cock standing up in a bathroom, but, hell, she'd played coercion games and flirted with choking play in a hallway less than twenty-four hours ago. This was nothing.

Her body was ready for more, too. Sex without Wyatt was like sneezing, a brief relief of tension. Sex with Wyatt left her boneless, not merely unsteady.

Once she had returned the dildo to its home, she stepped inside the massive shower. As she always did, she ignored the finer shampoo Wyatt continuously kept in stock for her and went straight for his drugstore brand. She was surprised he hadn't realized yet that she didn't use his fancier offering. Her choice was a gesture originally born of nostalgia, and one that she continued when she visited him, out of some bizarre desire to…get closer to him? Create another tie to him?

The tension that had seeped out of her in the wake of her orgasm reinvaded her limbs. That was the problem with orgasms. Their effects were never permanent.

You'll be okay, you and Wyatt. Like she'd said to her mother, they were doing things differently this time around, mostly because they were adults. Because of their maturity, they could avoid the mistakes they'd made when they were young.

You don't even know what errors you made when you were young. If you don't know them, how can you avoid them?

She turned and let the spray of the shower wash the soap off her face, chewing over this thought. She chewed while she got out of the shower, dried herself off, padded into Wyatt's bedroom, and dressed in a pair of panties and a bra.

Otherwise naked, she flopped on the bed. The shower had washed away her alcohol-induced bliss along with the sunscreen on her skin, leaving only alcohol-induced melancholy.

She stared up at the ceiling. It was boring and white. At home, she'd painted her bedroom walls and ceiling a bright blue, swirls of green and gold mixed in. Her life exploded with color. Red in her living room, blue in her bedroom, yellow in her kitchen. It looked like a toddler with ADD had been given a gift card for Sherwin Williams.

But it was hers. And if she were home right now, she'd be able to go into her closet and pull out the box that was more precious to her than the gold and silver and precious gems she kept in the safe in the floor beneath her bed.

Inside the box would be the faded and curling paper, creased and time-worn, that had traveled with her through a cross-country move and several small ones, which she'd snuck out to read during moments of depression and loneliness.

Wyatt's letters.

Letters he had written to her when they were teenagers and young adults, letters she had kept over the course of the decade they'd been apart. Once or twice, she had contemplated tossing the things, but something had always stayed her hand. Thank goodness. Months ago, their presence had been the final push she had needed to get on a plane and come find him; ostensibly to save her brother's hide, but really out of a deep curiosity to discover what had happened to the guy.

They were hers, a tangible monument to their previous relationship, so she got custody. But that meant they were far away, not here.

Tatiana sighed and curled up on her side, her hands stacked under her cheek. Not that she needed the physical copies to remember what was written—she only wanted to hold them in her hands. She'd read them so often, particularly since she and Wyatt had gotten together again, she could probably recite them from memory alone.

I want you waiting naked for me when I get home, all wet, like you always are.

She licked her lower lip. That was right after she'd started college. When he'd come home, she had been waiting naked for him in his apartment. With a set of furry handcuffs and a full bottle of lube.

I hope you take that part-time job at the library. I could pin you to a stack and fuck you, away from where anyone could see us.

Unf.

My apartment smells like you. Love you.

The faint smile around her lips was silly and not unexpected. Sweet, sexy, or funny, those letters never failed to make her feel as though she were being wrapped in a strong hug. What woman didn't like knowing that she'd been loved like that?

He sounded so…happy in them. And though she didn't have written proof of it, she knew that she'd been equally happy, pleased with her tough, secretly squishy, lustful boyfriend. As happy as they were right now. Well, before last night.

So what had gone wrong?

It's strange that something you can't remember would destroy your relationship.

Her smile faded. With a few words, her mother had slapped Tatiana in the face with her deepest worry.

Restless, she flopped onto her back again. Yeah, she wished she had her letters. Maybe they had a clue in them. After all, those had spanned almost the entirety of their relationship. Or at least the bulk of it, after she'd graduated high school.

The bulk of it, until that last year.

Tatiana squinted. He'd never given her anything in that last year. No goofy notes tucked into her backpack. No folded-up letters in her desk. No scribbled love notes on her pillow. Made sense, since that was the year everything had taken a turn for the worse. Not the sex. They had always had sex.

Everything other than sex. She could vividly recall their stress points, those problem areas that they'd both circled around again and again. Some of the issues had been important, some not at all. In her head, she'd always considered that last year as the year everything had imploded, when their anger and fights had escalated beyond a level they could control.

Because you fought. You never talked.

She stilled. Hmm. Well, well, well. How utterly profound. Where on earth did that come from?

Of course they'd talked. They talked a lot.

Not that last year.

Tatiana inhaled, replaying their history as an observer instead of a participant. Her screaming, yelling, and turning into a shrewish caricature while he sat in stony silence, made cutting remarks, or stormed out in disgust. The only times they hadn't run away from each other was when they fell into bed.

Just like last night.

Tatiana rolled to sit up, her heart pounding.

We're also not fighting.

If you figure out how to sustain that whole no-fighting thing, let me know.

They'd never fought, ever. At least, they'd never fought *right.* When things had gotten really dicey, when their frustration and disagreements became overwhelming, they'd resorted to cutting at each other with words before running off to lick their wounds. They never resolved or apologized or compromised on anything.

Tatiana opened her eyes and met her own gaze in the mirror over her vanity, bleakness turning them a stormy green.

How smug she'd been, thinking the best way to make things work was to bite her tongue and stay sweet.

We're not fighting. The fighting had never been the problem. The lack of talking anything through? Big problem.

They weren't avoiding the mistakes of their past. They were repeating them.

Chapter Nine

WYATT FOLDED BACK the cover on the tablet and handed it back to his chief of security. They had an event scheduled in their ballroom for the upcoming weekend. Normally, Wyatt didn't concern himself with the nitty-gritty of every wedding, bat mitzvah, and anniversary party that went down at Quest, but the birthday party was for a particularly good customer, a CEO whose parties often turned into a raucous celebration. A little consensual debauchery was all well and good, but Wyatt wasn't in the business of burying bodies for anyone.

Protecting rich people from themselves and each other was a second full-time job. After all, they had to stay rich to continue lining his pockets. "Make sure you vet the outsourced security personally."

His employee nodded. "Yes, sir. And I'll get right on fixing the cameras on your floor. I'm sorry we didn't catch that on our own. Someone will be up today."

Though Wyatt had developed a certain fondness for that blind spot, he didn't want any cracks on what his eyes in the sky could see. While he was sure the bigger target for a criminal was the vault and the floor, his money was insured. Tatiana was not. "Good."

He slipped out of the security office and made his way up to his own. Esme, his assistant, glanced up when he entered. "Anyone call?"

"No, sir. It's pretty quiet."

He glanced at his phone, which had yet to give a silent vibration, signaling a call or text from Tatiana. "I'll catch up on some work then."

"I thought Tatiana was in town."

"She is."

"Oh."

Wyatt couldn't blame the other woman for her confusion. Normally when Tatiana was anywhere in his vicinity, he was raring to clear his desk off quickly so he could go be with her. Since he'd spent the last decade as a chronic workaholic, it was an adjustment to want to be with someone more than he wanted to build his pile of money.

Sometimes, he worked from his laptop upstairs, so he could watch her while she twisted metal and manipulated jewels in the bright sunlight streaming into the penthouse.

She complained that made her self-conscious, but since she didn't kick him out, he figured she liked it.

"She's busy. With her parents," he explained. *And we sort of stupidly fought yesterday, and now I don't know what to do.*

Esme's plucked eyebrows flew up behind her thick spectacles. Plump and rosy-cheeked, she looked like—and was—a cuddly grandmother. Her eyes danced in merriment as she turned slightly in her swivel seat. "Oh, why don't you join them? I really can hold down the fort."

"I have no doubt about that." In the past few months, Esme had taken on increasingly more of his responsibilities. "I saw her parents yesterday. I'm waiting for her to be done now."

Esme smiled. "Ah. Once was enough, huh? My Ben used to be like that, with my family."

Wyatt liked Esme's husband, whom he'd met at various get-togethers that he'd attended. They were so kind and wholesome, sometimes Wyatt wondered why the couple weren't milking cows in some perfectly idyllic place like Iowa.

He leaned against the doorjamb. "Really?"

A small dimple creased her cheek. "Ben couldn't stand my mother." Esme shook her head. "My god, the fights we had. Took a few years of banging their stubborn heads together for them to find anything in common, but they came to be friendly. Makes for an uncomfortable Christmas, if you can't get along with your in-laws."

Could he be friendly with Tatiana's parents?

He caught himself about to sneer. Well, seeing as how he couldn't even think of them without making a face, probably not. "I can't imagine you and Ben ever disagreeing over anything."

She raised an eyebrow. "How boring it would have been if we'd spent the last thirty years agreeing on everything."

"Boring?" No, that sounded perfect to Wyatt. He was aggressive, and he had a temper, but it took a lot to get it started, and yelling and shouting wasn't his style. The world knew to fear him when he glared or spoke quietly, and that was how he liked it.

"Sure. Fighting can be fun."

It was not fun. Fighting was painful. Angry. Something to be avoided.

It used to drive him crazy, Tatiana's need to confront every little problem, usually loudly. She'd gained control over her temper, because when they were younger, it had snapped fast and boiled hot. His neighbors had once complained to him, *We can hear your woman down the block when she gets mad.*

"I think you and I have different notions of fun."

"Well, maybe not the actual fighting itself. After." A secretive smile spread over Esme's lips. "That's the fun part."

Wyatt had come to think of Esme as a maternal figure in his life. So he hoped she wasn't somehow referring to make-up sex. He forced a smile. "If you say so."

"Oh, come on. Doesn't it feel good, that catharsis? Feeling like you solved something?"

He didn't feel like he'd solved anything, fighting with Tatiana last night. "Maybe I haven't been fighting right," he responded lightly.

Esme chuckled. "That must be it."

Wyatt nodded to her, walked inside his office, and closed his door. He sank into his seat but didn't bother turning on his computer.

He pulled his phone out, placed it on his desk, and glanced at the blank screen again. As if staring at it would make it vibrate.

Groaning, he dropped his head into his hands. All day, all he'd been able to think about was the way Tatiana had looked when he'd left this morning. Wary, drawn, closed-off. God, he'd hated that. It wasn't the girl he knew, with the sassy mouth and the take-no-shit attitude. Fun? No, this wasn't fun.

Wyatt rubbed his chest. That goddamn dinner last night. Couldn't they pick up and move on? Did they have to drag the awkwardness out for days? He'd gone, hadn't he? What more did she want from him?

He was veering dangerously into petulant territory. Wyatt picked up the letter opener on his desk and turned it around in his fingers, watching the sunlight flash off the silver.

Maybe she doesn't want to have to feel scared to tell you her family is in town.

He stopped, the letter opener balanced on his knuckles, his pouty, self-indulgent mental wanderings drowned out.

Huh.

He tugged on that stray thought, pondering it. Oh, those instincts of his were screaming. Disassociating and assessing the players in any game was his specialty, a trick which had served him well over the years. In business, however, he wasn't emotionally involved. With Tatiana, he was fucking emotionally enmeshed, which made disassociating extremely difficult.

She shouldn't have been scared to tell him.

He circled that, examined it for weaknesses, for ways to slip out of it. Poked it for accuracy, prodded it for truth.

The statement held up.

So, why? Was her nervousness valid? He barely even spoke about her family.

When he played poker, he created an elaborate system in his brain, a diagram, the appearance of each card telling him something about another. The cards were turning over now, and he barely breathed, fearful of losing the epiphany.

She shouldn't have been nervous.

She'd been nervous because he treated her whole family like pariahs.

She'd been justified in dreading telling him.

He'd been a dick.

Wyatt blinked. He'd refused to dignify her Christmas invitation with a response. Refused to see Ron, though her brother lived a stone's throw away. And then, when he'd had no choice but to face her parents, he'd acted like some fucking teen rebel without a cause, angry at the world and angry at them for daring to impose upon his precious time with her.

He shook his head in disbelief. Was he fucking crazy? He had learned how to use charm to win over some of the wealthiest people in the world, to encourage them to open their bank accounts and bleed their wallets all over his building. He should have had her mother laughing and eating out of the palm of his hand, her dad giving him his grudging approval, her brother singing his praises for the part he'd played in reuniting the siblings and not sending him to prison.

Instead he'd done exactly what her father had accused him of doing. Forcing her to choose between him and them, because he wouldn't even dream of letting their worlds collide. He didn't know if Tatiana loved him yet. He wasn't sure if he loved her. But this wasn't some sort of fling they were having. He was trying to build something here. Why had he thought he could shut out her family forever?

He tapped on his phone to pull up his messages and texted her. *Where are you?*

He turned the letter opener around and around while he waited for her answer. Tatiana had a tendency to turn the ringer off and then forget to turn it on again for days. Annoyed, he'd doctored her phone during their last visit so her camera flash went off when he texted or called.

Her reply came a few minutes later. *Upstairs.*

Wyatt stared at the phone, a chill sneaking through his blood. She'd come back to his place without letting him know? Without sending him a teasing note or tempting him with the promise of a nooner or an office blowjob?

He saw his life split in two directions, somehow understanding the import of this decision. One where he did nothing, sat here, and avoided the awkward conversation and her renewed anger over this whole debacle.

That was a tempting path. Tatiana's temper cooled as quickly as it heated up, so he knew he could get away with it. The stilted conversation would soon ease, especially if they were both naked.

The other, going up and eating crow. Telling her he was sorry for making her feel like she couldn't tell him her family was around.

She might yell. Or even throw things.

Stop being a coward.

Oh, but he was. At least where Tatiana was concerned.

His phone beeped again. *Are you working?*

Wyatt's jaw hardened. A coward he might be, but his desire to please this woman was stronger. All she had to do was crook her little finger, and he'd run. It would be terrifying, if it wasn't so thrilling.

Chapter Ten

WYATT DIDN'T NOTICE anything amiss until he closed and locked the door of his home. He dropped his laptop case to the floor and stared at the sight in front of him. "Hi."

Tatiana glanced up at him, her hair sliding over her bare shoulder. "Hello."

He rubbed his hand over his mouth, trepidation taking a back seat to amusement and arousal. Yes, he enjoyed watching her work. He would have enjoyed it a lot more if he'd ever seen her work like this.

She lay on her stomach on the carpet in front of the floor-to-ceiling windows, dressed in nothing but a pair of skimpy mint-colored bikini panties and a matching bra. In one hand, she held something that flashed green, a pair of small pliers in the other. Her other work materials were scattered about. Chains of gold and silver snaked over the carpet, twining through a field of crystals.

He came to stand above her. Nudging a string of pearls aside, he sank down to sit, unsure of what to say. This wasn't a business associate he had to calm down or a customer who was unhappy. There were no social rules that he was aware of that would help him navigate this path and bring them back to their previous state of bliss. "What's up?"

She looked down at her hands and ran the unfinished piece through her fingers. "Not much. Working."

Her skin was flushed. He traced his finger along the bridge of her nose. "You look like you got some sun."

"Went to the pool at the Wynn."

With her mother. *Don't be a dick.* Wyatt schooled his face so it remained expressionless. "The Wynn's pool is acceptable," he said grudgingly, high praise for him.

"We went to the topless one."

He nudged her bra strap. "I see a tan line."

"My mom went European, not me."

He did *not* want that picture in his head. Ever, ever, ever. "Ah."

She gave him a small smile. "If you'd been there instead of my mom, I might have."

He flicked her nose. "If I'd been there, I would have made you."

"I know." Her reply was contemplative, not throaty and sexy.

They both looked away. Their silences hadn't felt like this before, filled with unsaid words.

A flash of something shiny in her hair caught his eye. "You have something here." He picked out the green crystal that had gotten caught. The sunlight reflected through the prism, and he froze. "Tatiana."

"Yeah?"

He held the stone up. Small but perfectly cut, the color

was vibrant. “This is an emerald.”

“Yeah. Everything gets stuck in my hair, huh?” Her competent, scarred hands fidgeted with the piece she was working on. Smooth semi-precious beads, darker in shade than the emerald he held, had been strung together, probably the beginning base of some larger piece.

He glanced around. Jesus. He didn’t have to pick them up to know that the various stones he’d assumed were red and blue and clear crystals were worth a lot more.

He dragged his avaricious gaze away from what he now realized was a treasure chest of jewels. “Tatiana, why is there a king’s ransom lying around?”

“Told you. I’m working. Working helps me think.”

“You’re naked.”

A bare shoulder lifted in a delicate shrug. “Working pantsless is the best way to think.” Her words were measured and precise.

Since she was usually meticulously careful with her expensive materials, he figured there was only one explanation. “Are you drunk?”

She squinted at him. “No. I might have been, earlier. But I’ve sobered up.”

He placed the emerald on the carpet with a final caress, trying to resist the urge to gather all of the materials and go stick them in his safe. He paused. “Wait. Don’t tell me you got on a plane carrying all of this?” His voice rose as he spoke. Was she kidding him? Thank God he’d insisted on picking her up from the airport. What if she had slipped inside a cab with an unscrupulous driver who drove her into the desert and mugged and killed her?

An unlikely scenario, he knew. But even a .001% probability of something bad happening to this female made his palms sweat.

She rolled her eyes. "Calm down. It's just money."

This from the woman who fretted for hours if her weekly budget didn't balance perfectly. His concern grew. "Tatiana…"

She braced her hands under her and rose to her knees. He got sidetracked by another small jewel falling off her to the carpet, his heart seizing at the potential loss of revenue. "Whoa. Careful there. Why don't we clean this up, and…"

She was wrapped around him before he could finish his sentence, her arms encircling his neck, her legs wrapped around his waist. She pressed her nose against his. "Hi."

Forget the goddamn jewelry. Her eyes were clearer and more flawless than the purest emerald. "Hi."

Wyatt adjusted himself so she could straddle him better, and slid his hands up her back, his fingers flirting under her bra strap. He glanced down between them. Her breasts were plumped up against his chest, the cups almost revealing the areolas. It would take a flick of his fingers to unhook her bra and pull those nipples into his mouth.

"You didn't ask me what I was thinking about."

Attention caught by the words and the serious tone of her voice, he looked up from her breasts. "I think I might know." *I was an asshole. And I'm probably going to be an asshole again at some point. But forgive my latest display of assholic behavior.*

She kissed him, her lips soft and sweet. He tasted strawberries and wine and her. Hours could be spent on this, hours where they wouldn't have to fight, hours where he could get drunk off of her.

Tatiana pulled away, too soon, and he tensed until every muscle was locked, aware of what was coming. *You deserve this. Let her get it out of her system.*

"Why did we break up?"

Caught off guard, he could only stare at her. "What?"

"Why did we break up? Back when we were kids?"

What did this have to do with anything? "I—Lots of reasons."

"Do better than that. What were they?"

He opened his mouth and closed it again. He didn't know. No, he knew. But he couldn't verbalize it.

Fuck that anyway. It was ancient history, and hardly relevant right now. "Does it matter?"

She fiddled with his tie, loosening it. Her sparkly pink nail polish was starting to chip. That would drive her crazy. "My mom asked me that today, and for the life of me, I couldn't answer it either."

He took a deep breath. "Tatiana. Why don't you get dressed, and we can—"

"No!" She had the element of surprise on her side, so she was able to knock him backward so he lay flat, a hundred and fifteen pounds of furious woman on top of him.

Yes, it was the surprise. He winced at the twinge in his lower back. It wasn't that he was getting old and slow.

"I don't need to calm down. I don't need to relax. I am not hysterical."

"Okay." He wrapped his hands around her upper arms, trying not to flinch at the loudness of her voice.

He didn't want to be here. No, he wanted to be here, on the carpet, with Tatiana on top, but he didn't want to be *here*, in this moment.

Her breasts trembled with the force of her emotions. "This is important. I know that you hate that I'm confrontational and loud, but this is important."

He clenched his jaw. "I do hate when you're loud." The admission was dragged out of someplace deep inside of him.

She blanched. He closed his eyes in order to block out the sheen covering her own. The sight made him want to rip his chest open and offer her his heart.

But when she yelled in anger, it was all he could do not to run.

Her small hands patted his face. They were callused from the work she did, a contrast to the rest of her soft, delicate body. "I told you to leave. That last time. Do you remember?"

How could he ever forget? The scene played out behind his closed eyes. A younger version of the woman on top of him, angry and crying and screaming at him. *I can't take this anymore, Wyatt! We're done. Get out.* "And I did." They'd never spoken again. Not even to exchange the things they'd kept at each other's places. A week later, after packing everything in his rusty Civic, he'd headed west.

"Don't you ever wonder what happened to us?"

"We were young. We weren't able to handle that kind of a serious relationship."

She tsked. "That diminishes us both."

"We had problems. We didn't know how to deal with them." Wetness dripped on his cheeks. Her tears. God, how he hated her tears.

"I think we still don't know how to deal with them."

WHEN HIS EYES flew open, Tatiana swallowed. They were

hot and anguished, the cold and controlled Wyatt gone.

She adored this man, the man he'd grown up to be. She probably loved him, though she refused to even contemplate that seriously until they got past this stumbling block in the middle of their path.

"We didn't have many serious problems, not 'til I graduated high school." They'd fought then, but they'd been fights that had often ended in steamy make-out sessions in the backseat of Wyatt's car, quickly forgotten and forgiven in the midst of their rioting hormones.

Wyatt looked so uncomfortable, Tatiana almost let him up. But he was a big boy, and she figured if he really wanted to run, he could toss her off and run already.

His nod was curt. "I remember our problems."

"Do you remember us fighting?" She placed her finger over his lips. "Or really, us apologizing, or using what we fought about to move forward? I remember the former. Me yelling. And you, either making sarcastic comments that only made me madder or storming off until we both cooled down." Her shrug was jerky. "I can't sustain my mad for long. So I would calm down. And we'd push that problem aside until something else happened. Nothing would ever get resolved."

He scrubbed his hands over his face. "I'm… I don't know what to say. Is that really how you remember things? That we broke up because we *didn't* fight?"

"More like, we fought, but not in any constructive way." She grimaced. "Do you know what I mean?"

He stilled, his gaze far away.

"Wyatt?"

He shook his head. "Nothing. I-I said something earlier

to Esme...." His thumb traced over her cheek, wiping away the wetness of her tears. "Come here." He pulled her closer until she was lying down on top of him. Her face rubbed over the fine cotton of his shirt. She gave a spare thought to the snot and makeup she'd leave on it, but she knew he wouldn't care.

His hand smoothed up her back, his fingers scratching her skin the way he knew she loved. "I do remember you yelling."

She winced. "I know."

"I don't want this to end." His voice was quiet. "I know we haven't been together long, but I'm falling for you."

"Are you? Or are you only falling for me when it's easy to fall for me?" The question was brave of her. Brave, because she feared the answer so much.

"What kind of a question is that?"

"Look at our track record. We're not good at handling things when the going gets tough."

"That's not true. Some marriages don't last as long as our relationship did."

"But it didn't last forever," she pointed out.

"That doesn't mean we can't make things work now."

She softened, attuned to his upset. "I don't want this to end either. That's why I think it's important to not repeat the mistakes we made before. We have a second chance, Wyatt. We shouldn't blow it."

There was silence as he rubbed his fingers over her neck, but she could practically feel Wyatt's clever brain thinking.

"I hate shouting," he finally said.

No, he never yelled or shouted. He motivated employees by treating them with respect and hitting them with his icy displeasure.

"I know," Tatiana replied.

"I've gotten better at handling my reaction, but…you make me feel like I'm a nineteen-year-old again. That's great when it comes to my cock, but probably not for my emotional maturity."

Her lips curled up. "Yeah."

Wyatt hesitated. "One of the first things I did after I was financially stable was visit a psychiatrist."

She tensed, eager to look him in the eyes after words like that, but he held her pressed tight to his chest. She gave in after a brief moment, willing to give him whatever he needed.

"It wasn't about you. Not entirely at least. I was in a bad place, overall. Most of it was tied to my dad and the way I was raised." He paused. "I stopped going to see her after a few visits because I got busy, but it was helpful anyway. It was the first time I ever spoke about my family to anyone."

She didn't dare breathe, for fear that he would stop talking. Over the course of their long previous relationship, Tatiana could count on one hand the times Wyatt had talked about his father. She'd never been allowed to meet the man, though she'd known of him by reputation and had caught glances of him around town.

He'd moved out of his dad's house when he was eighteen. At that time, she'd been titillated by the idea of her cool older boyfriend living on his own. When she'd matured and made comments about their estranged relationship, Wyatt's rebuffs had been so intimidating she hadn't pushed for more.

"Talking about it helped me sort of put things in perspective. Helped me process why I react the way I do to things sometimes. You're right. It's true, I shut down when people yell, but it's probably because…" He breathed out roughly, his chest rising and falling beneath her cheek. "I don't remember my father when he wasn't shouting. Some people get mean when they drink, but he would get loud. Loud and angry. I hated that. Hated the noise."

She licked her dry lips. "I'm so sorry." Guilt churned within her, every moment she'd ever raised her voice to this man replaying in her head.

"It's not you. You were and are being yourself. I'm the one who—" He made a frustrated sound. "Stands to reason that I hate fights, right? Confrontation is fine, I have to confront people every day, but usually I hold the power there. It's different when I can't…"

"When you can't what?" Tatiana prompted him when he closed his eyes, his dark brows drawn together, as if in pain.

His adam's apple bobbed. "When I can't walk away." He looked at her, stricken. "You're right. I'm the one who screwed everything up last time."

Unable to handle his distress, she shook her head. "No. It was my fault. I had no idea I was traumatizing you." But she should have. She'd been an overdramatic idiot sometimes, but she'd known that he was emerging from a dysfunctional household. She sniffed, and a tear splashed onto his thick forearm.

He pulled her up. His eyes were red, though she saw no tears. "Hey, don't cry." He searched for words. "I did walk away back then. The minute I started to feel uncomfortable. Just like I tried to walk away last night, when I could tell you were angry. I'm the ass."

She cupped his face. "You're not an ass."

Clearly wracked with guilt, he shook his head. "Should have told you then."

"I may not have understood. I was pretty dumb, Wyatt."

He snorted. "Not dumb. Young."

"And so were you." She grasped his shoulders and searched his gaze. "We aren't any longer, though."

"No. We aren't." He took a deep breath. "I don't only want you when it's easy or convenient. Please, believe me. This isn't easy. But I'm here."

Tatiana pressed her lips together. "That's promising, because I'm not sure if I could keep this up forever. I was trying so hard to keep everything smooth and happy for the past few months. Stay nice. Don't get mad. Don't get cranky." She sighed. "It was *exhausting*."

His hands stopped in midstroke on her back. "I was doing the same thing. I'd get bugged by something, but instead of talking to you about it, I'd shove it down."

"We can't live like that. I mean, we're doing this, right? Knowing that it won't always be smooth sailing and that we'll have problems?"

A hand curled over her ass. "We're doing this."

The spurt of pleasure at his cool announcement was not unexpected. "Then we have to figure out a way to learn to disagree. Or I'm going to stab you one day when you squeeze the toothpaste from the middle."

His fingertips slipped under the waistband of her panties. "That would not be pleasant."

"We should set some ground rules. I think you do well

with structure."

His chest vibrated beneath her. The tension that had gripped him had lessened, she could feel it. "I do."

"I won't yell at you anymore." She dropped a kiss on each cheek to punctuate the solemn vow. "I mean, I might, but I'll make a conscious effort not to. And if I start to turn shrill and it's bugging you, say the word and I'll put myself in timeout."

He raised a dark eyebrow. "Like a safe word for fighting?"

She seized on the concept. "Yes! Exactly like that." She thought about it. "The safe word is 'bacon.'"

"You pick the most bizarre safe words."

She kissed him, her tongue flicking against his teasingly.

He pulled back, solemn. "I'll work on not disappearing every time things get heated. Today was miserable."

"I'm going to safe word you if you try to run away," she threatened.

He hugged her closer. "Either that or take your top off, and I'm sure I'll stick around."

Tatiana narrowed her eyes. "Oh no." She propped herself up on his chest and shook her finger at him. "That's another avoidance technique we need to get rid of. No solving problems with sex."

"Aw, shucks, Ms. Tatiana," he whined. "Really?"

"Really." Her breath caught when he craned his neck up and captured her finger between his very white teeth.

Slowly, he sucked her finger into his mouth, his cheeks hollowing. He pulled back, his teeth scraping over the pad. "But angry fucking is kind of hot."

"I can still slap you during sex even if I'm not pissed at

you."

His eyes flashed, and his hands went to her hips. He dragged her down his body until she could feel his erection. "I think you can tell how I feel about that."

She grinned. Their problems weren't at all solved, but her chest felt curiously light. "Liked that, did you?"

"You hit like a girl. Which, during sex, is perfect."

His cock was notched into her slit. If it wasn't for her panties and his trousers, he'd be inside of her. "I'm not going to angry fuck you so you won't run away."

His sigh was deep. "Fine. I won't run away. You can even tie me up if I look like I'm going to bolt."

Aww, yeah. That brought some lovely images to mind. "Sold," she responded immediately. "Can I tie you up now?"

He laughed but stopped when she rubbed her pussy against him in a slow grind. His eyes darkened and dipped to her cleavage. "I told you. I'm not going anywhere."

"I don't want to argue with you. I want to fuck you."

"Trust me, I'll stay put even if you don't tie me up."

"Please?" She nibbled his ear, inhaling the scent of him, posh cologne and rugged manliness.

He attempted to resist, the tease. "That isn't how we usually do things."

"But I want it." She tugged at his earlobe with her teeth.

"You're making so many valid arguments today."

Tatiana sat up and tugged at his tie. "Get up."

"Are we done talking?"

"We're never done talking. I just think it's unfair when we don't let our bodies talk, too."

"We don't want to be unfair." He brought himself into

a seated position and waited for her to unknot and slip his tie free. She shuddered at the sound of the silk swishing against itself, knowing that restraint was approaching.

His restraint, not hers this time. Oh, the novelty.

"This is hot." She set the tie aside and unbuttoned his shirt.

He shrugged it off. "What is?"

She rubbed her hands over the crinkly sprinkling of dark hair, thrilled to find the rough brown points of his nipples hard and waiting for her. She bit at the nipples, sharp nips designed to echo the way he went at her own tits.

He hissed and pressed her head closer. "Harder."

She set her teeth and tugged at the nub, and he groaned.

Tatiana lifted her head. "I feel hopeful and reassured. About us. That's hot. I want to kiss you and lick you and fuck you. Seal the deal, you know?"

"Sealing deals is very important. Please, proceed." He wrapped his hand around her neck and brought her lips to his. The kiss was desperate and harsh, both of them needing an outlet for their adrenaline and cathartic relief.

Yeah. Their bodies really needed to have their own pow-wow.

He kissed and bit his way down her neck. She tilted her head to give him better access, whimpering when he nipped at the curve of her breast. He pushed her tits together and buried his face between them, rubbing his skin against her as if to absorb her scent.

He paused and drew away, his glittering black eyes matching the glitter of the small emerald he held beneath his teeth. She gave a half laugh. "How did that get in there?"

Wyatt had a fine appreciation for money, but he pulled

the stone out of his teeth and tossed it aside, all of his attention on her. "If you want me tied up, you better do it now, before I search you for more gems."

Gulping, she stood, his tie in her hand. "Take off your pants." She heard the sound of a zipper rasping open and fabric hitting the floor behind her as she headed to the dining room. She grasped a heavy chair—and, as an afterthought, a napkin from a place setting—and brought it back to where he stood, naked.

She paused, appreciating his hard muscles and thick, long cock. He wrapped his hand around it and stroked down, well aware he was taunting her.

Tatiana shook her head. "Sit down?" She cleared her throat. "I mean. Sit your ass down, Caine."

Smirking, he strolled over, waiting for her to unfurl the napkin and carefully cover the seat. "You don't have to be so fastidious."

Trying to recover her aplomb, she gave him a sultry look from beneath her lashes. "But things might get wet."

He licked his lips, his gaze dropping to the crotch of her panties. "Things are already getting wet."

"They are."

She walked around behind his chair and eyed the way his big hands looked crossed. When she tightened the silk around his thick wrists, her panties became damper.

"You're, uh, tying those a little tight."

"It wouldn't be fun if you could get out easily."

She came to stand in front of him and stroked his face with the back of her hand.

His eyes were roving all over her as if he didn't know where to look first. To congratulate him on his willingness to experiment, she pulled the thin triangles of her bra down so her nipples were fully exposed. "Sorry for the tan lines," she purred.

His cock jerked. "Which swimsuit did you wear today?"

"The pink one."

"I like the pink one. I'm booking the adults' pool here one night."

"No one would see us?"

"Unless you want them to." His watchful eyes caught her swift inhale. "Ah. You like that thought. It's the watching thing, right? You want them to watch me fuck you until you can't walk straight. You want them to see you beg for this cock."

She bit her lip, almost hard enough to taste blood. "Yes."

He cocked his head. "Do you want other people to touch you, too?"

Tatiana nodded, once. Her hands cradled her breasts, massaging the heavy weight. "Only if you want them to touch me."

"What if I wanted you to suck off another man while I fucked you?"

Her hand drifted down her belly, under the waistband of her panties. Her mouth felt swollen and empty. She licked her lips. "I would…I would be okay with that."

"And if it was a woman? If I told you to play with another woman's tits and pussy?"

Her belly contracted, and she toyed with her swollen clit, imagining it was another woman's. "I would be okay with that, too."

"You would do that for me?"

"No." Getting fucked while others watched. Wyatt, barking orders at her and another man. Or another woman. The security of knowing he wouldn't judge her for her appetites or for her fantasies. That he wouldn't push either of them past their limits. That he was the one she would be going home with at night. Hot. "I would do it for me."

His arms strained against the bonds, the muscles in his biceps becoming more defined. "Fuck yeah." The words were guttural, his entire focus on the fingering she was giving herself. The tight material of her panties constrained her. "God, woman…get over here and untie me, and I can get you off in two seconds."

He could, too. The man only had to look at her, and she could explode. Not that she would tell him that. She praised him plenty. Anymore, and he'd be impossible to live with.

Happiness bubbled up inside of her. Oh, she knew a happy ending wasn't guaranteed, but when was it ever? Their talk was a pretty good step in the right direction, this acknowledgment that they were both flawed, this sign that they could and would work together to fix their respective issues and compromise.

He groaned, the sound tortured. She stopped, panting. Tied-up Wyatt was pretty damn sexy. It suited the man, this air of helpless desperation. Almost as much as sexual dominance suited him.

Note: find your own version of neckties to keep handy. She'd like to see him bound by one of her studded belts. Or, better, a pretty pink scarf.

She dragged her hand out of her panties and up her stomach, leaving a trail of her own wetness. "Did you say something?"

"Get. Over. Here."

Enjoying the reversal of the power structure, she tipped her head and pretended to think about it. "Um. In a second."

She turned her back on his growled, "Tatiana," and walked to the bedroom. Halfway there, she paused, reached behind her, and undid her bra, letting the material fall to a heap on the carpet. Her panties got the same treatment. She was gratified at his hiss over the sight of her ass.

"You're earning yourself a paddling, sweetheart."

"Easy to threaten when your hands aren't free, darling."

Chapter Eleven

WYATT WAITED FOR Tatiana to return, a mass of wants and needs and lust and tenderness. He worked his wrists against the material binding him, not so much in an effort to get free, but out of impatient eagerness. Even if he'd wanted to, getting free might be a challenge. Surprisingly, Tatiana knew how to tie a knot. Wyatt tugged at the necktie harder, odd pride surging through him. *My woman can immobilize me.*

Sexy.

His dick was hard enough to pound nails, a direct contrast to the mush of his heart. He tilted his head back, breathing deep in an effort to dispel his arousal. All she had to do was walk back in here, and he'd go off.

His need was the only thing keeping him from grinning like a foolish sap. He felt young and optimistic, and all because they'd acknowledged a problem between them and resolved to work on it.

The more he thought about it, the more he knew his half-joking words to Esme were spot on. *Maybe I haven't been fighting right.*

Their problems hadn't been insurmountable; they'd made them that way, building anger and resentment. They wouldn't replay history. It wasn't the first time he'd comforted himself with those words, but it was the first time he'd really believed he had a handle on what that meant.

He bit the inside of his cheek when she walked out of the bedroom. Would there come a time when he got tired of seeing her naked? If so, he hoped he died on that day, because life wouldn't hold much meaning.

He stiffened as he registered the items in her hands. "What do you think you're going to do with those?"

Laughter filled her eyes. He'd ordered a few sex toys since they'd started dating. Nothing fancy. He had no aspirations to outfit a dungeon, and they were both creative enough anyway.

Tatiana set a vibrator and a small box down on the table. Wary, he watched as she unwrapped the new toy from its packaging. "It's something I picked up when I went to this shop last week."

He swallowed when the cock ring was revealed. "Jesus Christ. Between this and your work supplies, I'm filled with anxiety at the thought of your bags ever getting searched at security."

She gave him a cheeky grin. "Well, it takes their attention off the five-ounce bottle of shampoo I sneak in."

She inserted the batteries. The few experiences he'd had with sex toys had been with the woman's pleasure in mind. Never had he had one used on him. That was clearly about to change. "What's the vibrator for?" Because he might be using the safe word if it was going somewhere in him.

"For me."

Better.

She rolled the ring down his cock until it was nestled against the base. It was snug, but not too tight. More arousing than the nubby, silicone material was the look of adorable concentration on her face. Her brow furrowed as she got it on.

She glanced up. "How does it feel?"

"Not as good as you."

"You'll have me. If you're a good boy. Are you a good boy?" She stroked up his dick. Her words were light, a conscious reversal of his favorite question for her.

Answering should have made him feel subservient. Yet as lightly as she'd spoken, she was craving his response as much as he always craved hers, creating a feedback loop of power and control. "Yes."

She squeezed his cock tight, her hand like raspy silk. "I bought this one because it has a vibration mode." She traced her finger down the length of his cock, following the vein, and rested it on the base of the device. "Should we try it?"

Yes. No. Out of his element, he shook his head but remained silent.

A mocking smile graced her lips. "I think we should."

Her hand moved, and his head blew off.

Or that's how it felt. The vibrations would have been enough to get him off, but the ring also clenched tighter, staving off his release. He gave a helpless moan. Was she trying to kill him?

She appeared wholly unconcerned with his imminent death. Tatiana picked up the vibrator and rolled it over her nipples, making them harder and longer. Desperate to regain an upper hand in directing this show, he used the only tool he had. "How does that feel?"

"So good."

"Better than my hands? My mouth?"

"Never."

"Put it inside you. Let me see how you do it when I'm not around."

Watching Tatiana play with herself was high on his list of favorite pastimes, maybe a close second to fucking her. She moved the vibrator down over her belly and inserted the tip between the lips of her pussy. The rubber silicone disappeared inside her, those pretty pink lips snug and tight around it.

The fucking ridiculous ring she'd placed on him was an instrument of torture.

"Tatiana," he growled. "Come over here, and I can give you something better to put inside of you."

"Cocky."

"Exactly."

She gave a breathless laugh and tossed the vibrator aside. Instead of coming to him, though, she walked a few steps away to sink down onto the carpet in the middle of her jewelry supply.

She picked up the piece she'd been working on, the string of green beads, and glanced at him from beneath her lashes. "I think I do need something better inside of me."

No. No, she wouldn't. Would she?

"I was supposed to be finishing a commissioned necklace, you know. But no matter what I did, it was frustrating me." She gestured to the materials haphazardly scattered around. "So I figured I'd finish up this other project."

The piece she held was too short to be a necklace, too

long to be bracelet. Her fingers fondled the smooth, round beads. Wyatt gnashed his teeth. "Tatiana."

"I know you can buy sex jewelry, but that seemed silly when I could custom create it for myself. It's nothing fancy. No precious stones. But the beads are a nice size, I think."

"Don't you dare."

"Ooh. I love it when you use that warning tone. Maybe you should count to three." A naughty smile on her lips, she widened her legs until every pouting, pink inch of her pussy was visible to him, and leaned back against the window. She held the string up so the light shone through it, the color of each bead deepening. Tatiana blew on it to warm it and dragged it down her body. "One," she whispered.

His heart stuttered. He barely breathed. The first bead disappeared inside her.

Her stomach clenched. "Two."

They both moaned when she pressed the second bead inside her pussy. Sweat dripped into his eyes, and he shook his head to clear his vision. No, nothing could impede his view of this.

Her movements were sluggish as she reached for the third bead. Wyatt strained against the tie that bound him, his efforts to get free no longer half-hearted. Why the hell did he buy such good quality neckwear?

She paused, and he saw his opportunity. "It's too much, isn't it, baby?" he said, desperation making his words loud. "Your little cunt can't take it. Come over here. I'll make you feel so good."

Her red lips curved up. "You'll make me feel good anyway." She stroked the third bead between her fingers before pressing it to her pussy lips. "Three."

"Fuck. Me."

"Ohhh, God." She fell against the glass behind her and groaned again. "God."

He was out of persuasive words. "Tatiana. Please."

She licked her lips and gathered herself. Moving so she was on her hands and knees, she crawled over to him. She had to stop twice to catch her breath.

"They're moving inside of you, aren't they?" he rasped, unable to stop himself. "Rubbing against your walls. Driving you crazy."

Her only response was a whimper. Through his haze of need, he realized that the power balance was at that delicious point of equality. He might be bound, but she was as hungry as he was.

Good. That was how it should be.

Somehow she turned her submissive crawl into a slinky stalk, finally coming to her knees in front of him. She pressed a chaste kiss against the tip of his dick, rubbing it over the softness of her lips.

He couldn't bite back the words. "Please. Please."

She ran her tongue up and down the length of his cock.

He loved her hunger, like she couldn't get enough of him. But right now he needed something more.

"Please what?" she whispered, her breath on his cockhead making his eyes cross.

"Please. Fuck. Me."

She shifted and gasped. "But something's in the way."

"I'll get them out. Just untie me." God, the vibrations were killing him.

He shouted when she sucked his balls. No, that wasn't going to help him. "They feel so good," she murmured.

He struggled to follow the conversation. "I'll make you feel better. Always."

Her hands were shaking as bad as his. He ordered his muscles to remain still while she pulled the vibrating ring off him, the tightness destroying him.

"Hands," he prompted, when she stopped as if at a loss. Her heavy-lidded eyes blinked up at him. "Cock," he reminded her. He didn't blame her for her inattention. He was reduced to one-word orders, his entire being focused on getting his erection inside of her.

She nodded and stood, almost toppling over. Her skin flushed anew, and she used his shoulder to steady herself as she walked around the chair. He tried not to fidget while she worked on the knot that kept him helpless.

The second he felt the material give he exploded out of the chair, whirling around to haul her close. He picked her up easily, and she cried out, her head tipping back. "Don't come," he ordered her, brusque.

"BUT I HAVE to."

"You can in a second." He pressed his lips against hers hard. Their tongues tangled fiercely. He swallowed each sound she made as he walked the short distance to the bedroom, the beads moving and pressing deep.

He kicked the door closed behind them and dropped her to her feet. "Get on that bed."

She took three large steps back. "Make me."

That cruel smile was made more harsh by sharp arousal. "My pleasure."

She gave a very undignified yelp and spun around. It took him two long strides to catch her, pick her up as if she weighed nothing, and throw her on the bed face first. He was there a second later when she tried to roll over, planting a hand between her shoulders. "You've been toying with me."

She turned her head to speak, her ability to be coherent nearly impossible. Jesus, she'd outdone herself. Who knew that her jewelry supplies held such possibilities? "You liked it."

A spank landed on her buttock, close to her pussy, and she shrieked at the resulting jostling. He did it again, the bastard, just to hear her cry out again. "I'm buying these. I want more. Beads in every color and size." Another spank, even closer to her pussy. He grabbed her ankle and arranged her legs so she was more accessible. "Make you wear them all day, you fucking tease." The next slap landed on her pussy.

All she could do was squeal her appreciation for that plan.

Wyatt turned her over, his six feet of muscle looming in the darkness, the curtained-off room the perfect cocoon of debauchery. She could only lie there and twitch from the aftershocks.

He placed his hand on her lower belly. "Let's make sure they're all there. I want my money's worth. Three, right?" His other hand dipped between her legs, unerringly finding her slit. With his thumb and forefinger, he grasped the end of the chain, and tugged. "One."

She grasped the sheets in tight fists. "Oh, oh, oh."

"Don't come," he reminded her, more in control of his body now that he could control hers.

His directive was ridiculous and impossible. She shook

her head, frantic, but he ignored her to slip his long finger into her, alongside the hardness of the chain. He found the second bead and prodded at it, rubbing it against her too-sensitive inner walls. "Two."

Her pussy clenched on the bead as he eased it free. She was making animal-like sounds, her legs splayed wide open, but she couldn't care less how she appeared.

She panted, staring up at the ceiling but seeing nothing. "Please."

"Not yet. One more, I think. I want to make sure I get all three. You've modeled them so nicely."

Her back arched as he pulled the last bead out. "Three," he said softly. Ever so slowly, he dragged the string up her mound to rest over her swollen clitoris. "Now." He pressed and rubbed.

She cried out in relief and pleasure. Her muscles tightened and released as the orgasm exploded through her whole body.

Tatiana may have blacked out—she wasn't sure. When she was alert again, she found Wyatt standing by the bed in between her splayed legs, ripping open a condom.

She didn't need to hesitate or think about her words. This moment felt right. "My birth control is effective now. So if you want..." She stopped speaking when the condom went sailing through the air. Okay then.

Grasping her by the waist, Wyatt shoved her up farther on the bed. "If I want?" he muttered. "Hell. Yes. I fucking want. I've been counting down the minutes since we went to go get those blood tests."

It had been a sterile and practical step, but that afternoon at the lab had been one of the more romantic moments of Tatiana's life.

His throat worked as he climbed on top of her. She pressed her hands over his shoulders, amazed to find him shaking. "You waited 'til now to tell me this?" He fitted himself to the entrance of her pussy, and pushed. There was a tug of resistance, a little stretch as he forged inside. He didn't give her time to wait, simply surged in, filling the space that always yearned for him.

They both stopped and groaned. "I wanted the time to be perfect," she managed.

"Perfect." His hands fisted on either side of her head. "God, I love fucking you bare. Do you like it?"

A nod.

"Say it."

"I love it when you fuck me bare."

"And do you want me to fill you with my come?"

He pulled out and slammed back in, not at all careful of her smaller size. The best way to fuck.

She gave a strangled cry. "I want you to fill me with your come."

"Fuck, yeah. I'll fill you right up."

"Yes." She scratched her nails down his back, harder when he purred and leaned in to her touch, hard enough to draw blood.

"Love it. Love it when you claw me."

He was close, she could tell by the drunken pleasure on his face and the way his hips sped up, the uncoordinated motions growing jerkier and more haphazard. She gave him some resistance, pushing against him, and sure enough, that only made him more wild. He snarled and grabbed her hands, pinning them above her head as he rutted on her body.

That first orgasm had rung her out, so she hadn't planned on another. But the intense look he wore, the feel of his hot, thick, naked cock inside her—it was too much. She came on him, and it spurred him into climaxing. One thrust, a second, and he held himself still, so deep inside her it triggered a delicious sort of pain.

He collapsed on top of her, their sweat mingling together. Below, their fluids mixed together in a different way. Unexpected tears stung her eyes.

It took him barely a second to register her tears, and despite what was his certain exhaustion, he drew up on his elbows to kiss them away. "You okay?"

She sniffed. "Nostalgia. We haven't been together like this since…"

"I know." He rested his forehead against hers and smiled. "I like it."

"I bet you do."

"Not because I don't have to wear a condom. I never minded wearing one. I'd rather be careful than fuck a woman without." He kissed her lips, the meeting slow and soft and restful. "Because it's you I'm not wearing one with. That's… It means something. Doesn't it?"

"Yes."

He searched her gaze. "No more tears."

The order was autocratic and arrogant. But since the underlying tenderness was more than apparent, Tatiana let it go. "Okay."

He gave a satisfied smile and kissed her forehead. "Now." He stretched over her head and brought his hand back to show her the string of beads he held. "I love this new line of yours. Let's talk about a price. I'll warn you, don't think you can cheat me. I'm well aware of where these have been."

Chapter Twelve

"I HATE IT when you leave the toilet seat up."

"That's not a legitimate gripe. Every woman hates that."

"I don't care what every woman hates. I care what I hate."

Wyatt dropped a kiss on the top of her head. "Fine, fine."

Tatiana hid her smile and snuggled closer, his chest the perfect pillow for her head. The curtains were still closed, but weak sunlight was peeking through the cracks. "Airing grievances is fun."

"You know, Esme said fighting could be fun, and I laughed at her." His hand stroked over her arm.

"What do you think now?"

"I think I'm in a good mood, so maybe it's got something going for it. And you make everything fun."

They lay in companionable silence. Sleep hadn't been something they'd done much of during the night, but Tatiana felt recharged and refreshed. Between bouts of sex, they'd talked. Some of it silly, some of it serious.

All of it made her optimistic for the future. Optimistic and horny. Because apparently, hopefulness was some sort of weird aphrodisiac for her.

"Tatiana." Wyatt's voice was hushed.

"Yes?"

He hesitated. "I didn't like being surprised by your parents."

She stirred, ready to apologize anew, but he shushed her. "Let me finish. I didn't like it, but I get why you did it."

"You do?"

"Yeah. I actually realized yesterday that I was a massive dick."

She craned her neck up so she could see him. "You aren't a dick."

"I am. I would have told you this last night, but you were lying there and then we talked and then the beads." He shrugged, as if this sentence made sense.

It did. "Yes. I know. Always the beads."

His face remained serious. "I hate that I make you feel so defensive about your family."

"I love them."

"I know. And I'm happy you have them. I'm happy they love you."

Tatiana rubbed his belly, the crisp hairs tickling her fingers. "I'm not asking you to adore them. But it would be nice if you wouldn't avoid them like the plague. Or wince when I talk about them. Or act like seeing them is some ordeal that you have to suffer through. It's getting hard to keep my world with you and my world with them separate."

"Yes. We're together too much now."

"My mom already apologized." She grimaced. "I can't

speak for my dad. But take some heart in knowing that he's been a jerk to every guy I've ever dated."

"I don't blame him. You're too special not to be protected."

She tightened her arm around him, eager to get things off her chest now that he'd brought the topic up. "You don't have to be defensive or protective of me around them. You should all be on the same side—mine. If they say something out of line, trust me to stand up for myself. They'll get over being annoyed at me, but it's harder to forgive an outsider who suddenly comes in and tells them they're doing it wrong."

His lashes dipped. "Fair enough. I promise I'll make more of an effort."

He sounded so grimly determined, Tatiana had to smile. "It doesn't have to be right this second."

"No. No, but maybe we should…invite them to brunch."

Aw. Wyatt didn't even sound like he was gargling that much glass at the concept of breaking bread with her dad. She paused, hating to ruin the moment. "They're actually busy today. Ron is dragging out his barbecue grill in their honor."

He exhaled. There was a weighty moment of silence before he spoke. "Okay. I guess we're going to a barbecue, huh?"

She hadn't expected that. "No. Maybe it's too soon…"

"Tatiana, come on. I'm not some child. Let's get this over—" He stopped. "Sorry. Rephrase. Let me show you I can be better."

His words held only sincerity. How could she resist?

Her smile came from the depths of her soul. "Okay."

"What time does this thing start?"

Tatiana sighed, already missing the warmth of the bed. "If I tell you, you're going to whine about how we're already late."

He slapped her on her behind. "Then get up."

Tatiana took a second to deliver a tight hug. "Thank you. I appreciate it."

"Do you want to appreciate it with me naked?"

She considered that. "That'll make us late."

"Then maybe not right now. Go get dressed so I can try to charm the pants off your family." He cringed. "Never mind. I still have to forget that I've heard your mother's name and toplessness in the same sentence."

She chuckled and clambered out of the bed, headed for the bathroom.

"I expect tons of appreciation after we get home," he called out.

THEY ARRIVED BEFORE her parents did. Wyatt parked his relatively humble Mercedes behind her brother's car. Tatiana hadn't been surprised that he'd driven them, instead of enlisting Sal. A chauffeur would only make him stand out in her family.

She laid her hand on his thigh when he would have moved to exit. He wore jeans and a soft, faded shirt that may have once been blue but was now a shade of grey. She'd seen him in casual clothes before, but usually when he was visiting her. Here, he was too careful of his image to fully relax in something the old Wyatt would have easily worn. "It'll be okay. Really, be yourself."

He gave her a tight half-smile. "Sure."

She linked hands with him as they walked around the side of the house, into the gated backyard.

It was family only today—her bizarre, mixed family, consisting of a half-brother she'd only discovered a few years ago, his wife, his son, his in-laws and their children, and her parents. Tatiana knew her parents would be in heaven. They would have loved a large family, but it hadn't been meant to be.

They had, however, happily adopted Ron and his brood into their hearts. Her brother looked so much like her, they were wired to love him. For his part, Ron was happy to accept extra parenting, particularly since their birth mother hadn't spared him much attention either.

Peter, her baby nephew, was the first to discover her and Wyatt's presence. He toddled over on unsteady legs and came to clutch her calves. Not much of a cuddler, he quickly backed away. She was a standard presence to him, but Wyatt was not, so obviously the kid was fascinated. Standing a foot or two away, he raised his hands in the universal sign to be picked up.

Wyatt cast her a confused glance. "What does it want?"

Tatiana rolled her eyes. "Pro tip for you, Caine. Kids are he or she, but rarely it."

He looked down at the baby. "Pete, right? So it's a boy. Why is it wearing pink pants?"

"Peter's parents believe that children shouldn't be limited to certain colors because of their gender."

"Oh. They're those kind of people, huh?"

"Wyatt."

"Yeah, yeah. I know." He crouched down and picked up

Peter, holding him gingerly like one might a bomb. He glanced over when he heard her stifled giggle. "Quit laughing. It's not like you're any more used to children than I am."

That was true. She hadn't been around a ton of them, and so far, at least, no intense maternal craving had hit her ovaries. If it happened at some point far down the road, that would be fine, but at the moment a kid wasn't really in her cards.

Though…Tatiana studied Wyatt as he endured Peter's unintelligible babbling and curiosity. There was something rather sexy about a large man holding a baby.

"Hey…guys." Caitlin addressed her cheerful greeting to her, but her shocked eyes were riveted on Wyatt.

"Hey." She gave her sister-in-law a hug and took a moment to whisper in his ear. "Be cool, please."

She felt the change in Caitlin's demeanor right away. She loved the other woman to pieces, especially for the way her pragmatic calmness was a solid counterpoint to her brother's dreaminess.

Caitlin stepped back, a determined smile on her face. "Mr. Caine, how great to see you."

"Please, call me Wyatt." Only Peter was holding his lip so it came out more as, "Pwease, wall we Wyeff."

Caitlin winced and rescued Wyatt from Peter. "Sorry. Petey's always intrigued by a new face."

"That's fine. Handsome boy you have there."

Easily seduced by praise for her son, Caitlin beamed. "He is, isn't he? Well, come on back, guys. Burgers are on the grill, and there's some cold beer in the cooler."

"I hope it's okay that I came," Wyatt said to Caitlin, as

they followed her across the yard to where Ron was manning the grill. "I know you may not have been expecting me."

"Only because we know how busy you are. We knew you'd come if you could." Caitlin was a pretty decent liar when she needed to be, Tatiana thought.

"I'm reducing my workload. I'll be able to socialize with Tatiana—and her family—more now."

Caitlin's smile reached her eyes this time. "Hey, that's awesome."

Ron spotted them as they approached, and he froze. Caitlin hoisted her son higher on her hip. "Ron, look who's here."

"So I see." He took the hand Wyatt held out. "Mr. Caine."

"Wyatt."

Ron's eyes ping-ponged between her and Wyatt. "Wyatt. How, um, cool that you came."

Caitlin curled her hand around Tatiana's arm. "Why don't I show you where to put that pasta salad, honey?"

Tatiana blinked down at the forgotten container they'd picked up at the store on the way to the barbecue. "Oh, it can wait."

Caitlin's tug became stronger. "But my mother hasn't seen you in forever."

And more urgently, Caitlin wanted to grill her, Tatiana assumed. No surprise, since Wyatt's lack of interest in her family had hardly been subtle.

"Go on." Wyatt gave her a small nod.

She cast him a worried glance, but gave in to Caitlin. If she wanted him to get along with her family, she supposed she had to allow him some time with them. "Oh. Sure."

THERE WAS A strained silence between him and Ron after the women walked away. Wyatt straightened, searching for something to say. God knew they couldn't talk about their relationship pre-Tatiana. Wyatt wasn't the most astute person, but he knew embezzlement wasn't a good topic for a Saturday barbecue.

It was too bad he had some sort of weird history with every member of Tatiana's family. His luck was atrocious sometimes.

"You have a nice house," he finally said. The place was modestly sized, but the yard was large. Good for a kid and a dog.

"Thanks. Got it for a steal as a foreclosure." Ron wrinkled his nose. "A while ago. Before uh—Your money wasn't spent on this house."

"Oh. Good." Wyatt cleared his throat. "That's good."

They eyed each other for another long moment. "Do you want a beer?" Ron asked.

Boy, did he. He reached into the cooler Ron gestured to and withdrew a bottle, using his shirt to twist the top off. He paused when he noted Ron watching him with fascination.

The boy glanced away. "Uh. Sorry. It's like seeing a teacher outside of school, you know? Tatiana said you weren't always rich, but I didn't think you wore anything but a suit or drank anything but fancy wines."

"My Armani was at the cleaners," he replied dryly. "And for the record, my favorite drink when Tatiana and I were young was Natty Ice. And it wasn't for the taste."

The younger man's face split into an affable grin. As far as Wyatt could tell from observing Ron as an employee and from their few run-ins, that was Ron's default mode—cheerful, happy. Like a Labrador.

Wyatt didn't fully understand that. He wasn't exactly a dour person, but the only time he felt truly happy was when he was with Tatiana.

And he still wasn't so…openly jovial.

"This is weird, huh?" Ron scratched his arm.

Oddly enough, a flush rose up the back of Wyatt's neck, though he wasn't the one who had stolen tens of thousands of dollars. He took a gulp of his beer. "Yeah."

"Had to meet up sometime, though." Ron flipped a burger. "Tatiana talks about you all the time."

He looked across the backyard at where Tatiana was speaking to a frail, elderly woman. "Does she?"

"Sure. It's obvious you're serious about each other. Or heading that way." Ron took a deep breath, and regarded him steadily. "So it's a good thing we're breaking the ice sooner than later. I said it to you over the phone but didn't have the opportunity to say it to your face—what I did was stupid and foolhardy and I'm sorry. I was desperate."

Desperate enough to embezzle funds from him. Wyatt fought back the instinctive aggression that surged through him. He hated the reminder that he'd been bested by a baby-faced card dealer. The money was secondary. The hit to his ego? Epic.

Call him a territorial prick, but no one *stole* from him.

Ron nodded at the woman talking to Tatiana. "My mother-in-law. Cancer. Bad enough, but it ate her life savings. Mine and Caitlin's, too."

Wyatt nodded. "Tatiana told me." He hadn't cared much about the sob story. He'd already decided to cut the kid a break because of his relationship with Tatiana. After letting him sweat, of course.

"Yeah. Not making excuses. There were other options. Could have figured something out. I've always been someone who leaps first. Stupidly, sometimes."

"We all do stupid things." The words were meant to humor, but they emerged sincere. The elderly woman drew his gaze back. He'd never stolen, sure, but had he ever had that sort of motivation? If Tatiana had been in a position where she desperately needed money, could he have taken it from another?

Maybe. At the least, he might have been tempted.

"Yeah, but mine could have really screwed my family's future." Ron shook his head. "I'd react differently today."

Wyatt tucked his hands into his pockets. "Good."

"Yeah."

"You have a new job, now, right?"

"Yes. Did Tatiana tell you?"

No. He had someone keep tabs on the guy. Since Wyatt didn't think spying on your girlfriend's family was socially acceptable, he made a noncommittal response.

Ron shot him a sideways glance. "The place isn't as nice as yours."

Wyatt inclined his head. "Few are."

"But it's not bad. Pay's decent, and I do love working at casinos. The excitement, you know? Something's always going on."

He did know. Wyatt took another sip of beer, well aware that his next words were stupid and rash. "If you decide you want to come back to Quest, and there's an opening, you're welcome to apply."

Ron's jaw dropped open. "What?"

"You heard me."

"Is this...? Are you making this offer because you're dating my sister?"

"Yes." Wyatt shrugged when Ron frowned. "Does that bother you?"

"I don't want any favors because I'm related to your girlfriend."

"Don't be stupid. All of my decisions, from the second I traced the money to you, were influenced by the fact that you're related to her. Favoritism is the only reason you aren't in jail right now. It's a little late to get riled up about it."

Ron opened his mouth, but stopped. He shook his head. "But you didn't know she and I were related when you traced the money to me."

Wyatt paused mid-sip. Oh, shit.

Green eyes, so like Tatiana's, sharpened, and Wyatt glimpsed the intelligence the younger man hid behind his jocular attitude. "Am I missing something?"

Wyatt lowered his beer. "I thought Tatiana told you."

"Told me what?"

"Ah." He glanced over Ron's head, but Tatiana had her back to him. He'd known when Caitlin had dragged her away that the other woman probably wanted to gossip about him, and maybe give him and Ron a chance to break the ice privately, but weren't they done yet? Tatiana needed to get back here now.

"Hey. Told me what?"

Goddamn. "I knew you were related for a while before you stole from me," he said grudgingly.

"For a while? How long is a while?"

Wyatt shifted his weight. "From when I sent you that anonymous packet containing information about Tatiana."

Silence greeted him. "That..." Ron wheezed. "That was you?"

"Yes." Really, had the guy never wondered? Had someone delivered a long-last sister to him, Wyatt would have dug around.

"But...why...? How...?"

"Look, it's no big deal. You can ask your sister for details if you want." And then Wyatt wouldn't have to talk about it.

"Why didn't she tell me?"

Wyatt lifted his shoulders. "I don't know. I assumed she had."

"Can I...can I hug you?"

"What? No." He stared at the other man. "*No.*"

A big grin split Ron's face. "Aren't a hugger, huh?"

"No. No, I am not."

Ron nodded, his smile not faltering. "I'm going to go hug my sister, then. I want to hear more about this, and something tells me you won't tell me much. Mind watching the grill?"

"Sure."

"And I'll let you know about that job. If I do come back to work for you, I'll work my ass off, that's for sure." Ron held his hand out.

Wyatt accepted it, pleased to find the younger man's grip firm. "I wouldn't expect anything less."

"In the meantime, I think it's good for us to get to know each other. I'm perfectly happy to have you over any time to grab a beer, with or without Tatiana. I don't know if we have a ton in common, but I have no objection to trying to be friends."

Used to subterfuge in his business dealings, Wyatt paused, searching for an ulterior motive, but only found guileless honesty in Ron's face. "Thanks."

"Unless you hurt my sister, of course." Still grinning, Ron tightened his hand, using it to pull Wyatt forward. For a brief second, Wyatt wondered if the other man *was* going to hug him.

Instead, Ron slapped him on the back. He was shorter than Wyatt, but bulkier.

So Wyatt felt that slap.

Ron dropped his voice. "Tatiana means a lot to me. So I hope you understand that this brotherly threat to treat her well is both expected and sincere."

That was a warning any man could respect. Wyatt nodded. "Got it."

"Good." Affable grin back in place, Ron handed him his tongs. "Be back in a few. Don't let the meat burn."

Wyatt looked from the tongs to the meat. He hadn't manned a grill in a long time, but he hoped it was one of those masculine skills that one never quite forgot. Like changing a tire, or unfastening a bra. Cautious, he poked at one of the patties.

"Why, hello, Wyatt."

Wyatt dropped the meat. Janet and Nikolai stood at his elbow. Nikolai's scowl wasn't out of the ordinary. Janet had a reserved smile pasted on, that ever present tinge of worry darkening her eyes.

What will you do to her?

No. He yanked himself back from his instinctual defensive response, substituting reason for emotion. Why shouldn't Janet be concerned about whether he would hurt her baby? He didn't know how much Tatiana had told her about their difficulties, but Janet wasn't a stupid woman. She'd probably witnessed the aftermath of their last relationship. He knew their breakup hadn't been any easier on Tatiana.

He wasn't a kid, to be miffed or insulted by her justified caution. A woman's mother had the right to fret over her daughter. It was Wyatt's right to do his best to win her over. He could do that. Forget the past. Focus on the present. "Hello."

"Are you in charge of the grill?"

Charm them. He relaxed his stance, feeling his way. "Indeed I am. I think Ron's planning to pin it on me if anyone gets sick."

Janet's smile widened. "He's slick, that one."

"You don't have to tell me."

"Oh." She blinked. "Was that a dig at how he embezzled money from you?"

The loud question had to have been heard all over the yard. Wyatt bit his cheek. "Well, he did embezzle a lot of money. But I'd say it was more a good-natured tease."

"That's acceptable. It's wonderful that you're here, isn't it, Nikolai?"

The larger man eyed Wyatt. "Yes." His words said one thing. The lasers his eyes were shooting at him said another.

Janet stepped closer to Wyatt, and shocked him by pulling him into an embrace.

Was he wearing a sign begging for hugs today?

After a brief hesitation, he realized that this wasn't…terrible. And it wasn't unfamiliar, either. Janet had hugged him a time or two when he was younger. Since his mother had died when he was ten and his father was, well, his father, parental affection had been foreign to him then. It had been easier to build resentment against perceived slights than to enjoy and crave such a thing.

Maternal kindness wasn't quite as bizarre to him now. He accepted and even appreciated it when it came from Esme and her family. He'd changed. And that was good.

Unsure of where to put his hands, he awkwardly patted her back. "Thanks. It's nice to see you again."

She was tall enough that she didn't have to lean up to whisper in his ear. "You're a good boy, Wyatt. You always have been. You keep making my baby smile, and we'll be solid, you and I."

That note of amusement made her sound so much like Tatiana, Wyatt did a double take. He gave her a cautious squeeze, amazed that it had been so simple. "Thank you." She thought he was a good boy? She always had?

Well.

She pulled back and smiled. "Nikolai. Remember your promise." She looked over his shoulder, raised her hand in greeting, and called Tatiana's name.

For a few seconds, he and Nikolai stared at each other. *This is like a gauntlet. With the meanest, angriest bastard at the end.* "My wife and daughter yelled at me. Because of you," Nikolai finally said, his voice accusing.

Measure your opponents. Ron respected kindness. Janet,

her daughter's happiness. Nikolai…

Strength.

Call it manipulation, but Wyatt considered his ability to read people a necessary skill. He dipped his head and hardened his own tone. "Tatiana and I fought. Because of you."

"My wife called me a belligerent fool."

"Tatiana said I was an asshole." He actually didn't remember if Tatiana had called him that, exactly, but it sounded right.

Nikolai grunted. "You are," he muttered. "I don't like you. I never did."

"I know."

They glared at each other.

"Why are you here?" Nikolai asked.

"Because you're important to Tatiana. And she's important to me."

"Words."

"You doubt me? I'm certainly not here to see your pretty face."

Nikolai sneered. "You will hurt her."

"Never." His response was instant.

"You hurt her last time."

He glanced Tatiana's way in time to see her brushing a lock of honey-blonde hair out of her eyes. His heart clenched. "Losing her was like losing my right hand," he replied quietly. "It won't happen again."

"Turn the burgers."

Jolted, Wyatt looked down at the grill and flipped the patties.

"Janet said you must be smart. To have become so successful in such a short time."

"I'm not stupid."

"Show me. Because if you do hurt her…I know people." Nikolai tapped the side of his nose with a menacing smirk. "And I will assume you are very stupid."

Wyatt decided not to tell Nikolai that an alleged Russian Mafioso often patronized his establishment. "I understand."

Nikolai grunted. "You are destroying that meat. Even the vegan can see this."

Wyatt gritted his teeth and flipped the burger.

"Better. You do not use a grill much when you are busy running a den of sin?"

Wyatt cast him a glance. "Glass houses, Nikolai. Tatiana mentioned you like to gamble."

"Recreationally. Not as a profession."

"Let me guess. Blackjack is your game."

Nikolai snorted. "Tatiana told you that too?"

"No. You seem the type. Quick, constant thrill. You have a mathematical mind, so you count the cards, which ups your probability of success. You like winning. Still, you'd do low stakes. Not because you're worried about losing the money, but because Janet scolds you." Wyatt smiled when Nikolai glowered. "I'm really smart."

"Lucky."

"That too. And it's not a den of sin." No, it totally was, but Nikolai didn't need to know that. "It's an honest business."

"I suppose it pays better than the construction and waiter jobs you used to do."

Call him crazy, but Wyatt was almost starting to enjoy

himself. "Those were honest jobs, too."

"Hmph."

"Tell me something: are you going to be this difficult whenever we run into each other?"

"It depends. Do we have to run into each other often?"

"As much as Tatiana wants."

Nikolai didn't speak for a long moment. When he did, his voice was gruff and low. "Do not screw things up, boy. Very rarely does any man get a second chance."

"I know."

Nikolai cleared his throat. "Good." He snatched the tongs out of Wyatt's hands. "Now go sit with the women. I will handle this."

Chapter Thirteen

ENGLISH EXPERTS WOULD probably argue that the words meant the same thing, but in Tatiana's brain, there was a difference between being happy and being content. She'd been happy for the past few months with Wyatt, at times deliriously happy. Too happy, she'd thought, but it wasn't that. There was no such thing as too happy.

There was such a thing as too anxious. The anxiety over their chances of success, over waiting for the other shoe to drop, had made it impossible to enjoy that happiness. Constantly worrying was, as she'd told Wyatt, exhausting. What would happen when the bubble finally burst? When life threw a roadblock in their path?

They'd survive, bitches. That's what.

She hadn't felt content until today. Not just happy, but secure in their relationship.

Contentment trumped happiness.

Sleepy from her good mood and full belly, Tatiana turned her head so she could see Wyatt's profile. "Was it terrible?"

Wyatt gave a faint smile, his attention on the road. "Not

as bad as I thought it would be, no."

She rested her hand on his leg. "My family loves you."

"I feel like I've been asking you this a lot lately, so don't take it the wrong way, but are you drunk?"

Tatiana chuckled. "Nope."

"Your dad asked me if I'd written you into my will yet." He cast her a sardonic glance. "FYI. If and when I do, I'm tying that bequest up so he won't have any extra motivation to hasten my demise."

"Eh. You can give my share to a groundhog sanctuary or something. I don't need it."

His face softened and he shook his head, his expression both fond and exasperated. "I don't think you still have any idea how much money I have."

No, she did. Beyond the fact that she couldn't care less about having funds beyond a level that made her comfortable, the thought of Wyatt dying made her too upset to give two fucks about what she'd get out of it. She'd feel the same even if they weren't together. "I don't want to talk about this," she answered, making a conscious effort to modulate the sharpness of her tone.

"Okay." His voice was gentle.

Tatiana sniffed, eager to get back to their playful banter. "Anyway, he only threatens to kill people he likes."

"If you say so."

"Remember, it's a good sign that he didn't pop a blood vessel when my mom invited you to their anniversary party."

"No, he only growled when I accepted."

Tatiana stretched, feeling like a lazy cat. "Because he likes you."

He covered her hand with his. "Happy?"

She smiled. "Better. Content."

He eyed her. "Good."

"Thank you."

"For being civil?"

"For trying so hard to make this work."

He squeezed her hand. "Don't thank me. It's what I want."

She stuck her tongue out at him. "I'll thank you if I want to."

Wyatt gave a great sigh. "Fine, if you insist. You should probably get down on your knees."

"If that's how you want me to deliver my appreciation."

"Always." His hand tightened on hers when she tried to slide it up to his crotch. "Maybe not when I'm driving."

"Man. I will feel so appreciative next month when you come with me to that anniversary party." She paused. "We could stay with my parents."

"Uh, I'm not sure if—that is, isn't that nice B&B still there, on Delaware? You used to always talk about how you wanted to go there."

She bit her cheek at the note of desperation in his words. Poor Wyatt. He was trying so hard. "You don't want to stay under my dad's roof with me, Wyatt? It's not like it would be awkward, since we'd be in separate beds, at opposite ends of the house." She dropped her voice to a whisper. "Though you could sneak into my room, once everyone's asleep."

"Your father would stand outside your bedroom with a machete."

"You could always go by way of the window. Like you

used to. Remember that trellis?" God bless that trellis. Really, why on earth would you put one of those things next to your teenage daughter's window? Her parents had practically been begging for her to sneak her sexy boyfriend in. "Though you're bigger now. It may not hold up."

His thigh tensed beneath her hand. "Wait. Whoa. Does your bedroom look the same?"

She pretended to think about that. "Oh, gosh darn. I think it does. You mean the white canopy bed and ruffled comforter?"

Wyatt grunted. "Fuck. And the dainty little furniture?"

She nodded. "And that big mirror on top of my dresser. The one that lets you see the bed."

He shuddered. "We're staying with your parents."

"And you'll crawl in my window?"

"Hell, yes." He removed her hand from his thigh and grasped the wheel. "Quit talking. Don't move. I need to get us home."

She inched her skirt higher up her thighs. "Can I touch myself?"

Wyatt shot her a glance. Since he didn't protest, she snaked the material up the rest of the way, revealing her thong. "I've been going crazy," she murmured.

"Don't. Talk."

Tatiana spread her legs as wide as she could. "You don't want to know why I've been going crazy?"

His jaw was tight, eyes fixed firmly ahead of him. "Tatiana."

She ignored the warning in his voice and dipped her fingers to her pussy. Stroked them in, back out. Held her hand out to him.

He looked. Looked again. Gave a groan. "Jesus."

She rolled the beads between her fingers. "You bought them. Thought you'd want to make sure they don't go to waste."

Wyatt plucked the string from her hand, shifted, and tucked it into his pocket. "Keep that dress up. But don't touch yourself anymore."

"You don't want me ready?"

"I don't want you ahead of me." He cranked the A/C up, placed his hand, wet from the beads, on her thigh, and pressed her legs wider. "There we go. Keep those pretty legs open."

The air hit her overheated flesh, and she moaned, tilting her head back. "Finger me."

"No. Wait."

"How much longer?"

When she shifted her legs, he surprised her with a slap on her upper thigh. "Don't move. Soon. Now, hush, or I'll slow this car down."

No, he couldn't slow the car. Not when she was getting revved up.

They didn't speak for the next five minutes, Wyatt hyper-focused on his driving, breaking a few laws to get them back to Quest. Despite his order, she flipped her skirt down when they came within its vicinity.

He parked in front, and Tatiana got out, murmuring her thanks to the valet who held her car door open. Wyatt tossed the man the keys and grasped her hand, leading her through the front door and lobby.

"I have never been so annoyed to live here," he muttered, as he had to force a smile for an employee.

She stifled a laugh. "We could have gone around back."

"I couldn't drive anymore."

They rode the elevator up, both of them twitchy. When they disembarked on the top floor, Tatiana gave a yearning glance at the wall where he'd oh-so-deliciously ravished her a couple of nights ago.

Wyatt noticed her regard. "They fixed the cameras."

She looked at him, appalled. "Why would you go and do something like that?"

"Trust me," he replied grimly. "At the moment, I have no idea."

It took a second for him to open the door, but it was more than she wanted to wait. He grasped her around the waist, yanked her in, and pinned her against the back of the door. Tilting her head back, he sucked her neck hard. "I love living here, but I'm starting to note definite disadvantages."

"Not being able to fuck in a hallway is not something most people consider when figuring out where they should live."

"I'd consider it. Someday, we'll live somewhere else. A house, maybe. And I'm going to fuck you in every hallway."

"No cameras?"

"Maybe cameras. But I'll be the only one who sees that footage." They kissed, their mouths hungry. He angled her head, stroking deeper, one hand dropping to her ass and squeezing through her dress.

The words he'd spoken reverberated in her head. Perhaps they'd been a casual throwaway statement, but unless she asked, she'd obsess over them forever. When they broke apart, Tatiana tugged at the bottom of his shirt. "So *we're* going to have a house?"

He yanked at the shirt, bringing it off over his head, revealing his leanly muscled chest. "I assume so."

Tatiana raised an eyebrow and scraped her nails down his chest. "You can't assume something like that."

"Sure I can. Baby, you're nuts about me." He unbuttoned and unzipped his jeans, shoving his boxer briefs off with them, revealing his long, hard cock and rock-solid thighs. "You're going to move in with me. You won't be able to help yourself."

"Is that right?" Oh, the arrogance on this man. She'd take him to task more seriously when she could concentrate better on the conversation. It was difficult when there was so much cock and muscle to look at. Bless him and his early morning workout routine.

"Like you can't help how wet you get when I look at you." He grabbed her skirt and tugged at it, letting it drop to the floor. Her panties went next, and she was lifted up easily. He stepped forward, his penis rubbing against her thigh. His stubble scraped her cheek when he went for her mouth. "Like you can't help how you squeal when I fuck you with this big, thick cock."

She did squeal when he entered, though she tried to stifle it. No need to inflate his ego. He was already inflated. All over.

"See?" he whispered. "Some things are a given."

She was so wet, he slid in and out of her without resistance. She grabbed his shoulders and wrapped her legs more firmly around his waist. His heavy arms and body held her in place while he fucked her slow and steady.

She panted. "I don't want you thinking I'm easy."

"No." He leaned down and bit her nipples through her shirt and bra. "You never have been. Oh, Jesus, that's it. Squeeze me."

She tightened her inner muscles, liking the helpless groan he gave. Yeah, some things were a given.

"So tight. Your pussy's begging me, isn't it?"

It was. It would always need him, slut that it was. "Yes."

"Yeah." He gave her long, hard thrusts, his face harsh. He pressed her back against the door, angling his body so his shaft rubbed against her clit. "You feel perfect like this. Naked. Hot. You're so wet."

"Mmm." She scratched her fingernails over his scalp, loving the way he stretched into her touch. "We'll save a fortune on condoms."

"Your frugality is sexy."

Tatiana clenched her pussy, the small revenge easy. "Shut up and fuck me."

He uttered a choked laugh and started hammering into her. "Like that?"

"Yes."

"Huh?"

"Yes!"

"Yeah. I'll pound you through the door." He scraped his teeth up her neck. "Keep milking my cock with that tight cunt. I'll fill you up. Make you drip with my come."

Her mind shorted out, everything reduced to the shove of his big cock inside of her, her vocabulary shrinking to filthy words of praise and desire, words like *faster, harder, use me, fuck me.*

"God," he muttered, right when she was close, so close. "Fuck, yeah." He licked his fingers and brought them between her legs, massaging her clit while he drilled her.

Her muscles seized up, and she shrieked. He brought his mouth down on hers, groaning. He thrust until he was balls deep and froze, moaning again, his face helpless and a little crazed.

Wyatt collapsed against her, pressing her to the door, his breath coming hot and heavy on her neck. "Mm."

After a few moments, he straightened and slipped out of her, still holding her wrapped around him like a monkey. After walking into the living room, he placed her on the couch. Since he hated it when she was clothed, he wasted no time pulling off her top. He pushed her down, coming to lie on top of her.

His cock lay against her thigh. He was still semierect. The man was a machine. She arched up, so he could fit better into the notch between her legs.

"See? Can't resist me," he murmured, smug. "Only a matter of time before you move yourself in."

Tatiana shook her head. Smart man, to broach the subject of his heavy handed plans for their future during and after sex. During, she was lost in a haze of hormones, and after, her spine had the consistency of pudding. Either way, it was difficult to work up the requisite level of worry. Still, she made an attempt to bluster. "I suppose I'd be the one who would have to move, to accommodate your job, huh? I have a life in San Francisco. Work, friends."

She expected him to issue some chauvinistic comment designed to rile her up, but he only frowned. "It would be difficult for me to leave here for long periods of time. But I suppose we could compromise, try living both places. I'd have to be on site for the busy season, and I may need to fly back on weekends when we're at your place."

She blinked. When had they gotten to talking logistics, implying this was a done deal? "Wait. What?"

"I'm invested in this company." He shrugged. "But I'm invested in you, too. I thought I'd made that clear."

"No. Not that. I mean, yes, that too. I can't believe that you'd even consider living in both places…"

"Why not? You make a valid point. It's unfair for me to ask you to uproot yourself without even thinking of the alternative."

She stared at him, flustered, touched, amazed, and scared. "You're serious about this."

"Of course."

"But…but we can't just move in together."

"Why not?"

"Because it's only been a few months."

"Plus…what? Years of knowing each other?"

"It doesn't work like that."

His eyes narrowed, and Wyatt-the-shark edged out Wyatt-the-lover. "It's the sensible next step."

"We don't know if we can live together."

"Well, exactly. We don't right now. Unless and until we live together, we won't know. Besides, long-distance is a pain. It's harder to be a normal couple when we're both in a hurry to get to the fucking."

"You think we'll fuck less if we live together?" Ha! Good luck with that. She didn't want to live in a world where she didn't want to jump Wyatt's bones.

"God, I hope not. But maybe we'll go a few hours in between." He donned a hangdog face, utterly out of place on him. "I'm not a kid anymore, you know."

She stroked her fingers through his hair, the black strands like crisp silk. "But…what if we fight?"

"We might." He grasped her face between his hands. "I told you. I won't storm off. I'll stick around. It won't be like it was."

"We say that we'll make these changes, but you know that won't happen magically overnight. Acknowledging a problem doesn't make it go away."

"No, but we can work on it." He kissed the tip of her nose. "What are you really scared about?"

"I'm not scared." Yes, she was scared. She was terrified. Being hopeful that they might have a shot was a far cry from taking the plunge and merging their lives together completely. "I'm…being cautious."

"That's not a word I'd use to describe you."

Tatiana smacked his arm lightly. "I don't want to hurt. Like before," she said awkwardly. "What if we have some other problems?"

He rested his forehead against hers, his long lashes veiling his eyes. "Then we deal with them. If we want this to work, we make it work."

The thought of living together was terrifying and thrilling. More terrifying than leaving her family and everything she'd ever known to forge a life for herself across the country. More thrilling than selling her first commissioned necklace. It could be the most wonderful decision she ever made.

Or it could blow up in their faces and leave them with more wounds.

Yet…for the first time, Tatiana could visualize it. Not only the good parts, but the bad, too. Waking up, laughing, loving, fighting…a steady cycle. Lather, rinse, repeat.

"I'll think about." She glared at him when he opened his big, fat, argumentative mouth. Did he not get what a big concession that was for her? "It's a big step, okay? Let me think about it. Don't push me."

He rested his head on his hand and blinked at her, earnest. It was difficult for him to look meek. Like a tiger donning a kitten mask. "Yes ma'am."

Tatiana narrowed her eyes, immediately suspicious of his easy acquiescence. "Wait a minute. This was all you were hoping for, wasn't it? For me to consider it."

"Oh, no. I was certain you'd drop everything and move in with me. After all, it's not like your work is important to you. Plus, you're so eager to live off my money. You only threaten to shove my credit card up my ass on Wednesdays."

"Oh, hush." She scowled at his teasing, trying to hide her own smile.

He allowed his satisfaction to surface. "Over-ask. Under-expect. Master negotiator's first rule."

"Ugh. Men."

Wyatt slid his hand up her thigh, his erect cock slipping inside her. "Not men. Man. Singular."

Languorously, she stretched. "Mine." She ran her foot up his thigh, the hairs tickling. "My man."

"Yes." He rocked. A hand stroked up her arm, slick with sweat and the lotion she'd applied earlier. "All yours. God. You're so wet."

Tatiana moaned when he hit that sweet spot deep within. Wet from her. And from him. "I should clean up. I'm dirty."

"No." His breath brushed her lips. "That's how I like you."

Bet On Me

Chapter One

"I CAN'T WAIT to see that dress on my floor."

A smile curved Tatiana Belikov's lips, her shoulders relaxing. Presumptuous men were hardly new, and over the course of her thirty-odd years of life, she had mastered the art of teasing them or cutting them down with a single look, depending on her mood.

However, since her dress would be shucked off the instant she entered her home, for comfort if nothing else, this wasn't a case of baseless male arrogance. It didn't mean she wanted him to think she was easy. "Your floor? Aren't you always telling me it's *our* place? That would make it our floor."

Wyatt Caine's hand slid over her hip. "I will deed my entire penthouse—no, the whole casino—over to you if it would entice you to strip somewhere."

"If that's the way you do business, it's amazing you aren't bankrupt."

"To be fair, I'm not usually dying to fuck my business partners."

She brushed her fingertips gently over his hand. "You'll

have to wait." Her voice was as low as his, mindful of their surroundings.

Wyatt Caine gave a rough groan. "I know."

She glanced down at the strapless white silk sheath, satisfied with her choice. Classy, elegant, sexy-conservative. A foil for the deceptively simple gold and emerald necklace she wore. Not only did it ensure she stood out amongst the elite black-clad crowd attending the exhibit, it had the added benefit of driving Wyatt crazy.

Wyatt loved her in white. Loved her in anything he could soil.

"You want me to die of blue balls," her lover grumbled.

"I'm not sixteen anymore, and I know that can't actually happen."

"You didn't believe it at sixteen either." His fingers clenched her hip, wrinkling the silk. "But I'm telling you, I'll be the first documented case."

"The horror." She scratched his skin. "Patience. It won't be long now."

"It's already long."

Tatiana bit back her laugh and gave him a final pat on his hand before she disentangled herself. Wyatt wasn't the only one wrestling with temptation.

They'd spent the entire last month living in San Francisco, and she had grown accustomed to seeing him in more casual wear. Tonight, he wore black tie, and he wore it well. So well, she wanted to rip it off him. Tatiana shook her head to clear it of the images of what lay beneath his clothes. Broad shoulders, narrow hips, flat stomach, and yes, his long, thick…

She sighed. After a year together, one would think they

would be less sex crazed. Weren't they supposed to be past the honeymoon stage?

She blamed it on his ass. His round, taut, bitable ass.

And of course the fact both of them had sex drives that were...overly healthy?

Not now. "Stop distracting me. I have to work."

Wyatt slid his hands into his pockets. Damn it. Mentally, she slapped herself to keep from craning her head around to leer at the way the fine fabric stretched over the aforementioned ass.

"I didn't mean to distract you," he said.

"Bullshit," she replied. Wyatt was a breathing distraction, and one she was all too tempted to cling to tonight in an effort to calm the butterflies in her stomach.

But standing around and hiding behind her boyfriend would hardly sell her art. She frowned at him. "Get us something to drink."

An expression that looked suspiciously like a pout formed on his face. His face was closely shaved, his high cheekbones and chiseled jaw revealed without the scruff he'd sported when they were in California. His hair had been recently cut, and the short, dark strands were begging for her hands to mess them up. "I don't try to get rid of you when you come to one of *my* events."

"Because when we go to those things, I don't follow you around and whisper dirty things in your ear."

"Oh, really?" Wyatt raised his voice a couple of octaves higher and adopted a breathy quality. "Wyatt, I thought you should know I'm not wearing any panties under this dress."

"Shh." Hopeful no one had overheard, she glanced

around. Okay, fine. Maybe she'd whispered a few dirty somethings in his ear a time or two.

She allowed herself a moment to reminisce. That had been the best gala she'd ever attended. She'd scored a wine basket in the silent raffle, and then she'd scored with Wyatt in the janitor's closet. "Point taken. Now go get us something to drink. Shoo."

Wyatt sighed, but there was a light in his eyes. She loved that light. She saw it more and more often, a sign of his satisfaction and pleasure.

She was starting to love a lot of things.

She fiddled with the hem of her dress. No. No. Too soon. They'd had problems, deep problems with communication, and a yearlong commuter relationship and a couple months of living together wasn't long enough of a trial period to be certain of anything. Including love. They needed time to ensure they could make things work before they started throwing that word around.

Yeah, she had this mental speech down pat now.

"Fine. I'll go get us a drink."

She shook off her brief second of melancholy and squared her shoulders. "I'm going to mingle. Find me."

"I always do."

She allowed him a few steps before she spoke, mischief prompting her. "Hey. Guess what?"

He glanced over his shoulder in time to see her smooth a hand over her hip. No panty lines marred the drape of the white silk. His gaze dropped there, and he bit back a curse, heat flaring in his eyes. "You're killing me."

She added an extra twitch to her ass when she strutted away, confidence in knowing he was watching giving her the boost she needed to stroll through the exhibit when all she really wanted to do was go hide in her safe, familiar studio back home.

People ebbed around her. Some looked at her, some barely noticed her, others did a double take or stared. *Good. Let them stare.*

Staring was good. Staring meant attention, and attention was never a bad thing in her line of work. She preferred the attendees talk about her pieces, but talking about her was acceptable, if it resulted in sales.

She didn't do showings often, only once or twice a year. The owner of the gallery she had previously arranged all her exhibits through in California had counseled her on the importance of exclusivity. Supply and demand.

A waiter passed in front of her, and she eyed the tray of shrimp before deciding her nerves would punish her if she tried to down anything more than the handful of small appetizers she had already consumed.

She flashed a meaningless, cool smile at an older couple who paused to survey a bracelet. Usually, her work would have been under glass, but since this line contained a functional element, the gallery manager had made the decision to leave the pieces uncovered. She expected a certain degree of curiosity tonight from the people who grasped the concept underlying her new line. They had deliberately kept things subtle, but the clues were there.

Will they like it? Maybe it's too scandalous. Maybe you should stick to designing pretty things.

Once her inner bitch started, she wouldn't sit down. *Maybe you'll only be able to find success back home. This is a new state, a new city, a new population who has never heard of you. What are you thinking?*

She swallowed the lump in her throat. Perhaps she was making too much of things, but it seemed vitally important that her first showing in Vegas be a wild success. This was Wyatt's home; he was well known here, though maybe not amongst these circles. More importantly, as of three months ago, it was her home.

"You lucky bitch."

Instant warmth spread through her, quieting her annoying internal monologue, and she turned to greet the woman who had cursed her. "Akira. You came. I wasn't certain if you were in town."

Akira accepted the hug Tatiana gave her like a queen deigning to recognize a peasant's offering. Yet her arms tightened imperceptibly around Tatiana, a rare display of warmth Akira only bestowed upon her friends.

At first glance, no one would associate Akira Mori with friendliness. Slim and tall, she was all angles from the cut of her cheekbones to her narrow hips to her razor-sharp brain. Since Tatiana owed her success partially to the woman, she knew better.

Eight years ago, the stunning female had stopped in front of her booth at the craft fair where Tatiana had been showing her jewelry, out of place in a vintage Chanel dress. She had touched a necklace and snorted. *Girl, you're better than this place. Dream bigger.*

Easy to say. Easier to do when you had a wealthy, internationally notorious patron suddenly wearing your designs.

Akira based her operations in San Francisco, but she could be in any city at any given time checking on her established nightclubs and bars, or breaking ground on a new one. Vegas was a favorite spot of hers. Tatiana had been hoping she would be able to come tonight. Friendly faces were always welcome.

"You know I like to see what you have cooking. Sorry I didn't RSVP. I had to go to London to launch the new club, wasn't sure I would be back." Akira flicked her nails, shoving aside her multimillion-dollar empire with a wave. "But enough about me. Let's get back to you being a lucky bitch."

"I am lucky, but I'm hardly a bitch." Tatiana thought about that. "Most of the time. I'm not a bitch most of the time."

"Well, I can't call you a whore, darling. That's everyone's pet name for *me*." Shiny black hair slid over her shoulders, and she pointed in the general direction of the bar. "Tell me I did not see you making googly eyes at the infamous Wyatt Caine?"

Tatiana cocked her head. "Um, I know we haven't had a chance to see each other this past year because we've been traveling so much, but I could have sworn I told you I was dating him."

"You said you were seeing your old high school flame. You said he moved in with you. Wyatt Caine does not need to move in with anyone."

"We moved in with each other. We're splitting our time between here and my place."

"That's sickeningly progressive of both of you." She scowled. "He's as rich as me. Maybe even richer than me."

"Are you mad you're not the richest person in my life?"

"Damn straight. I should be the richest person in everyone's life. Does he fuck as good as he looks?"

A cough came from somewhere nearby, and Tatiana gave a wry smile. She had spent her whole adult life trying to be discreet about her hunger for sex, so Akira's open and uninhibited pleasure-seeking had taken some getting used to. Once she had, Tatiana had quickly learned to admire her lack of shame. She leaned in. "Better."

"Lucky. Bitch." A dangerous light entered Akira's eyes. "I'm having a party next Friday."

Tatiana raised a brow, excitement stirring. "Oh? Here?"

"No. At my house."

Akira's house parties were rare, but they were legendary. Probably because they were little more than exquisitely catered orgies.

Tatiana had attended two over the years when she'd been between boyfriends, but she personally had too many trust issues to fuck complete strangers. The first one, she'd clung to the shadows and watched with wide eyes and a heaving bosom. The second one, she had gotten tipsy and made out with Akira in front of a handful of voyeurs.

That had been exciting. The lurking had been exciting too, and had fueled more than a few restless nights. If she had a steady boyfriend she trusted implicitly with her…

If she had Wyatt with her? Oh my.

No, she had no issue with complete strangers watching her do anything with him.

Reading her thoughts, Akira spoke. "Come. Bring him. I want more contacts in the Vegas market. I also want to see him naked."

"I wish." Tatiana shook her head, regretful already. "We need to be here next weekend. Wyatt has an event he can't miss."

"Damn it." Akira arched a perfectly plucked eyebrow. "I would be happy to host something smaller this week. Locally."

"Something smaller, huh?" Tatiana pursed her lips, amused and intrigued. "I don't know…"

"Sorry if I'm overstepping." Akira traced Tatiana's necklace with her gaze and then a fingertip. She reached the loop around her neck and gave a gentle tug. Tatiana stiffened and swayed toward the other woman. "I assumed that if Caine inspired your new line, he must be rather creative. Not a vanilla kind of guy."

"I'm so happy you understood the concept behind the pieces," Tatiana murmured, catching her breath. The woman's lack of boundaries was intoxicating, the sexuality she oozed firing Tatiana's imagination.

Akira flashed a megawatt smile. "Honey, the day I can't identify sex toys when I see them is the day you can bury me six feet under."

"To answer your other question, no, Wyatt isn't…vanilla." Tatiana whispered the last word, since the gallery manager had circled around, within earshot.

"So. Let's get together." Akira bit her lip and leaned in closer, lashes fluttering flirtatiously. "It'll be fun."

Akira's fragrant perfume twined around Tatiana, teasing her with promise. It would be more than fun.

Tatiana glanced Wyatt's way, but he was hidden from view. The man had been working so hard lately. Managing his business from her home wasn't a cakewalk, and yet he had done it without complaint. For her. For them.

Sometimes she thought she would burst with the secret of her love for him. She might not be able to tell him yet, but she could do something for him. Something mind-blowing.

Tatiana met Akira's expectant gaze. "I'll call you tomorrow."

"Good girl." Akira narrowed her eyes, calculation replacing seduction. "In the meantime, I'll go introduce myself now."

"I thought you came to see my new line," Tatiana teased. All of Akira's hedonism hid an ambition that put Wyatt's to shame. No surprise networking took precedence over shiny things.

"I saw it. Already bought a bunch. You'll be busy."

Tatiana wanted to collapse in relief. Akira didn't buy crap, even from her friends. The offhand comment was more valuable than any ringing endorsement or review.

Even if no one else buys anything, you did okay.

An artist's insecurities were a terrible thing. Right up there with relationship insecurities.

Akira took a step away before spinning back. "I won't steal him away from you," she blurted out. "Either now or later."

Tatiana bit the inside of her cheek. She supposed Akira might have to occasionally deal with jealous females, but she was hardly one of them. "Whore, please."

LAST WEEK, WYATT had visited Tatiana's studio, a sun-drenched warehouse not far from her small apartment. While she worked, her fidgeting hands became deft and sure, her focus laser sharp. A fascinating thing to watch.

This was a different aspect of her work, and it was no less interesting. His clever, dreamy, occasionally vulgar girlfriend had tugged on her more polished persona to schmooze wealthy patrons and solicit the highest price for her art. Prices even he, despite his deep pockets, raised an eyebrow over.

Wyatt allowed himself a small smile and leaned against the bar, content to take his time getting their drinks. He was in no hurry to rush back to her right this minute. She was speaking with a tall, strikingly pretty Asian woman, and for the first time since they'd walked into this place, she appeared at ease. No need for him to attempt to distract her from her nerves.

He had thought posing as her arm candy would only entail looking on proudly. Like him, she was heavily invested in her work, and he hadn't believed anything could shake her confidence in her finished product.

He was wrong. Worry had created shadows in her eyes and a line between her brows. Was this how she was during every show? Maybe it was an artist thing.

Glasses clinking on the bar behind him prompted him into turning around. He pulled out cash for the pinot noir and whiskey and thanked the bartender.

"No problem. Sorry for the wait. Always know it's a good show when people rush the bar later in the evening."

"It is a good show." He hoped so. If Tatiana was fretting this much without knowing the sales, he feared she might be despondent if she didn't do well. That would, of course, make all the attendees blithering idiots. He might be biased, but though everything Tatiana made was stunning, she had outdone herself with the pieces she had crafted over the course of the past year.

You're my inspiration, she'd murmured against his ear

last week. He would have chalked that up to cooing nonsense, had he not been testing a prototype for her at the time, running a string of pearls between her legs.

Such a clever girl.

"Hello there." The husky female voice came from his right.

He sipped his whiskey and glanced over to find the woman who had been speaking to Tatiana. "Hello."

She held out a hand. "Akira Mori."

The name rang a distant bell. Her hand was slender, but there was nothing delicate about her firm grip. "Wyatt Caine."

"I'm aware." She tilted her head. "I'm a friend of Tatiana's."

Tatiana might have mentioned someone named Akira a time or two, but Wyatt couldn't quite recall what those conversations had revolved around. "Good. She could use more friends here." Here, in the room, as well as in Vegas.

He was a fan of anything that made Tatiana feel at home in this city. Persuading her to even consider living with him had been a herculean task. He was a bit of a loner, but she needed friends to be happy.

"I didn't realize she was dating you. It's a surprise."

"Is it?"

"I've heard of you. You don't seem like her type," she said frankly.

He raised an eyebrow. Who did this blunt stranger think she was? "We've known each other a long time. I suppose Tatiana would know best what her type is."

"She's lovely."

"She is."

"Unexpected."

"Unexpected?"

"She looks like she'd be a simple woman, but she has so many layers." The woman's black eyes were cold, merciless. "I don't have many friends. I like to ensure the ones I have are taken care of."

This was the most bizarre conversation he had ever taken part in. Was this woman warning him? In that case, he should probably tell her that Tatiana's family had made pointing out his inferiority an art form. He was well aware she was a prize. "It's a pleasure to meet you, Ms. Mori, but I really need to…" He trailed off. "Wait. Mori? Are you related to—?"

"Yes."

"Your father is—"

"Yes."

"That makes you—"

"Yes."

"Ah." He nodded. "Akira Mori. I've been to one of your clubs."

"Good. You have excellent taste."

No wonder this was weird. He had heard Akira Mori was blunt to the point of being rude, and more than a little eccentric. He scanned his mental databank on the woman, stiffening when he recalled the context in which Tatiana had spoken of her. "You and Tatiana are close?"

Akira picked up the wine he had ordered for Tatiana and took a large gulp. "As close as I am to anyone."

"I've heard about your parties."

Her lips curled. "Most people have."

Wyatt worked his jaw. "Tatiana will not be attending

any in the near future."

A delicate sneer crossed her face, freezing when he calmly continued. "Not without me."

She stilled. "Oh really?"

"Yes." He knew Tatiana was too passionate to have been celibate during their years apart, but whatever she had done then was her business.

What she did now was his business.

Akira studied him, her fingers tapping the glass. "You're okay with that, then?"

Tatiana would enjoy herself, little exhibitionist that she was. Lately, his entire life was consumed with pleasing her. Giving her pleasure through sex? Easy. It was whether he was pleasing her in other ways that kept him guessing. Was he making the same mistakes he'd made before? Was she happy? He had tried to mesh their lives together while respecting her world, but he'd had to fly back numerous times during the one month they'd spent in San Francisco. Each time, he'd wondered if she'd still be waiting for him when he returned.

Or would she realize, like everyone else had always known, that she could do so much better? Yes. Sex was easy. It was all these other details that made him feel like he was trying to hold water in his hands. "I want whatever Tatiana wants."

Akira watched him. "The gossip mill is pretty quiet about you."

"Is it?"

"Except that you're a cold bastard."

"That's deserved." He was a cold bastard. Except when he was with Tatiana.

He scanned the small space. With his height, he was able to spot her amongst the sea of other attendees. Her honey-blonde hair was gathered on top of her head in a sexy, haphazard manner that looked like it was one pin away from tumbling down her back. Her tight, curvy body was poured into that simple white dress. The dress, under which she wore no panties. His fingers itched with the desire to wreck her.

She was talking to the gallery manager. Her eye roll was so subtle, if he hadn't been watching her, he would have missed it. His woman was bored. Probably hungry, too, since nerves and fear her dress wouldn't fit had kept her from eating before the show.

She shifted, and Wyatt glanced at her three-inch heels. Silly fuck-me shoes that provided little arch support. Her feet were paining her.

Tatiana gave a strained smile and nodded. The light glinted on the chain around her neck.

His eyes narrowed. The necklace was new, a delicate gold braid that was looped around her neck once. There was no closure on this necklace, as there were on most. Both emerald-tipped ends were left to dangle, though she had slipped them inside her bodice.

He focused on her chest, but the material of her dress was too thick to see the chain. Best guess? Those emeralds were snug against her nipples right now. Teasing was what they were designed for, after all.

Bad girl.

A reckless urge rose within him. He couldn't do anything about her shoes or her belly, but he could play the good arm candy. Boredom and stress were foes he was always up for vanquishing. It probably wasn't the sanest idea, but sanity and rational thought generally fled when faced with the chance to play with Tatiana.

"You don't look cold." Akira leaned close to him, until he could feel her breath against his cheek. "You don't look cold at all."

Over a year ago, he might have been tempted by this strange, uninhibited, beautiful woman. But that was before Tatiana had stormed back into his life.

He glanced at Akira. "Excuse me." He turned back to the bar, pulled out a pen, and quickly scribbled a note on a napkin. He folded it up and snagged a passing waiter. "Can you ensure that the woman…right there…in white gets this?"

The man nodded and accepted the napkin.

Akira waited for the waiter to walk away before speaking. "Funny. I can't see Tatiana's teeth from all the way over here. How do you know something's stuck between them?"

Wyatt twitched his tie into place before smoothing it. Of course she had read over his shoulder. He'd be annoyed if he didn't feel like she was some odd kindred spirit. And if he didn't have to attend to his woman in the most delightful way. "It's been a pleasure to meet you," he said formally. "If you don't mind, I need to find the restroom."

A flash of amused mischief lit her eyes, replacing the icy speculation. "My, Caine. People have you pegged wrong, don't they?"

"I try not to get pegged at all."

"Hmmm." She shook her head. "You people and your layers. Take my word for it, it's so much easier to be shallow and one-dimensional, you know?"

"I wouldn't know." He eyed her. "And I don't think you do either."

She merely smiled. He had only taken three steps when she spoke again. "FYI. The ladies' room is in the opposite direction."

Chapter Two

TATIANA BARED HER teeth in the mirror. What the hell had Wyatt been talking about? She'd made a horrified excuse upon reading the napkin the server had delivered and fled to the bathroom, but her teeth were perfectly fine.

The door opened, and she blinked at the man who entered. "Wyatt?"

He ignored her and walked into the ladies' room, big and dark and far too masculine for the ivory marble and rose-gold fixtures. He pushed open both empty stalls and then came for her.

"Wyatt, what the hell are you doing in the—*mmph*."

He sank his hand into her hair and yanked her close, taking her lips in a hungry kiss. It was rough and forceful, his teeth biting, his tongue rubbing against hers.

One hand slid down her back and grabbed her ass, kneading the flesh. She ripped her mouth away, breathing heavy. "Wyatt, this is the ladies' room."

"I don't care." Denied, he drew his mouth down her throat, latching on to the patch of skin at the hollow and sucking it between his teeth, hard enough that she knew she'd have a mark tomorrow.

Normally she sneered when a grown man left a hickey on a woman. Such an adolescent thing to do. However, Wyatt had never left marks in visible places when they were teens, for fear her parents would see.

She kind of loved it on the rare occasion he did it now. It was a sign of his lack of control. A sign of their mutual lack of consideration for whether the world saw his possession of her body.

"I know you don't care." Her eyes nearly rolled back in her head when he sucked harder. "I don't think the women who have been drinking wine all night will be so blasé. Alcohol's a diuretic," she babbled.

He licked and kissed his way down her chest, where her dress made the most of her small assets. "Need this." He scraped his teeth over the slope of her breast, and she jumped.

"Wyatt. I'm working."

"*You* need this." He raised his head until his gaze locked with hers. Those black eyes were glittering feverishly, almost glazed over. "Say the word. Or we fuck here. Now."

The word. Their safe word, which thus far she had used exactly once, during a bout of overly energetic sex that had resulted in a leg cramp.

So she knew what the word meant. The word meant he would stop on a dime and let her return to the regular world, no questions asked, no hard feelings, no crankiness. She could walk out the door and rejoin the people milling around outside and commence worrying about her career and her life's work.

Or…

Her stomach clenched, her nerves morphing into a dark excitement. "It's wrong."

His hand slid down her hip, wrinkling the pristine fabric. "So it's perfect."

"Wyatt…"

He passed his hand over her leg and pushed the skirt of her dress up. The silk slithered over her leg until his palm met bare thigh. "Hot damn. I love your body." His hand squeezed her thigh, as if testing it for jiggle.

"I've gained weight since I started living with you, you know," she admonished.

"Not at all."

The man had made it his goal in life to get her to eat whatever it was he deemed a sufficient quantity of food. Once she'd accused him of trying to fatten her up so he could eat her.

He'd thrown her on the bed. And eaten her. "I have," she insisted.

"But I give you such a workout."

Those so-called workouts left her too satisfied to roll out of bed and make it to the gym. All she wanted to do was lie around and eat chocolates. So she did. And the scale went up. "Cardio only."

"Maybe for you. Holding you down while I fuck you is killer strength training."

"I should hold you down while I fuck you next time."

He stroked his hand up her leg, his fingertips finding the lips of her pussy, the thick digits catching the hairs there. "Good luck with that."

She pushed her hips the slightest bit forward. "We shouldn't."

"Mmm." His finger flirted with her pussy. "You don't sound sure about that." Wyatt's words were absent, his eyes on his hand between her legs. "Spread those thighs for me."

Against her better judgment, she obeyed. His middle finger sank inside her.

She choked out a laugh. "Casanova. I feel like we're back in that old Honda of yours and you're wooing me into giving you what you want."

"I did some fine work in that Honda."

"But only with me," she said archly. He had been a senior when they met, and she knew he'd had girlfriends before her, but they'd mutually picked each other's cherries.

"Of course. You inspire me." His lips teased hers, the delicate touch a sharp contrast to the thick finger buried unmoving inside her pussy. He liked to kiss like this, bare brushes of his lips against hers, not because he wasn't eager to taste her, but because he liked it more when her hunger eclipsed his and she forced a deeper touch.

He'd started like this the first time in the backseat of his Civic, though then it hadn't been deliberate, but a sign of his nerves and uncertainty. He'd leaned in a bit, and she'd cradled his cheeks and brought him closer, both of them clumsy and filled with hormones, nervous someone would discover them parked on the side of the road.

She'd slipped her tongue inside his mouth, and he'd grown bolder, drawing his hands up from her waist, palms brushing the sides of her breasts. It had taken multiple make-out sessions before she could convince him deepening that illicit touch was okay.

He was comfortable reading her silent cues now. That was one of the best things about Wyatt—they might play he was the greedy barbarian, but at the end of the day, it was always about what she wanted. What she needed.

All she ever needed was a man like him.

She sank her fingers into the hair at his nape, which was too freshly cut to get a good grip on. She scraped her nails over the skin there and brought him closer, pressing her tongue inside his mouth, the first aggressor.

With her silent permission, the rein he kept on his control broke. He thrust once with his finger before pulling it away, leaving her open and empty. One big hand wrapped around her throat to tilt her head, angling it. He bit her bottom lip as he drew away, scraping the flesh and soothing it with rough licks when she whimpered.

"You taste like champagne and strawberries," he rasped. He licked his lips. "And maybe some of those bacon-wrapped scallops."

She snorted a laugh. Only Wyatt could make her laugh when he was fingering her. "Not as romantic."

"If you want romantic, you came to the wrong man."

Another lie. The man was a romantic down to his bones, though he concealed that mushiness well.

He must have seen the smirk on her face, because he scowled. "I am not romantic."

"Okay," she soothed.

"Stop using that tone. Like you're humoring me."

She made her eyes very big. "Okay. I'll stop humoring you."

An adorable growl ripped from his throat. "Would a romantic man bang you in a bathroom?"

He would if he knew her. Romance was a subjective thing.

Wyatt left her to unbuckle his belt and unbutton and unzip his pants. His dick looked thick and delicious when he pulled it out, engorged and curved. The tip flared wide. She knew what that cock felt like in her mouth, her pussy, her ass, and she'd never be able to get enough.

She swallowed, not surprised that he had her salivating. Oh man. She loved his cock.

If only she could hide her appreciation. Arrogance coated his every word. "Change your mind?"

She pouted. "I can control myself."

"Liar." He stepped closer and worked her snug skirt up farther. He pushed her legs wider, until the tip of his cock brushed against the hair on her mound. "You're panting for it."

"Maybe," she allowed. There was no maybe about it, as he would find out when he discovered her rapidly dampening pussy.

He guided his cock so the flared head pressed against her clit and rubbed it there in a small circular motion that had her moaning. "You're right, Tatiana. Maybe we should stop. Someone will miss you soon. Maybe come looking for you."

She bit the inside of her cheek so hard she tasted blood. "They could."

"That would be terrible for business." He brushed the back of his hand over her nipple, silk and emeralds rasping against the engorged tip.

"It would."

"So what's your decision?" He teased her by sliding his cock between her pussy lips, the wet glide forcing her up on her toes to seek a deeper connection.

She struggled for the space of one second. She had made the rounds and mingled, and the crowd tonight was accustomed to eccentric artists. If she disappeared for fifteen minutes, no one would remark upon it. "Make it quick. And don't mess me up."

He wrapped his big hands around her waist and lifted her. The room spun in a dizzying circle before her back was pressed against the door. "Done."

"Oh my God."

He sank inside, letting her weight and gravity do its job. Her head dropped back, but his hand on her neck prevented her from rapping her head against the door.

And it kept her hair from getting mussed. Talented, this man.

He sucked her earlobe before worrying it between his teeth. "Good?"

"Damn it, Wyatt. We could have waited." She pressed her hips forward, seeking more of him, but he held her too tightly for her to find satisfaction.

"Even a second would have been too long."

He pulled almost all the way out before shoving deep, not giving her a chance to get accustomed to his size. She was wet, but not enough to make it easy for him. He had to work to get her to accept him, and he was up for the challenge, twisting his hips to get her to take more of him.

He gave a rough groan, far too loud for Tatiana's peace of mind. "Shh."

A reckless smile spread over his lips. "Keep me quiet."

Her pussy clenched on him, and he grunted. She slammed her lips over his, swallowing the sound of his pleasure.

One hand on her throat, the other hand on her hips, mouth fused over hers, he fucked her hard and fast, their breathing deepening with every rock of his penis inside of her. Their moans were captured by each other's mouths.

The door bumped her back. For a second, she thought they were making it rattle in its frame. Odd, she thought, for such a heavy piece of wood.

Then she realized the slab was opening inward. Someone was trying to enter.

Her head shot up, lips separating from Wyatt. He blinked, reason replacing some of the passion on his gaze. Accustomed to being in charge, he took immediate action, pressing both of them harder against the wood, his cock driving deeper into her, his hand slamming the moving door shut.

Wyatt opened his mouth, no doubt ready to take care of the situation. In horror, she slapped her palm over his lips. This was the *ladies'* room. No woman had a baritone like Wyatt, she was certain.

"I'll—I'll be a minute, I'm sorry. I'm not feeling well," she stammered out.

There was a pause in the hallway before they heard the sound of footsteps walking away. His lips curved under her hand, and he bit her palm.

"We're going to be arrested," she whispered.

He circled his hips. "Worth it."

"This is risky."

"And you love it. You're as wet as I am hard."

He was right. She did love it. A normal person's ardor would have cooled at the interruption, but she'd never been able to call herself normal. Tatiana studied him from beneath her lashes. "You have two minutes."

"All I need." He avoided crushing her dress beyond repair by gripping her hips. She'd wear bruises there tomorrow, but that would be just fine.

His hips picked up speed and his eyes fluttered shut, his lashes making crescents on his cheeks.

He was waiting for her. She cupped his face and brushed her thumbs over his lips. "Do it," she whispered. "I'll get mine later."

She would. There was no doubt about that. She might trip him and ride him the second they got home.

He bit her thumb. "Later?" He shoved deep, making her thighs tremble. "What kind of man would make his woman wait 'til later?"

"You always make me wait for it."

He licked her thumb, soothing the sting. "Only if I know you need to."

He forced her to stand, pulled out, and steadied her when she would have fallen.

"I don't need to wait now?" she breathed.

"No. It's past time." He tugged at the bodice of her dress, revealing her strapless white bra.

His lips quirked. "Padded. No wonder I couldn't see the necklace." Wyatt yanked at the bra until it was bunched beneath her breasts.

She glanced down. The necklace ended in hoops, small nooses that were looped around each nipple. A tiny emerald tightened the golden braid. Her nipples were rock hard, constricted by the metal.

He admired the sight. "You should march out right now. Model this for your guests. Show them how clever you are."

"I only want you to see this one. It's my favorite," she purred.

He dipped his head to tongue the abused nipple. She bit her cheek as he drew strongly and his hand found her pussy, sinking inside and fucking her with two fingers. "Wyatt," she whispered. "Someone could come in. Hurry."

He sank to his knees. "Turn."

She obeyed, eager to get off. He caged her hips and arranged her so her ass was in the air, her back arched, and she had no choice but to use the door for balance. Her breasts hung down like ripe fruit, the gold of her necklace glittering.

Wyatt scraped his teeth over the exposed skin of her buttock. He spread her legs farther, his breath gusting over her. Two fingers smoothed over her pussy and widened into a V to hold the lips apart. His tongue slid over her clitoris, and she cried out.

"Poor thing." He licked delicately, prodding the small nubbin. "And you wanted me to wait. It would hurt to walk around with this, wouldn't it?"

"Yes," she hissed.

"Your hard little nipples, too. They would ache. Let me make it all better." He opened his mouth and sucked in her clit. She let go of the door to reach behind her and grab his head. He shook it once, a clear warning. Muttering a curse, she returned her hand to the wood.

He stretched his hand out and found the chain that hung between her breasts. Tugging it tightened the metal on her nipples. She shrieked and came against his tongue, her pussy contracting on the talented muscle. He gentled his touch, letting her ride it out for as long as she wanted.

He held her when she would have collapsed on the tile, guiding her down so she was cradled against his lap. "Wait, my ass." He flicked her nipple.

She opened her eyes, breathing deep. "Oh my God, Wyatt. Someone must have heard me."

"Doubtful. This room is far enough away."

She dropped her voice to a whisper, though it was far too late for that. "What if whoever tried to come in here is still outside?"

He shrugged. "There's a unisex bathroom two doors down. She most likely went there."

Oh. Well. It had still been damn illicit, she consoled herself.

"Your friend. Akira? She might have figured out what we were up to."

Tatiana shrugged. "She won't be scandalized."

"I didn't think she would." He licked the side of her neck. "One day I want you to tell me exactly what you did at those parties. I want every detail."

She purred and stretched. "It would get you off, wouldn't it?"

"Especially after I punished you for being such a bad girl."

"Maybe we could go together, sometime," she ventured. "You can watch me being bad."

He was silent for a long moment, and then his hoarse voice answered. "That would be acceptable."

A secret smile crossed her face. She staggered to her feet, and he followed. Only then did she take note of his wet, still-hard penis. "You didn't even come. After all the work you did to get me alone in here."

He braced himself with his back to the door and redid his pants, grimacing when he tucked his cock inside. "I'll take it out on your ass when we get home."

She glanced in the mirror. Her face was bright red and her breathing rapid, but once she tugged her bra and dress into place, she looked none the worse for wear.

No one would know what she'd been doing right under their noses. Whee.

"Let me clean you up."

"No. Leave me messy." She leaned in and brushed her lips over his in a chaste kiss. "It'll keep me wet."

His hot breath coasted over her cheek as he dipped his head and gave a breathless laugh. "Damn, woman."

She cast him a mischievous glance and worked her dress down over her hips. There were a few wrinkles in the silk, but nothing that would be noticed. "You want me ready for you, don't you?"

Wyatt straightened his tie. "Always."

Tatiana opened the door a hair, breathing a sigh of relief at the empty hallway. "Come on."

He followed behind her, not cowering or tiptoeing. With every step, Tatiana could feel her tension returning.

There was no need for it. The gallery manager had informed her everything was going well, that sales were mounting. Those who understood the functional element of her jewelry were titillated. The ones who didn't were simply taken with the sensual designs.

Wyatt's hand closed over her nape as they came to the end of the hallway. "Hey. Do I need to find another place to fuck you?"

"What?"

"Relax."

She stared at him. "Did you arrange this encounter to calm me down?"

His hand tightened, and he gave her a wolfish smile. "And because I wanted to show you what happens when you tease me with your tight little body."

I love you. "Thanks," she choked out, but the word was inadequate. He had known she was upset. He had known, and he had tried to take her mind off her worries.

His hand slipped into hers, and he squeezed. "It's a good show. A great show."

A burst of pride ran through her. Pride in her work, but also pride Wyatt got to see people's reactions to what she did.

Oh, she knew he was aware she had a good deal of commercial success, but it was different from his world, where she could see the obvious fruits of his labor—the massive casino, the lavish grounds, the obsequious people.

The signs of her success were muted. Partially because she liked it that way.

That need for him to see her accomplishment might be the reason she was extra nervous tonight, as silly as it was. As if Wyatt would think less of her if she didn't sell oodles. "People do seem to like my designs," she mused.

"They love it. And you."

She took a deep breath as they reentered the gallery. "Only an hour left. I only have to do this for an hour."

"An hour. And then I'll be bending you over the closest waist-level surface, no matter where we are." He released her hand. "Just focus on that."

Chapter Three

THE SLAP ON her ass woke her from her stupor. Tatiana groaned and buried her head beneath the pillow, accustomed to this kind of wake-up alarm. "Go away." Accustomed. But not appreciative.

"No. You told me to wake you before I left."

She peeked out of the decadently soft bedding and winced at the weak sunlight entering the room. Wyatt stood beside the bed, already showered and dressed, looking dark and dangerously handsome in his expensive suit. He knotted and tightened his tie.

When she'd drifted off to sleep last night, she *had* told him to wake her in the morning. Or had it been morning already when he had finally let her rest?

Whatever. It had been too late to be cheerful about rising now.

Tatiana shut her eyes. "I changed my mind."

Unsympathetic, he finished adjusting his neckwear and hauled off the comforter, the air-conditioned room leaving goose bumps on her naked skin. "You always tell me to ignore you when you say that."

Damn it. She knew herself too well. A gusty sigh left her lips. "I am not pleased."

"Imagine being the one who has to get your ass out of bed every day, sweetheart," he said dryly. "It's hardly a barrel of monkeys for me."

"Liar. You like this, you sadistic bastard." She rose on her elbows, resigned to getting out of bed.

He grinned but didn't respond, far too fresh for her mood. Ugh, morning people. They were the grossest.

"What are your plans for the day?"

Correction. Talkative morning people were the grossest. Silent, she narrowed her eyes at Wyatt until he sighed and handed her the mug of coffee sitting on the nightstand. Steam curled from the top. She inhaled deeply and took a bracing sip.

Five large gulps in, she was able to open her eyes and focus on Wyatt, who was slipping his shoes on. She liked watching him put his wingtips on. It was like watching a knight put on his suit of armor.

The fanciful thought made her smile. "I have a ton of work to do. Three commissions I want to get out of the way before orders from the show start pouring in." She said it with a satisfaction she hadn't been certain she would feel today. Her agonizing had been for naught. Every single piece had sold. The attendees had loved her new line. The gallery manager had said she would call Tatiana today for a full run-down.

Happiness coursed through her. There would be more orders and more shows in her future. Her new city loved her.

Wyatt smiled. "Sounds good. We should see about setting up a studio for you here. The spare bedroom doesn't have nearly the light that your workshop does."

Her heart stuttered. She took a sip of coffee, giving herself a second to think, before responding in the same carefully casual tone he had used. "That would probably be a good idea."

Wyatt glanced up at her from beneath his lashes. "Yeah?"

Another sip. "Yeah."

"Well. Okay then. I'll see if I can set up something with a realtor this weekend."

"Okay." She set her coffee on the nightstand before walking on her knees over to him and grabbing his face.

"What are you doing?"

"Giving you my favor, sir."

His lips quirked, but he didn't protest her kiss. It was long and slow and sweet, and he pulled away with obvious reluctance. "I have to go." He rubbed his thumb over her lower lip, his face as soft as she had ever seen it.

"I know." She pressed another kiss to the corner of his mouth. "Fare-thee-well, sir."

He eyed her. "Sometimes I wonder what goes on in your brain."

"It would scare you."

"Undoubtedly." His lips turned upward, and he leaned in, gave her another quick kiss, and left, a jaunty swing in his step.

She flopped back and stared at the ceiling, listening to the empty apartment. A studio. A studio right here. Knowing Wyatt, he would lecture her on all the financial reasons to buy a place instead of renting it, and she probably would end up doing that.

So permanent. She swallowed. A home was a home, but a studio was her favorite place in the whole world, where she was free to slip inside her work and give her imagination free rein. It was a big step.

Relax. It's not like it's marriage.

Her lips twisted. After she and Wyatt had broken up so long ago, Tatiana had decided she wasn't the marrying type. Men married good girls. Sweet girls. Girls who weren't bitchy and quirky and forgetful and a little bit slutty.

Except Wyatt liked all those things about her…

She shook her head. A studio. That's all they were talking about. Not a ring. *Quit doodling hearts on your notebook, Belikov. Get it together.*

That was something she'd gotten good at as she grew older. Throttling back her emotions, not overreacting to some stimulus, not leaping to conclusions. Keeping things slow, for fear that going too fast would result in implosion.

That was what would maintain her sanity. And keep their relationship on track.

Just. A. Studio.

Chapter Four

A STUDIO. NO, it wasn't a lifetime commitment, but a studio meant something. He was certain of it.

Wyatt was whistling by the time he entered his office, and grinned when he spotted Esme sitting at her desk. Bespectacled and pleasantly plump, the woman was deceptively soft looking. She was his defensive line, his eyes and ears, and the only reason he was able to work remotely from San Francisco at all.

Anyone who could facilitate his life with Tatiana was his savior. "Morning, Esme."

"Sir." Uncharacteristically somber, she stood. "I've been calling and texting you for about ten minutes."

He sobered immediately, his hand flying to his coat pocket and pulling out his phone. He cursed when he noted that he'd left the ringer on silent, having forgotten to turn it back on after the exhibit.

Tatiana's bad habits were rubbing off on him. This sort of thing was unacceptable when his business did not sleep. "I'm sorry. What's the problem?"

"You have an unexpected visitor."

He groaned. "Who? Tenchi? Adams?" His two biggest investors were generous, as well as being giant pains in the ass. Surprise visits were nothing new.

"No. It's…I don't know. I put her in your office. You don't have any meetings scheduled this morning, but I thought it best to not have her sitting here where anyone could…" She licked her lips, looking supremely uncomfortable.

It wasn't like Esme to be so flustered. "Why is that?"

Esme twisted her hands together. "It's a child. A little girl."

Wyatt frowned. "A child? How did she get up here?"

"The front desk called me and said she was here to see you, that she said she was related to you. I saw her on the camera and thought you may wish to handle this privately."

"Related to—" Wyatt shook his head, mystified. "I don't have any family, so if she's claiming to be a distant cousin or something…"

Esme squared her shoulders, as if bracing herself. "She looks a great deal like you, sir. Even Jaya at the front desk remarked upon it."

"What are you saying?"

Esme stared back at him, some of her composure returning. "I think you know."

"No, I—" Light bulb. He froze. "You're not implying some little girl is mine. Right?"

Esme looked down at her desk and straightened a piece of paper on the already neat surface. "I'm not implying anything. She looks like you," Esme repeated calmly. "And claims to be your relation."

"She's not. I don't have any…" He swallowed his bile

and tried again, struggling to force the last word out. "I don't have any...kids." Even the thought of having a child turned his stomach into a lead weight. Who was the mother, if he had a kid?

Not Tatiana.

Jesus. Tatiana. His muscles tightened as if readying for a blow. Ten minutes ago, he'd been thrilled she'd agreed to look into getting a studio here. What would be her reaction to an illegitimate child? Not good, he was willing to bet. She didn't want kids right now. And, well...that was more than okay with him.

The last time he'd felt an emotion like this had been over a decade ago, when he'd watched Tatiana walk out of his life.

From very far away, he heard Esme speaking to him, in a low, discreet voice. "If you like, I can get to the bottom of this for you and handle it."

Like Esme handled his mail and his phone calls. Like she handled his unwanted visitors.

The woman's eyes shifted to the door leading to his office, and Wyatt swung his incredulous gaze to the girl standing there. Black hair with the same silky shine as his was bound in a neat braid. Her eyes snared him, big and dark and fringed with lashes so thick they made her look like she had eyeliner on.

When he'd been her size, those lashes had gotten him teased to the point of fistfights. Hers probably broke hearts.

Let Esme handle it. He wasn't the first rich man to have a paternity scare. He doubted any of them dealt with it themselves.

The girl took a single step. "Hi."

What the fuck is wrong with you? Listen to yourself. You're not the man I know, if you would simply dump this on Esme.

His conscience didn't sound like Jiminy Cricket. No, that was Tatiana's sharp tone ringing in his brain. He gave a shake of his head and spoke to Esme. "No. No, thank you. I'll see what this is about. Make sure we're not disturbed." He turned to the girl. "Hello," he said, internally wincing when he heard the harsh note in his voice. *Just a child. Don't scare her, moron.* He dialed it back, making sure his next words were gentler. Soft and soothing wasn't his style, but he could manage it for this kid.

His…kid?

He shoved that thought out of his mind, because otherwise panic would render him mute again. "How are you?"

"Good."

Esme cleared her throat, and Wyatt jerked. Inside. Esme had been right to put the kid inside his office. It would take about five minutes and one person not on his payroll for rumors about his illegitimate child to start flying.

His business model was based on discreet depravity. That meant keeping his nose clean. No one wanted to trust their secrets to a man who couldn't keep his own.

Mobilized into action, Wyatt strode toward his office—and the girl. "I'll call you if I need you, Esme. Don't disturb us."

"Yes, sir."

The girl backed away as he entered, her brown eyes very big. He closed the door behind him, the noise too loud.

"Well." Wyatt clasped his hands behind his back, unsure what to do with them. Or her. He fell back on manners he used for adult guests. "Would you like a seat?"

"Okay." Gingerly, the girl sat on the sofa he gestured to, her hands tugging at the hem of her bright yellow T-shirt.

Other than her coloring and eyes, she also shared his chin and face shape, but her small bone structure had nothing in common with his, and her nose was a cute little button.

Each difference calmed him, each lack of similarity helping him breathe enough to think and regain some of his usual control. He took a few steps closer, so he could stand behind the chair facing her. He gripped the back of it. "My assistant didn't give me your name."

"Ellie. Short for Elizabeth."

Esme had given her a can of soda while she waited, he saw. That was good, the cynical side of him whispered. If TV was right, he could score a DNA test off that. His private investigator would know, surely.

He'd always been careful with his sexual partners. He'd never had to deal with the threat of a paternity suit before.

Until now.

This was…okay. He could handle this. He could be charming when he wanted to be, and he drew that skill around him, the polish he'd adopted over the past few years settling over him. All he had to do was be the man everyone expected to see. No one ever questioned that. No one looked deeper. "Ellie short for Elizabeth. My name's Wyatt Caine. What's your last name?" He was picky enough he remembered the names of every woman he'd ever gone to bed with.

She pressed her lips together. "Caine."

He nodded, thinking for a second she was merely repeating his own name back at him. But she stopped and was staring at him expectantly, and he realized…

Her name. She was telling him her last name.

That didn't mean anything. "How old are you, Ellie?" he said, and mentally swore when the girl flinched. He forced a smile and came around the chair, dropping into it so it would put him on her level. Her fists were clenched in her lap, one red Converse tapping the floor.

"Nine."

Nine. Which would make sense, the smug voice of his conscience whispered. Because her conception could have fallen within that window of time when he'd been in the arms of one woman after another, desperately trying to forget Tatiana. He'd always worn protection. But protection failed.

He placed his hands on his knees. He was too big, too awkward. His office was too stark and modern for this fresh-faced child. She belonged in a suburban split-level with two caring parents and a golden retriever. "What can I do for you, Ellie?"

The flutter of the rapid pulse in her throat was evident, as was her nervous swallow. Still, she met his gaze squarely, intelligence brimming in her eyes. "I'm sorry to bother you, but we were in town, and I wanted to meet you."

A dull roaring echoed in his ears. "Okay."

"I don't think I was supposed to know about you, but I overheard my dad telling my mom your name."

She'd overheard…what?

What. The. Fuck. "Your *dad* told your mom my name?"

"Yeah." Her button nose scrunched up. "Until then, I guess I didn't really think about the fact that I had a brother."

Chapter Five

"BROTHER."

Her head tipped, and it was like looking at his own almost arrogant expression. "You didn't know about me, did you? Dad said he hadn't talked to you since before I was born."

Well before this girl would have been born. The last time he'd seen his father had been the morning of his eighteenth birthday. He'd risen early, having packed the night before, and walked past the man passed out on the sofa.

Some kids saved for college. All he'd been looking for post high school was his own place.

He raised a finger, hoping to get a moment to collect his thoughts. Wyatt rose, went to the door, and opened it a crack. "Esme, can you order us something to eat and drink?"

His assistant studied him. He gave a slight shake of his head, and relief filled her face. "Yes, sir."

He closed the door and strolled back to the chair, dropping into it with deceptive casualness.

A sister.

A tiny, helpless little thing who looked like him and was the same age as him when his mother had died and his father had become an alcoholic stranger whose son's existence had pained him.

Dear God.

Ice spread through him. Coldness was good. Since Tatiana had come back to him, he'd chipped away at that protective layer, but he welcomed the frozen layer surrounding his emotions right now.

"What's your father's name, Ellie?" He sounded flat and emotionless to his own ears, but he couldn't work up the ability to fix that.

"Sam Caine." She dug into her back pocket and pulled out a rumpled photo. "I thought you might need proof."

Wyatt stared at the piece of paper in her hand before stretching out to accept it. Proof. Yes, the man in the photo was definitely his father. Older. Happy. Smiling at a baby he was holding in his arms.

It was hardly a DNA test. Wyatt's finger tightened on the photo for a brief second, creasing the corner before he handed it back to Ellie.

"I knew he was married before he met my mom, of course, and that he had a son. I don't have any other siblings. When I found out your name, I investigated you."

"Investigated me."

"The Internet. That's how I knew where to find you. We live in Tucson. I'm just visiting here for the weekend."

The Internet made kids dangerous, and the fact that this girl was here alone led him to believe she was already a bit of a problem.

"How old are you again?"

"Nine."

"You're very precocious for a nine-year-old." Not that he knew many nine year olds. But her precise speech and sharp gaze didn't seem childlike at all.

She tilted her head, her brief initial flash of timidity gone. "Precocious is muttering adorably insightful things. I'm really smart. Especially with computers."

Fascinated despite himself, he ran his hand through his hair. "Great."

They sat in silence for a minute. "So. Your parents are…married." The word felt distasteful on his lips. The old man had gone into an alcohol-soaked depression after Wyatt's mother had died, neglecting his only son. Screamed, cried, raged at his only son. Made that kid feel like he was nothing.

"Yes. They're married."

Bastard like that didn't deserve a second chance at a family. Not after he'd screwed with his first one.

Wyatt had turned out okay, outwardly. He was successful, he donated to charity, he wasn't an alcoholic or abuser himself. But he wasn't normal. He never would be.

No one understood that, not even Tatiana. Living with a dysfunctional parent was like taking a piece of wood and letting it sit in the rain. It warped it. It could be stained and sanded and cut, but that damage would always be there.

He focused on the pragmatic details. "Did your mom drop you off here?"

Ellie looked down and ground the toe of her sneaker into the carpet. "Um, not exactly."

His stomach knotted. "Your parents don't know you're here, do they?"

She sighed, a soft gust of air. "No, sir."

Polite. "How did you get here, Ellie?"

"I had my allowance money. I took a cab."

Wyatt bit back his immediate response to that, because it involved vulgar words. Vegas wasn't the hotbed of depravity that the world made it out to be. Still, he wouldn't want his nine-year-old hopping into a cab by herself here. Hell, he didn't like it when Tatiana took public transportation, and she was a grown woman. Anything could have happened to the girl.

Not his kid. Maybe not even his sister. It wasn't his place to scold her. The knock on the door interrupted them, and Esme entered, carrying a tray.

The woman would never cease protecting him, playing waitress so more staff wouldn't see Ellie. He cleared his throat. "Esme, this is my... This is Elizabeth."

Without missing a beat, Esme dimpled at the girl. "What a pleasure. I wasn't sure what you'd like to eat, so I had them send up some doughnuts and bagels and fruit."

"That's fine," he assured her.

Ellie thanked Esme. After the older woman left, she daintily picked up a bagel and nibbled at it.

She ate like Tatiana, he noted. All delicate and birdlike. He made a fist and rested it on his thigh. "Is there a reason you didn't want your parents to know you were coming here, Ellie?" The ugly scenarios played in his mind, fueled by history.

"Well, my dad looked so sad when he was talking about you." She placed the bagel back on her plate. "I didn't want to bring you up and have him be upset."

His muscles locked. The sound of tears and shouting

rang in his ears. "How does your dad get when he's upset?" *Does he cry? Does he scream? Does he tell you he wishes he was dead? Does he ask you to kill him, because he'd be happier that way?*

She ripped off a piece of the bagel and shredded it. "He gets quiet, and he tries to pretend he's okay, but I can tell he's not."

"Quiet."

"Yes. He's a quiet guy, but I can tell he's usually happy. His sad quietness has a different feel to it."

You do not share the same father.

It could be a coincidence he and this girl looked alike. She could have obtained that photo somehow or doctored it and this was an elaborate scam. Because there was no way the man she was describing was his dad.

He was careful not to let his suspicion show. First things first. He wasn't about to have the police show up because he was harboring a runaway. "Your parents are probably frantic."

"I left my mom a note."

He raised an eyebrow. "Really. Do you think she'll read the note and go about her day?" Because if so, the kid really did need protection from neglectful parents.

Ellie winced. "No. She's probably not up yet, though. Her best friend is getting married this weekend, and she was helping with wedding stuff until late."

He pulled his cell phone out of his pocket. "Then you should call her."

Ellie made a face and reached into her backpack to retrieve a green phone. "I guess you're right."

Did most nine year olds have their own phone? Though

if his kid ran off on a regular basis, he'd glue a phone to her hand. A phone with GPS.

She rubbed the screen with her thumb. "Maybe we should hang out a bit more before I call," she said hopefully.

"Are you scared?" *Will they hurt you?* If Sam Caine was her father, maybe he had graduated to using his fists. Maybe her words about how he was a happy, mild-mannered man were BS, a child's wishes.

His stomach knotted. Or maybe the mother was the monster.

"Scared? No. Well, yes."

His muscles tensed. "Ellie…"

"My dad might get sad, but my mom's going to lecture me forever. And I'll probably get grounded."

He let his shoulders relax. Lecturing and grounding sounded like appropriate parental responses. If she was telling the truth.

Ellie pushed a button and held the phone to her ear. He could hear ringing and then a woman's groggy voice. "Um, hi, Mom. It's Ellie."

There was a burst of chatter. "No, I'm not at the hotel. I came to see… Mom, calm down. I'm fine. I came to see…" Ellie shot him a glance, "…Wyatt."

There was dead silence for a moment. Ellie nodded. "Yes, that Wyatt. I heard Daddy telling you… I know. I know." A resigned expression crossed her face. "Yes, I know I shouldn't have gone off on my own. That sounds fair. I'm okay. Yeah, I'm at his hotel. He's been really nice. I… Okay."

She lowered the phone. "Is it okay if she talks to you?"

His initial response was no. He did not want to talk to

the woman who was allegedly married to his son-of-a-bitch father. Not today and not ever.

But it was remarkably hard to convey that to a child. So he took the phone and held it to his ear. "Hello."

"Mr. Caine." The woman's voice was stilted and formal and carried a hint of a Southern accent. "My name is Carol. I am so sorry, and I apologize for my daughter." In the background came the sound of clothes rustling. "I am on my way right now to get her."

Wyatt glanced at the girl. "It's not a problem."

"She is okay, right? I can't believe she just walked out in a strange city." Her voice thickened.

"She looks none the worse for her adventure."

"I didn't think you knew about her." The woman's voice softened. "I've been lobbying for you to meet, but certainly not like this."

"It's fine." His father's new wife. He was speaking to his father's wife. His mother had been dead for so long he could barely remember her. But this woman had taken her place. If Ellie was to be believed at all, she had made his father…happy.

A bead of perspiration slid down his forehead. He was distantly annoyed at the small evidence of his lack of control.

"Perhaps when I get there, we could have breakfast…"

He angled his body away from the girl, lest the sight of her crack the icy barrier that had solidified around his heart. "I am rather busy. I'm afraid I don't have time for that today."

"Of course." The woman was silent. "My husband…your father, he…"

"We will see you shortly, then."

The woman hesitated. "Yes. Yes, of course."

"Do you need directions?"

"No, we were sightseeing, and I'm aware of where your casino is. I'm not far. We're at the Holiday Inn Express. I'm getting in my car right now."

"When you arrive, come around to the back entrance. Ellie will be waiting there." He gave her rough directions. "You can avoid the traffic in front." And gossipmongers wouldn't see the child.

"Okay. Thank you for looking out for her."

That sounded far too familial, and he didn't know how he felt about that. "It was what anyone would have done."

"Of course. Thank you. I'll be right there."

He hung up without saying anything further and handed the phone back to Ellie.

The two of them stared at each other for a brief moment.

"I'm grounded for at least two weeks, Mom said. No TV too," Ellie announced glumly.

"You probably shouldn't be running off in strange cities. There are people out there who could hurt you." *Unless you have a reason to run away.*

"I guess." She glanced up at him through her tangled lashes. "It was worth it, though. I'm glad I got to see what you looked like. I couldn't even find many good photos online."

"You probably shouldn't be running amok on the Internet either." There were more than a few salacious articles printed about him.

"It's how I learn things. I need to learn things." The girl

slid off his couch and grabbed her backpack. It was cheap but in good condition. After his mother had died, he hadn't gotten new school supplies until he was old enough to walk to the store and buy them himself. "That's also why I wanted to see you. My dad told my mom that you were like me."

"Like you?"

"A genius."

He scoffed. "I'm no genius." School had been fine, and he hadn't had to expend much effort to grasp concepts, but his life had been all about survival back then. That meant most of his time had gone into working and paying bills.

"Sure you are. You're old, but you're still pretty young to be in charge of all of this." Her lips twisted, the cynical expression out of place on such a baby face. "My parents are great, but I don't really feel like I belong. It's nice to see that I'm not so unusual. It's okay to be different if you have someone you can be different with. You know?" She held out her hand. Slowly he extended his own hand and grasped hers. Her grip was firm—for a nine-year-old.

"Thanks for seeing me."

"It's been a pleasure, Ellie." A rush of protectiveness pierced his armor at the feel of the small, breakable bones in her hand. They shook once and then paused, as if they were both pondering what the next move was.

A hug? No. Rejected. He was not a hugger.

After a long moment, her hand slipped out of his. "I hope I get to see you again. But I understand if I won't."

He couldn't guarantee her that she would. If she was legit, a fraternal visit would require him to arrange it with her folks. With his father.

Ha. Ha. No.

Wyatt cleared his suddenly scratchy throat. "Just. Give me a second, okay? I need to go to the bathroom. And we'll head down to see your mother." His father's wife. Allegedly. He swallowed down bile.

"You don't want to see her," Ellie guessed. Shrewd kid.

Since he appreciated candidness, he replied truthfully. "No. I don't."

She nodded and hitched her backpack higher. "Okay."

He went inside his attached bathroom and turned the taps on, uncaring that he was dripping water on his suit when he splashed it on his face, struggling to distill the thoughts running through his head.

Calm down. Think. You're at the table, the cards have been dealt. Who are the players?

His father. His father's wife. Their child.

Who's the most important player?

The girl.

He glanced into the mirror, not recognizing the wild-eyed man staring at him, his hair and face wet.

Yes. The girl.

What do we need to know about this player?

First: was her story legit? Easy enough, that part.

Second: did she need him? Did she need help?

The child glowed with health, and she looked well cared for. His clothes had never been as neat and pressed, and her arms were round, like she didn't know what it was like to scrape together a dinner when all the cupboards were bare and parents were absent.

Still, appearances could be deceiving, and no one knew better than him what kind of father Samuel Caine could be.

No one knew better than him how hard it was to hope someone would help, that someone would believe that his parent was abusive even though there was never a mark on his body.

What if this poor kid was being abused, her sharp mind wasted on parents who diminished her?

People could change. People could grow and learn from their mistakes. His current relationship with Tatiana was based on that premise, so he had to believe it. But his father? God.

What will you do with the information you find out about this player?

Help her? Take her? The panic he'd experienced on thinking he was actually her father resurfaced. What the fuck did he know about being part of a family? Nothing. He was only now learning how to be someone's partner.

Worry about that later. Gather the information first.

He inhaled deeply. Mobilized, he wiped off his face and went back into his office. "Ellie—" He cut himself off, stymied by the silent room.

Frowning, he jerked open his office door to find the waiting room empty of everyone except Esme. "Where is she?"

Esme glanced up in surprise. "She said that you told her to wait in the lobby for you."

Part of him was annoyed. The other part was impressed.

If this is how she lies now, she's going to be a monster when she's a teenager.

"I didn't." He strode out the door and downstairs. When he got to the back entrance, he didn't find Ellie sitting on the bench outside, or a strange woman waiting.

Gather the information.

He yanked out his phone and dialed his security, not bothering with pleasantries when someone picked up. "Check the entrances and tell me if you saw a dark-haired female child leave in the last five minutes. About nine years old."

He waited impatiently for the guard to run through the footage. The woman finally spoke. "Yes, sir. A young girl exited the back entrance three minutes ago and got inside a Toyota Camry. Do you want me to run the plates?"

Goddamn it. "Yeah. Get back to me."

He dialed his private investigator on his way back to his office. The man picked up as he walked past Esme and shut his office door.

The PI had a small, exclusive operation, and Wyatt used him mainly because he was certain Jared wouldn't spill his client's secrets even if his skin was being peeled off his body. "Mr. Caine."

"Jared. I need you to find out everything you can about a young girl." He glanced around, though he was ensured privacy in his office. "Elizabeth Caine. Nine years old."

"Date of birth?"

"I don't know. Parents are allegedly Carol and…" he forced the words out, "…Samuel Caine. They supposedly lived in Tucson."

Jared paused. "Any relation?"

"Samuel Caine is my father." Dispassionately, Wyatt rattled off the man's date of birth and social security number. He'd had the number memorized by the time he was twelve because he'd needed it to handle their various household finances when his father was unable to.

If Jared was surprised by the news that his biggest client even had family, he didn't betray it. "Very well. Everything?"

Wyatt dropped into his chair. "Everything. I want to know where the girl goes to school, her medical records, her shoe size. I want every piece of information on the parents as well."

"Not a problem."

"As soon as possible."

"I can get you anything that's public records immediately. Confirmation that those records are accurate and any more information may require mobilizing someone in Tucson, so it may take a day or two."

"As soon as possible," Wyatt repeated, and hung up.

He placed his phone carefully on his desk and steepled his hands. Now what?

Now you wait for information. Once you have information, you can move.

His phone buzzed. He peered at it. Tatiana. *Feel up to playing with me tonight? We leave at eight, sharp.*

He stared at the text for a long moment. Wyatt was well aware of what he should do. A proper boyfriend would call Tatiana or head upstairs right now and tell her everything that had happened. Let her soothe him. Let her handle all of those bubbling emotions he was so inept at processing.

Only...they wouldn't just talk about today's bizarre encounter. He'd have to open his veins. Whine about his childhood. Lay all of his weaknesses out in front of her, regardless of whether the kid's story checked out.

He squeezed his eyes shut. The past year, he'd been consumed with wooing her. Getting her to trust him. Care for him. He needed her in his life, and never before had a goal been so important. Never had a goal seemed so challenging.

Adult Wyatt had to be enough for Adult Tatiana.

He opened his eyes, staring bleakly. He wasn't enough. He had told her that. Her family had told her that. She didn't believe them, for whatever reason.

Lucky for him. But it meant he couldn't reveal his foibles now. Not his childhood scars. Not his fear he would never be able to be a part of a functional family. Not yet. Not until she was in too deep.

It was a manipulative tactic, but he was a manipulative man. Wyatt swallowed, his self-loathing tasting like ashes.

She's going to be pissed. His difficulty expressing himself had been a major problem when they were kids, and he'd promised he would do better.

Though, to be fair, what was there to tell? He wouldn't hide a sister from Tatiana, but Jared hadn't yet confirmed the kid was related to him. Even a birth certificate wouldn't prove anything until Jared could verify it was the real deal. That could easily take until tomorrow.

He drew the frigidness around him, settling it over his emotions. Business as usual today. First order of business was ensuring he was distracted this evening as well.

He picked up the phone. *Sounds perfect. Can't wait.*

Chapter Six

SHE SHOULD HAVE brought her sketchbook with her, Tatiana decided. It was her distraction of choice when she had to wait somewhere. And it was better than her usual haphazard M.O. of scribbling on whatever surface was at hand.

She frowned at the doodle she'd made on the napkin. The design had been in her head all day, nagging and poking at her while she'd hunched over a desk and set stones.

Damn it. Even haphazardly sketched on a napkin precariously balanced on one leg, the ring was perfect. It would be exquisite if she cast it.

With a small growl, she seized the paper. Her fingers only made one crease before she changed her grip and tenderly folded it. She stuck it and her slim pen back into her purse and drummed her fingers on the leather of the seat in the limo.

She had expected Wyatt to come upstairs to shower and eat first, but he had left her a message a couple of hours ago telling her he had gotten tied up and would meet her at the car. He had sounded sufficiently distracted, so she assumed it was something big.

Still…Tatiana checked her watch. Fifteen minutes late? For Wyatt, that was a lifetime.

The door opened, and she straightened as Wyatt slid in to sit next to her. "Hey, you—oh."

His lips came down hard on hers, the kiss desperate and more than a little wild. One hand slid behind her head, holding her still for him. His tongue thrust inside, taking her mouth as easily as he took her body.

It was a different kiss than the one she had received when he'd pushed into the ladies' room last night. That had been deliberate seductive aggression. This was out of control. One thing Wyatt rarely was.

"Wow." She gave a breathless laugh when they parted. "Miss me?"

He didn't respond, only leaning his forehead against hers, his hot breath gusting over her lips. His lashes were long arcs on his cheeks. She cradled his cheeks and tilted him away, noting the deep furrow between his eyebrows, the lines bracketing his mouth. "Hey. Are you okay?"

He inhaled and opened his eyes. They were glassy for a second, but his lashes swept down, concealing them. "Yes. Yes, I'm fine. Sorry I'm late. Long day."

She studied him for a minute. Tension strummed through him, so obvious she would have had to be blind not to notice. Blind, or not in love with him. "Would you rather go home? We can watch a movie—"

"No," he replied quickly. "No. That is, I wanted to see what you had planned tonight." His smile was forced, not fooling her. "Sounded intriguing."

"Wyatt—"

"Stop." A muscle in his jaw twitched. "Please. Don't ask me anything. I need… I want…"

Need me. Want me. Gripped with the desire to soothe whatever had left him so disturbed, she ran her thumb over his cheek. "Tell me."

He caught her finger and bit down on the pad of it. "On your knees."

WYATT HALF-EXPECTED Tatiana to raise an eyebrow and make a saucy quip at his guttural command. He didn't know if he could take that right now.

He had kept himself together all day, and other than Esme, he was certain he had fooled everyone he came into contact with. They might have thought he was more brusque and preoccupied than usual, but no one would consider he was distressed about personal matters. Because he didn't have a personal life.

Except Tatiana.

One glimpse of her blonde head and he'd lost his control. He had to bury himself in her taste, wrap it around him, a layer of heat to keep him from freezing to death. A quick blast and he could return to normal.

She didn't move for a second, considering him, and he almost howled. *Please don't ask, don't talk, help me get it together…*

Slowly she cast a glance at the divider up between them and the driver and slipped to her knees. She wore a dress of some frothy pink material which made her look like a sweet piece of cotton candy. When he got his tongue on her, she would melt like spun sugar. He swallowed, the taste of her nipples and pussy burned into his memory.

She ran her palms up his thighs and pressed, until she had made a place for herself. Her nails scratched him through the material of his pants.

Tatiana dropped a kiss on his inner thigh. "Are you sure everything's okay?" Another kiss, closer to his hardening cock.

"It will be," he managed.

Her lips skated up his leg. Her lips covering her teeth, she mouthed the head of his cock through his slacks and underwear. She compressed her lips, and he grunted at the pressure. Never enough.

His fingers flew to the fastening of his pants, but she was already there. "Let me," she murmured.

He couldn't deny her. Not now. Not ever.

He hissed in a breath when she pulled out his semi-erect dick from the tangle of pants and boxer briefs. She nuzzled it against her cheek, her expression dreamy. With one finger, she stroked the tip of it, teasing the sensitive head. He closed his eyes and leaned his head back against the leather headrest, ready to let her sweet mouth take him away.

The phone in his jacket pocket rang, and his eyes sprang open.

"Who is it?" she whispered, as if the other person could hear.

"No one important." No one who couldn't wait.

"Find out." She ran the tip of her nail down his cock.

He shuddered. "What?"

"Find out."

He didn't want to find out. Jared had assembled some

documents for him to view, but he hadn't wanted to so much as look at them until the other man could verify their authenticity. What if he had managed to do that already?

The ring came again, shrill. Tatiana sat back on her knees. He cast her an annoyed glance, but he pulled out his phone and glanced at the display. Relief. Not Jared. "IT," he said tersely.

"Pick it up."

"Goddamn it, Tatiana…"

"Pick it up, or…" challenge and mischief lit her eyes, "…I stop."

Catching on, exhilaration rushed through him. Yes, yes, yes. A game. A game was exactly what he needed.

Wyatt mock scowled, but she only smiled and circled his cock. One stroke down, then up again, her palm skating over the sensitive tip.

He answered the phone. "Caine," he growled.

She rewarded him with a small kiss to the underside of his penis, her shining green eyes laughing up at him.

"Yes." He tried to pay attention to what his head of IT was saying, but it was a garbled mess of words and syllables. Why was the man still at work? He needed less conscientious employees.

Tatiana had his dick in her hands. Nothing else existed in the world.

She flattened her tongue and licked him from base to tip, once, twice. The third time, he arched up, and she drew him in. Her slender hand slid down the part of his shaft she couldn't get in her mouth, her saliva lubricating her fist. His hard flesh pressed against her smooth, inner cheek. Hot. Wet.

"We can meet about it tomorrow," he interrupted the man on the phone. What was his name? Jim? John?

Oh, God, sweet forgetfulness.

She pulled away, leaving his cock wet and abandoned, and ducked her head.

"No, I don't want to—Fuck. No. No, not you." He clenched his thigh muscles as her eager mouth captured his balls. She sucked gently, and his hand gripped his phone hard enough to crack it.

Her tongue slid up the furrow between his balls, dragged against the underside of his cock, and then she paused, watching him expectantly.

He exhaled. She was rewarding him. Each time he spoke, she gave him a little more.

Clever. He'd remember it the next time *she* was on the phone.

Shooting her a glare that he hoped conveyed his displeasure, Wyatt readjusted the phone so he could hold it between his ear and shoulder. He sank both hands into her tousled curls, the strands curling around him like silk bonds. Little tease she might be, but she wasn't going anywhere until she sucked him off.

He gave a tug of her hair, and her cheeks flushed redder, her lashes fluttering. "Tell me more about this vulnerability," he said into the phone.

He used his grip on her head to bring him closer, and she rewarded him by engulfing half his cock in her mouth, sucking him in time to his muttered *hmms* and *oh reallys* and *yes*. As long as he uttered something, she was on board. The second he paused too long, so did she.

"That sounds great," he finally said, ready to the end the

game, his every muscle locked and strained. He didn't think he'd be able to take any more, and as much as he liked his IT guy, there were some things the man did not need to know. Namely that his girlfriend was the best cocksucker on the West Coast.

Now, if the man wasn't an employee…

"I'll call you later. Something's come up," he interrupted the man, and released Tatiana long enough to fumble the phone off and toss it onto the seat. The vibration of Tatiana's low laugh sent a zing of pleasure up his shaft. "Fuck, yeah. Give me a little hum."

She obeyed, and his stomach tightened, the sound traveling up along his cock. He guided her lower, until she was swallowing him whole. "You were teasing me. You have to pay for that now."

The sensation of her throat muscles closing around his cock, her muffled moans, her soft hair gripped in his hands…it was all too much. He released her for a second, let her come up for air, and then thrust again, harder and faster until his balls drew up and he came in a rush, spurting into her mouth. She swallowed every drop, only releasing him when he was spent.

"Fuck. Perfect," he gasped. She did this to him, turned him inside out. Sex with other women could be good, could be spectacular, but it could never be this.

He would be ruined without her.

He brushed his hand over her head, and she glanced up and gave a naughty grin. "I hope you have another round or two left in you. I'm not done with you tonight."

The limo chose that moment to come to a stop. Wyatt turned his head and looked out the heavily tinted window.

They had stopped in front of a building with the word *DECADENCE* emblazoned over the entrance. He had heard of it. It was an upscale and exclusive place, catering to young celebrities, the hipster elite, and tourists with too much money to burn.

It was owned by Akira Mori.

"Tatiana…" He licked his lips. Crazy to presume anything. "What are we doing here?"

Tatiana was tugging his clothes back into place, and he took over the job, zipping and buckling his cock back in. Her nipples were tight beneath the bodice of her dress. His mouth watered.

He could taste them, right here. His driver knew better by now than to jerk the door open.

"What are we doing here? Hmm. Each other? Maybe?"

The hopeful note in her voice made his lips twitch, while the words stoked his desire. "Tatiana."

She busied herself tidying her hair, disguising the havoc his fingers had wreaked. "Whatever you want us to do."

"No. Spell it out for me. I want to be certain."

The dark excitement in her gaze made his nerve endings sizzle. "Want to invite a couple of other people to play with us?"

He licked his suddenly dry lips. "Akira."

"And her friend Remy." She shook her head. "I don't know him well, but Akira assures me he's trustworthy. And, well, Akira might act like a loudmouth, but no one would ever hear anything from her. It would be as discreet as we can get." Her lashes swept down. "We fantasize about an audience and watching other people fuck. I thought maybe we can try it. In a safe space. With safe people."

His voice was hoarse. "You don't have to do this for me, you know. I'm content with only you."

"I know." Her throat worked. That lovely, graceful throat that had swallowed his cock whole only minutes ago. "I want this. I want to do it for you, but I want to do it for me, too, because it's hot as hell. But it only works if we're both on board, so if you're not interested, you need to be honest."

Not interested? Was she insane? The thought of making those whispered fantasies a reality made him want to weep with joy.

He could drown himself in her pleasure, surround himself with hedonism and sex. Surround himself with Tatiana and forget the real world and the uncertain future.

How had she known? This was exactly what he needed tonight. "Don't be absurd. I'm more than interested." He brought her hand to his lips and brushed a kiss over the deceptively delicate palm. "What's on the table? Watching? Fucking? Touching?" They'd teased each other with that fantasy before—another man or woman touching her, making her come for him.

"Yes."

He raised an eyebrow. "Yes…"

"Yes. All of it. Watching them and having them watch us. As far as touching…we only fuck each other, but I'd be on board with some fondling or kissing or licking. I'll stop it if I decide it's too much or I don't like it. I don't know Remy well enough to let him touch me. But…I'm comfortable with Akira." She cleared her throat. "The house parties. You know."

His head spun, the blood having rushed to his cock

from her matter-of-fact recitation of her boundaries. "Oh, honey. How did I end up with you?"

"Just lucky, I guess."

A smile crossed his face. "That I am."

Chapter Seven

TATIANA CAST WYATT a glance as she led him inside the club. "Do you want something to drink?" It was crowded but not packed. There were a few patrons milling around, the DJ playing low-key music that would transition within the next hour or so to something louder and wilder.

"I'm good," he said, pitching his voice louder to be heard over the music. "Where are we going?"

"To the VIP area."

"Hmm."

Her skin was tingling with both excitement and nerves. This was big, bigger than anything they'd done before. She had been fairly certain he'd be on board, but relief had made her lightheaded when he'd immediately agreed.

He wasn't simply pretending to be into it, either. Tatiana would be able to tell if he was faking. The lines around his eyes had relaxed, the tension that had been strumming through him diminished. A shadow lingered, but she had effectively distracted him from whatever worries he had brought home from work.

A BJ was a pretty good cure for stress, but impending

sex games could really blast through it.

Tatiana nodded to a bouncer who stood guard at a hallway. The other man stepped aside, and they went down the short hall until they reached a staircase. The music became more muted as they climbed.

Wyatt gripped her hand tightly as they came to the top of the stairs. An abandoned dance floor stood in the center of the room, surrounded by opulent leather chairs and sofas.

The room appeared empty, at first glance, and Tatiana entertained a brief worry that she and Akira had gotten their wires crossed.

"There," Wyatt said, his voice so low it was barely a breath. "On the sofa."

A shadow moved in the recesses of the dimly lit room. Tatiana peered into the darkness. As her eyes adjusted, she made out a couple locked in a passionate kiss. Akira and Remy had not waited for them.

Emotions swept over her, excitement and nervousness creating a giddy mix. She grabbed Wyatt's arm when he would have taken a step. He turned his head, the blue lighting casting his face into shadow. "I want to make sure, one last time, that you're cool with this."

The corner of his lip curled up. "I can sign a consent form, if you like."

Tatiana glanced at the couch, and arousal slid through her. "You and I, we've never done anything like this before." Whispers and thoughts and the danger of getting caught. Those were their favorite things. "I want to be certain you won't look at me any differently tomorrow morning."

He considered her for a brief moment before slipping his hand under her hair. He used the grip on her neck to pull her forward and delivered a quick, hard kiss. "There is nothing you can ever do that would make me look at you any differently. I'll never shame you for anything you do with your body. I won't let you shame yourself, either. We like what we like." He gave her the slow, bad-boy smile that had melted her heart at sixteen. "And right now, what I'd like is for both of us to enjoy ourselves. However that might happen."

"In that case…" She drew her finger up his chest. "Can you do me one more little favor?"

"What's that?"

She leaned in closer and licked his firm lower lip. "Pretend this was your idea," she whispered. "Make me want it. Make me crave it."

The flare of his nostrils was the only sign she had that he heard. He drew back and laced his hand with hers, and started walking toward Akira and Remy.

Slipping into the role the way some women might slip into a silk robe, she deliberately made her steps hesitant, so he had to tug her forward. She stumbled once or twice, but he never faltered in his long-legged strides.

He came to a stop in front of the couple, who were still engrossed in each other. Supremely confident, he sank into a huge leather armchair. Awkward, she hovered until he urged her to sit on his lap.

A bottle of champagne sat chilling in an ice bucket on the side table. Wyatt poured two glasses and handed her one. She accepted it automatically and sipped from the glass, mindful of Wyatt's cock pressing against her hip and his finger lazily tracing a pattern on her arm.

A handful of feet separated the sofa and the chair they

sat in. There was nowhere for her to look but straight ahead at Akira and the man she had drafted into tonight's games. When Tatiana had spoken with her on the phone earlier in the day, Akira had assured her Remy was sweet and uninhibited, and best of all, discreet. Tatiana didn't want their exciting night turning into a PR mess for Wyatt.

Tatiana wasn't sure how tight-lipped Remy was, but he was hot. His face looked like it belonged on a European model, and he was lean and toned under his expensive navy suit. When he shifted, his bald head shined under the light directly above them. His eyes flashed open, and she caught a hint of ice blue.

He was no Wyatt, she added loyally. But nothing to sneeze at.

Akira was...Akira. Glamorous as usual, she wore a short, silver, sequined dress that showed off her magnificent legs and breasts.

Tatiana took a bracing sip of champagne, the bubbles tickling her throat. Remy's long fingers stroked up Akira's leg, until he was flirting with the hem of her dress.

Tatiana didn't realize she was holding her breath until she let it out in a rush when the man slid the dress up. He broke his lips away from hers to say, "Open your legs."

Akira opened them a sliver, and he urged them farther apart, until her pussy was bared to them. Waxed and plump, her lips were red and flushed with excitement.

"She's pretty," Wyatt whispered in her ear. "But not as pretty as you."

Tatiana couldn't respond, not when Akira was moaning as Remy sank two fingers inside her. He thrust them in and out, and her hips moved, following the movement. He pulled his fingers out teasingly, letting Tatiana and Wyatt see the moisture on them. "You're so wet, baby," he murmured to the woman.

Akira whimpered, still ignoring the others in the room. "It's all for you. Fuck me, please."

Remy shushed her. "You know it's not that easy."

Tatiana knocked back another gulp of her champagne. If she stretched her hand out, she could touch the couple. She could finger Akira herself, or press her hand over Remy's cock. But that wasn't what she wanted in her deepest, darkest fantasy.

Remy pulled at the woman's dress, yanking it down to bare her firm, round breasts and tight light-brown nipples. How many times had Wyatt done that to her, making her dress little more than a useless belt, eager to get to her most erogenous zones?

Remy cradled Akira's breast. The two of them might have decided not to acknowledge their spectators, but by the way Remy lifted and presented the flesh in his hand, there was no doubt he was playing to his audience. His head dropped down and he sucked, his cheeks hollowing with every pull. The music downstairs masked Akira's sharp cry of pleasure.

Wyatt's hand brushed against her knee, and Tatiana shuddered as if she were the one whose breasts were being pleasured. "Having fun yet? Watching them?" he asked.

"Yes."

"But that's not all you want."

He squeezed her thigh when she remained silent. Not silent because she was ashamed. Silent because she was too busy tracking the flush spreading over Akira's chest and neck as Remy scraped his teeth repeatedly over her nipples, stretching the flesh with each pull.

"No," she replied, her voice hoarse.

"Tell me what you want."

She shut her eyes so she could focus on his words. "I want them to watch."

"Watch what?"

"Watch you fucking me." The words tumbled out. "I want them to watch you fucking me, and see me loving it, everything you do to me. I want them to see me."

Remy bit Akira's nipple harder and glanced at Tatiana, a small smile curling his full lips. "I see you, sweetheart. It would be hard not to."

The man was devastating when he smiled.

Wyatt nipped her ear, as if chastising her. "Tell me how you want it. I'll give you anything you want." He paused. "Except another man touching you."

Brilliant. Wyatt was spinning her hesitancy about Remy into his own decree. No wonder she loved him. "Yes, sir."

"Killjoy," Remy muttered. He shot Tatiana a bright grin and casually licked Akira's nipple.

Akira barely flicked a glance their way. Instead, she ran her hand up Remy's leg and squeezed. "Remy." There was a world of demand behind the word.

Wyatt shifted behind her, and his fingers found the tab of her zipper. Her dress gave way, loosening around her chest. Wyatt slipped the straps over her shoulders, working the material down until she was topless.

Akira finally acknowledged their presence, her gaze appraising Tatiana's breasts. Only her breasts. The woman's gaze didn't go any higher than that. She was objectifying her, turning her into a sexual prop.

Tatiana loved it. It left her free to treat Remy and Akira the same way.

Wyatt licked her earlobe. He brought his fingers to her mouth and stroked them over the lower lip. She allowed one pass, two, but she was hungry for him, and she opened her mouth and sucked in his forefinger. He inserted a second finger and thrust deep enough to trigger her gag reflex. She let it come, aware he liked the tightening of her throat on any part of his body.

His fingers left her mouth, and she inhaled as he dragged the wet tips down to her nipple, circling the areola before clamping down on the tip. He pinched her hard, because that was how she liked it, and he knew her body better than his own. The touch shot straight from her breasts to her groin, and she squirmed in his lap.

Wyatt gave a low laugh. "You're getting antsy, aren't you?"

Sex and sin were a living breathing entity in the room. Clothes were coming off, inhibitions cast aside. Of course she was antsy.

"Poor thing," he crooned.

Remy slid his hand behind Akira's neck and released the tie of her halter top. The dress fell to her waist, mimicking Tatiana's state of undress. "Up," he commanded her softly.

Akira stood, and with a practiced shimmy of her hips, her dress fell to the ground, leaving her in a silver thong.

It was more than what Tatiana wore under her dress.

Akira's eyes briefly met hers, and Tatiana was both reassured and excited by the hot arousal in them. She didn't want her and Wyatt to be the only ones enjoying themselves. That would hardly be fair, given how hard they were going to be getting off on this. Tonight, and many nights after, when it was a memory.

Remy slowly unbuckled his belt. "What did I tell you?"

The other woman was one of the strongest people Tatiana had ever met, wealthy and independent. But her voice was timid when she spoke. "Don't wear anything underneath my dress. Sir."

The cold dominant, the reluctant submissive. Tatiana's favorite kink, the one Wyatt catered to so perfectly. Wyatt slid his hand in her hair and pulled her head back until her neck was arched. His teeth closed on her skin, hard enough to bruise.

"You disobeyed me," Remy said, his tone a weak imitation of Wyatt's at his bossiest.

Akira's lashes fluttered. "I did."

"Get on your knees."

Akira turned to face away from them and descended to her knees, the act graceful. Two dimples flashed above the cheeks of her ass. Her hands worked at the man's fly, and she pulled out his thick, long penis. Tatiana only got a single good look as he donned a condom, before Akira opened her mouth wide and sank down on it.

Remy shoved his hand in her hair and pushed her down farther. "That's it," he rasped. "Take it deeper."

Akira did, sucking more of it in until Tatiana was truly impressed. She considered herself a cock-sucking artist, and she didn't think she had anything on her friend.

The hand fondling her breast squeezed extra hard, and Tatiana was brought back to her own man and her own game. "You like Remy, don't you? You find him attractive?"

Wyatt crooned.

Ah, the moody lover. Classic.

When she didn't answer quickly enough, he raised his hand and spanked her tit, the sharp slap against her nipple bringing a rush of blood to the surface. She gasped. "I do."

"Did you see his cock?"

Remy watched her with eyes gone vague from lust.

"Yes."

"Did you like it?" Wyatt spanked her other tit, and she moaned.

"I did."

His next spank was harder.

"Not as much as I like yours," she added.

"Who gave him to you?"

"You did," she lied.

"Who gives you everything you need?"

Tatiana ground her ass back against his cock, annoyed that two layers of fabric separated them. "You do."

"Fucking right." He dipped his thumbs inside her dress and shoved it off. She raised her ass to help him, and then she was sitting gloriously naked.

Some long-dormant remnant of modesty flashed through her, told her that it was wrong to be nude above a public place, wrong to get excited over an audience.

Wyatt's hands slid up her legs. Remy groaned. The second of shyness vanished as her adrenaline spiked.

"Fuck, she's pretty," Remy bit out. His blue eyes shifted between Tatiana and the woman going down on him with such excited fervor.

Wyatt made a self-satisfied noise. He stroked her thigh with the lightest of touches. "Open your legs. Give him a good look."

She inched them wider. She wanted Remy to see, wanted to slam her legs open wide. *Look what my man is going to get. You'll never touch it.*

But that would ruin all the fun.

"Wider."

She feigned reluctance. "I don't know, Wyatt."

His voice hardened. "I want you to open your legs."

Her lower lip pouted. "I don't want to."

His hand in her hair wrenched tighter, until her neck was arched at an angle that was just shy of painful. She whimpered, delighted.

"Whose body is this?"

"Yours."

"Mine. My tits." He squeezed them hard, and then his hands traveled downward until they were both on her inner thighs. He wrenched her legs open. He arranged her so her feet were flat on the couch on either side of him, her cunt spread wide open.

His hand cupped protectively over her pussy. "My pussy."

She whimpered and made a halfhearted attempt to close her legs. "Please."

"Please what? I want them to see it. See what a slut you are for my cock. Aren't you?"

"Huh?" The excitement and lust was overloading her system, making it difficult to think or verbalize coherently.

"Aren't you a slut for my cock?" He settled her against his chest, the fine fabric of his shirt a smooth contrast to her heated back.

"Yes."

"Say it."

"I'm a slut for your—for you." Not just his cock. For his hands, his mouth, his everything.

His lips curved against the skin of her neck. "You always have been."

"I always have been." She paused, reciting the next verb tense in her mind, too nervous to say it.

I always will be.

"Good girl."

He stroked his hand down her arm, stopping when he reached her gold bracelet. "I do love this piece, you know." He pulled the bracelet off and made quick work of bringing her hands behind her. With a couple of twists, the metal bound her wrists.

Since she had taken advantage of his distraction to close her legs again, he wrenched them open. "If you don't listen, I'll tie your legs open, too," he chastised. "Understand?"

She strained against the gold. She was pampered, used to the silk of his ties or scarves. This was brutal and cold. Perfect. "Yes."

Wyatt kissed her neck. "Remy, let that woman off your dick so she can see how pretty this pussy is."

Remy's hand tightened in Akira's hair. "Fuck you, no. The only way she's getting off my dick is if she makes me come." He shook Akira's head. "Did you hear that? Do you want to see what they're doing?"

A frantic nod.

"Then work for it."

Akira redoubled her efforts.

Remy relaxed further and zeroed in on Tatiana's pussy. "She is stunning, Akira. I'd love to get my tongue in her."

"Tough shit." Despite his cold denial, Wyatt slid his fingers up and down Tatiana's slit, holding her open, advertising her creaminess. Taunting the other man with what he couldn't have.

Remy's breath started to come faster. Clearly Akira wasn't fooling around anymore. His hips worked, thrusting up into her mouth. Akira made a choking sound, and Remy gave a mean laugh. "Fuck yeah. Choke on that dick."

"This is obscene," Tatiana breathed.

Wyatt rested his chin on her shoulder. "Good. That's what you like, isn't it?"

Yes. "No."

"No?" Wyatt spread her wider. "Aren't you wet?"

"I don't know."

"Does she look wet to you, Remy?"

Remy moaned. "Extremely."

Wyatt looked down her body. "I think he's right, sweetheart. Let me check." Wyatt's hand moved lower, two thick fingers sliding easily inside her before withdrawing. He held the shiny digits up so she could see the liquid on them. "Look at that. Your pussy's dying for some cock, isn't it?"

She shook her head. "No."

He brought his fingers to her lips, painting them with her own lube. "I think you're lying."

He inserted the two fingers into her mouth, and she sucked them, eager to tempt him into losing control.

He pressed his lips against her ear, his hot whisper making her shiver. "Do you know what I do to bad girls who lie?"

Remy hissed out a curse. "Shit, I'm coming." He stopped his partner's head from rising. "No. Not yet." He thrust up twice and tensed, his face contorting as he came.

He breathed out and relaxed when it was over, releasing Akira. She immediately sat back on her heels, head lowered submissively.

Remy tossed the condom in the wastebasket near the couch, stood and shucked off his clothes until he stood in front of them nude. His body was more muscular than Wyatt's, but he was shorter. His cock was pretty, thick even when half-hard, shiny with his come.

Wyatt chuckled. "I don't think you're listening to me, Tatiana."

"What?" she asked absently.

Remy sat back down on the couch and stroked Akira's head. "You did such a good job, Akira. Come up here and sit on my lap so you can watch."

The woman stood and moved hurriedly to Remy, as if she feared the man would change his mind. She straddled him with her back to Remy, her long legs on either side of his.

She was mirroring Tatiana's position. Tatiana inhaled, ready to combust.

"Tatiana," Wyatt said.

She immediately responded to the controlled violence in the one word. "Yes."

"What do I do to bad girls?" he repeated.

She licked her lips, savoring the taste of her own body. "You spank them."

"And then?"

"You fuck them," she gasped out, the words barely audible.

"That's right." He pressed his thumb on her clit and

rotated it. "I'm going to give you another chance. You want this, don't you? Want everyone to see what a slut you are for my cock?"

Yes, yes, yes. She breathed in deep, her thighs tensing. His touch was too light to make her actually come. "No."

He stopped, hands lifting off her needy pussy. "Wrong answer." He raised his head. "Akira. Come here."

Tatiana's breath stopped.

The woman glanced over her shoulder, not moving until Remy nodded at her and slapped her ass, the noise lewd and fleshy. Then she got down on her hands and knees, crawling over to their chair.

Wyatt leaned in closer and whispered in her ear. "Tell me if it's too much."

"I want it," she whispered, ready to pass out from excitement. "I'll tell you if it's more than I'm willing to do."

Satisfied, he looked over her shoulder at Akira, who was sitting between her open legs, her avaricious gaze on every inch of Tatiana's spread, naked body.

"I need an extra set of hands," Wyatt explained kindly. "Don't finger her or touch her in any other way. Hold her pussy lips open for me."

Dear God, was he trying to kill her? She rubbed her ass against him. His cock was steel hard at her back, but as always, he had iron control over his needs.

Fingers, softer than Wyatt's, brushed over the curls on her mound. Those slender fingers landed on either side of her pussy and pushed the lips open.

Tatiana strained against her bonds, tilting her head back, but he was a solid force behind her. That touch alone, that foreign, unfamiliar touch, was enough to shoot her through the stratosphere.

"Thank you, Akira," he said, ever the gentleman, and then brought his hand down with a sharp crack over her pussy.

Her body tightened, and on the second slap she came, twisting against his hard arm around her and the metal that bound her tightly.

She came back to earth to find Akira still holding her spread open. Wyatt lazily inserted three fingers inside her and thrust a few times, giving her clit time to lose its oversensitivity after her climax.

"You let her come like that?" Remy *tsk*ed. "Akira doesn't so much as think of coming without my say-so."

Akira's snort was low, but obvious. Tatiana gave a weak smile.

"I'm a kinder man than you," Wyatt explained.

"Obviously."

"That doesn't mean she gets away with two spanks though." He spoke to Akira. "Wider."

Cool air rushed over her pussy as the woman obeyed. He raised his hand and started, the blows of his cupped palm delivering the bite of pain she needed. He was careful not to let her get used to any kind of rhythm, alternating sharp, quick blows with longer grinds, using his other hand to play with her tits.

Akira's fingers sometimes moved, readjusting their position, and the glance of her long nails or the hot puff of her breath as she exhaled made Tatiana want to scream with agonized arousal.

Remy lolled on the couch like a pasha, his hand jacking his rapidly hardening cock. Silent now, he watched with a predatory gaze as Wyatt delivered his punishment and she took her pleasure.

She came three more times as he spanked her, until her world was focused to the feel of his hand slapping her wet cunt and the never-ending stream of climaxes it delivered. She didn't realize she was crying until he stopped and wiped her cheek. "Whoa. Okay?"

Not Wyatt the conqueror's voice here, but Wyatt her lover. She nodded and swallowed her tears. "Yes."

"Sure?"

There was real concern, worry that he had gone too far. She loved him for it, even if it was wildly unnecessary. She turned her head so only he could hear. "I'm having the time of my life, and if you put the brakes on this now," she whispered, "I may never speak to you again."

A dimple flashed, and then his coldness was back in place. "I don't think you can deny how hot you are now, can you?"

"No." Her voice was small. She gave a shuddery sigh.

"Do you want this?"

"Yes." Or that's what she tried to say. It came out as an affirmative squeak.

"Who owns this body?"

"You do." *Squeak, squeak.*

"Can I do whatever I want with it?"

"Yes."

"I can tell Akira to eat you out. Or I can have you suck Remy's cock."

Her breasts rose and fell. That last sentence was for show. Their boundaries, once set up, were ironclad until they said otherwise. So she didn't have to think about her response. "Yes."

"I can fuck you in front of these two."

Akira's fingers twitched on Tatiana's pussy, and she flinched from the burst of illicit pleasure. "Yes."

"I can invite everyone downstairs. And fuck you in front of them."

"Yes."

"Why?"

"Because I'm yours."

Wyatt's teeth sank into her neck. "Good answer," he growled. "Let her go," he said to Akira.

She released Tatiana and twisted to look at Remy, who nodded. "Come here, baby. You did a good job." He stroked his condom-encased cock from root to tip. "Let me reward you."

Wyatt wrapped his hands around Tatiana's hips and lifted her up to stand. She glanced over her shoulder at the rustle of clothing. With a few swift motions, he pulled his clothes off, kicking them aside to lie on the floor.

Bias schmias. Wyatt's body was better than Remy's. Long and lean, with those rippling, sculpted muscles, his chest adorned with the perfect amount of hair.

And that hard, thick cock. She shuddered. She *was* a slut for that cock. No lie.

He stepped close, the heat of his body seeping into hers, and he worked at the knotted metal between her wrists.

On the couch, Remy pushed Akira to her back, so one leg rested on the floor, the other wrapped around Remy's hips. He pressed inside her, and she moaned, her red lips forming a small O.

Wyatt pressed a hand between her shoulder blades.

"Grab the back of the couch."

Eager to please, she bent over, her hands finding the slick leather. The position left her with her breasts almost hanging over the other woman's face. Akira stared up at her, her hot black eyes objectifying Tatiana's body and cataloguing her every expression.

The smooth head of Wyatt's cock traced between the seam of her buttocks, stealing Tatiana's attention. "I want to fuck you in the ass," he growled. "But I don't think I can wait to lube you up properly."

Akira licked her lips, eyes falling to half-mast as Remy picked up the speed of his thrusts. Tatiana inhaled. "You can do whatever you want to me," Tatiana breathed. "However you want."

Wyatt gave a dark chuckle. His cock moved lower, and he inserted the tip into her pussy. "It seems a shame to waste all this sweet wetness. You're dripping for me."

Tatiana's fingers tightened on the leather as Wyatt sank into her, his dick impossibly large after her multiple orgasms. He started fucking her in long, hard drives, the thick head of his cock almost pulling out of her before slamming back in. He was brutal, almost uncaring about her own pleasure. Exactly what she needed.

Remy's scalp brushed against her arm on his next pounding thrust, timed, she realized, to mimic Wyatt's. "She looks nice getting fucked, doesn't she?" Remy murmured to Akira.

"So pretty." Akira gave a small, secret grin. "I want to fuck her, too."

Wyatt gave a rough growl, used his grip on Tatiana's hips to pull her up to stand, bent his knees and fucked up into her. A primitive mark of ownership. Tatiana tipped her head back and cried out at the savage pounding.

Remy slowed his thrusts to appreciate the show, his eyes locked on her bouncing breasts. "Akira helped you so nicely. I don't think you're showing your thanks."

Wyatt slowed and pushed Tatiana down. Her hands slipped on the slick leather, desperate to find a grip. He pulled almost all the way out and then powered so deep inside she sank lower, her breasts dangled over the other woman's mouth. "What do you say, Tatiana? Should we reward her a little for helping me punish you?"

Yes, yes, yes. She nodded frantically.

His hand stroked over her head, soothing her. "Then give her whatever you want her to have."

Her mind raced with erotic possibilities but finally settled on the simplest scenario. She lowered herself until her nipple brushed against the other woman's mouth. Akira's tongue darted out and licked her. Tatiana gave a sharp cry and arched her back, so her entire nipple could be given a similar treatment.

Akira's lips were full and soft, and there was no maidenly hesitation when she wrapped them around Tatiana. The woman knew what she was doing, sucking her hard and strong. Tatiana's body would have collapsed had two large hands not wrapped around her arms and steadied her.

"God," Wyatt bit out. "Take whatever you want. I have you."

Wyatt's short, rapid strokes told her he was close, and between the steady sucking at her tits, the restraining hands on her arms, the feeling of being watched and appreciated, Tatiana couldn't stop the high, keening cry she gave. His cock brushed over her G-spot, and she sobbed. "There. Right there."

"Yes. Right here." He circled his hips, working that spot until she tightened around the cock inside her and came.

Wyatt ripped out of her and whipped her around, shoving her to her knees. "Your tits. I want it on you."

He jacked his cock, her lube making him slick and juicy. A couple of pumps with his own hand and he came, long and hard, his semen landing on her chest, which was already slick with sweat and Akira's saliva.

He fell to his knees and reached for her, massaging his come into the skin of her breasts and stomach, even dipping below to make sure her pussy was marked with his semen. He rested his forehead against hers, breathing hard. "Mine," he sighed.

"Yours," she agreed.

Their lips met in a kiss that was tender despite the sounds of renewed fucking behind them and the pulse of music, louder from when they'd arrived, vibrating beneath their knees. She pulled back and brushed his hair from his face, unable to tear her gaze away from his. Not even when Akira gave a small wail.

He pressed a kiss against her thumb. "Thank you."

"I love—" No. She cut herself off. Not here. Not with other people in the room. This was far more intimate than sexual shenanigans. Far more serious than anything else they'd ever done.

They'd traded the word love back and forth as children, and she wouldn't diminish that. However, what she felt for him now was so much bigger than what it had been. Bigger than either of them.

When you get home. Tell him tonight. Yes. That felt…right. No more lecturing herself. No more denying both of them. Giddiness made her beam. "I loved it. Thank you."

His answering smile was just as goofy as hers. "Good."

"God, I need a cigarette." Remy's hoarse voice reminded them both they weren't alone. Tatiana glanced over to find him standing, hitching his pants up.

Akira sat up, her face and body flushed but her cool composure back in place. "No smoking in here. Outside."

Remy picked up Akira's dress and handed it to her with a chaste kiss against her cheek. "You can't make an exception for the man who just fucked your brains out?"

"Hm. No. My brains are still intact."

"Sounds like a challenge. Night is young, babe."

Her smirk was dangerous. "If you feel you need to prove something, I won't stop you."

He whispered something to her before he turned to Wyatt and Tatiana. "You guys sticking around?"

Tatiana shook her head. Wyatt had all her attention now. "We'll be heading out."

Remy gave a mighty stretch and a cheerful grin, undaunted. "Right on. Thanks for inviting me. It's been fun."

Wyatt inclined his head, arrogant despite their nudity. "Yes. Thank you for…" He trailed off.

Tatiana pressed her face against Wyatt's shoulder, hiding her grin at his uncharacteristic loss for words. "Playing along?" she suggested.

Wyatt glanced down at her. "Yeah. That."

"My pleasure. Seriously." Remy winked at her as he walked past them.

Wyatt tucked a strand of her hair behind her ear, the gesture tender. "Ready?"

She shifted, aware of her too-sticky body. The drive home wouldn't take them long, but the frothy material of her dress would make it an uncomfortable ride. "I need a Kleenex."

"There's a restroom up here." Akira had stood to languidly slip her sequined dress on. She pointed to the left.

Wyatt helped Tatiana to her feet before scooping up their clothes. He stepped into his pants as she clutched her dress close. Tatiana stood on tiptoes to press a kiss against Wyatt's jaw. "Be right back. I want to clean up."

He paused in buttoning his slacks to pass his hand over her ass. "Not too much."

"Oh, never. I know how you like me."

WYATT ADMIRED THE elegant line of Tatiana's back and the round curve of her buttocks as she scurried to the bathroom. He finished fastening his pants and pulled his shirt on, frowning silently when her naked form disappeared from view. He wanted to wrap himself up in her again.

"It's so cute when a man moons after a woman."

Oh, right. He would have to go home to do that. Wyatt concentrated on the buttons of his shirt. His brain was foggy with sexual satisfaction and the pleasant exhaustion that came from hyper-focusing on his partner's every response. Keeping his defenses up around Akira would be difficult, even if he hadn't had the day he had. "I should thank you for arranging this."

"I didn't do it for you." A naughty smile tipped her lips. "I did it for Tatiana, and for me, because I like getting my hands on someone that hot. Though watching you fuck was nice. You're good at it."

He paused and eyed Akira. On anyone else, the words could serve as a come-on, but he felt as though she was merely stating a fact. Curled up on the couch like a lazy cat, her bare legs tucked under her, she was sexy. Disheveled. Hot. But without Tatiana in the room, he didn't have a lick of interest in stripping either of their clothes off again. "Thanks," he said shortly.

"I told her she was a lucky bitch at the gallery, to land you. But it's the opposite. You're the fortunate one." Akira shivered, the sequins on her dress catching the light. "Is it always like that with you guys?"

Yes. Always.

"It doesn't hurt that she's head over heels in love with you, I bet."

He froze. "What?"

The single word cracked like a whip, but Akira didn't take offense. She raised a slender shoulder and uncurled her legs, coming to stand. "Oh yeah. She looks at you like you hung the moon. I thought she was going to write you a sonnet there at the end." Had he not been watching her so closely, he would have missed the flash of wistfulness that crossed her face. "You're smart, indulging her desires the way you do. Acceptance and a lack of judgment are very seductive to women like us."

Wyatt shoved his hands in his pockets. "She hasn't said she loves me." Something he'd desperately wanted not more than a week ago. Before he realized the flip side to the overwhelming joy it would bring: despair if Tatiana wised up and left.

"Whatever." Akira examined her nails. "I approve of you on a conditional basis, especially after tonight."

"Gee, thanks."

"It's a compliment, really. My conditional approval is something to covet." Akira's gaze sharpened. "That borderline panic isn't a good look for you. If you want to love her back, Caine, that's fine. But if you're not going to be able to do that, if you're not able to give her everything she needs, cut her loose. Like I said, I think highly of her. She deserves better."

Everything she needs.

Adult Wyatt has to be enough for Adult Tatiana.

His throat worked. What if he wasn't?

"Uh, am I interrupting something?" Tatiana walked up to him. Automatically, his arm went around her, hauling her close to ward off the creeping, returning chill. She was dressed, if a bit rumpled.

Akira smiled at Tatiana. "Not at all. We're discussing business."

"You aren't seriously conducting business at an orgy," Tatiana said, amused. She looked up at him, and he forced his lips up.

"Oh, you're so cute." Akira fluttered her lashes. "This isn't an orgy. This is hardly a baby orgy. An orgy-ette, if you will. A four-gy. And I do business everywhere." She slinked closer and drew her finger down Tatiana's arm until she reached her bracelet. Akira tapped it and pulled it off her wrist with a quick twist. Intelligent avarice glinted in her eyes. "I want this. Add it to my bill. See? Business and pleasure. We all win."

Tatiana grinned. "Consider it a present."

"Even better. I like free." Akira donned the piece and held it up to the light, admiring it. "Call me if you want to play again. Now go on. Remy's only in town for the rest of the night. Gotta make the most of it."

"She's a character," Wyatt remarked as they wound their way through the club. He had to pitch his voice higher to be heard over the music. The place was beginning to get crowded.

Tatiana's shoulder brushed against a stranger's. The gleeful smile she shot Wyatt was easy to interpret and lightened the heaviness in his heart. *This guy didn't know what we were doing right upstairs.* "Are you complaining my friends aren't more boring?" she said aloud.

"Not at all."

They spilled out of the club, both of them inhaling the cool night air. "It's not like I had to search far and wide for deviance. It seems to come to me." She eyed him. "Like you."

"Like me."

They reached the limo, and Tatiana slid inside. Wyatt crowded her in, and she leaned her head against his shoulder. He pressed a kiss to her tousled hair. "Tired?"

"Exhausted. But I'll never forget it," she said simply.

"Me neither." He swallowed, words rising up in his throat, the need to pour out his worries great. Damn Akira. He had been doing so well savoring his time with Tatiana, living in the moment. "Hey."

She peered up at him, her eyes limpid green pools. *Go home. Take the rest of the night. Deal with this tomorrow.* "Mind if we stop and grab a burger? You didn't think to feed me before our big adventure."

She yawned, loudly. "Look, I could either arrange an orgy or make you a sandwich. I'm not superwoman."

Chapter Eight

WYATT PRODDED HER into the shower when they got home, though all she wanted to do was stretch out and go to sleep. Lazy, she leaned against the shower wall and let him wash come and sweat off her body, watching him from beneath half-lidded eyes.

He opened a tube he'd brought in with him and smeared cream on his fingers. She hissed and stood on her toes when he brought his hand to her pussy. "Poor baby," he crooned. "Are you sore?"

"Yes."

He nipped her pouting lip, his fingers going deeper, soothing her inflamed tissues with the salve. "This might help."

"Do you seriously stay prepared for the off chance that you would wreck my pussy?"

"It's hardly an 'off chance'. More like a certainty."

She tipped her head back and moaned as Wyatt found and manipulated her G-spot, under the guise of treatment. His body kept the water from hitting her, but the steam kept her warm. "Wyatt, I can't."

He brought his fingers out, smeared more ointment on them, and returned to her pussy, brushing his slick fingers over her abused clit. "I know. I'm just trying to take care of you. I can't help it if this gets you hot."

Please. That faux-innocence wasn't fooling anybody. She took the tube from him and squirted a generous amount on her palm before bringing it to his cock. "Are you feeling rubbed raw, too?"

"Actually, now that you mention it…"

The shower was filled with the sound of their escalating breaths and sighs as they touched each other. Wyatt leaned one hand against the wall and curled it into a fist as she measured him in slow, steady strokes, stopping to put more ointment on both of their hands.

He rubbed her clit, and she gasped. "Need it harder."

He *tsk*ed. "I can't give it to you any harder, sweetheart." He surrounded her clit with two fingers and squeezed, working it gently. "I don't want to hurt you."

Oh yeah? Two could play this game. She glanced up at him and released his cock. "I don't want to hurt you either."

He stretched up to yank out the detachable showerhead. "Here. Ride this."

The first blast made her squeal, but he dialed it back so the stream changed to a pulsing massage on her well-used flesh. She clasped his wrist and directed the stream of water to where she needed it. "You creative bastard," she said.

His chuckle was lost in her loud moan as she came.

He shut the water off and scooped her up, toweling them both off before carrying her into the bedroom. He dropped her on the bed and followed down on top of her, covering her up.

He sat up, straddling her, and grabbed the lube from their bedside table. He poured a handful onto his cock and stroked himself with long, slow pulls before dribbling the slick oil on her inner thighs.

He moved them both onto their sides so they were facing each other and fit his cock between her legs. "Open up," he murmured. "Give me something hot to fuck."

His cock glided between her legs easily, and he worked it hard and fast. Even then, he was considerate, avoiding everything but the slightest brushes against her tired pussy.

"You're amazing," she said dreamily. "Did you know that?"

He didn't stop, but his hand clenched on her hip. He stroked her flank and kept thrusting. "Am I?"

"Mm, yes."

He let out a shaky breath and pressed down on her upper leg. "Tighter."

She clenched her inner thighs, and he groaned. "Jesus, Tatiana. You're the amazing one."

"No." She shook her head as much as her limited range of motion would allow. "You give me exactly what I want and need. You have no idea how rare that is. I do." She stroked her fingers over his lips and face. There were wrinkles and lines on him that hadn't been there when he was eighteen.

That was okay. She was different too. Somehow their differences were meshing together.

She pressed a kiss to his lips, and it was sweet and perfect. The perfect moment. "I love you," she said clearly.

He shuddered—this big, strong man shuddered in her grip as if he were helpless. He thrust twice more, and

Tatiana felt his warm come on her flesh.

He let out a long breath. "Say it again."

"I love—"

His kiss cut her off. He rolled her onto her back and thrust his tongue in her mouth, pulling back for a brief second. "Again," he demanded.

"I—*mmph.*" She was laughing when she came up for air. "You're not letting me talk."

"I can't help it." He kissed her again. "You shouldn't."

"Shouldn't what? Love you?" She snorted, and then ruined her indignation with a yawn. "Stop me."

He rested his forehead against hers. She stroked her hand down his back, pausing when she felt the fine tremor running through his muscles. "Wyatt?"

He pushed away from her and rolled to sit on the side of the bed. His hands cradled his head, his back bowed. Chilled, Tatiana drew the comforter around her. "Hey. Look, you don't have to worry about saying it back or anything. I mean, I get that it's kind of fast, and I'm not putting any pressure—"

"No," he said harshly. "It's not that."

She sat up. "Um. Okay." Nibbling her lower lip, she stared at his rigid back. His first reaction to her big revelation had been way more fun. *More kissies please?*

"Tatiana."

"Yes?"

"I think I have a sister."

Chapter Nine

TATIANA BLINKED, NOT certain she'd heard correctly. "What?" The muscles in Wyatt's back bunched, and he shot to his feet, pacing to the bureau. He yanked out a pair of boxer briefs and pulled them on. The tension she had so creatively worked out of him had returned, invading his limbs, a deep frown creasing his forehead.

She'd thought it was work stress. Easily remedied with a blowjob and group sex.

Maybe not.

"Did you say you think you have a sister?"

"Yes."

Baffled, she stared at him. "Since when do you have a sister?"

He ran his hands through his hair. "Since approximately nine years ago."

Her mouth was agape, but there was nothing she could do about that. "Uh. I think you may need to break this down for me. I don't think I'm following."

He returned to sink down on the side of the bed, facing away from her, his arms resting on his legs. "A little girl came to my office this morning. She claims to be my father's daughter from a second marriage."

The words falling from his lips were precise and clipped. This morning? All of this had happened this morning? He'd waited over twelve hours to deliver this major, life-altering news?

How dare he shut me out—

Whoa. Back up.

Nope.

Tatiana punched her inner teen girl into submission. No. This wasn't about her. She didn't get to make it about her.

Yes, Wyatt hadn't come running to her, and that did sting, especially since they had already talked about him being more open and not keeping things from her.

Yet, it wasn't like he'd gone about his day blithely. She thought of the way he'd kissed her when he'd first seen her earlier in the evening, the desperation and need in his touch.

Why hadn't he told her? That was the important question. She examined his body, his fists clenched tight.

Because it hurt him.

The girl hadn't just claimed to be his sister. She'd claimed to be a living, breathing connection to his father. The father Wyatt barely spoke about, after years of estrangement. Oh, her poor Wyatt.

It hurt him, and Wyatt wasn't good with embracing emotional pain. This was a man who handled his biggest emotions—fear, anger, sadness—by bundling them up and stuffing them in a subzero freezer.

He was braced now. Waiting for her to freak out or shriek. As if she wasn't a mature, intelligent woman.

She tugged the blanket tighter around her and scooted closer until she could layer herself over his back. "If you'd rather not talk about it," she said quietly. "We don't have to."

His shoulders tensed. "You're not mad?"

"No." She kissed his neck, right at his hairline. "We're in a relationship, not a mind meld. You're allowed your thoughts."

"I didn't tell you when I found out. You should be furious."

Anything she wanted to say—*you didn't have to, you had your reasons*—sounded snarky, though she meant the words sincerely. "This isn't like what we talked about before, about us communicating when we're angry," she said, choosing her words carefully. "I get that family carries a whole different set of baggage. Talk to me if it'll make you feel better. If you need some time, that's okay, too."

He turned so swiftly, she wasn't prepared for the weight of his body. He pushed her down on the bed and came up over her, holding himself on his elbows, his face very close to hers. "I…" he exhaled harshly, sounding frustrated.

Her heart gave a little pang. "Can I snuggle you right now?"

He jerked his head back and eyed her. "*Snuggle* me?"

"Sure." She wrapped her arms around his neck and pulled him down so his head was pressed against her chest. "Snuggling is crucial when we get news that throws us for a loop. I'll teach you. Here. Put your arm here, and then move your head like this. Ah, perfect."

They lay like that for a long while, Tatiana running her fingers through his short hair and staring into the darkness of the room.

"You sure you're not mad?" The words were muffled against her breasts.

She blinked rapidly. Did he think she was a monster?

No, that wasn't fair. Ten years ago—hell, maybe even a year ago—she might have happily lit into him for failing to tell her about this right away. Her kneejerk reaction when he'd just spilled the beans proved she wasn't immune to that kind of thinking.

She grimaced. She wasn't perfect, but she'd be damned if she acted like an immature twit anymore.

"I'll confess something," she said, struggling to find something to say, to open the conversation. "After our first night together, I went to see Ron, and I told him I would give him the money to reimburse you, but to continue paying you in installments so you wouldn't know."

He had stilled in her arms, but she was certain he was listening. Wyatt had been adamant about not taking her money to make up for Ron's embezzlement, even ripping up the check she had offered him. "It took Ron about a week to realize you and I might be headed somewhere serious. He told me he changed his mind and he paid me back what I'd given to him. I was annoyed with him, until I realized he basically saved us a massive argument." She lightly tugged his hair. "See? I kept something from you, too. I'm sorry about that. But family things can be weird."

He turned his head, though he didn't respond. His breathing grew deeper. So deep, she was startled when he spoke. "Do you remember how I said I never searched for you after we broke up because I didn't think I would be able to keep myself from showing up at your door?" he asked.

She held her breath. "Yes."

"I didn't search for my father after I left because I didn't care what happened to him."

The lack of emotion in his voice made her ache.

They didn't talk about his dad. What she knew about Wyatt between the time his mother had died and the time he had moved out was superficial.

As an adoptee, she knew better than most that love often transcended biology. She felt no emotion for her birth mother, beyond disappointment and an occasional wistfulness. Wyatt hated his father. And from what Tatiana had been able to piece together, that hate was justified.

"I pictured him showing up here, though. About what I'd say to him."

"What would you have said to him?"

His smile was grim. "Nothing I could say to a kid."

"You know, you're in luck." She attempted a lighter tone. "The population of people who meet long-lost siblings is pretty small, and you've got someone with experience in your bed."

"This isn't like when you met Ron."

"You're right. We were both adults, for one, and I didn't know enough about my birth mother to hate her. Maybe I went through some of the stuff you're feeling, though? The worry that it's not real. Wondering whether they'll like you, or you'll like them. Nervousness at the thought of a stranger being somehow connected to you."

He exhaled, his breath stirring the lock of hair that had fallen over her nipple. "I told Jared to find out everything he could about her. Make sure she is who she says she is."

"You think it could be a scam?"

"I don't know. I have money. Wouldn't be the first time someone tried to take it. May be the most creative way."

That was true. Though a fake long-lost sister was a bit of a stretch in the world of DNA tests. And getting a kid to collude was risky.

"When will Jared get back to you?"

"He sent me a file this afternoon. I didn't open it. Told myself I was waiting for him to get more details, but really…I didn't want to face it." He shifted, rubbing his stubbled jaw against her skin. "He said he would be in touch first thing in the morning with more."

"It's a Saturday."

"If you pay someone enough, they work on Saturdays," he said dryly. "I told him to go ahead and send an investigator out to Tucson."

Tatiana lifted an eyebrow. "To do what?"

"Dig through trash. Talk to teachers."

"Oh. Wow."

His brow furrowed. "Why? Is that…weird?"

"No," she replied hastily. "Not weird." More excessive than what most people would do, maybe. But perfectly normal for Wyatt. "I don't know how you kept from opening that file right away. I'd be dying of curiosity."

"I printed it. It's in my briefcase."

"Oh."

A grunt came from his lips. "I should look at it."

"We don't have to. Or, you can do it alone."

He raised his head. "Who are you?"

"What's that supposed to mean?"

"The Tatiana I know would be peppering me with questions and dying of curiosity. Who is this meek, accommodating female in my bed?"

"Um." She raised one finger. "First, I am always accommodating in bed. I think I proved that tonight." Another finger. "Second, how dare you. Meek? Call me bland, too, why don't you, and really insult me." A third finger. "And lastly…yes. I am dying of curiosity, and I want to know everything and see everything and then have a discussion about all the things I know and see." She pressed her hand to his face. "It's weird, how I can put aside my own feelings and consider yours. It's like I'm in love with you or something."

Ah. There. The corner of his mouth lifted the tiniest amount. "Are you tired?"

"Not anymore."

"Yeah. Okay. Let's get this over with, then." With that unenthusiastic decision, he rolled off of her and padded out of the room. She took the time to grab the robe off the chair near the bed and wrap it around her.

The light next to the bed gave off a dim glow. Wyatt came back in, carrying a thin file. He sat next to her and placed it on his lap. He stared at the top of the manila folder for a long moment. Inching closer, Tatiana placed her hand on his chest, right over his heart. "Okay?"

"Yes."

He didn't move. Slowly, giving him time to protest, she opened the folder. Her heart caught at the sight of the 8x10 photo. "Oh my God, Wyatt. She looks just like you."

"I thought so."

If this was some scam, Tatiana would be very surprised. The eyes, the coloring, the shape of her face. She knew those features.

Abruptly, she recalled something Wyatt had said to her when she'd questioned how he could have known Ron was her brother. *Do you really think I would confuse your eyes with any other human being on the planet?*

She lightly touched the school photo. "What's her name?"

"Ellie."

"Nine, huh?"

"That's what she said." Wyatt picked up the photo and placed it between them. "Nine years, four months…twelve days, to be exact." He fingered the birth certificate. "Elizabeth Anne Caine. Parents are Carol and Samuel Caine."

She flipped to the next page to reveal two Arizona driver's licenses. Samuel Caine had Wyatt's eyes and coloring, which made sense, given the appearance of the little girl. Tatiana had seen the man from afar when they were kids. Wyatt had never introduced them. For the majority of their relationship he'd been on his own.

"She showed me a picture of him, too. Holding her as a baby." The twitch of Wyatt's jaw was the only sign of emotion. She pressed tighter against his side, as if her body heat could warm him.

He turned the page, and she leaned farther over his shoulder to read the short bio Jared had scraped together on the small family.

Samuel Caine had moved to Arizona—she did the math quickly—two years after Wyatt had left him. Worked for the same construction company for the past six years. No arrest record.

He'd married Carol not long before Ellie's birth. The wife was a nurse, over a dozen years younger. No criminal record on her either. They lived in the suburbs, in a three-bedroom ranch home they owned.

A few other pages followed, detailing other parts of their life, like where Ellie went to school and what kind of cars they drove. Wyatt flipped through the papers and then simply stared at the painfully brief data for so long Tatiana felt it necessary to speak. "I guess there isn't much to go off of here. Once Jared calls—"

"That's my father. It's legitimate."

"Maybe—"

"No. It's really him."

"We can get a DNA test. On him, or Ellie."

"No need." His fingers tightened on the paper a split second before he ripped it clean in two. "No *fucking* need." He ripped it again, and again, before dumping the mess on the carpet.

He grabbed Ellie's photo. She tensed, prepared for him to tear into it, but he stilled. "Doesn't matter if she's his biological kid or not. She's living with him. I counted the days I could leave him, and now he's putting some other kid through eighteen years of misery?"

Speaking past the lump in her throat was difficult. "It was always miserable?"

"No." Wyatt bit off the word. "It wasn't awful before my mom died. They were decent parents, if inattentive. They were so disgustingly in love, they didn't have much room for me. I don't know if I was unplanned or what, but I was an afterthought. After she died…" Wyatt shook his head. "He might as well have crawled inside that casket with her."

Tatiana's parents were in love, but she'd never been left

in doubt that they desired her. Sure, she'd experienced pangs of self-doubt as a kid about her biological parents, and she'd had to struggle through some angst when her biological mother had made it clear she wanted nothing to do with her as an adult, but how bad would it have been to grow up with people who considered you unworthy of attention?

"I used to wish he had buried himself, too. On the day of my mother's funeral, when everyone had left, my dad got drunk. He smashed every photo frame in the house, every glass, every casserole some well-meaning neighbor had brought over. I hid in a closet. He screamed it should have been me. That he would have missed me less. He screamed until he passed out."

Her breath caught, thinking of a ten-year-old Wyatt hiding in a closet while his remaining parent yelled words at him no child should ever hear from their father. Her arms tightened around him. The pressure of tears stung her eyes, but she refused to let them fall. How *dare* anyone treat him that way?

Wyatt stared at the girl's face, oblivious of her enraged horror. "She's smart."

Attempting to focus, Tatiana shoved aside her anger. "Is she?"

"Insanely smart. The way she was talking…" He cracked a smile. "She got annoyed I called her precocious. Is it normal for a nine-year-old to know what that word means?"

"I don't know. Ask me when Pete turns nine," she said dryly, referring to her baby nephew.

"Guess neither of us has much experience with kids."

"The curse of only children." She rested her hand on his

bare belly, making small circles with her fingers, a motion designed to soothe rather than arouse.

"You know...there was a brief moment, when I first saw her..." He paused.

"What?"

"I thought maybe I was her father." He lifted his arm and wrapped it around her. "I thought about every woman I was with. Between my time with you now and then. That first time I slept with someone other than you, I felt...like it wasn't right. Like I was cheating on you. The second girl, too. And the third."

She rested her head on his shoulder. "I felt like that, too. For a long time."

"I didn't want her to be mine." The words fell between them. "I'm an adult. This kid has the courage to come into a stranger's space, and I was racing ahead, thinking of damage control. DNA, who the mother might be, what I would tell you, how you would react, whether you would leave me. What kind of a man does that make me?"

They were into some heavy shit here. Tatiana carefully considered her words. "A normal one, I'd say. A surprise child would throw anyone off-guard." They had discussed their views on children sort of obliquely in the past year. Though the world told her that her womb was slowly crumbling under the weight of her thirties, she was in no hurry. She'd be as alarmed if a kid showed up claiming to be hers.

Well, because of basic biology, probably more alarmed than a man.

"I don't know if that's normal." He scrubbed his hand over his eyes, and then kept it there, concealing his gaze. "I want you to love me. I want you to live with me. I want you enmeshed in my life. At the same time…I'm certain that eventually you're going to split. And I don't know if I can deal with that."

Struck, Tatiana swallowed. Last year, when they'd reunited, she'd asked him why he hadn't come looking for her over the intervening years. *I barely survived losing you once, and our parting was mutual then. I have people who depend on me now, who rely on me. You're a distraction I can't afford.*

Deep down, was Wyatt always bracing for her to leave him?

Well, why not? His mother had left. His father's love for her had turned him into an ugly, broken man, and he'd checked out on Wyatt. Those were the relationships that he'd had for reference.

"Wyatt…you're wrong."

His words were halting. "Sometimes when I'm with you, I feel like a fraud. Like you don't know how crazy my life was, and you don't know…" He grimaced. "I don't think I'm normal. And I don't want you to know I'm not normal."

"Not normal? Of course you're normal."

"You don't know me. I've never even told you about my childhood, and I've known you for a collective total of how many years?" He dropped his hand and smiled a hard, angry smile. "I wasn't going to tell you, either. Because I'm a manipulative asshole, and I was hoping you would eventually be in too deep for it to matter that I'm a shaky prospect, in terms of building a family and having a future.

"Your Akira said something to me tonight, about how if I couldn't give you everything you need, I need to cut you loose now, and I realized how dumb my plan was. I have to be enough for you. You should know everything. Before you tell me you love me again."

Whoa. "I don't think there's a person in this world I know better than I know you." She placed her finger on his lips when he would have spoken. "No. Fine. I don't know about your childhood, or your parents. But I know who you are. Nothing I learn about you will change that."

"I don't know what kind of father I'll be. You want kids."

This was not a talk she had been planning on having, but she was down with it. "I'm in this for you, not your sperm. You decide you don't want kids? Fine. Nothing wrong or evil in that, and when we get to that point in our relationship, we can mutually decide yea or nay. But don't think you'll be a crappy dad because your father was one. Look at how you are with Pete. You'll never convince me you're not a protective and loving man." Wyatt had warmed up to her nephew, especially once he had discovered the toddler loved Lego. The two of them had spent an entire Sunday afternoon building skyscrapers, Wyatt's looking rather suspiciously like Quest.

"He's easier to interact with now that he talks," Wyatt admitted.

"And as for my leaving you…" She shook her head, baffled. "I wouldn't, but even if I did? You'd be fine."

"No, I—"

"Oh, you'd be hurt. You'd suffer." She smoothed her hand over her hair. "I mean, really. Losing all this? It would be awful. But you're forgetting that I've already left you once. I survived. You survived. Eventually, we both thrived." Brushing her thumb over his lip, she gave a small smile. "If I died and left you with a kid? There is no way you would crawl into that grave with me. Partially because I would come back and kick your ass, but also because you're not that kind of man. You're not your father. You can love someone deeply, irrevocably, and still love yourself and others enough to live without them. You stay with people you love because life is better with them, not because you'll die otherwise. I know this for certain."

She expected him to fight her, but he clasped his hand over hers and pulled her close, until they were a hairsbreadth away. "I want to argue with you," he whispered.

"Don't bother. You'll lose." She leaned in and kissed him, slow, drugging. He followed her lead, letting her set the pace.

They were both breathing hard when she pulled away reluctantly. While forgetting all of reality in each other's arms was tempting, Ellie was between them.

Literally. Tatiana touched her wrinkled photo. "Wyatt?"

He followed her gaze. "Yeah?"

"What do you want to do?"

"I want to see her again."

She nodded immediately. "Okay."

His words were halting. "No, I don't really want to. I want this to go away. But it won't, and I feel like…I should make sure she's okay."

And the man thought he didn't know how to be a part of a family. He was protective of everyone weaker than him.

Wyatt continued. "She said she was curious. Maybe it was more. She seems to be well cared for, but sometimes things happen to kids, and they don't leave any marks on their bodies."

The words were emotionless, falling in the room with the weight of a thousand confessions. She bit the inside of her cheek to distract herself from the pain in her heart. God, he was killing her tonight. "Yes," she managed. "Did Jared find out how long she's in town for?"

"The weekend. Ellie said it was her mother's friend's wedding." He shifted. "It's the two of them. Her father is in Tucson."

Good, she thought fiercely. She might punch the man if she saw him. "You know where they're staying?"

"Yes."

She nodded. "Okay. We could go in the morning."

"We were going to go look at studios for you."

That's right. They'd discussed that…Tatiana blinked. Dear Lord, had that only been this morning? "I'll call the realtor. We can go on Sunday afternoon."

"I don't want to—"

"Wyatt. It's fine. The studio can wait a day." She kissed his cheek. "I was thinking of buying instead of leasing, anyway. So I don't want to rush into a space, you know?"

"Buying."

She shrugged, trying for an air of casualness, though she knew now how much the concept of permanency meant to him. "Makes more fiscal sense."

His Adam's apple bobbed. "Yes. I agree." He placed his finger under her chin and lifted it, searching her gaze. "Thanks."

She kissed him firmly. "My pleasure."

"I'm sorry I ruined the big night you planned."

"Nothing about this night was bad." Her words were

honest. She felt as though she'd been through the emotional wringer, but every step they'd taken tonight had been about making them stronger.

They would never be invincible, but they could damn well be close.

"Still…"

"Wyatt. Remember how you helped me at the gallery when I was nervous? Let me be as good of a girlfriend as you are a boyfriend."

"I fucked you in the bathroom."

"Yeah, you got something out of that. I get something out of this. I don't want to hear anything more about it."

His chuckle was rusty. "Fine." He stirred. "I don't know if I'll be sleeping. I'll go out to the living room so you can rest."

"I won't be either. I kinda feel like sketching." She sat up. "Why don't you pop in a movie, and I'll see what we have for snacks."

"You don't have to—"

She shushed him and slid off the bed, grabbing her sketchbook off the nightstand. Her fingers itched for a creative outlet for the swirling mess of feelings inside her. "I want to. I'm wired and a little hungry. You got a burger on the way home, and you didn't feed me at all."

Wyatt's laugh was hoarse. "Look, I could feed you or dump all of my baggage on you. I'm not superman."

Chapter Ten

WHEN HE'D BEEN young and trouncing pros double and triple his age on the poker circuit, commentators had wondered if Wyatt had a pulse, he was so calm and emotionless under pressure. Today, his palms were slick as he drove to the hotel where Ellie and Carol were staying, despite the distraction of Tatiana's light patter.

Poor woman. No way had she been prepared for the emotional shitstorm he'd rained down upon her last night. In the wee hours of the morning, she'd finally dozed off in his arms while they sat in front of the television. He'd spent the time until she woke watching infomercials and stroking her hair.

His eyes were gritty and bloodshot from lack of sleep, his body vibrating with the kind of energy that came from caffeine and nerves. He'd chosen his clothes at random, and would have walked out the door with mismatched shoes if Tatiana hadn't stopped him and gently pointed it out.

He stole a glance at her pensive profile. The morning sun formed a halo around her, turning her into a golden angel. He knew what she'd growl in response to that observation, if he dared to voice it. *I'm no more an angel than I am a whore.*

Correct. There was nothing ephemeral about her. She was too earthy and ribald to be an angel, and he wouldn't make the mistake of putting wings on her and slapping her on a pedestal. Didn't mean he couldn't consider her his personal savior.

Part of him was alarmed at the needy, insecure mess that had come spewing out of his mouth last night. Another part of him was so relieved the cat was out of the bag and that she was still by his side, he didn't have much room for shame.

The rest of him was too preoccupied with this upcoming meeting to worry about his relationship.

His stomach tightened as he edged his sedan into a spot between minivans and SUVs.

His sister was inside this family-friendly hotel. Jared had called an hour ago, while he and Tatiana had been pretending to eat breakfast. The private investigator had sent over more information supporting the blood tie between him and Ellie. Not that he needed more proof. As he'd told Tatiana, the fact that the kid lived with his father was enough for him to dig deeper.

That didn't mean he was a great family man, as Tatiana seemed to think. It meant he was the only one in the world who had an idea of all the ways the kid could be suffering. A child was a child, at the end of the day. Helpless.

A rush of protectiveness infused him. She hadn't asked to be Sam's daughter, or his sister, but it looked like she was both. And he could do for her what no one had ever done for him.

His sister. He wanted to test the words out loud, see how they sounded on his tongue. He hadn't claimed a family member in so long, it felt strange.

Wyatt swiped his hand over the back of his neck. It was fine. This was not a big deal. He'd dealt with billionaires, millionaires, politicians, mafiosos. A little girl and her mother should be a cakewalk.

A soft touch landed on his arm, and he started.

"Wyatt," Tatiana said, anxiety creasing her brow. "We don't have to do this, you know. We could work out some sort of meeting through our lawyer, or communicate over the phone. Or I can go and talk to them without you."

This woman. He wrapped his hand around the back of her neck and wrenched her close, pressing his lips against hers in a brief but desperate kiss. "No," he murmured. "I'm okay. I've got you."

"That's right." Her smile was a shadow of its normal self, worry for him obvious. "Your lucky charm."

"The ace up my sleeve."

"We can work out the appropriate gambling analogy later. Shall we?"

He took a deep breath. "Yeah. Let's go."

Wyatt tucked her hand into the crook of his elbow after they exited the car, not wanting to lose contact with her.

Needy.

He buried the chastising voice, replacing it with Tatiana's expected, exasperated words. *Yeah, you're needy now. I might be needy tomorrow. That's how it works.*

They had parked on the side of the hotel, and they made their way around the perimeter toward the front. This establishment was light years away from Quest. It filled its advertised purpose: a safe, affordable place for families to stop and rest while they were on vacation together. The type of hotel he had never been to when he was Ellie's age. Or at any time after his mother died. Family vacations had stopped then.

The sound of shrieking children grew louder as they neared the outdoor pool. Caught by the noise, he glanced at the area and faltered, finally stopping dead in his tracks and bringing Tatiana to a halt with him.

Samuel Caine looked older than the driver's license photo Jared had sent over, with silver threaded through his midnight hair and wrinkles on his face. His dark head was bent close to another, one that wasn't graying. Wyatt watched his father smile at Ellie as he rubbed sunscreen on her arms.

That wide-open smile was foreign to Wyatt. He hadn't seen his father grin like that since before his mother had died. Even before her death, that level of happiness had been reserved for his mom, not him. Samuel flicked his finger against Ellie's nose, and his smile widened.

Ellie reached up on tiptoes to kiss her father's cheek, and something broke inside Wyatt.

They should go. They had to go. His father wasn't supposed to be here.

Jared was more than capable of keeping tabs from afar, and there were other ways to ensure the child's safety. Maybe he would seek the kid out when she was older. Or speak with her if she contacted him again.

Ellie ran off to the pool, and Samuel straightened from his crouched position. As if sensing a gaze on him, he glanced over the heads of the riotous children and parents.

Ice ran through Wyatt's veins as matching black eyes met his.

To his credit, Samuel looked as shell-shocked as Wyatt felt. His father took one faltering step, and then another, and another, until he was at the wrought-iron gate to the pool. He reached down, twisted the handle, and opened it.

Tatiana squeezed his arm and he jerked, having forgotten she was standing next to him. "Your call," she whispered. Of course she had recognized his dad. The man still looked disgustingly like him.

Wyatt would happily turn and walk away forever, grateful to never encounter this man again for the rest of his life.

Don't grow up to be weak like me. Please.

Words the old man had often sobbed out during his drunken crying jags. In the beginning, Wyatt had watched wide-eyed and silent, or cried himself. Later, he grew so desensitized, he would step over the man to go make himself a sandwich or to take care of the bills.

The words had stuck with him, though. Wyatt eyed the hand holding the gate open, rage flushing through him. Fuck no. Everything he'd done in his life had been done partially to prove he wasn't weak like this bastard.

He tightened his grip on Tatiana's hand and squared his shoulders, girding his loins to walk the short distance.

When Wyatt had left home, he had still been an inch or two shorter than Samuel. They were the same height now. Roughly the same build, too. Construction had kept the man whipcord lean. Wyatt had worked on a crew when he'd been younger. He'd spent the past decade trying to replicate that workout in a gym.

"Wyatt," his father said. Wyatt controlled his instinctive

flinch from the familiar gravelly voice. "I didn't think..." He trailed off.

They stood in frozen silence, cataloguing each other for a long moment, before Tatiana delicately cleared her throat.

Samuel tore his gaze away and looked at Tatiana. "Excuse me. I—" His brow furrowed. "I know you. You look familiar."

"My name's Tatiana Belikov." She held out her hand. Automatically, Samuel grasped it. "Wyatt and I dated in high school."

To Wyatt's surprise, a dull red flush worked its way up Samuel's neck. "I'm sorry. I should have remembered."

A good parent would have remembered. He and Tatiana had only been dating for six months when he moved out of his father's home, but that was more than enough time for a functional adult to have met a child's girlfriend.

"I never introduced you two," Wyatt said flatly. "So it's not a surprise you can't remember."

"Ah. Yes." Samuel had trouble meeting Wyatt's gaze.

He should have trouble with that, Wyatt thought viciously. "I came to see your—" he choked on the word wife, unable to think past his mother, "—family. I didn't think you were here."

"I flew in last night after Carol told me about Ellie's adventures." The other man squared his shoulders. "I was going to come see you today."

Bullshit. The guy hadn't tried to see him when they were within driving distance of each other.

Tatiana cleared her throat again. "Why don't we sit down somewhere?"

Samuel jerked, as if he'd been prodded into recalling

where they were. "Yes. Please, that's a good idea."

Wyatt forced himself to put one foot in front of the other to follow the older man to a patio table where a pretty, plump blonde watched them with worried eyes. The nurse, Wyatt thought. His mother had been a blonde, as well. The old man had a type.

He glanced at Tatiana's honey hair, disturbed to think he and his father shared a preference for anything or anyone. But he'd always be attracted to Tatiana, even if she turned her hair pink and her eyes purple.

"This is my wife, Carol," Sam said quietly.

Wyatt nodded and gave a brusque handshake to the woman. "Wyatt." He nodded to Tatiana, who smiled warmly at the other woman, no doubt trying to diminish some of the awkwardness. "This is Tatiana."

"How nice to meet you both," Carol responded, but worry lines creased her brow, belying her words.

"Wyatt?"

He turned at the now-familiar, eager voice. Ellie wore a hot-pink one-piece, with neon goggles pushed up on her head. Her dark lashes were spikey from the pool water, her hair hanging in wet ropes down her back.

"Hello, Ellie."

"What are you doing here? I didn't think I would see you again."

"You snuck out yesterday before I could speak with you."

"I thought it was best." Before he could respond to that cryptic and oddly mature pronouncement, Ellie glanced at Tatiana. "Is this your girlfriend?"

"Yes."

"Hello," Tatiana offered. "I've heard a lot about you."

"You dated in high school," Ellie announced.

Wyatt raised a brow. "How did you know that?"

"Found pictures from your senior prom. Your alumni board is pretty active online." Ellie surveyed Tatiana. "You were a lot fatter then."

Tatiana's lips twitched. "I was going through an awkward phase."

"Ellie, for God's sake…"

Ellie glanced at her mother. "Sorry." The word was dutiful, as if Ellie was used to apologizing. "Why aren't you married yet, if you've been dating for so long?"

"We took a break for a while," Tatiana replied.

"Ellie, can you give us a minute, please?" her father interjected.

A mulish pout crossed the girl's face. Some people might loathe seeing that expression on a child's face but something within Wyatt eased at the sight of it. He had never disobeyed or become stubborn with his fragile father. He had learned early to avoid anything that could trigger a drunken rage.

"But I want to talk to Wyatt," she whined.

"Later." Samuel reached into his pocket and pulled out a handful of quarters. "Here, go play video games."

The girl snorted. "Those arcade games are for babies. The graphics are terrible, and I can beat them in a few minutes."

"Elizabeth," her mother interjected. "Do I need to remind you that you are still in trouble from your antics yesterday?"

Ellie's pout disappeared, and so did the quarters. "No,

ma'am. I'll come back soon." With a wave to Wyatt, she trudged away.

Wyatt wanted to smile at the forlorn sigh Ellie tossed in for good measure, but he was far too overwhelmed by his own demons.

"Would you like to go inside?" Carol asked.

And prolong this? No thanks. Wyatt shook his head and sat down at the patio table. Tatiana's hand slid off his arm, but only to link her fingers with his.

"First, I'm sorry for what Ellie did yesterday," Sam Caine spoke, his voice low but pitched high enough to be heard over the din of kids.

"She has a mind of her own," Carol said, exasperated but affectionate.

Wyatt nodded. "She's smart."

"Brilliant," Samuel confirmed matter-of-factly. "She's taking high school classes. But that doesn't mean she's allowed to run off in a strange city. She knows not to try it again." His father shifted. "I didn't think she even knew enough about you to find you. I kept tabs on you, of course. But I thought to wait until she was older to tell her who you were."

Wyatt flinched, and Tatiana's hand tightened on his. Tabs? His father hadn't kept tabs on him even when they lived in the same zip code.

"It's fine," he said shortly.

"I'm sure it was a shock to you. That wasn't how I imagined the two of you meeting."

"You imagined us meeting?" The disbelieving words slipped out before Wyatt could stop them.

Samuel looked down at his large hands, his thick lashes

veiling his eyes. "Since the day she was born. I thought, by this time, I would have contacted you. But somehow the days went by, and then the years. Still, I figured I would come here eventually. Tell you about Ellie. Ease you into meeting her."

Carol shifted. "Sam knows how he was to you, Wyatt. It torments him—"

"Carol," Sam growled.

"No. This may be your only chance to speak with him." Earnest kindness radiated from her. "Sam knows he made mistakes in his life, and he's spent the last decade trying to make them up. Not a day goes by that he doesn't think of you. He is so proud of your accomplishments."

"Enough, Carol." Sam kept his eyes on Wyatt, arrogance in every line of his expression. Wyatt knew that look well. He saw it in the mirror often. "She's right," he said to Wyatt, surprising him. "I am proud of you. I have been keeping track of your success. And I'm sorry."

The apology was simple.

Too simple. Too easy.

Did the man think that one "I'm sorry" would wipe out years of neglect? Fix his past, change who he was?

Fuck him.

Wyatt's lips barely moved. "I thought you were dead."

The other man flinched, and Wyatt continued. "I didn't keep tabs on you. I didn't care what happened to you. And if Ellie hadn't come to see me yesterday, I would have continued not caring what happened to you." Wyatt looked at Carol but addressed his words to his father. "Your wife reminds me of Mom."

Out of the corner of his eye he watched his father tense.

"Your mother was a good woman. So is Carol."

Wyatt refocused on his father. "I came here because my private investigator confirmed that Ellie was who she claimed to be. And all I could think, after I discovered that, was that Ellie may have come to me solely because she wanted to get away from you."

Samuel blanched.

Carol's face turned red. "Excuse me? My daughter is a happy little girl and loves her father very much. That's absurd."

"Why?" Wyatt studied his father coolly, though his blood ran hot. "When I was her age, I loved him more than anything in the world. And I would have paid someone to get me away from him."

Tatiana drew in a shaky breath next to him but otherwise didn't speak, didn't correct his rampant rudeness. She was merely there, a support beam for him to lean on and extract strength.

Samuel's chest expanded. "I'm not like I was. I've changed."

"Have you?"

His father's jaw worked. "I know it's no excuse. I loved your mother so much. When she died, I lost my mind. I crawled into that bottle, and I wanted to die."

Wyatt glanced at Tatiana, recalling the words she'd spoken last night. Whether he said the words aloud or not, he loved her. More than he'd loved her when he was a kid, though that seemed impossible. If she died, he would be bereft.

Bereft. But not dead. Not crippled.

Crushing relief made his hands shake. He fisted them to

hide the tremor. He hadn't fully believed Tatiana last night, unable to process through his turmoil. She was right. He wasn't his father. Not in this. He'd already faced his worst demon, having her leave him once in his life.

He would take care of his business. He would take care of the people who relied upon him. And if he had a child? He would fucking take care of that child. Because that was what you did.

Wyatt looked at his father. "What are you going to do to Ellie if her mom dies?"

Carol drew in a sharp breath. "You are out of line. I trust my husband."

"My mom trusted him." The words spilled out of him, ugly and vile, like he was opening his veins and pouring bitter blood onto the ground. It needed to be done. Let it soak into the concrete, stain the pool black.

Tatiana's here. She shouldn't hear this.

Let her hear.

"I doubt she thought that she was leaving me with a weak alcoholic. Have you told her? Have you told Carol about how you'd drink all day and all night? How I had to make my own breakfast, lunch and dinner, and yours, too? How I had to pay the electrical bill when they threatened to turn it off? How you would cry every night? How you told me, when I was eleven, that you were going to kill yourself, and you grabbed a knife…" He lashed out to grasp the other man's wrist. Samuel didn't resist when Wyatt wrenched his limb over to display the thin silvery marks on his inner arm. "Not hard enough to die, though, right? Not deep enough so I could go live with a distant relative or take my chances in the system. Just to spray enough blood to terrify me."

His father had turned gray. "I will not do to Ellie what I did to you," he whispered. "Ever."

Wyatt nodded, anger and adrenaline making for a heady mix. "Damn right you won't." He released the other man's arm and leaned forward, his legendary control long gone, his mouth taking over. "Because unlike me, she now has someone who can look out for her. I will keep an eye on you and her from now on, and if I hear even a hint that you've fallen off the wagon? If anything happens to your wife and I see you reverting back to your usual ways? I will come and I will get her, and she will be mine. I have the money and the power to make that happen. Do not doubt it." Words he hadn't planned on saying. Words that felt right.

Carol straightened, her brow furrowing. "Are you threatening us, Mr. Caine?"

Wyatt turned to her. Good. She had some backbone. He hated to think Ellie was being raised by two weaklings.

Before he could speak, Tatiana did. "It's not a threat. It's a promise." Her face was composed, as if she wasn't a bit fazed by any of these revelations. "I don't know how much of Wyatt and Samuel's history you're aware of, but he has the right to doubt your husband. He has the right to question him."

Anger tightened the older woman's lips. "This is my child…"

"Stop. They're right." Wyatt's father spoke, cutting off his wife. Samuel smiled at Carol and stroked his finger over her cheek, the tenderness coming from this man utterly foreign to Wyatt.

"You see the best in me. You always have. But the things

Wyatt said, the things I told you about that time, they barely scratch the surface. There are so many incidents I don't remember. But I have no doubt Wyatt does."

Wyatt had to keep himself from sneering, those memories crashing around his brain. A raw, exposed nerve. That was what he felt like.

"I never hit him or physically abused him. But I'm certain that's not much comfort." Samuel spoke to his wife, but his gaze was on Wyatt.

His eyes were so clear, free of the redness brought on by booze and misery. Wyatt couldn't remember ever seeing them like that. "I would have rather you punched me, sometimes," he admitted, the words torn from him.

His father nodded, suddenly looking very tired. "Yes. I don't blame you. I understand your concern about Ellie. I know you don't want to hear this, but I'm proud you're the kind of man who would be concerned about her."

No, he didn't want to hear that. He didn't need his father's pride.

Samuel continued. "I have changed, and she is a happy, well-adjusted girl. But if you wish to keep an eye on her, I won't complain."

Suspicious, Wyatt searched the older man for some ulterior motive. His wife's outrage seemed far more normal than this easy acceptance.

Oh. There it was. That emotion in Samuel's black eyes. Wyatt had seen it in the eyes of men who were uncertain about the hand they held but were determined to brazen it out all the same.

The same emotion he occasionally experienced, though he buried it, replacing it with arrogance. With new suits.

With fancy gadgets.

Fear.

Fear that he was faking it, that he wouldn't be able to live up to the image of the man he projected to the world. Fear that he would regress back to what he had been.

No, he didn't like having anything in common with this man who had fathered him.

Wyatt swallowed his sneer and gave a short nod. "Good." He glanced at the small alcove where Ellie was dutifully playing an ancient Pac-Man game. He was on such a roll, speaking without thinking, he continued on with it. "I would like to see her."

"Sam and I already spoke about this," Carol said, her earlier friendliness cooled. "If you wish to have an occasional visit, supervised, that would be fine. But you won't be permitted to express your issues with your father or me to her. We won't have a source of negativity in this family."

Fair enough, and far more generous than he'd expected. "You'll have to be the one to supervise," he informed Carol. "Not him."

"That sounds fine," his father responded humbly.

No more. He couldn't sit here anymore. Eager to move, Wyatt nodded and stood. His hand automatically went to button his jacket before he realized he had dressed casually today. "Very well. Thank you for your time. I'll be in touch."

He raised his hand to Ellie, who had whipped around at the screeching sound of his chair on the concrete. She abandoned her game and came darting back to them. "Are you leaving?"

"Yes," he managed.

Her little face fell. "Oh."

Tatiana spoke to Carol and Sam, her tone saccharine sweet now. "Could Ellie come visit before you leave?"

The older couple exchanged a look, and Carol nodded. "I can bring her tomorrow evening."

Tatiana beamed at them. "That sounds wonderful." She fished in her purse. "Um, hang on, I know I have one in here." She pulled out a handful of mints, a stick of gum, a lipstick, a broken earring and a pen before finding a tiny stack of tattered business cards. Peeling one off, she handed it to Carol. "That's my cell number. We can go to the pool maybe, or have dinner. Get to know each other."

Tatiana would have the other woman eating out of her palm by the end of the day, he suspected. It would help to smooth over his faux pas of questioning her parenting skills today.

He caught the shadow of a bored grimace on Ellie's face. He awkwardly patted her shoulder. "If you want, you can see my security setup. I'll show you how we catch card counters."

Her eyes gleamed. "Okay."

He didn't hug her. Maybe he would one day embrace this tiny scrap that shared his genetic material. Not today.

After a final nod to his father and Carol, he and Tatiana left the pool.

He made it to the car, and without a word, Tatiana took his keys and pushed him into the passenger seat. His hands were shaking, he realized. No. Not just his hands. His entire body, deep tremors that wracked him from head to toe.

"Oh, Wyatt," Tatiana murmured, and then her hands were framing his face, worried green eyes looking into his.

"It's okay, honey. We're going home." She gave him a quick kiss before settling into the driver's seat and starting his car.

Home. The word stayed with him, his mantra, as they drove the short distance back to Quest. Whenever he saw the soaring building that was his casino, his chest filled with pride and excitement. He'd done that. He'd turned a rundown, forgotten establishment into one of the greatest well-known secrets in the world.

It was the first place that had ever belonged to him, but it hadn't been home. Not until Tatiana had come into it.

He glanced at the woman sitting next to him, a frown knitting her brow. Fate had brought her to his doorstep, rocking his careful plans, messing up his life, turning it upside down. Turning him into a creature of impulse instead of one of logic.

Making him happy.

They pulled up to the back entrance, and Tatiana stopped the car, coming around to open his door. She hustled him inside and through to the elevator.

She pressed the button for the top floor, and he reached forward and placed his hand over her ass, weighing and measuring the firm roundness. She froze.

"Wyatt," she said, her lips barely moving. "Cameras."

Goddamn cameras. Couldn't a man fuck his woman in his own elevator, for crying out loud?

Nonetheless, he gave her ass a squeeze before letting go. His palm burned, a welcome reprieve from the numbness that otherwise encased him.

He wanted to bury himself inside her, forget this iciness. Another shiver wracked him. Her arm was there around him almost instantly. So much smaller than him, yet her concern propped him up. "Hang in there."

Somehow he managed to stagger to their suite. And then they were in his bedroom, and she was removing his clothes. He wanted to be charming, to be smooth. Or alternatively, do what he did whenever bad memories threatened to overwhelm him—grab her, toss her up against a wall, and fuck her.

He couldn't though. Submissiveness wasn't something he enjoyed on him, but he had no other choice.

She knelt to get his pants off, and he stepped out of them, dumb and mute as she manhandled him into the bathroom. "Already showered," he managed through numb lips.

"I know. I think we need to be warmed up." She pushed him into the shower and turned the heads on. How many times had they been in this shower together now? A hundred?

She cleaned herself, and then it was his turn. She lathered up the soap and washed his chest and belly, her hands making circular motions. She ran the washcloth up over his chest and down his arms, lifting each one to wash the sensitive underarm area. Her hands slicked over his side, before descending to her knees. She avoided his cock, which was a feat since it was staring her straight in the face. Instead, she washed his thighs and calves, all the way to his feet.

She signaled for him to turn around with a tap on his thigh, and he dumbly obeyed, facing away from her. She started at the top again, moving the sudsy towel side to side across his shoulders and his spine.

His gaze focused on the shampoo bottles on the marble

shelf. One was his, a standard two-in-one, a brand he'd been using since he was thirteen. There were two other pink bottles from the high-end salon downstairs, meant for a woman. "Why do you always use mine?"

"What?"

"You used to hate my shampoo when we were younger." He braced his hand against the tiled wall. Her hand was ghosting over his buttocks. "Remember? But you only use your own when we're at your place. When we're here, you always use mine."

She was silent for a beat, but then she responded. "I like to smell like you." Her teeth closed on the flesh of his ass in a delicate bite. A tease. A mark of ownership. "And it reminds me of who you were. And who you are now. I like—I love both of those people."

"Who am I?"

"I've been thinking about that ever since you spilled all that nonsense last night about how I don't know you. So silly. The world may swallow this rich and cold image, but I don't. You're warm, and you let me get away with murder, all while pretending you're in charge, because that's what I like. I'd even say you let me manipulate you, but there isn't a doormat bone in your body. I might occasionally despair over that, but it's good in the long run. You like the toys money buys you, but deep down you're in this for the challenge and little else." She pressed a kiss over the flesh she'd bitten. "That's who you are. I'm getting a pretty decent deal."

He shuddered and turned around to look at her. Her eyes met his evenly. Never a supplicant, this woman. Not even on her knees. He leaned back, the tile cold on his back.

She grasped his hands, lacing his fingers with hers. Her tongue lapped at his hardening cock, tasting him.

He shuddered and tightened his fingers around hers. She responded to the subtle plea by opening her mouth wide and engulfing the head of his cock, swallowing half of him. He thrust forward, always dying for more contact, more warmth, but she backed away.

Her honey-blonde hair was wet from the water, her green eyes shadowed. "Let me," she said quietly.

He couldn't refuse her. Not now, and not ever.

Wyatt let her. Let her take charge and command him, let her control him the way she let him pretend to control her. Under everything, it was always this, wasn't it? He was always hers.

He didn't know how much time passed with his body silently straining as she sucked on him lazily. It could have been minutes or days or weeks, with the steam swirling around him and her mouth ruling his life. All he knew was that she pulled away as he was grinding his head into the tile behind him, struggling not to come.

She stood, somber, and turned off the water, holding her hand out to him. "Come on."

The warmth was gone, and he'd do anything to return to it. He followed her docilely and let her towel off her body and then his, shuddering when she swiped the rough terrycloth over his cock.

Christ. She was going to kill him for sure.

As much as his cock was dying to get back inside her, he knew it would be best to wait. Wait, and he would be rewarded. Wait, and she would give him everything.

He followed her to the bedroom and waited as she

pulled back the comforter. After lying down on the white sheets, she motioned to him. It was all he needed. He covered her and made a space for himself between her legs.

He buried his face in her neck and inhaled the scent of her and him mingling together.

"Now?" he asked, humble.

She scraped her nails down his back. "Yes."

He sank inside one inch, then two. She closed her eyes, and he stopped, needing that connection. "No. Look at me."

Her eyes sprang open, and their gazes locked.

So familiar. He sank in a couple more inches. She was tight, like she always was. As tight as that first night, all those years ago, when he sank inside of her. When he'd looked into her eyes and felt the coldness recede, like he was coming home.

Akira had been right. He was the lucky bitch.

He dipped his head until his forehead rested against hers and his body forged into her. "How do you want it?"

"However you want it."

He shook his head. "No. Tell me."

Her hands clenched into the muscles of his ass. "Deep and slow."

He nodded, honored, and gave her exactly what she wanted, pulling out almost completely before sliding back in, helped by the lubrication of their bodies. Her pussy resisted the thick head of his cock on each downward drive. She made him work for it, and he was happy to accommodate.

Wyatt had been ready to blow a few minutes ago, but he controlled himself now, taking care to give it to her right, judging by her breathy moans. He wanted to fuck her like this forever, but his body took over his best intentions, and soon he was hammering into her as she mewled and cried out beneath him. Her nails scored him. He grasped her hands, and this time he was the one to hold her down, giving her something to struggle against.

Words broke free from his mouth, needy, grasping. "You're mine."

Her lashes fluttered open, her eyes dazed and filled with pleasure. "Yes."

He worked his cock over her sweet spot until her face went slack with pleasure. "Always. Say it."

"Always," she gasped, her cunt tightening on him as she came in a rush. He worked himself deep and held himself there. Call him primitive, but he loved the way it felt when he came inside her, when he knew that if she arose from the bed right after, some of his semen would trickle out of her.

So fucking hot. His ass clenched, and he spurted in her again, filling her completely.

When he was done, he rested his head on her shoulder. She was wrapped around him like a monkey, arms and legs tight. He shifted them to their sides so he could do the same to her.

"Do you remember when we first met?" she asked.

"You dropped your books at my feet."

"Do you remember what you said to me?"

Mystified as to why she was bringing this up now, he shrugged.

"I thought you would make fun of me or sneer. You were older than me, and every girl at that school thought you were the hottest thing on two legs. You said, 'Don't worry about it. It happens,' and you then helped me pick them up." She kissed the corner of his mouth. "It was a small kindness, but you won me over right then and there. There is nothing wrong with you. Nothing twisted. You were a good man then, and you're a better man now."

He rested his forehead against hers and breathed deep, exhaling the bitterness and anger.

She continued, her voice soft. "You judge yourself too harshly. And though I think you have a healthy sense of self-esteem generally, you are blind when it comes to this. Living with a dysfunctional parent may have left scars, but it didn't make you dysfunctional, too. Look at you. Look at what you've become."

He scoffed, disregarding the hotel they lived in, the millions of dollars changing hands as they spoke. "That's work."

"No." Her lips tilted up. "There's me. I'm a prize, baby, and you've won me over twice in this lifetime." She stroked her hand over his cheek and said very seriously, "That should give you an idea of how amazing you are, if nothing else."

A hoarse laugh escaped him. "You are indeed a prize, Belikov."

She found the perfect spot to rest her head, under the hollow of his throat. "Oh, Caine. You have no idea."

Yes. If she left him, he would survive. But God would he grieve for this.

Dumbass, she would say. *You're so worried about me leaving you, you can't even fully enjoy that we're together now.*

No more.

Simple words. The moment was important. It should be

marked by a speech, or a grand gesture. Tatiana loved grand gestures.

He didn't have the energy. Shrugging off his insecurity and deep-seated fear was exhausting. Embracing a tentative future, terrifying.

He could give her something, though. "I love you, you know," he said. He hadn't said it to her, not even after she had told him. What a ridiculous oversight.

She kissed him on his shoulder. "I know. Of course you do."

Chapter Eleven

WYATT OPENED GRITTY, tired eyes and stared at the late-afternoon sun peeking through pulled drapes. Jesus. How long had he been asleep? He couldn't remember the last time he had slept during the day.

Then again, he'd had a rough couple of days.

He rose on his elbows and pushed aside the comforter Tatiana must have covered him with. He would rather be covered with her.

Finding her was the first step to achieve that goal. He stood, his legs a little wobbly after his long nap. He swiped his jeans up off the floor and donned them, zipping them up as he made his way out of the bedroom.

He followed the faint noise of silverware to the dining room, stopping when he spotted Tatiana. Her hair was blown out, and she was wearing makeup. But the most unusual part of her outfit was her dress. The emerald-green frock teased his memory. A halter bodice made up the top, with the skirt consisting of strips of fabric that played peekaboo with her skin.

Their first night together. During this decade. She'd

worn this dress.

He cocked his head. As he recalled it, he'd destroyed the dress, so this must be a replacement.

She straightened a place setting and noticed him. Nervousness flitted across her face before she beamed a smile. "Hey." She came over and kissed him on the cheek. "Good morning, sunshine."

"More like good evening."

"You needed the sleep." She busied herself straightening his hair, which was cut so short, he hardly needed it.

He glanced at the dress and then the table, which was set with china. The candles in the center were lit, despite the sunshine from outside. "Am I…underdressed? For something?"

"For dinner. An early dinner. And no." Her busy hands went to her skirt, and she twitched a strip of material in place. "I wanted to wear this."

Okay. "Oh."

"I made us dinner."

"You did?"

She pouted. "Don't sound so shocked. I can cook, you know."

Her gentle tease made him smile. "I know. It's just that you never do." He walked closer with her and surveyed the table. "Ah. That looks like breakfast."

"I was preoccupied. I didn't want to concentrate on some complicated recipe. This is easy, and you like it."

"I do like it." He looked at his bare chest. "Maybe I should put on a shirt."

"No, no, sit." She indicated a chair. "I don't mind the view."

He sat down and watched, bemused, as she served him fluffy eggs and crisp bacon before serving herself and settling at his right.

"Eat," she said. There was a nervous lilt to her voice that put him on edge.

They needed to talk about everything, he knew that. As much as he'd benefited from getting these things off his chest, he wasn't looking forward to another emotional bloodletting. The scrambled eggs tasted like dust in his mouth. He swallowed, eager to get this over with. "Tatiana, perhaps we should discuss..."

"Oh, fuck it." She put down her fork and looked at him, earnest but apprehensive. "I know I'm not doing this right. It should be a dinner, not a breakfast, and it should be after, not before, but I can't wait. This is too much." She picked up a folded piece of paper from next to her plate and slipped out of her chair. After a moment of consideration, she got down on a knee and fumbled the piece of paper open. "This should be a ring," she muttered. A flush lit her cheeks. "But I didn't want to wait to cast it." She smoothed the paper over his lap and peered at him expectantly.

Wyatt picked up the piece of paper, aware his hand was shaking. Though it was only a drawing, he knew the ring would be magnificent when she created it. He wasn't much for jewelry, but he could see this piece on his finger for the rest of his days.

"It's going to be made of platinum," she said, the words tumbling out. "And there will be tiny chips of diamonds along the top edge here, so it looks like a solid line. Because you pretend to be flashy and over the top, but you're not like that, not really, so you can wear it with a tux or with jeans."

He placed his palm over the sketch. "Tatiana," he asked, each word very slow and careful, "are you proposing to me?"

She swallowed and finally met his gaze. "I am."

He stared at her. "You know it's supposed to be me proposing to you."

"Well, we're pretty nontraditional all around, you know."

The joke was a valiant effort, but he was too flummoxed to respond.

She sobered. "I haven't slept. Thinking about everything. How you think you aren't normal. And how you're always braced for me to leave you. How you thought I wouldn't want you if I knew how crazy your family was."

He gritted his teeth, hating the picture she was painting of him, but he remained silent. He'd seen a psychiatrist when he was making enough money to go to one, and though his visits had ended when he'd become overly consumed with work, she'd pointed out that he exhibited some textbook behaviors of a person who had come from a dysfunctional home. Fear of abandonment and rejection? Check.

"And then I thought…" she said, her voice so soft he had to lean forward, "…I don't want you to always have to be in charge of everything. That's not fair. You do so much for me. I want to do this for you."

"You don't have to propose to me so I feel secure. I'm not that weak."

"I'm proposing to you because I want to marry you. No other reason."

A memory teased him. His mother's old music box.

When it was wound up, a pair of skaters would dance the perimeter, come together for a brief moment, and wander off again. He remembered he'd wondered if he and Tatiana were like that. *Crashing together, twirling around, maybe drifting off. But always returning.*

It was about time he stopped agonizing that they might drift off, and started to enjoy the whole crashing-together part. A smile crossed his face. "I should have known you would take the reins."

"Only because I don't want you to have any doubt I want you. If it's still not clear, I do want you," she said simply. "I love you. I always have. I always will. Nothing you say or do could make me change that. And in case you're wondering…" she nodded at the ring, "…that's been in my head for a long time." She smiled. "I took the initiative by practically slamming my books on your feet when I was a kid. Figure I should keep this streak alive, yeah?"

"Thought that was an accident."

Her chin rose. "Please. There wasn't even anything there to trip on. No, I wanted you to look at me. Even if there was a chance you would laugh at me."

"I look at you." He stroked her cheek, his heart so full he thought it might cease operating. "Give me a second. Stay right there."

"UH, I'M KIND of waiting for an answer here," Tatiana called after a minute or two had passed. She shifted, the carpet rough on her knees. This was not protocol for a proposal, right? Shouldn't he have squealed with joy and accepted by now?

Okay, maybe squealing wasn't something Wyatt would

do, but he should have definitely accepted.

He came back into the room, holding a small box, and she cast him a disgruntled look.

"You're kind of leaving me hanging here, Wyatt."

He matched her position, getting on his knees in front of her. "I thought getting serious would scare you off."

She regarded him steadily, without a hint of reproach. "I don't scare easily."

"I know." He gave her a lopsided smile. "I do. It's what kept me from not seeking you out for all those years, even when I should have. The stakes are too high when it comes to you."

"Silly. I'm the surest bet you'll ever find."

He ran his thumb over the top of the plain wooden box. "Even thinking it might scare you, I was still getting ready for this." He flipped open the lid.

Tatiana assessed the small fortune in jewels with a professional's eye. She picked up a diamond and held it to the light. "These are beautiful."

"For the past couple of months I've been collecting them."

She squinted. "Is this my dowry?"

He snorted. "No. I don't have a family ring or anything to give you, and I didn't want to get you something someone else made. Thought you should have some choice in it. It is your area of expertise."

"I get to design my own ring?"

He grinned at her delight. "Who could do a better job than you?"

"No one." Ah, there was the shriek. It came from her, not him, but that was okay. "I can't wait!"

He shifted the jewels to the side and pulled out a tattered piece of notebook paper. "There's this, too."

"What's that?"

"The marriage proposal I drafted when I was nineteen."

Her mouth dropped open. "What?"

"And you thought you had all my letters."

She had kept every single letter he had written her during the course of their seven-year relationship.

Well, clearly not every single one. "You kept it? All these years?"

"Of course. For the same reason you kept my other letters. I liked to have the proof. To know I loved someone the way I loved you."

Vibrating with curiosity, she held out her hand. "Let me see."

Supremely satisfied to have bested her, he considered her demand before shaking his head. "No. I don't think so."

"You're joking."

"No. I have to keep some surprises in this relationship. And you could learn to benefit from delayed gratification."

"This is torture. Not delayed gratification."

"There's that hyperbole I love so much." He tucked the paper back into the box. "I figure our twentieth? Twenty-fifth anniversary? I'll let you read it. It's great. Some of my best work."

"I hate you."

"No. You don't. Now, what's your answer?" he teased.

"Nuh-uh. What's yours? I asked first."

"But I've clearly been planning this."

"But you were moving at a snail's pace, overthinking it."

"Thank God I have you to save me from thinking."

She opened her mouth and closed it again, eyeing him suspiciously. "I hate it when you cleverly insult me."

"I could never insult you." Still smiling, he held up the box of loose stones and that mystery letter. "What if I asked you properly?"

"Hmm." After considering that, she nodded. "Very well. Make it pretty."

He cleared his throat. "Tatiana Belikov, you crazy, unconventional woman. I've loved you forever. I love that you're kinky, and dirty, and filthy in the bedroom…" he paused, thinking, "…and out of it. I love that you let me be myself. I love you. Will you marry me?"

She regarded him seriously and folded up the sketch she'd made of his ring. His smile was gone now, his eyes grave. As if her response would be anything other than what it was.

"Wyatt Caine, you're crazier, dirtier, and kinkier than me. Luckily, that seems to work for both of us. Of course I love you, doofus." She tucked the square of paper into his jeans like a dollar bill, her fingers brushing against his belly. "And I'll marry you if you marry me."

He gave a small *oof* when she launched herself at him, knocking him backward to the carpet. He rested his hands on her waist, his face soft. He looked younger than he normally did, carefree and relaxed.

That was how she felt, like she was sixteen again. No, not sixteen. Her love for him was deeper now, more faceted. No less intense, but with a stronger foundation. Not because he was more loveable, but because life had changed both of them.

She'd found her heart again. There may not be any certainties in life, but this time, she was going to hold on to it with all her strength.

He stroked his hands up the back of her thighs. “I’m going to put in my wedding vows that you can’t wear panties.”

The words cut through the seriousness of the moment. She leered down at him. “If that’s how we’re doing things, I’m going to demand head every morning forever.”

“That’s going to be a given. Don’t waste your vows on that.” He flipped her over, using his lower body to pin her to the floor.

She ran her foot up his calf. “I want a filthy wedding night. With toys.”

“I don’t need no toys. Have you seen what I can do with a pen?”

“What if you used the toys on me while someone watched?”

He paused, going from semi-hard to full mast in about three seconds. “Fucking hell, Tatiana.”

“Yeah.” She lifted her head to lick a flame of sensation along his jaw. “I thought so.”

“We’re getting married next week,” he said emphatically.

She snorted. “Good luck with that. I have to shop for the dress, which will take forever. Figure out our flowers and food. I suppose we could do it here, so the venue is taken care of.”

“Of course we’ll do it here…” He thought of the stellar quarter they’d had, helped in part by the booking of their facilities and ballroom. “We might have to do it on a weekday if we want to have it anytime in the next six months. Or try to pressure someone into switching."

"That's so long away."

He was glad he wasn't the only one who was impatient for her to be his.

"And I don't want to waste my wedding-night idea on a non-special event."

He gave a half laugh and pressed his forehead against hers. His dirty little Tatiana. She was probably already imagining someone watching while he taunted her with a vibrator. Most men might be annoyed that she wanted more than his eyes on her on their wedding night, but he wasn't most men.

And she definitely wasn't most women.

Thank God. He exhaled, the remnants of bitterness inside of him relaxing their hold on his soul. The future. She was his future. They were strong. They had a shot.

All he ever needed was a chance. He could do a lot with that.

"My mom will also want to help plan," she said, almost apologetically.

He nodded. "Maybe by then Ellie could come." He shrugged, as if it didn't matter.

She kissed his lips. "Well, yeah."

"I'll have to invite my business associates, too."

"Mine as well. And friends…" Her forehead wrinkled. "This is going to be a production, isn't it? It's good we have a long engagement, so we have time to plan it."

"Yeah," he agreed, though his heart wasn't in it.

"Or we could go down to one of those chapels and get hitched right now."

He stilled at her joke. She blinked up at him and shook

her head. "But that would be crazy."

He was silent.

"Right? That's crazy, Wyatt."

He considered it some more.

A dangerous glint entered her eyes. He knew that look. It had usually preceded some nutty idea, like painting her dorm room chartreuse or climbing out of her bedroom window. "It's super impulsive."

"Yes." He waited. There was very little convincing that needed to be done here. Not when she was sporting that look.

"That's not like you."

"No." He grinned at her. His face was going to ache if he kept up this much smiling. "But it's very like you. And you are a terrible, terrible influence on me."

"My parents would be so sad."

Weak. She couldn't even put up a robust argument for him to knock down. "We don't have to tell them. We plan a big wedding, throw the party." He leaned down and whispered in her ear, "But you would be mine today. And we could have that wedding night tonight. I have a friend. A discreet one, whom I'm certain I could coax out to play."

She shuddered. "Akira might still be in town, too."

"So many eyes on you. You'd like that, wouldn't you? Everyone watching as I make you mine—"

"Okay, enough. Enough. You brilliant bastard. Let me up. We can find an ordained Elvis in about five minutes."

He got to his knees and helped her up, pausing before he stood. On his knees, he wrapped his arms around her waist and pressed his face against her abdomen.

She stroked his hair. This. This felt right. She was his,

his perfect match. A whirlwind of life, love, sex, and chaos.

The world should know it.

He kissed her belly before rising. "I'm going to get dressed."

The tip of her tongue touched the corner of her mouth. "Wear a tux. I like you in a tux. Should I change into something else?"

He drank in the sight of her, in the dress she'd worn the first night she'd walked back into his life. "You're perfect as you are."

"Hurry up." She gave a whoop and twirled in a circle, her skirt fluttering around her. "Don't make me wait."

"No." He grinned and strode to the bedroom. "We're done waiting."

Epilogue

Ten Years Later

"I THINK THIS one's crooked."

Thirteen-year-old Dee Caine picked up the hand mirror and studied the braids her father had painstakingly put in her hair. "It's okay."

"No, see?" Wyatt readjusted her hand and pointed to a section on the back of her head. "Crooked."

Tatiana glanced up from the newspaper she was reading. "I could do it." She had been half-joking, but the instantaneous "No!" she received from Father and daughter wasn't very nice.

She sniffed. "I am an artist, you know. I have excellent hand-eye coordination."

"Sure you do," Wyatt soothed. "Just not with Dee's hair."

"It's *my* mother who taught you," she muttered.

"Yes," Wyatt said calmly. "After she gave up on teaching you."

Tatiana rolled her eyes and hid her smile at the conspiratorial wink shared between Wyatt and Dee. She might huff and puff, but at the end of the day, the special bond between the two of them warmed her.

Dee had been six when they'd adopted her, a couple of years after their wedding. As a favor to a friend, Tatiana had agreed to do children's lessons for a local San Francisco charity that brought artists into elementary schools.

She hadn't known Dee's parents were long-gone when she'd drifted over to help the girl assemble her project. Within a couple of the weekly lessons, the shy, kind-hearted girl had wormed her way into Tatiana's heart. When she had discovered Dee was in need of a family, it had seemed the most natural thing to consider adoption.

She had worried over Wyatt's reaction. *Guess what, honey. I'd like to adopt a child, this specific child. She's beautiful and sweet, and we bonded over sparkly things.*

They had progressed to a point where they discussed children openly, and they were both less panicked by the thought of offspring. But adopting a six-year-old was far different than having an infant, complete with a nine-month gestation period that might give them more time to get used to the idea of a family.

Surprisingly, though apprehensive, Wyatt had been open to the idea. She credited the handful of visits he had with his sister, visits which had increased in warmth exponentially each time. Plus, he'd promoted Esme, who had taken over a number of his day-to-day tasks at the casino, leaving him with more free time than he knew what to do with.

By the time they met with the adoption agency, Wyatt had come firmly on board. And when he and Dee had finally been introduced…

Tatiana smiled as she watched him critically analyze the girl's hair. Dee had been solemn and quiet, eager to please and hungry for love. Wyatt needed to be needed, his gruffness masking a deep core of tenderness. It was a match made in heaven.

The stomp of small feet preceded the sentence Tatiana heard practically every morning. "I can't find my book bag."

Tatiana sipped her coffee and responded with her usual reply. "It's next to the door. Where you kept it last night."

John slipped into his seat at the breakfast table and stared blearily at the bowl of cereal in front of him. A preemie at birth, he was still small for six, and his feet didn't quite touch the floor. He yawned as Tatiana nudged his spoon closer. Poor baby. She sympathized with his aversion to mornings.

"You don't have much time, kiddo," she said gently.

Brushing floppy red hair out of his eyes, he sighed and picked up his spoon. John had come to them in a more conventional way—once they'd decided they were ready to take on the responsibility of another child, they had contacted an agency in Vegas. John had been a cranky two-year-old when he'd tumbled into their home.

He was messy and loud and rash. Tatiana stroked his hair back from his face. He was perfect.

Dee placed her mirror on the table. "Mom, can we see them again before we go to school?"

Her gaze met Wyatt's where he lounged against the counter, and he smiled. He smiled readily now, real smiles that warmed his eyes. After a full decade married to each other, he still wouldn't admit that he was a romantic, but the love she saw in his eyes every time he grinned? Aw. No way a non-romantic could manage that trick.

"Sure." She pulled out her phone and opened the picture before handing it to Dee.

Delight filled the girl's face, her dark eyes flashing. The child had a maternal streak, and Tatiana knew she was counting the days until the new little ones made their appearance.

"I wanna see!" John demanded, and Dee pushed the phone across the table.

John picked up the phone, chewing absently on his cereal. A frown creased his brow. "How much longer?"

Wyatt checked his watch. "One week, twelve hours, and approximately thirty-four minutes."

The precise time was a running joke between the two of them that rarely failed to make John giggle, but this time he continued to scowl. "What if they don't like us?"

"Of course they'll like us," Dee said, so confident of her place in life, Tatiana wanted to rejoice. "We're going to be their family."

Tatiana moved to pull John into her arms, but she needn't have bothered. Wyatt was already there, standing behind him. He leaned down to kiss the top of his son's head. Casual affection came as readily to him as smiles now. He was a hugger, at least where his family was concerned. "It might take them some time to warm up to you. They might be scared because they're in a new country and with a new family, but I'm sure you'll help them."

John thought this over, his brow smoothing. "Yeah. Okay. Can I have sugar on my cereal?"

"Absolutely not," Tatiana said briskly, clearing her throat to hide a sniffle. "Your teacher almost killed me last time I sent you to school sugared up."

The car horn interrupted her. "Aunt Ellie's here! She said she'd drive us." Dee jumped up from her seat and grabbed her bag. John followed, picking up the nutrition drink Tatiana had placed next to his breakfast. The kid was always hungry but rarely able to sit still long enough to finish a meal.

Wyatt scowled and moved to the huge picture window overlooking the front of the house. "If she's with that new boyfriend of hers, tell her I don't want him driving around with you," he called after the children. The only response was the front door closing, which made his frown deepen.

He turned back to the window, shifting to try to see Ellie's car. Tatiana refolded the newspaper and set it on the table. "Wyatt."

"Hmm."

"Get away from the window."

"She needs to concentrate on school. For that matter, she needs to go back to school."

Having graduated college the previous May, Ellie had decided to take a year to figure out her options and work at Quest. Plus engage in a harmless flirtation with the rebel son of one of Wyatt's competitors. Tatiana had shamelessly encouraged both of these endeavors.

"How is she going to go to grad school if she insists on dating that loser?" Wyatt lifted his hand at her snort and pointed it at her, still straining to see out the window. "I don't want to hear it. Not one word about irony. Or the shoe being on the other foot. Not one word."

She bit the inside of her cheek. "My lips are sealed."

"Your dad's lips weren't when he was here last week."

Wyatt deepened his already deep baritone. "See, boy? Now you know my pain when you sniffed around my little girl."

"That's because it's Daddy's sole joy in life to torture you."

"There is no comparison between me and this kid. Boy has a terrible reputation. I have half a mind to sic my PI on him, but Ellie would kill me."

"So would I." She admired him standing there. The years had been kind to him. She had gray hairs popping up every day, while he got a spot of distinguished silver at the temples. Middle-aged pudge had settled around his stomach last year, an event which had so horrified him he'd gone on an exercise regimen that would have made a Navy SEAL weep.

He wore a suit, but with the day-to-day busyness of their lives, he had to trust in his assistant to ensure they were the latest style. Wyatt rarely cared about image or appearance. Not when he could spend his free time wrestling with his son or helping his daughter with homework. Or, for that matter, seeing to his wife.

Speaking of which. "Wyatt."

"Hmm."

"We have fifteen minutes."

He finally turned away from the window, shooting her a quizzical look. "Fifteen minutes for what?"

"Fifteen child-free minutes. Before you have to leave for work." She shoved back from the table and stood. "What should we do with that time, hmm?"

A light lit his eyes. "I can think of a few things."

She gave him a slow grin. "Which room?"

"Surprise me."

With a squeal, she turned on her heel and made for the foyer. He gave her a head start, but by the time she hit the stairs, he was fast on her heels.

He grabbed her around the waist before she could make it to their bed. With his foot, he slammed their bedroom door closed. Important, though the house was temporarily empty. Between the housekeeper and the kids, the large place never stayed empty for long.

He picked her up easily and carried her the rest of the way to the bed, tossing her on it hard enough that she bounced twice before settling. "The bedroom," he mused. "How very conventional of you."

"I'm an old married lady," she said, lowering her lashes demurely. "I have to be conventional."

His hands were at the fastening to his pants, unbuckling and unzipping. "How much time do we have now?"

She glanced at her watch. "Twelve minutes. We're getting slow."

He climbed on top of her, his muscular thighs bracketing hers. Wyatt's big hands stroked down her sides and captured her leggings. He sat back and worked the stretchy fabric down, taking her panties with it. "That isn't much time. We should hurry and get to the good stuff."

"Good thing I kept myself ready."

"Did you?" His hand stroked up her leg, finding her pussy. He froze, and his eyes flared as he dipped a finger inside her. "Oh. Yes. Smart girl. You've been wearing this all morning?"

"Mmmm. I'm nothing if I'm not a dutiful wife."

"I'm so glad you know your place."

"On my back?"

"Naked. Spread. Wet." His talented fingers found the end of the emerald colored beads and tugged. She gasped as he fucked the string of beads back and forth, the friction of the smooth balls driving her crazy. "Not conventional at all," he muttered.

"You'd be bored if I was."

"I would. This design is one of my favorites. Simple. Elegant."

"I know how much you like it."

He tugged the beads out, her pussy clenching to keep them inside. He filled the emptiness, guiding himself in. They had a healthy sex life, and not just healthy with all the demands they had on their time, but healthy in general. Still, every time he sank inside her, she felt like it was the first time, that second of discovery and lust and eagerness still there.

He framed her face and brought his lips to hers. "It's going to be like this when we're eighty, isn't it?"

"You'll be eighty. I'll still be young and beautiful."

"That goes without saying." He brought his hand between them. She didn't realize he still held the beads until the round balls rolled over her clit. She shrieked, arching up, which drove him deeper. He gave a tortured groan and thrust harder, faster, the friction sending them both into climax.

When the spasms had subsided, Wyatt lifted his head from her shoulder. "We're getting too good at quickies."

Tatiana traced her fingers over his back. "Out of necessity, but I'm hardly complaining."

He rolled over and slid off the bed, righting his clothes as he went. Tatiana yawned and stretched, supporting her head on her hand so she could watch him return to office-ready wear. *Good thing his clothes don't wrinkle easily.*

"It's going to be more of a necessity when these two new ones show up," Wyatt remarked.

She gave a little bounce. "How much longer? How much longer?"

He grinned. "One week, twelve hours and…" he checked his watch, "…eleven minutes before we get on that plane to Russia."

"I can't wait."

His smile broadened. "Let me see them again."

Not at all surprised at his eagerness, Tatiana fished her phone from the wreckage of the bed. Wyatt pulled up the photo and stared at it, his expression softening. She climbed on her knees and looked at the two little girls who would be coming home with them soon. Katerina was four, Anna three.

Tatiana had wondered if Wyatt would prefer they adopt infants, but when she'd questioned him about it, he'd stared at her as if she were crazy. "What would I do with a baby? They can't even talk."

Tatiana cocked her head and smiled at the little girls' solemn faces. "Are you worrying they won't like you, too?" she teased.

He snorted. "No. Of course they'll love me."

Her heart swelled so much, she had to hide her face in his back, lest she embarrass him. That kind of deep, inner security in their love had taken years, and the project wasn't over yet, but she adored that he was capable of appreciating his own worth. Not only as a businessman, but as a husband and a father.

Unaware of her emotions, he continued. "No, I was thinking they have your coloring, and they'll probably be as pretty as you. I already worry about Ellie and Dee. When did I get to be responsible for so many girls?"

"Quit being sexist. You can worry about John, too."

"I caught him trying to use my razor on his eyebrows yesterday. Trust me, I worry plenty."

She chuckled. He twisted around and surprised her by bearing her down to the mattress, his gaze intense. "Listen, Ellie's on break. She can watch the kids this weekend. Or Ron would take them. We won't have a chance like this for a while after Kat and Anna come. Why don't you and I slip off? Back to the penthouse for some alone time."

"Alone time of the non-quickie version?"

He lowered his head and kissed her, long, drugging kisses. "Filthy alone time," he whispered against her lips.

"Ooooh. I like that."

"I thought so." His hand groped around the bedsheets until he found the beads. He placed one hand on her stomach and slipped the orbs back inside her, holding her still when she writhed. "In the meantime, you can have this."

"So generous," she murmured, loving the sensation of being filled. His finger dragged over her clit, and she purred at the surge of pleasure.

"I try."

"I'll set things up for the weekend."

"Perfect." He gave her a final kiss and pushed himself off the bed, surveying her with a self-satisfied grin. "How did I wind up with you again? Luck, right?"

She extended her arms over her head and arched her back, displaying her body for him. "You and I, we make our own luck, Caine."

From the Author

Thanks so much for reading the Bedroom Games Series! I hope you enjoyed it.

Did you love Akira? So did I. Watch her meet her match (and maybe throw one of her infamous house parties) in A Gentleman in the Street.

If you're looking for other books of mine that are similar in heat level and genre to The Bedroom Games Series, I recommend the Pleasure Series or A Gentleman in the Street.

If you would like to know when my next book is available, please visit me at www.alisharai.com, follow me on twitter @AlishaRai, or find me at facebook.com/alisharai.

Happy Reading!

A Gentleman in the Street: Excerpt

AKIRA MORI WAS partial to a certain kind of man: the kind you fucked raw and dirty until your voice was hoarse and your skin slick with sweat. The location wasn't important—up against a brick wall, in the back of a car, on a kitchen island…

Jacob Campbell is not that kind of man.

Bullshit. Every man could be that kind of man. Or at least that was what she wanted to believe, when she was currently eyeing a delightfully sweaty and half-naked Jacob.

The late-afternoon sun flirted with smooth, tan skin. Muscles flexed and danced as he raised an ax and brought it down in a rhythmic cadence. Wide shoulders tapered to a narrow waist. His abs were flat and ridged with muscle, his chest powerful and shiny with sweat. Worn jeans hung low on his hips, revealing a thin line of paler skin.

Had she ever seen him without a shirt? No, she didn't think so. Thank God for small favors or she would have forgotten long ago their contentious relationship didn't allow for tracing that tan line below his hipbones with her tongue.

If he came out to the sticks to bare it all like this regularly, she would happily sacrifice the two-thousand-dollar high heels currently sinking into the dirt to play voyeur.

In theory, at least. She shifted, conscious of the mud clinging to her precious babies.

He won't thank you for your appreciation.

She pushed the thought aside. Tight-lipped disapproval would come soon enough. Akira leaned back against the tree behind her, the better to settle in for the show.

How did he get an ass like that sitting around writing books? She had a desk job too. Even with her predisposition to slimness and inability to sit still, she had to work out like a fiend not to succumb to office spread.

He brought the ax down with a loud thwack and left it there, leaning over to pick up a bottle of water from a nearby stump. He turned, and she was treated to a view of his profile. Too-long dark brown hair tangled around his face. His throat worked as he swallowed the water. He'd grown a beard since she'd last seen him. She hated stubble burn, but he looked so good with facial hair she could not imagine minding some scrapes on her inner thighs.

She must have made some sort of noise; his head lifted. There was too much distance between them, but she knew his hazel eyes would darken to the same color as the leaves on the trees the instant he caught sight of her.

It always took her a second to collect herself when he turned his stare on her, a brief instant to remember what role she needed to play. She assured herself time and again he would never spot that smidgen of vulnerability. No one could.

Better she laugh and taunt and outrageously flirt to the point of irritation. Better he think her an empty-headed, useless, sex-crazed twit than guess the mortifying truth: she'd wanted this man for over a dozen years.

He was the first to end their staring contest and move, capping the water bottle. She clenched her hands behind her as he walked toward her, letting the rough bark scrape her sensitive knuckles.

Get ready. Shields in place. Ice ran through her veins and steel grafted to her spine.

He stopped a foot away from her. It was rare for her to find a man taller than her, especially when she was wearing her high heels, but Jacob easily topped her. If she extended her arm, she'd be able to touch him, run her fingers over his deliciously muscular stomach.

She worked up her most blinding smile, the one that could stop traffic and launch a thousand ships, that could destroy a man or make him feel a thousand feet tall. "Hello, Brother Jacob."

Other Books by Alisha Rai

Bedroom Games Series

Play With Me, Book One

Risk & Reward, Book Two

Bet On Me, Book Three

Campbell Siblings Series

A Gentleman in the Street

Pleasure Series

Glutton For Pleasure, Book One

Serving Pleasure, Book Two

Managing Pleasure, Book Three

Veiled Series

Veiled Desire, Book One

Veiled Seduction, Book Two

Single Title

Night Whispers

Hot as Hades

Never Have I Ever

Cabin Fever

Made in the USA
Coppell, TX
11 April 2021

53567174R00265